the
playgroup

janey fraser

arrow books

Published by Arrow Books 2011

4 6 8 10 9 7 5

First published in Great Britain in 2010 by
Arrow Books
Random House, 20 Vauxhall Bridge Road,
London SW1V 2SA

www.randomhouse.co.uk

Addresses for companies within The Random House Group Limited can
be found at: www.randomhouse.co.uk/offices.htm

The Random House Group Limited Reg. No. 954009

A CIP catalogue record for this book
is available from the British Library

ISBN 9780099558194

The Random House Group Limited supports The Forest Stewardship
Council (FSC®), the leading international forest certification organisation. Our
books carrying the FSC label are printed on FSC® certified paper. FSC is the
only forest certification scheme endorsed by the leading environmental organisations,
including Greenpeace. Our paper procurement policy can be found at
www.randomhouse.co.uk/environment

MIX
Paper from
responsible sources
FSC® C016897

Set in Sabon by Palimpsest Book Production Limited,
Falkirk, Stirlingshire
Printed and bound by
CPI Group (UK) Ltd, Croydon, CR0 4YY

the playgroup

Janey Fraser is a writer and journalist who has also written five novels under the name Sophie King. She lives in Devon with her husband.

This book is dedicated to

William, who insisted on taking his
cricket ball to playgroup.

Lucy, who cried because she was
too young to go to playgroup.

Giles, who was always trying to escape
from playgroup.

My husband, who has taught me
to take time out to play.

Also to the real Puddleducks playgroups
and Corrybank primary schools everywhere,
who do such a great job both for children
and parents.

ACKNOWLEDGEMENTS

I am indebted to my agent Teresa Chris. I am also very grateful to Gillian Holmes for her clever eye; to Marissa Cox for her publicity expertise and everyone at Arrow. Also to The Romantic Novelists Association, with particular thanks to Katie Fforde, Kate Furnivall, Linda Mitchelmore and Margaret James.

THE PUDDLEDUCKS PLAYGROUP NEWSLETTER
SEPTEMBER ISSUE

Welcome back, everyone! If you're new, we'd like to give you an extra-special hello! Here, at Puddleducks Playgroup, we understand that your first day might seem daunting. But we're around to make sure you settle in – and that includes nervous parents!

We've got all kinds of activities to keep you amused and also help you learn! There's our new Pyjama Drama group and our weekly Wriggle and Giggle Musical Movement group. This term, we're very fortunate to have Kitty Macdonald (of Britain's Best Talent fame) who will be running a music workshop morning and helping us with the end-of-term nativity play!

Please also put the following date in your diary: on September 30 there will be a Parents' Social in the main hall, so book your babysitter now!

Here is some advice to make the autumn term go with a swing.

VITAL DO'S AND DON'TS

DO make sure every item of clothing is clearly labelled – including underwear!

DO fill in the enclosed medical form, especially the allergy section.

1

DO *fill in the Emergency Contact form together with your doctor's details.*

Please be aware that this term, we have a new security code which has been fitted on to the main door. If you are late, you will need to ring the bell so one of the staff can let you in.

Right! That's it! We hope your little Puddleducks will have a splashing – sorry, smashing! – start. If you have any questions, please don't hesitate to ask.

PS. Do any of you mums have a secret talent? If so, we'd like to hear from you. At Puddleducks Playgroup, we welcome outside speakers who can tell us about their own area of expertise. So if you're an artist or a writer or a singer or even if you have just come back from an interesting holiday, please get in touch.

THE PUDDLEDUCKS SONG

We are the little Puddleducks
We love to learn through play.
It keeps us bright and busy
All *(two beats)* through the day!

Chapter 1

'Mrs Merryfield, Mrs Merryfield. We went to More-ishus. And it *rain*ed.'

'Hi, Gemma! Nice tan! Listen, I'm pretty certain Molly is dry now but just in case she's not, there's a spare pair of pants in her sandwich box. That's the one with the picture of a giraffe on it – sorry I didn't have time to label it.'

'Morning, Miss Merryfield. Had a good break? Darren, have you said hello to your playgroup leader?'

'Gemma, I'm *so* sorry. But we've just had Beth checked again and it turns out she's allergic to wheat as well as salt, sugar, any kind of additives and – get this – any food that's yellow. Weird, isn't it? So can you make sure she doesn't have any biscuits at breaktime?'

The stream of traffic on the first day of term was always hectic with the children running up to swing on her arms, wrap their small warm bodies round her legs, bobbing up and down, unable to stand still for a second and announcing in breathy excited voices exactly what they'd been up to in the holidays. It was like lots of different hands playing piano notes at the same time.

The parents too would understandably want to chat, some calling her Gemma because they felt they

5

knew her, while others preferred a more formal address. As for the children, she'd given up explaining that she was a Miss. In their minds, any woman like their mum had to have a Mrs in front of their name.

And there were so many people milling around, all needing something different from her. For a start, there was Darren's mum squatting down by the play-dough table to settle in her three-year-old, who was nervous about coming back after a whole summer off.

Then there were mums like Kyle's who arrived in skinny tops and casual jogging bottoms (so casual that they looked as though they'd just rolled out of bed and were going back to watch daytime TV) and just waved goodbye to their children without a second glance. Kyle's mother always dressed her son in a skimpy Power Rangers T-shirt, winter and summer, even though Gemma kept asking her to bring in some-thing warmer. It had got to the point now where she just lent Kyle something from the Lost Property box when his arms went blue.

And of course there were the one-offs like Clemmie's mum, who used to be a model, and arrived every day in beautifully cut trousers, earrings and flawless foun-dation complete with lipliner. 'Don't forget your handbag, Clemmie darling. It's got your oatmeal snack in it so we can keep an eye on those naughty calories.'

Some parents came from the council flats down by the bottom end of the canal. A good smattering came from the smart houses up at the top end where house prices had been known to go into seven figures. There were also a lot of in-betweeners from roads where you could park your car in the drive and those where you couldn't. It was a testament to Puddleducks that families who could have afforded to go private were actually keen to send their under-fives to a state playgroup like this one.

Mind you, there were times when she felt she *did* run a private one-to-one service.

'I'm reely sorry to bother you, Gemma. But Mikey's lost his favourite sweatshirt and we think he might have left it behind here last term. Could you have a quick look for it when you have a second? You can't miss it. It says, *Granny went to Adelaide and came back with a new Grandad.* Not very funny, actually, under the circumstances but I'll tell you about that one later.'

'Miss Merryfield? Could I have a word? Poppy is *awfully* upset because she only got *three* gold stars at the end of last term for her letter outlines and Alex got *four* even though Poppy can do lovely p's and q's whereas Alex, I couldn't help noticing from his worksheet over there, still gets his b's back to front. We did a *teeny bit* of practice during the holidays. So I wondered if you could bear this in mind because it *does* make a difference to her confidence, don't you think?'

'Morning, Mrs Mayfold. Did you have a good holiday? Lucky you, having eight whole weeks off.'

Merryfield, she tried to say to Sienna's mum, who was always getting her name wrong, partly because she usually conducted a conversation while checking her iPhone for emails at the same time. As for the long holidays, like most teachers, Gemma was used to digs like that. She'd actually spent quite a lot of time preparing for the new term. Besides, as Miriam had warned her before going on maternity leave, you couldn't win with Sienna's mum, who always criticised everything. She was already complaining to the father behind her about someone's parking outside.

Gemma's eyes softened. She liked Toby's dad, although he was married so of course she didn't like him *that* way. No, it was because he was one of that increasingly common breed of fathers who looked after their children while their wives went out to work. It wasn't, they had both told her confidentially at the last parents' evening, what they had intended, but redundancy and the cost of childcare had made it work out that way, and actually it was panning out quite nicely, because it meant he had more time to be with the children.

'Sorry to bother you.' Toby's dad, always polite, was pushing a packet of tablets into her hand. 'It's the last of Toby's antibiotic course. It was just a chesty bug and he's not infectious any more, but he does keep making some rather bad smells because of the medicine and . . .'

There was a squeal behind him. 'Chesty bug? Are children allowed into playgroup if they're sick?'

Gemma's heart sank. When it came to going back to playgroup after an illness, there was always a fine line between 'almost better' and 'completely better'. The mother who had squealed, in what sounded like an American twang, was new. Poor thing. She'd need reassuring.

'Have you got a letter from the doctor to say that he is fit for playgroup?' Gemma smiled apologetically. 'You might remember that we need that now.'

Toby's father nodded enthusiastically, delving into his jeans pocket and bringing out a scruffy envelope along with a nappy wipe, a black dog-poo bag (clean), a tissue (not so clean) and a smattering of small change which then scattered all over the floor.

'Oh my word!' The alarm was evident in the twang. 'Danny might try to eat those coins. He's always putting things in his mouth.'

Danny! It was coming together now. This was the American mother who had already rung her twice with all kinds of questions. Were the Puddleduck sweatshirts optional, because polyester made Danny's skin itch? Did the staff ratio conform to the current guidelines here in the UK?

'Please don't worry, Mrs Wright,' soothed Gemma, looking past her to where Danny had already shot off to the messy corner, where one of her helpers was introducing the new intake to the joys of splashing in bowls of soapy water and measuring containers.

The painfully skinny woman with the short, spiky haircut and a worry groove on her forehead frowned. 'It's Carter Wright without a hyphen. Not just Wright.'

'Sorry.' Gemma smiled, mentally kicking herself for not having memorised the register properly. 'I do understand it's difficult leaving your son for the first time. All our parents find that at first. But we do take great care of the children. I promise.'

Toby's dad, bless him, was nodding enthusiastically again. 'Honest. Toby's our baby and I didn't know what to do with myself when he started here – only two and a half, he was – so we got a dog. I know, crazy isn't it. By the way, congratulations.'

Gemma's heart threatened to stop. 'I'm sorry?'

'Congratulations!' repeated Toby's dad, beaming. 'I gather you're our new pre-school leader while Miriam is on maternity leave. What did she have?'

Gemma's heart began beating again. 'A boy. Nicolas. That's Nicolas without an h.'

'Great news! Did you hear that, everyone? Miriam had a healthy baby boy! We ought to rustle up a parent collection.'

Gemma watched Toby's dad springing into action and already wheedling donations from some of the other parents as they finally drifted out of the exit door, through the enclosed outdoor play area and get on with their own lives until 11.30 pick-up time. Some of them were, at the same time, reading spare copies of the playgroup newsletter she'd brought in. Miriam had said that was a great idea, although, at the moment, Miriam thought everything was a good idea apart from giving birth again.

Trailing behind them was the American mother with the spiky haircut, reluctantly looking back at her son who was now blowing bubbles. 'You don't think he'll try to eat that stuff, do you?' she asked Gemma plaintively.

It was all she could do not to give the poor woman a hug. 'He'll be fine. Please don't worry. We'll take good care of him.'

'DON'T WANT TO STAY! DON'T WANT TO STAY!'

Oh dear. By the door was a screaming human tourniquet of Gap meets Boden as Daisy, who had just been presented with twin baby sisters, entwined herself around her mother's legs. The American woman gave her a look that said, *Is this what they do when we're not here?* and turned away, head bowed, towards the car park.

'She's been really clingy ever since these two came along.' Daisy's mother's watery brown eyes appealed to her. 'I can't leave her like this!'

Gemma could have said the usual stuff about not worrying because most children stopped crying once their mothers had gone. But she also knew that if she was a mother herself, that wouldn't really help.

So instead she had another trick up her sleeve.

'Daisy?'

Gemma pretended to be surprised by the voice which came from the back of her throat, her lips hardly moving. It was an action she'd been working on over the summer, much to her landlady's amusement.

'Daisy? It's me. Mouse.'

Daisy opened her eyes a fraction as Gemma knelt down with her hand inside the hand puppet made out of an oven glove, felt scraps and sequins. Mouse was the class's favourite toy. When they had Quiet Talk Time, during which the children would sit in a circle and take it in turns to say something about the day, it was tradition that Mouse would be passed around at the same time and they were only allowed to talk if they were holding him. It worked brilliantly in stopping other children – even Billy – from interrupting.

Animal distraction had been a trick that her grand-mother had taught her. So far, it hadn't failed to work.

'Hello, Daisy.' Gemma crouched down so she was on the same level. 'I wonder if you can help me. There's something very tiny inside my pocket and it's trying to get out.'

The yelling got louder. Daisy's puce face was now firmly buried into her mother's feet so the poor woman was in danger of falling over, complete with twin slings.

'Oh no!' Gemma somehow managed to make her voice loudly authoritative and yet calm at the same time. 'Mouse says he's got a terrible headache from all this noise. He wants you to stop and see what he's been getting up to in the holidays.'

Slowly, she pulled out the felt finger mouse she had made: a smaller version of the glove puppet, created from fabric remnants sold by the craft shop on the high street. Bending her finger up and down to indicate distress, she made whining noises so it seemed that miniature mouse, with his red-sequinned eyes, was crying. Daisy lifted her head very slightly in concern.

'It's Mouse's new baby and it's his first day at Puddleducks Playgroup,' explained Gemma. 'Poor baby mouse is feeling a bit scared and wants you to help him make a pasta calendar with the rest of us, or maybe do some leaf printing. By the way, he says he loves your daisy tights!'

There was a sudden painful knock on her shoulder. '*Me!* I want to hold Mouse. *Me. Me.*'

Gemma liked to think of herself as a patient teacher, but Billy would have tested the fortitude of St Trinian.

Last term, she'd had to see his parents when Billy had given another child an impromptu bowl-shape haircut with the aid of a plastic Christmas-pudding dish from the playbox and a pair of so-called safety scissors.

'You can hold another baby mouse,' said Gemma, delving in her other pocket for the spare she'd made in case this happened. Daisy had stopped crying now and was tenderly stroking Mouse's whiskers, which were loosely sewn on with large tacking stitches in brown thread. Sewing had never been one of Gemma's strong points.

'No!' Billy had grabbed a plastic hammer from the toy toolbox now and was banging it against the Wendy house with huge, angry thwacks. 'I want the big proper Mouse.' He pointed to Daisy's. 'Not this stupid one.'

If Billy's mother hadn't already dumped him and left in indecent haste without even an anorak for break time, she might have felt tempted to call her back.

'Tell you what, Billy,' said Gemma suddenly. 'Remember how you promised not to cut anyone's hair any more?' Billy's hammer-banging intensified and was now to the count of four instead of two. 'Supposing I said you could give Mouse a trim?'

'Wot?'

For a four-year-old, his tone of voice was more suited to one of those rough police dramas in which her friend Kitty had once been an extra as a singer in a sleazy nightclub. 'Well, maybe after Music Mania, I could show you how to tidy up Mouse's whiskers. We might make him a new outfit too.'

Billy was very keen on dressing dolls, something

that his dad, a 6ft 2in. builder, had raised at the last Parents' Evening.

'All roight then.'

Fantastic! She hadn't expected him to cave in quite so fast.

'Would someone please take that child's batteries out!' said a voice behind her with a definite fed-up edge. It was Bella, her young assistant, who was, as usual, dressed in clothes more suited to a catwalk than a playgroup, with those high heels and short stretchy black skirt that had attracted the eye of that Scandinavian au pair. 'By the way,' sniffed Bella, checking her register, 'everyone's here apart from someone called Lily without a surname. She's one of the new ones, isn't she?'

'Yes, she is. Maybe she's not coming. I gather there was a bit of a question mark over her.' Gemma tried to sound normal, but Beryl the headmistress's words were still ringing round her head from their meeting last term: *There's something very important I need to tell you. It's about one of the new children who will be starting in September.*

'Well, if there was any doubt, she ought to have given up her place. There are enough people on the waiting list.' Bella's voice had an irritated click in it that matched the sound of her smart red heels, which had, she'd informed Gemma earlier, cost her nearly a month's wages.

'Actually,' said Gemma in a low voice, 'there aren't. Not now. Beryl says that the Ofsted report on the main school has put parents off sending their children to Puddleducks.'

14

Bella's beautifully threaded eyebrows rose in consternation. 'But that's outrageous.'

'I know.' Gemma glanced up to check that Jean had sat all the children round in a circle with their various tambourines and shakers made out of plastic washing-up bottles and beans, ready for Music Mania. 'So we have to prove that we're the best playgroup in the area if we want to keep going.'

'It's that serious?'

She nodded. 'There's something else too.'

But before she could say anything, there was a ping, indicating that someone was at the door. She'd been waiting for this. 'I'll go,' said Gemma, leaping up, her heart thudding in her throat.

This was ridiculous. She treated all the children the same, whatever their backgrounds, as she had told Beryl. Even so . . .

'Miss Merryfield?'

She nodded, transfixed by the husky voice that was coming out from this tall, elegant, wafer-thin vision in sparkly jeans, black satin jacket that looked more like a man's DJ and beautiful, soft-looking pale pink cashmere scarf that was entwined round the woman's neck, partly shrouding what little face there was on show, thanks to the huge dark sunglasses which were so shiny that they reflected back Gemma's startled expression. There was also the overpowering smell of the woman's trademark perfume that she'd read about in Kitty's well-thumbed copies of *OK!* and *Hello!*

'This is Lily.'

Only then, to her shame, did Gemma glance down at the child who was standing between them. Her mother's pale manicured hands were on her shoulders; the two of them looked like flowers in a vase, one tall and the other short. The little girl had a chalky-white, almost translucent complexion. Her dark straight hair, cut in a precise bob, framed startlingly bright blue eyes.

'Be good.' For a minute, the stranger's gravelly yet somehow feminine voice was so bewitching that Gemma almost thought she was addressing *her*. 'Someone will be here at lunchtime to pick you up.'

The beautiful woman glanced at her. 'I won't be here in person very often. You understand, don't you?'

Gemma nodded. My boss has already explained, she tried to say, but too late. The woman had slipped out, and in the distance she could see a huge, black, highly polished car waiting. Gently, she bent down towards Lily. 'Do you like music like your mummy?'

The girl nodded.

'We've got a xylophone over here. Shall I show you?'

They turned round and almost went smack into Bella, who had come up to see what was happening. 'Was that who I think it was?' she breathed, glancing out of the window at the blacked-out limo pulling away.

'Shhh,' said Gemma fiercely. No one, her grand-mother used to say, was more placid than Gemma except when it came to defending others. 'You can't tell anyone. Or else we'll all be out of our jobs. Even more important, we could be putting a child's safety at risk. And no, I'm sorry. I can't tell you why.'

16

Chapter 2

Much as Gemma loved to chat first thing to the parents and reassure them – especially today, the start of a new term – she also loved it when they went, leaving her and Bella and Jean in charge of twenty small people.

Some, like Billy, charged around with big broad grins, making buzzing sounds more appropriate to the aviary at the local zoo where Molly's mother worked, while others zoomed into their favourite areas.

There was something for everyone. The toy garage which Toby loved; the sandpit tray (Alex's); the computer with the CBeebies site (Sienna's, who always asked 'why?' when told anything); the dressing-up corner (Clemmie's); the messy corner with bowls of spaghetti and jelly so children could experiment with texture (Billy's); the Wendy house (Darren's) and the red, knee-high tables where they cut up playdough with play scissors (everyone's).

This was 'free play time'. Gemma had helped Miriam organise this for the past three years since coming to work at Puddleducks, but now she was on her own! The realisation both excited and daunted her. Ever since she could remember she had wanted to work with small people, partly because her own grandmother had run a nursery, coincidentally not far from here.

'You're a natural with children,' her grandmother used to say, which was why Gemma had insisted to her father, a university lecturer, that she didn't want to follow in his footsteps even though her grades were so good. What she really wanted to do was take an Early Years degree course so she could work at a playgroup or, as so many were called now, a pre-school.

'It's more structured than you think,' she had tried to tell her father over the years. And it was. Puddleducks had to follow quite a tight curriculum that helped children learn through play.

Right now, in fact, it was time for the numbers game. She nodded at Bella, who had rather worryingly confessed last term that she was thinking of going into PR, and also at Jean, whose own children had grown up and moved away. Jean found that working here helped to ease that awful empty-nest feeling. 'OK, everyone. I want you all to sit down in a nice tidy circle. It's time for our bed game! Who wants to show our new Puddleducks how it works?'

Billy's hand shot up towards the ceiling. 'Me, me,' he demanded urgently, as though straining to go to the loo.

Billy! They all agreed that one day, this one (who was much bigger than the others for his age, with hair that seemed to grow in a zigzag fringe and always needed cutting) would go far. Whether that would be up or down was anyone's guess.

'All right, Billy. Can you fetch the Puddleducks

18

blanket and lie down.' She looked around the circle of children. 'Clemmie, I can see you are listening nicely. Would you like to lie down next to Billy?'

Not needing another invitation, Clemmie tottered over in high heels, wearing the princess costume that she always nabbed from the dressing-up box every morning. Thank goodness for DFTB, otherwise known as Dad From The Beeb, who was constantly topping the box up with costumes like cast-off Teletubby outfits.

'We need three more helpers,' sniffed Bella, checking her nails as she spoke. 'Danny, can you lie on the other side of Billy?'

No problems with that one, thought Gemma as she watched the new boy run over and dive under the blanket, giggling. What lovely long blond eyelashes!

Two more and they were ready. 'There were five in the bed,' they all sang. 'Then they all turned over and one fell out. That's right, Danny, you fall out. Not so hard or you'll hurt yourself. Now everyone, how many are left in the bed? Yes! Four. How many fell out? Yes. One. So what does four and one make? That's right. Five.'

By the end, Gemma's throat felt a bit sore, but the children loved it and it was a good way of helping them to get the hang of mentally adding and subtracting through play.

'Awful news about Brian, isn't it?' said Jean quietly as she helped Gemma get the mid-morning elevenses ready while Bella was in charge of the story-reading circle.

Had she missed something? Brian was the kindly

if somewhat absent-minded head of Reception year at Corrybank Primary, round the corner, otherwise known as Big School. Many Puddleduck children went on to the main school, which was why there were so many joint activities such as assemblies, after-school club and, of course, the traditional nativity play just before Christmas. Brian and Miriam had been the lynchpins for this.

As Jean gave her the news about poor old Brian, who lived in her road ('that's how I found out, you see'), Gemma's eyes filled with tears.

'Apparently someone called Joanna Balls is taking over,' continued Jean importantly. 'You can imagine how difficult it must have been to get someone at short notice. Comes from an inner-city London school, or so I've been told. She'll find Hazelwood a bit different, won't she?'

Gemma, still too upset to talk, nodded. How grateful she was to be living in this smallish, pretty market town just an hour from London, with its coffee shops and canal and church halls with so many courses that you could spend every evening doing t'ai chi or yoga or whatever you wanted.

She was lucky too to have her flat at the top of Joyce's house just a ten-minute drive away, even though her landlady was constantly asking why a nice girl like her hadn't found the right man yet. How do you know I haven't? Gemma wanted to reply, but instead she just made noises about still being young at not-even-thirty-yet.

But the best thing about being at Puddleducks, far from the family home in Devon, not to mention

Cambridge, where she had done her degree and met Kitty, was that no one knew her. Not the real her, anyway.

'Surprised no one's informed you, given that you're the acting pre-school leader now,' added Jean critically. 'Mind you, it only happened last Tuesday.'

Gemma tried to get her thoughts straight. 'I was in Greece until yesterday with my friend Kitty. And when I got back my laptop was playing up again, so I haven't checked my emails. No, Molly, it's not time for outdoor play yet so just sit nicely. You need the toilet again?'

Molly nodded solemnly. 'My mum says I'm con-sonated.'

Thank God for children! They made you smile even when you weren't feeling like it. By the time she and Molly came back (having needed that spare pair of pants after all), the others were already sitting up at their red tables and chairs for their mid-morning slice of toast and plastic mug of apple or orange juice, depending on tastes and allergies.

'Mrs Merryfield, Mrs Merryfield, can I have a cappuccino instead like Lars does at breakfast?'

Johnnie's Scandinavian male au pair was the subject of much nudging amongst the younger mothers. Clearly his tastes had rubbed off.

'No, Johnnie,' said Gemma kindly but firmly. 'I keep telling you, sweetheart. It's not on the menu, I'm afraid. Finished, everyone? OK. Let's line up by your pegs, everyone, and put on our coats.'

Danny was really settling in, she noticed, as she watched him head for his peg with the picture of a dog and the word '*Dog*' written underneath it. That had been one of her ideas: to put the picture of an object that began with the child's name, and then the word itself.

Lily, however, was being very quiet, hanging back and clinging to the soft pink woollen comfort blanket which she'd brought in and had shoved up inside her jumper.

'That looks like a kangaroo pouch,' said Gemma lightly, kneeling down next to her. 'Do you know what that is? Look, there's a picture of a kangaroo on the wall. It's got a pocket in the front of its tummy to carry its babies in.'

Lily stared at her with those china-blue eyes, almost as though she didn't understand what she was saying. Mentally Gemma checked her notes. There had been nothing unusual about Lily. Nothing to say she was autistic, like the four-year-old they'd had last year, who could only communicate by pointing to a wallet of pictures which both she and the staff had carried. Yet there was something about Lily's behaviour that didn't seem quite right.

'Tell you what. Why don't you go outside with Clemmie? She can be your buddy. Clemmie! Hold Lily's hand, can you?'

Clemmie shook her head fiercely, clinging on to the princess tiara as though Lily might try to nab it. 'How about you, Danny, then? You're new like Lily. You can explore together.'

Danny made a buzzing noise like a bee and flew towards them, arms outspread on either side until he stopped right in front of Lily. 'Hold hands,' he demanded in an East Coast twang that Gemma suspected came straight from his mother, and together they walked out into the playground where Jean was helping children on to trikes and Bella was organising a game of hopscotch.

Gemma watched Lily look trustingly up at Danny and wondered if, one day, she might have one like that. Would she, mused Gemma, slipping into her favourite delicious daydream, have a daughter who looked like her? It wasn't that she was particularly proud of her own blonde hair or her nose which turned up a bit too much at the end, or even her eyes, which a Certain Person, back in her Cambridge days, had described as one of her best features. No. It was because it would be so nice, one day, to hear someone say, 'You must be mother and daughter.' As she'd told Kitty enough times, she simply couldn't imagine life without children of her own.

It was nearly picking-up time now for the morning session. Together with Jean and Bella, she helped round up the children, making sure they all had their snack boxes to go home with as well as two lots of gloves and their coats and the right shoes. Amazing how many went home with another's left shoe by mistake! Last term they'd had two Puddleducks who kept swapping their underpants, which resulted in a few M&S/Primark mix-ups.

'You nip out before the afternoon session,' urged Jean, seeing her glance at her watch. 'I know you've got things to do in town. I can clear up here.'

Jean was so sweet! And it would help. It really

would. She simply couldn't put this off any longer. 'Thanks so much.' Gemma gave Jean a quick hug that made her colleague flush. 'I won't be long. Promise.'

Nosing her grandmother's old green Morris Minor out of the playgroup car park with its large blue and white duck sign, Gemma joined the lunchtime queue down the road towards the town centre.

Now, as she edged towards the roundabout, she saw Alex and his mum in one of her long, flowing cheesecloth skirts walking past, waving excitedly with their matching red hair and freckles. HM, Miriam called her. Not Her Majesty as the rather upmarket Bella had assumed, but Hippy Mum.

The traffic was stationary so, very quickly, Gemma waved back. Children found it so exciting to meet teachers out of school! It was as though they assumed staff were locked away in the supplies cupboard along with all the materials.

Spotting a parking space, Gemma made a mental note to grab something from the supermarket so she could get free parking and then . . .

An ominous crunch sent shudders down her spine. Shaking, Gemma glanced into her mirror but couldn't see anything. Yet she had definitely hit something. Feeling sick, she opened the side door. Please don't let it be a child. Or a dog. Or a . . . motorbike? And not just any motorbike. A big red and black steaming piece of metal with souped-up handlebars and a seat that should have been high up off the ground but was now lying on its side.

'What on earth do you think you were doing?'

A tall well-built man – with a hint of dark stubble on his chin, dressed from head to toe in black leather, glared at her. Under his arm he carried a red helmet with a large black stripe running through it. He would have been good-looking, Gemma thought, if he hadn't been scowling so ferociously.

'I'm so sorry.' Gemma stared down at the bike, still unable to believe what had happened. Thank goodness Morris the Minor wasn't damaged. 'I just didn't see it.'

'How could you have missed it? It was right behind you. Didn't you look in your mirror?'

'Yes of course I did, but your bike isn't the same height as a car, is it?'

'That's because it's a bike and not a car,' he growled.

'If it's broken, I'll pay for it,' she ventured.

He was already on his knees, having a good look and running his fingers over the bodywork and the winged back as though the motorbike was a person. 'You're lucky.' He spoke over his shoulder without looking at her. 'She seems to be all right.'

She? OK, so she called Granny's car 'Morris', but it somehow seemed a bit odd for a man who must be, what, in his mid-thirties, to refer to his bike as a 'she'.

'Sure?' Gemma glanced nervously at her watch. She had about a nanosecond to go before her appointment. 'Because if you don't want me to pay for anything, I need to go.'

The back of his head nodded curtly. I'll take that as a yes, thought Gemma as she sprinted along the side of the supermarket and into a dark brown building on the high street.

By the time she came out, Gemma felt both scared

and excited. Soon after Christmas, they had confirmed. It would all be sorted by then.

Meanwhile, no else, she told herself, while automatically checking her precious silver chain to make sure it was still round her neck, must know about this, apart of course, from Kitty. To her family, the rest of the world and in particular to Puddleducks Playgroup, Gemma had to make sure that she was known as Miss Merryfield, the dependable, warm, uncomplicated nursery-school acting head.

Chapter 3

Nancy Carter Wright sat in her car outside the playgroup, watching the remaining stragglers trooping in with their array of brightly coloured snack boxes and coats, which Nancy had learned to call 'anoraks' in a bid to fit in.

How could Danny have behaved like that?

Her mind went back half an hour to when she had queued up along with a male (!) au pair who kept texting, while some kid in oversize spectacles balanced dangerously on a wall above a woman in pink slippers who was actually breastfeeding her baby in front of everyone.

Danny had been sitting in his stroller quietly, his legs dangling over the edge, making her uncomfortably aware that Sam was right and that their son probably was getting a bit too big for his stroller, or rather 'pushchair', as she'd learned to call it now.

Then some woman who looked as though she belonged more in Haight-Ashbury with that long cheesecloth skirt, dangly green earrings and bright ginger hair arrived with her rosy-cheeked kid on one of those three-wheeled cycles which looked really dangerous to her. The doors had opened at that point and they'd all gone streaming in, apart from one mother with twins around her neck and a toddler at her ankles.

'Don't cry! It's all right, precious. Mummy will stay with you. She won't go just yet!'

Nancy had stared with longing at the woman who was comforting her daughter in the lovely blue and white patterned daisy tights, whose face was blotchy with tears. Danny, on the other hand, had shot off, still in his coat, towards the messy corner where he had sat down next to the child who'd been walking the wall and immediately began playing cars. Traitor!

'Shall we hang up your jacket, Danny, before you start playing?' suggested one of the helpers, the name *Bella* on her beautifully pressed Puddleducks sweat-shirt over a rather tight skirt. 'Look. Your peg has a picture of a dog next to it. D for Danny and D for dog, see?'

He hadn't even given Nancy a backward look as she'd kissed him goodbye and promised that she'd be back at lunchtime, on the dot.

Now, as she sat in the car, making sure that he didn't try to run out and see where she'd gone, she wondered what on earth she should do to fill in the time. Sit here with her book? Go for a walk?

It was one of those bright September days that her mother-in-law, who lived in Norwich, referred to as 'a summer autumn'. But despite the lovely warm sunshine that filtered in through the car window, Nancy couldn't bring herself to leave.

What would Danny be doing right now inside that place? Would he still be in the messy corner, with its bowls of jelly that kids were actually encouraged to

28

run their hands through and 'examine the texture'? Just think of all those germs that must be lurking inside, the ones that she called 'monsters' to try and get Danny to see that he really must wash his hands every time he touched something.

Nancy shuddered. She could just see Danny's small bewildered face now. He'd be feeling completely lost in that old-fashioned hall with its notices about Mothers Union and Sunday school and something called the Women's Institute.

He'd be yanking at the sleeve of that girl who seemed far too young to be in charge of all those children. This Gemma, with her sing-song voice and bright yellow bangs, would be too busy with the other kids so Danny would be making his way across the hall and out through the door which someone was bound to have left unlocked after these latecomers, and then what? He'd try to make his way back along that busy high street and maybe he'd cross the road to try and get home.

The picture, which was all too clear in her head, sent cold shivers down her back. Perhaps she'd just sit and read her book right here in the car park. That way she could also keep an eye out for Danny in case he came looking for her. It was only two and a half hours. And then she could go in and collect him. Anything rather than go home and be in an empty house.

Sitting in the car didn't help either, though. Glancing furtively across the car park, she decided to take a quick peek in at the window. She was sure no one would notice; not if she was careful.

Nancy felt a huge lump forming in her throat as

she saw her son standing in a ring of children, each earnestly singing that song on the bottom of the newsletter. They were doing actions too.

'We are the little Puddleducks'

They were pointing to themselves now.

'We love to learn through play.'

Here they were counting on their fingers while skipping.

'It keeps us bright and busy'

They were grinning at this point and pretending to sweep the floor with an imaginary brush.

'Orrrrrlllll through the day!'

Here they were stretching out their arms on either side.

Nancy felt a pang of jealousy as she slunk back to the green and white four-wheel drive that Sam had bought her as protection against the forthcoming winter weather. She should have done more playing with Danny when she'd had him to herself all day. Now he'd be bored at home if he was having so much fun here.

At 11.25 on the dot, Nancy clambered stiffly out of the car again, having sat there for two hours, miserably listening to the radio.

'Blimey, you're here early,' said a small, plump woman with the sort of clear braces that Nancy had had as a child. 'Your kid's first day, is it?'

Nancy nodded.

'I'm usually late but I had a dentist appointment round the corner so no excuses, right?' She nudged Nancy in that familiar fashion which seemed to come naturally to some English women.

'I know you from somewhere!' She searched Nancy's face as though looking for clues. 'Weren't we at antenatal together?'

Nancy thought back to the days when she and Sam had just moved to Hazelwood. She was six months pregnant, and the doctor had suggested classes. She hadn't found anyone there who seemed a natural friend but then again, back in Connecticut where she had grown up, she'd always been a bit of a loner, preferring her own company and books to the fussy clothes and make-up and dolls that the other girls were into.

After Danny's birth, Sam had encouraged her to go to the group's weekly post-natal gatherings. But it wasn't safe! Everyone knew that you came out of a doctor's surgery with more germs than you went in with, so why should these groups be any different?

In fact, that was one thing that was really worrying her about playgroup: that Danny would go down with all the bugs that were bound to be hovering dangerously in the air. Maybe she ought to buy him one of those face masks that the Japanese wore in airports. So sensible, she mused, completely forgetting the woman in front of her.

'Nancy, isn't it?' persisted the woman. 'You've cut your hair. That's why I didn't remember you immediately.'

The urchin look, as the hairdresser had called it, was meant to make it easier for her in the mornings by giving her more time for Danny.

'I'm Brigid.' There was a gummy grin. 'And that tall gangly woman with pink streaks in her hair and

31

the pushchair is Annie. Right. Doors opening, everyone. Brace yourselves!'

Nancy shot in, searching for Danny and wondering at the same time why this woman could remember her name while she failed miserably to remember hers. Motherhood made you forgetful; her American parenting magazine told her that. A sign of post-natal depression, her mother had said warningly in a recent letter.

'Did you have a nice time, poppet?'

But Danny was ignoring her. Instead, he was playing hide and seek in the playhouse with a scruffy kid wearing a Ben 10 T-shirt and a No Fear cap with a smear of red paint down the side.

'We haven't seen you for ages,' the gangly mum was saying as Nancy tried in vain to get Danny's attention. She had a pushchair next to her containing a small muffled-up pink bundle with a tiny button nose that gave Nancy a short sharp shot of envy. 'I'm Annie, remember? Brigid and I thought we'd go to Break and Flake down the road for a sandwich. No, Matthew. Don't poke your sister's eyes. She's asleep. Want to join us?'

Somehow Nancy found herself agreeing. Leaving her car, she persuaded Danny to get into his pushchair so he didn't run alongside the pavement like that unruly boy Billy in the No Fear cap, who turned out to belong to Brigid with the clear braces.

'Only just started at Puddleducks, have you?' asked Annie as they walked down the hill.

Nancy felt herself colour up in that unflattering red patchy way that she'd developed as a teenager and

32

never got rid of. It hadn't been so obvious back in Connecticut, where her natural tan had offset the plainness of her looks. In England, her skin was the same colour as uncooked pastry.

'Kind of.'

Brigid shot her a look. 'But your boy's nearly four, isn't he, like ours, and they've been going for ages. Blimey, I'd go nuts if I had Billy at home all day.'

'I just felt,' said Nancy, her accent twanging slightly in the way it always did when she was trying to keep calm, 'that he wasn't ready before.'

There was an awkward silence during which she could almost hear them thinking 'overprotective mum'. Well, at least she was keeping her son safe in his pushchair, which was more than the other two were doing. How could they let their children edge along the pavement like that in some kind of daredevil game?

They were at the café now and sitting down at one of the outside tables. It was, Nancy had to confess, quite nice. One of the reasons they had moved to Hazelwood was that it was just an hour to London, which meant Sam's commute wasn't too bad. Then there was the town itself, which was really pretty and bursting with good dress shops, an art gallery and an ancient church with arch-shaped windows that advertised yoga sessions outside.

'Want out!' Danny yanked at his pushchair straps in a way he had never done before. If that was what playgroup taught him, she wasn't impressed. 'All right, but you have to sit still,' she said firmly as she lifted him out, putting him on the chair next to her.

33

'Mum! Ice cream!'

Danny was pointing to one of those stalls on the street that might or might not be properly refrigerated. 'How about a nice healthy rice cake,' Nancy offered, getting out the packet she always carried in her bag.

Danny held out his hand reluctantly.

'What's the magic word?' she reminded him.

He grinned, displaying that same winsome charm that his father had won her over with. 'Chocolate!'

The other women snorted with laughter. Why was it that some English women acted like pigs?

'No Danny, it's "please". You know that.'

'He's all right,' interrupted Brigid. 'Now, what do you think of Puddleducks? Great, isn't it? Coming to the social evening, are you?'

Nancy shook her head firmly. 'I couldn't possibly leave Danny.' She was dead sure of that one. 'The last time I did that was when he was six months old, and this neighbour of mine left the side of his cot down when she checked him.'

'And you haven't left him since then?' demanded Brigid. 'Jeff and I go out for a drink every Friday but then my mum sits for us.' She laughed loudly. 'Completely mad she is but I don't know what I'd do without her. You got family here?'

Nancy shook her head. 'My mom is in Connecticut.' She paused, wondering whether to mention her father, who was now in Vancouver with his third wife, and decided against it on the grounds that it might lead to more nosy questions. After all, their relationship added up to scarcely more than an occasional exchange of Thanksgiving phone calls. 'But Patricia, my mother-in-law,' she added with a sudden need to feel more conventional, 'lives in Norfolk.'

'Blimey!' Brigid's expression indicated that Norfolk might as well be as far away as Connecticut. 'My mum lives next door. We've got one of those cottages by the canal. You know, the ones that used to be council. Miriam lives there too. She's the real Puddleducks play leader, but she's on maternity leave at the moment and that's why Gemma is in charge until Christmas.'

Alarm bells began to ring in Nancy's head as her new friends prattled on. The real playgroup leader wasn't there? That explained the young girl whom she hadn't met when checking out Puddleducks last term. A flash of doubt passed through her. Was this girl really experienced and responsible enough to look after her Danny?

'So we thought we might join some kind of class. Maybe yoga. What do you think?'

Nancy became aware they were both looking at her in that funny way again. 'Sorry? You lost me there.'

Gangly mum was grinning. 'Now that the boys are at nursery, we thought we'd do something for ourselves for a change. Want to join us? Matthew, I told you not to poke her eyes. Now she's wide awake, you little monkey!'

Nancy suddenly felt horribly aware of that overwhelming suffocating feeling that submerged her every now and then and made her want to run home, shutting the front door on the world outside. 'I'm not sure about doing a course,' she wobbled.

35

Brigid was looking sorry for her now, which was even worse. 'But don't you think it would be a good idea to do something with your time, Nancy? Didn't you used to be a scientist or something brainy like that before Danny was born? No, Billy, you've just been to the toilet. You can't need to go again.'

It was time to go home now. Definitely time. 'That was ages ago,' she managed to say, though her voice was sounding even wobblier than before. 'I can't go back to work now. Things have changed and besides, I want to be there for Danny when he comes back from nursery.'

Annie reached out and touched her hand. 'We're not talking about going back to work, Nancy. Just a class.'

'No!' She whipped her hand away. 'And before you start preaching to me, why don't you look after your own son? Look how near the road he is. He could get run over and if he did, it would be your fault!'

Their horrified faces looked as though she'd just slapped them with a packet of baby wipes. Too late, Nancy realised she'd said too much. Overcome with embarrassment, she whipped Danny out of his chair, dumped him in the pushchair and sped off down the high street as fast as she could. It was only when they got home that she realised, with a horrible pang, that she'd forgotten to pick up her check.

Chapter 4

The whole upsetting incident, coupled with Brigid's remark about her being a scientist, disturbed Nancy for the rest of the day, taking her back to a life which she had tried so hard to bury in her mind in order to concentrate on this one.

Yet, as she attempted to persuade Danny to have an afternoon nap after his exhausting morning, she found herself remembering.

When she'd met Sam, she'd just started working as a researcher in the Physics department at Harvard, partly thanks to a teacher at school who had noticed her natural abilities as a scientist, and encouraged her to take a degree. For her part, Nancy loved the clean pristine qualities of numbers. There was only a 'right' and a 'wrong' with maths and science; none of these woolly interpretations practised by her friends in the Arts faculty.

She loved her work, really loved it, but then along had come Sam, who'd been a friend of a fellow researcher, and that was that. For her, anyway. She had been totally smitten and he . . . well, he had liked her. But she couldn't help thinking that if Danny hadn't happened, before they'd even had a chance to celebrate their first-meeting anniversary, they might not have got this far.

Now as Nancy snuggled up in front of a CBeebies DVD with Danny on her knee, nuzzling his head, she wondered if this was why Sam had been so cold and distant in the last year. Was he regretting his decision to stand by the rather plain American girl whom he'd got pregnant with slightly indecent haste? Parenthood had taken both of them by surprise, and not just because of its speed. It was all so much more difficult than anyone told you.

Why, thought Nancy as she switched off the set after the buzz of the twenty-five-minute timer to prevent Danny getting hooked, couldn't kids behave like numbers?

'That's right, Danny. Play with your counting bricks!' She piled them up in their correct order. 'See? One, two, three . . .'

If only you could do the same with children! How she wished she could add up their columns or quirky characteristics and pack them neatly into their rightful places. Maybe she simply wasn't cut out for motherhood. Her own mother certainly had had her doubts and not just about her parenting abilities. 'Marriages often fall apart when children come along unless you know what you're doing. Remember, dear, that if it doesn't work out you can always come back here.'

The words had made Nancy stiffen. She wasn't going to end up bringing up Danny alone, as her own mother had done when her father walked out all those years ago.

Maybe that was why Annie's words about the classes had rankled. Perhaps she *did* need to do something else while Danny was at playgroup. But what?

38

Ideally, she'd have liked another baby, but unless a peck on the cheek could be considered as sex, that would be impossible!

Besides, Danny always insisted on coming into bed with them at night and his small restless body, flailing between them, made intimate relations both physically and emotionally impossible.

Yet, if she could give him something to make him sleep for just one night, she might persuade Sam to . . . Then she could have another baby. At least she would have something to do when Danny was at school all day.

That was when the idea came to her. A seduction plan! The boldness made her flush. Later tonight she'd cook a really nice chilli con carne, which was one of Sam's favourite dishes. She'd try, really try, not to run upstairs every half-hour to check that Danny was still breathing in the red fire-engine bed they'd had imported from Bloomingdales, and then they might actually have some time to themselves.

Meanwhile, she still couldn't get rid of that niggling fear about the new playgroup fill-in. It had been haunting her ever since the girls had mentioned it.

If Gemma Merryfield was only 'acting leader' for the older, clearly experienced Miriam whom she'd met when first looking round, did that mean she hadn't had her CRB check? Nancy was an expert on the Criminal Records Bureau, thanks to Google, as well as everything else on playgroups and pre-schools.

There had been a terrible case recently in the papers where one playgroup hadn't checked an employee's record and a child had been abused. The idea made her want to vomit and the more she thought about it, the more it seemed possible that this could happen again. Surely it was only sensible to make a phone call just to check out the situation?

An answerphone! How irresponsible of them not to have someone at the playgroup, manning it twenty-four seven.

'This is Mrs Carter Wright. My son Danny has just started with you and I have an urgent question about security checks on staff. Please could you ring me. DANNY, DON'T DO THAT!'

Dropping the handset, Nancy raced towards her son, who had gone puce. Just in time, she managed to hook her index finger down his throat and extract a horseshoe-shaped electric-blue brick. Instantly, his colour returned to normal.

'That's it!' Tears of relief shuddered through her as she pulled Danny towards her, rocking him back and forth and breathing in his special smell. 'That brick is going in the bin. It could have killed you. We'll write to the manufacturers just like we did with the felt shapes that you nearly swallowed, and tell them their lines simply aren't suitable for under-fives.'

Only then did she see the phone lying on the ground. As she went to put it back, she heard with dismay the click that meant that the Puddleducks Playgroup answerphone had recorded everything. Absolutely everything.

It was an hour later, after Danny had zonked out on her lap – if only he'd had that nap earlier – and she'd gently lowered him on to his bed and draped a pale blue cover over him, when there was the sound of the key in the lock.

Sam? But he wasn't usually back for hours! Nancy put down the wooden spoon and groaned. She'd taken advantage of Danny's exhaustion to get tonight's big seduction meal prepared well in advance, so she could put it in the oven ready for when he was home. Now Sam would see the surprise and it would all be ruined.

'You're early,' she said, wishing too late that her words had come out in a friendly fashion rather than in that accusatory tone.

Her husband put his head round the kitchen door. 'It's because I've got to get up at the crack of dawn tomorrow.'

Not again! She was tired of these early breakfast meetings in the City which meant that she felt obliged to get up to see him off, even though she'd only had a few hours' sleep herself, thanks to Danny's nocturnal habits. Even so, Nancy couldn't help feeling slightly sorry for her husband. He looked tired and his tie was slightly dishevelled. Too late, she wished she'd changed out of her sloppy beige sweatshirt that still had egg and soldier stains down the front from Danny's tea yesterday.

She made towards him to give him a kiss, but he was already frowning at the pan on the range. 'What's that?'

'Chilli,' she said reluctantly, knowing that the surprise was well and truly spoiled now. 'Thought I'd make something different tonight.'

His face took on an irritated look. 'But I told you.

41

I had a lunch today with clients so I didn't want dinner.'

'No.' She felt her hand shaking on the frying pan. 'You never said that.'

'I did.'

They glowered at each other. 'It's half done now, so someone's got to eat it.' Nancy was trying not to cry. 'I've got your son to bed early and . . .'

'He's your son too.'

'Maybe, but he's got your awkward bits.'

Oh dear. She hadn't meant to say that.

'And he's got yours.'

Stop, she wanted to say. We're behaving like a pair of children ourselves.

'Listen.' He gestured that they should move through to the sitting room and sit on the cream sofa they'd bought from Harrods when she was pregnant, before realising that this might not be the perfect colour for a small body prone to releasing smelly substances from both ends.

'I've been meaning to talk to you.'

His words carved a knife through her chest. This was almost exactly what her own father had said to her all those years ago, when he'd explained why he was going.

'I've got another trip coming up.'

Not another! Sam was always being sent out to Singapore, sometimes for as long as three or four days, which meant she had to cope with Danny all on her own.

'I've been asked to sort something out in the Ho Chi Minh office. You know, Vietnam.'

She cut in. 'I know where it is. I'm not stupid.'

'Did I say you were?' He got up from the sofa and looked out of the window at the garden swing they'd installed for Danny. 'It's until Christmas.'

'That's nearly four months away!'

'I know it's a long time to leave you.' He had turned round now, and was looking at her as though she was someone else other than his wife. 'But I think it might do us some good. Don't you?'

She began to shake. 'What do you mean?'

'Come on, Nancy.' He sat down again and took both her hands. His grasp felt cool and calculated. 'We both know things haven't been right for a long time. This will give us a chance to think.'

Part of her wanted to pull away her hands, and the other part to hang on to him to stop him going. 'Are you having an affair?'

Even as she said the words, she knew it wasn't possible. Sam just wasn't that kind of person.

'No. But I think you are.'

She stared at him, stunned. 'What on earth are you talking about?'

He was looking at her with that same strange cool look that, together with his blond hair, made him seem more Scandinavian than English. 'With our son. You love him more than you ever cared for me.'

'That's crazy.'

'You spend,' said Sam, getting up again and walking away from her into the kitchen as though to put space between them, 'every waking moment talking about him. You worry that he isn't eating; that his cold might be potential pneumonia; that he isn't talking as much as he should be; that he might choke in his sleep, which is why you allow him to come into our bed at night; that he might come to harm at this new playgroup, which is why you haven't sent him until now. In fact, all you ever do is put him first.'

Nancy was so stunned she could hardly speak as she ran after him. 'But he's a child. He needs looking after. You're a grown man.'

Sam nodded. 'Exactly. And you know what? I love Danny as much as you do, but you haven't been the same since he was born.'

'Nor have you! You expect life to go on as normal, but that doesn't happen when you have a three-year-old.'

'Nearly four, Nancy. Nearly four. Most couples are on their second by now, but how could we ever manage with two when we can't cope with one?'

He didn't even want another child! Nancy felt hot tears trickling down her cheeks. Sam put out a hand to wipe them away, but she turned from him. As she did so, she moved against the cooker and somehow knocked the saucepan handle flying.

'I'm sorry.' She began dabbing the sauce off her husband's suit with a piece of kitchen roll but it stuck in white paper bits all over his jacket. At the same time, they could hear the tiny telltale sounds of footsteps coming down the stairs.

'Mum! Mum!'

Without even looking at Sam, Danny went straight to her, trailing his blue cover and burying his head in her stomach so she could feel his warm sleepiness.

'See what I mean?' said Sam quietly. 'He ignores me completely.'

'It's only because he doesn't see enough of you,' hissed Nancy. 'Four months in Vietnam is going to make it even worse.'

Sam shrugged. 'Nothing I can do about it.' He rubbed his hand on Danny's head, but their son clung to her even more fiercely.

'Think I'll sleep in the spare room tonight,' said Sam softly. 'I won't disturb you then.'

'What?'

'Didn't I say? My flight is first thing tomorrow morning.'

Chapter 5

Joe Balls dropped the last remaining sticky sweet into the bin. Poor old Brian Hughes wouldn't need those any more, just as he wouldn't need the half-eaten packets of out-of-date Bourbon biscuits in his middle drawer.

It had been the end of a long day. Just as well the main school didn't start until tomorrow, due to 'staff training' which the head had cancelled at the last minute. Another sign of disorganisation, although it had given Joe extra time to prepare for tomorrow, not to mention clearing out Brian's stuff from his desk and locker, which no one else had bothered to do.

It was then that he heard the voices from the room next door. The first high-pitched one he hadn't heard before, but the second, the sort of heavy, breathy, ten-a-day type which he couldn't bear in a woman, definitely belonged to the school secretary. Diana Davies, but do call me Di, had introduced herself when she'd turned up at midday. He himself had been there since 6.15 a.m. On the dot.

'What's he like then?' said the high-pitched one.

'Imagine a cross between a northern Colin Firth with a slight paunch and Mr Grumpy and you might get the picture! Really dishy even if he does act a bit stern and, get this, no wedding ring! Some of the mums are going to love him!

'Mind you, goodness knows what time he must have got in. You know how early I usually am? Well today, I was running *slightly* behind and you could see from his face that he thought I should have been here before. Right now, he's clearing out Brian's desk. Probably should have done it myself but to be honest, it didn't seem right to nose through the poor man's things.'

There was a cluck of approval from the other woman. 'Such a shock. I couldn't believe it when I heard.'

'I know.' The voice dropped but Joe, who'd had plenty of practice at picking up low conversations, still managed to tune in. 'Makes you wonder if this one is any good, if they managed to get him in at such short notice.'

If there was anything that his years on the fourteenth floor of the second biggest bank in the world had taught Joe, it was to deal with backbiters immediately.

Slamming shut Brian's top desk drawer to make a noise and alert the two gossipers that he was there, he strode across the room, bending his head to avoid the ridiculous pot plant with the knobbly crooked stem.

Poor old bugger. Brian, he meant, not the plant, which would have to go, along with all the other mess that had been left behind. Streamlining and grade boosting. That's what the Reception year at Corrybank Primary needed. It was, after all, why he had been given the job in the first place. A touch of overall business acumen wouldn't be amiss either, even if that hadn't been in his job remit.

It would also help, in his opinion, if the whole playgroup concept was tidied up. Some areas seemed to call it a pre-school instead. Frankly, it was confusing.

'Mrs Davies?'

The plump woman with a low-cut blouse, a crinkly pale bosom which preceded her by several inches and a black polyester skirt that was far too tight for her age (which, Joe reckoned, had to be around seven squared), jumped. 'Goodness, Mr Balls! I thought you said you were going to examine the supply cupboard.'

'I have.' He nodded shortly at the owner of the squeaky voice, a skinny woman with the hair-tucked-behind-the-ears style which, he suspected, she might just have been sporting since her teenage years. Ditto her canary-yellow sweatshirt, which looked like school uniform. 'And you are . . . ?'

'Penny. I'm one of the teaching assistants.'

Joe couldn't help feeling a flash of scepticism. In his experience, 'teaching assistants' could be very varied in terms of abilities, ranging from bright graduate mummies at the top end, down to inadequately educated parents who used commas when they ought to have used full stops. One of his arguments at his interview for this job was that there should be a more uniform entry qualification for TAs.

'Do you mind telling me what your qualifications are?'

The woman fiddled with the buttons on her yellow sweatshirt. 'I don't actually have a teaching qualification but I did an English A level before I had my kids.'

'Right.' He nodded that short sharp nod that had

earned him the reputation of 'Balls by name, balls by nature' on that fourteenth floor. In fact, as Ed always said, his bark was far worse than his bite, but the problem was that once he started, he couldn't seem to stop. Like now. 'Want to know what my qualifications are?'

Both women were looking at him, their mouths open. 'Four A levels. First-class degree from Durham. MBA in Business Studies. Ten years working for the second biggest bank in the world. Three years teaching at one of the toughest primaries in east London which released me to step in as acting Reception head here at Corrybank after Brian Hughes' heart attack. And that is why I was able to come at such short notice, as you put it just now.'

Joe stopped abruptly. He had a nasty feeling that he might have been shouting or raising his voice without realising. The two women were now flushing awkwardly. In his experience, women could do this in one of two ways. The attractive kind that made them look vulnerable, or the blotchy kind that made them look as though they had measles, which now applied to both of them. Joe felt ashamed of himself for such thoughts.

'I'm sorry, Mr Balls,' breathed Di heavily, fiddling nervously with her too-tight polyester skirt band.

Joe waved her apologies away. That was another thing he'd learned on the fourteenth floor. Disarm your enemy with surprise and painful truths, but then forgive them graciously so they became part of your team. 'Let's just forget it, shall we?' He nodded at Penny to show he included her in his pardon too.

'After all, our main job is to get Corrybank back on its feet, isn't it?'

Joe suddenly realised he was talking as though he was in charge of the whole school. 'I'm sure you'll agree,' he added hastily, 'that the Reception year is possibly the most important. We need to catch our children quickly and get them into the right learning frame so they continue to make good progress right on through into secondary school.'

Much turkey-neck nodding, which reminded him of an aunt whom he and Ed used to visit religiously every Christmas. 'And do you know how we can begin?'

Two sets of worried eyes were on him. He needed to restore relations, and fast. 'By getting rid of that yukky plant in my office. It's a health and sanity hazard.'

Penny in the yellow sweatshirt twitched nervously. 'It's a yucca. And don't you mean health and safety, sir?'

He nodded tersely. 'It was meant to be a joke.'

Both women let out a simultaneous peal of false laughter. Ed had always said Joe was hopeless at trying to be funny on purpose.

'You can also arrange for someone to empty the bin, which is already overflowing with the contents of Brian's desk. I had to clear it myself.' He shot a look at Di to show she wasn't off the hook yet.

'Sorry, sir, but it didn't seem right somehow . . .'

'Really?' Joe couldn't bear it when people didn't face the obvious. 'Mr Hughes isn't going to be coming back, is he? We can hardly leave his office as a shrine.

In fact it's just as well we've all come in before term starts. There's a staggering amount of random paperwork that still appears to be on his desk.'

Di looked as though her forehead was about to overflow with tiny specks of sweat. It reminded him of the water cycle that was on his syllabus to teach the Reception year when they arrived. He'd feel better then, he thought. Children were so much more interesting and straightforward than adults.

'By the way, sir. You were meant to have got this before but I'm afraid it sort of got mislaid in the kerfuffle after Brian was taken ill.'

Joe glanced down at the untidily stapled paper she'd thrust into his hand.

Puddleducks Newsletter?

Di's voice got deeper and breathier. 'Puddleducks is the name of the playgroup round the corner, sir. It is linked to Corrybank and . . .'

'I'm well aware of the tie-up between the two, thank you.' Joe glanced down again at the newsletter, which, he could see, was written in a far too familiar and jaunty style. So unprofessional, with all those exclamation marks. 'Who wrote this?'

'Gemma Merryfield, sir. She's the . . .'

'Acting head of the playgroup.' Joe flashed one of his more charming smiles. 'I made it my business to know who the main players were before I started.'

Penny looked upset. Well done, Joe, he told himself. Now you've implied she isn't important. 'There are some changes I need to make to this,' he began.

'Changes?' Di's eyebrows, which were, he observed, faintly pencilled in as though the originals had disappeared, rose. 'It's too late for that, I'm afraid. They've already been posted.'

'Snail mail? Why weren't they emailed? Do you know how much a stamp costs nowadays?'

The teaching assistant was stammering now in an effort to produce an explanation. This wasn't the kind of start he had wanted, Joe told himself. Forget the northern Colin Firth. Both women probably saw him now as Mr Grumpy crossed with a three-pronged Halloween figure.

'Gemma Merryfield,' said Di coolly, 'thought it would be a personal touch. Besides,' she added primly, 'not all families are on the Net.'

Really? From his experience during the last three years at an inner London school, most of the kids there were glued to Facebook.

'Actually,' added Penny, smoothing down her yellow sweatshirt in an action that seemed to go with a sudden boldness in her voice, 'we've had quite a few phone calls for the PS bit.'

The PS bit?

'There,' Di's squat, unpainted index finger stabbed in the general direction of the bottom of the page in front of him.

Do any of you mums have a secret talent? If so, we'd like to hear from you. At Puddleducks Playgroup, we welcome outside speakers who can tell us about their own area of expertise. So if you're an artist or a writer or a singer or even if you have just come back from an interesting holiday, please get in touch.

Penny was virtually jumping up and down now with a schoolgirl excitement that made Joe feel embarrassed on her behalf. His banking days had taught him to be wary of unrestrained enthusiasm. It was usually the sign of someone going over the edge. 'We've got one Puddleducks parent, Molly's mum,' she was babbling, 'who's a keeper at the zoo near here.'

Joe frowned. 'But what relevance does that have to the curriculum?'

'It's all part and parcel of showing children how the world works.' Di was colouring up again as she spoke. 'Well, something like that anyway.'

'I can see that.' Always let someone know you can see their point of view, he reminded himself. 'Fond as I am of figures, I can see that children need more than hard-nosed facts. But talks from monkey keepers?' He gave a short laugh. 'Don't you think all that is a bit amateurish?'

Clearly not, from the stony look on Di's face, and her silence, which said more than any words could. An unfamiliar cold wave of uncertainty passed through him. Had he made a mistake in coming here and leaving the sharp end of teaching in London? The thought made him shudder. Maybe this was not the clever career move it had initially seemed to be.

When Joe had first been emailed by someone rather high up from the local authority, asking if he would consider a post that had just come up to cover an emergency in a lively town that was 'only an hour from London', he had, to be honest, been quite tempted. His time at the inner-city school had ceased to be the challenge it had been at the beginning and he was aware that as a late entrant to the teaching profession, he needed to build up his CV.

Hazelwood had seemed just the ticket. No need to move, since he could just about commute from the flat he had bought in Notting Hill after Ed. The job would also be a challenge of a different kind.

'If you can turn this place around, it will be a real feather in your cap, Mr Balls,' he'd been told at the interview, and he had felt excited shivers down his spine.

And now, here he was, discussing zookeepers! 'Talking of Gemma Merryfield,' said Joe, in what he hoped was a conciliatory tone, 'I see from Brian's diary that he had a meeting booked with her this evening, which I intend to keep. So if anyone calls for me, would you kindly tell them that I will be at the playgroup until,' he checked his watch, 'at least 6 p.m.'

Di sucked in her breath. 'I think we'll both be gone by then, Mr Balls.'

He felt another flash of annoyance. A school was a business like any other, and whatever their rank, staff ought to be prepared to work late. 'That's a shame. I was going to ask if you would like a working supper at one of the cafés in town.'

The invitation was meant as a friendly gesture, but from their shocked faces he might as well have asked them to jump from that fourteenth floor; something one of his colleagues had once threatened to do over a deal that had gone badly wrong.

'I've got my Sid to cook for, thanks,' said Di hastily.

The teaching assistant was beginning to stammer again. 'I've got to walk my . . . my dog.'

'Really!' Di's eyes flashed interest. 'I didn't know you had one. Oh, I see . . .'

Pretending not to feel hurt, Joe returned to his office and began taking down the calendar bearing pictures of Hazelwood's Top Twelve Beauty Spots that Brian had pinned on the wall next to his desk. Poor bloke hadn't realised then that he wouldn't be there to turn over to the September page.

After that, it would be time to tackle Miss Gemma Merryfield about the newsletter and her ideas for next term. Then he needed to spend another four hours (or as he liked to think of it, two hours squared) on his own proposals. Nothing like numbers, thought Joe happily as he walked briskly down the high street towards the first turning on the right. Good, clean and simple figures which made you feel that everything was nicely in control.

Chapter 6

Puddleducks, Joe had discovered during his brief recce earlier on, looked as though it had jumped out of a Caribbean brochure, with its whitewashed walls and cheerful yellow and red flowers painted childishly round the windows and doors.

Above the doorway was a faded Girl Guides sign, and the words 'Memorial Hall' in chipped green paint. But below that, on the doors, someone had painted a giant blue and white duck with an apron on. Quite sweet really, if you liked that kind of thing.

There were voices inside too! Laughter. Not the sarcastic type like that of the fourteenth floor, or the short sharp snorts of despair in the staffroom of the inner-city primary. This was the genuine variety and for a reason which Joe couldn't put his finger on, it disturbed him.

'Don't worry about it! Mistakes happen!' This voice sounded as though it was laced with exclamation marks. It was the sort of voice, noted Joe, that managed to somehow sing and laugh at the same time. How did people do that? When he spoke, it was always in a gravelly tone. It had been one of the things that Ed had apparently liked about him.

'Once,' continued the voice, 'my mother dropped us off the day before term was due to start and didn't wait to check we'd gone in. It was different in those days. My brother and I just played in the fields and went home, pretending we'd been to school for the day!'

'Really?' This other voice had a south London edge to it, suggesting the owner wasn't a local. As a native Tynesider and proud of it, Joe had been shocked when he'd moved to London and found that the inhabitants on the north side of the river, especially the bits that were merging into Buckinghamshire and Bedfordshire like Hazelwood, regarded themselves as a breed apart from those on the south side of the Thames.

'I feel so stupid. It's this new job of mine. They know I have to leave early for nursery pick-up but then my boss – who doesn't have kids himself – put all these files on my desk and I didn't like to say no. It won't happen again, really.'

Her voice had a tearful edge to it. 'I'm sorry, Honey. You must be starving.'

The singing voice chimed in. 'Actually, I gave her one of my sandwiches. Hope that's all right.'

'It had cold sore in it!' piped up a shrill voice.

Both women snorted with laughter. 'I think you mean coleslaw, Honey!'

Joe silently groaned inside. Don't say the child was actually *called* Honey. He'd thought it was a term of endearment rather than a first name. Why was it that people down south didn't seem to give their children proper Christian names?

'Better get cracking now,' continued the laughing sing-song voice, which, he suspected by now, belonged to this Gemma Merryfield. 'I've got a meeting with the new Reception head at the big school. None of us have met her before, although someone said that . . .'

Her? Clearly this was his cue. 'Good evening,' he began, walking into the hall. Then he stopped. Joe never forgot a face but surely, in this case, there had to be a mistake. Either that or it was some pretty big coincidence. Was this the girl from the car park?

'As you'll see,' he continued, still staring at the sing-song blonde with the fringe, wearing a Puddleducks sweatshirt, 'the head of Reception is male rather than female.'

The girl flushed. 'I'd been told to expect someone called Joanna Balls.'

It was one more example of this place's inefficiency! '*Joe* Balls, actually.' Stiffly, he put out his hand to shake hers while taking another good look. There was no mistaking that nose which turned up a bit too much at the end. Or those strangely compelling muddy greeny-blue eyes which had stared at him only a few hours earlier when he'd nipped into town for a sandwich and found that some idiot had reversed into his bike.

And unless he was very much mistaken, the penny had just dropped at her end too. 'You're the new acting head of Reception?' she said in the sort of voice that sounded as if she was hoping to be corrected.

He found himself nodding curtly, willing himself not to bite off her head about the bike. It was, he'd since told himself, something that could have happened to anyone. Anyone, that is, who hadn't been looking properly.

'I'm really sorry about your bike.'

Immediately, he flashed her a look that was meant to indicate 'not in front of a mother'. Too late! He could sense the excited frisson of interest already.

'I'd better get going while you have your meeting,' interrupted Late Mum. Fantastic. No doubt all this would be fuelling tomorrow morning's parent-at-the-school-gate gossip. 'See you tomorrow. Honey, say goodbye to your teacher!'

Joe watched Gemma waving goodbye to the child, who was dancing off with her mother, purple mittens jiggling at her side at the end of their elastic arms. He had to hand it to her. The rather enthusiastic Miss Merryfield might not have great motor control when it came to reversing, but she seemed to have a way with the kids. Maybe he'd been a bit tough with her.

'You always get *one* who either turns up very early or very late,' said Joe in what was meant to be a 'let's forget the motorbike scene' tone.

Gemma laughed nervously but he could see that the smile didn't reach her eyes. He'd worried her and now he was going to have to upset her even more.

'I was really shocked to hear about Brian,' she cut in before he could begin. 'So sudden! He was such a good Reception head and always went to so much trouble to make sure he knew the children before they came up.' She stopped suddenly. 'I'm sorry. I didn't mean that you won't be such a good head.'

There was an awkward pause and then there she went, rabbiting on again. He could almost hear the exclamation marks in her sentences, just like the newsletter. 'It's just that it's all a bit of a shock, like I said.

I only heard recently and I'm still getting my head around it.'

'That's life,' he said, more crisply than he'd intended. 'Meanwhile, I thought we ought to discuss a few things.'

Joe made a sign that she should sit down. The only chair near her was child-sized and red plastic. He himself took the adult one, which put her at even more of a disadvantage. Not very nice but tactically necessary.

'I'd like to start by discussing your newsletter.' He drew out the poorly stapled pages of A4 from his jacket pocket. 'Did you run this past anyone for approval before sending it out?'

'Not exactly, but . . .'

'Did you or didn't you?'

'Miriam, who used to run the playgroup but is now on maternity leave . . .'

He cut in without meaning to. 'I know about that.'

'Well, Miriam said I could have a free rein.'

'Tell me. Does a free rein include using a plethora of exclamation marks and inviting zookeepers in?'

She coloured. 'We've always had parents coming in to give talks. Last term, we had a mother from Goa who showed the children how curry powder is made.'

'And is that really important from an education point of view?'

She shot him a look. 'Do *you* know how curry powder is made?'

He had a sudden vision of the curry house with pink and blue neon lights off the Holloway Road that he and Ed used to frequent every Wednesday. It had been their favourite.

'Not exactly. Besides, that's not the point.' He waved the newsletter in front of her. 'May I ask why you posted these instead of emailing them and saving money?'

Her expression became wary, making her look older than the twenty-three or -four he'd first put her at. 'Not everyone has access to a computer.'

'Come on!'

'I mean it!' Those greeny-blue eyes were almost glaring at him. 'Besides, it's nice to have some old-fashioned traditions. Parents can pin this on the kitchen wall.'

'Just as they could do with a printout.' He took a document from his briefcase and put it in front of her. 'Let's move on. I'd like you to take a look at this.'

She glanced at the paper for a minute and then up at him from her child's chair. The ridiculous height difference meant he could see she had very carefully lined the inside of her eyelids with soft violet. For some inexplicable reason, this disturbed him.

'Britain's Top Ten Playgroup of the Year Award?'

He nodded.

She frowned. 'I've never heard of it before.'

'That's because there isn't one.'

The violet lines crinkled slightly. 'I don't understand.'

'You will. In precisely one week, one of the biggest banks in the world is going to be announcing that it is sponsoring the competition and awarding a rather large sum of money to the ten best playgroups in Britain. Of course, the money will be useful, but it will be the prestige which really counts.'

'How do you know this?'

Because he had persuaded his old boss at the bank to push the idea? Because he had told them that banks needed to do something to restore their reputation in the public eye? 'Trust me. I just do, although sadly, despite my inside knowledge, there is no guarantee that we will win.'

Gemma stood up as though she presumed the meeting was over, although maybe she was just uncomfortable in that small chair.

'Hang on. I haven't finished yet. There's something else, something extremely important, that I need to say. It's about one of the new Puddleducks.'

He lowered his voice. 'I know Beryl's already talked to you about Lily but I just want to run an idea past you. I think we need to talk to the other parents and explain that it's vital they don't talk to the press about her. Do you agree?'

Chapter 7

Joe called Mike as soon as he could find a suitable place to pull in on his way home, but it was Lynette who picked up the phone.

'Still out, I'm afraid.' She gave a small sigh. 'Did I tell you he's having to do some private tuition? We're finding it a bit tough at the moment.'

Immediately, Joe felt bad. Money had never been a problem when he'd been in the City and even now, he was comfortable. But that was because he didn't have anyone else to look after. Once, after one of his bonuses, he'd offered to help them out – after all, Mike and Lynette were his best friends – but they'd clearly been offended and the subject hadn't been raised again.

'How was your first day?' Her voice was so soothing and inviting that Joe found himself telling Lynette all about biting Gemma's head off in the supermarket car park and then finding she was the playgroup leader.

'No!' Lynette's voice had a disbelieving thrill in it. 'You'll have to take her out to dinner to apologise!'

'But she was the one at fault,' he protested. 'In fact, they all are. Everyone's so disorganised.'

'Is that so?' Lynette's voice took on a slightly different edge. 'Or is that just Joe Balls, Mr Perfectionist speaking? Don't take this the wrong way, will you? But it sounds as though Hazelwood is a very different kettle of fish from your London school. If I were you, I'd go easy. You don't want to get off to a wrong start, do you?'

Joe began to feel rather uncomfortable. He'd always been able to talk to Lynette, ever since they'd all met at university back in the nineties. In fact, if Mike hadn't beaten him to it, he might have asked her out.

Instead, she'd become his best female friend and her advice was usually sound. 'Wrong start?' he repeated ruefully. 'I've got a feeling that it might be a bit late.'

'Nonsense.'

'No. I mean it.' Joe felt his voice become uncertain. 'What if Mike was wrong when he suggested I should go into teaching? Sometimes I don't think I've got the patience.'

'You have!' He could almost see her now, sitting at the foot of the staircase, talking to him and flicking back her shoulder-length auburn hair in the way she did without thinking. Sometimes he thought that if he didn't have Mike and Lynette, he wouldn't know where to turn.

'You've got workplace skills, Joe, and that's what schools need nowadays. Look how amazing you were in that London school. I still remember coming along to that maths quiz you put on.'

Her voice became muffled as though she was covering the handpiece. 'Mike and I had to pick our way through condoms in the playground to get there. Neither of us could work in an environment like that,

I can tell you. And what about that boy who threatened you with a knife in class? You dealt with him brilliantly, just as you'll be able to deal with all these new problems. Just take it slowly, Joe. And don't be too quick to judge others. Try to show that softer side that lurks underneath.'

Maybe she was right.

'Changing the subject,' she was adding in that soft voice of hers, 'have you heard from Ed? I hope you don't mind me asking, but Mike and I couldn't help wondering.'

'No. Have you?'

He could almost hear her shake her head. 'Not a word. Mind you, I do think that . . .'

Whatever Lynette thought was suddenly drowned out by the sound of fierce arguing in the background. His godsons! Nothing could have made him prouder than when Mike and Lynette had asked him to do the honours not just once but twice.

'Boys, don't do that!' Lynette's voice was rising. 'No, Charlie, that's NOT your battery and do be quiet, I'm trying to speak to your godfather on the phone. Sorry, Joe. I've got to go. But you *are* coming down in a couple of weeks for Fraser's birthday, aren't you? Great. See you then. Bye!'

IMPORTANT NOTICE!

We know you've already had the Puddleducks September newsletter and although we don't want to drown you with more paperwork, we want to tell you about a Very Exciting Opportunity that has come up!

You might have read, in the press, about Britain's Top Ten Playgroup of the Year Award, which has just been launched by Bank With Us. Playgroups throughout the country have been invited to find a brand-new project that will involve the whole community.

For instance, it might be a reading project where we invite local businesses to donate books and then come in to hear the children reading.

This is the example that Bank With Us has given us, but we want to find something more exciting and different! So we're asking you to think of something that will help Puddleducks Playgroup win!

The prize is a staggering £20,000 to spend on equipment and resources but I'm sure you will agree that although the money would be very helpful, it's the prestige which will count. So, over to you! Please send your ideas into us, in writing!

PS. Just another reminder that there are still some spaces left for the After-School club, which is only open to Puddleducks and Corrybank children.

PPS. Below is another song we plan to sing at the end-of-term concert/nativity play. If you can practise it at home, along with the Puddleducks Song, that would be very helpful!

THE PUDDLEDUCKS TOOTHBRUSH SONG

We are the little Puddleducks
We love to clean our teeth.
Up and down, round and round,
Behind and underneath!

And again with actions!
We are the little Puddleducks
(children point to themselves)
We love to clean our teeth.
(toothbrush action)
Up and down, round and round,
*(bend down, straighten up and do finger circles in
air)*
Behind and underneath!
(look behind and then on floor)

Thanks, everyone!

Chapter 8

Gemma woke early on the second day of term, conscious that she'd just had a really weird dream. As she rolled out of bed and stumbled towards the bathroom that she used to share with the other lodger – so nice to have it all to herself now! – it came back to her in bits. There'd been something about a motorbike. A red and black bike with a metal wing-like structure that swept up at the back behind the seat as though it belonged to a rocker . . .

In her dream, the bike had taken off all on its own but as she'd begun chasing it down the road, she'd suddenly realised there was a child sitting on it. A very pale girl with dark hair and solemn blue eyes. Just at that point, she started to fall down a hole in the pavement.

Falling, according to Kitty, who was big on dream interpretation, meant a fear of losing control.

Gemma shivered as she peeled off her pjs and stood under the shower waiting for the hot water to kick in. No prizes for guessing why she'd dreamed of a bike like the one that belonged to Joe Balls (wow – had they got off to a wrong start there!) and a pale, dark-haired girl who looked like Lily.

Personally, she'd thought Joe's idea of talking to the parents about the need for discretion had been a good

69

one, but Beryl had vetoed it by email late last night, saying it would draw attention to the situation. After all, not all the parents realised exactly who Lily was.

Gemma closed her eyes, feeling the heat of the water finally surging over her. Even so, the niggling worry in her chest remained as she drove to work. Something didn't feel right, she thought, which was why she wasn't totally surprised when she arrived at Puddleducks to find the American mum with short spiky hair waiting at the door, clutching the other end of her son's Velcro wrist harness.

We don't start for another half an hour, she wanted to say, but the distraught look on the woman's face stopped her.

'Sorry I'm early. Danny, stand *still*! You can't go inside right now. Mrs Merryfield isn't ready for us yet.'

Miss Merryfield, please! Sometimes it just wasn't worth correcting.

'It's just that . . .' Her hands were twisting in an anguished fashion. 'I needed to make sure . . . You're new, aren't you?'

Gemma was taken aback for a second. 'I've been at Puddleducks for three years. But I've only just taken over as acting playgroup leader, if that's what you mean.'

The woman was nodding energetically. 'That's exactly what I meant. I don't mean to be rude but I wanted to make sure that you've been checked. Danny, I said stop fidgeting like that.'

Checked? Visions of an infectious diseases clinic shot into her head.

Mrs Carter Wright was still nodding furiously. 'That you've had your security checks.'

Was this what it was all about? Some people, thought Gemma, might have been affronted. Put yourselves in the parents' shoes, Granny had always said. If she'd been a mother in a strange country with different rules, she might be worried too.

'Yes I have.' Gemma almost wanted to pat the woman's hand comfortingly. 'We all have to. Everyone does who works here, including the cleaners. So you don't have to worry on that score.'

She glanced at her watch. 'I know you're early but if you want, why don't you come in with Danny now and you can watch us get ready. It might reassure you to see what we do.' She squatted down beside Danny, who was trying to yank off the wrist harness. 'Shall we show Mummy that lovely Wendy house you were playing in yesterday with your new friends? We could do some letter outlines too!'

Bella arrived shortly afterwards to find Mrs Carter Wright standing awkwardly over her son while he played peekaboo behind the playhouse curtains.

'Is that our new FM?' she hissed.

Gemma gave her a disapproving look. One thing she hadn't liked under Miriam's leadership was her boss's penchant for labelling mums. FM stood for Fussy Mum. There was, Miriam used to say heavily, always *one*. Then there was AW Mum, which stood for Always Working, like Freddie's mum who sent her son pictures of herself in the office via his kiddy iPhone, which he wasn't meant to have at school.

Occasionally there would be a DM (Drunk Mum)

after the social evening. Usually they had a very watered-down punch on offer, containing more orange and lemon squash than anything else. Last term one of the mothers had brought along her own bottle of 'water', which turned out to be vodka.

'I'm sho shad that Oliver is leaving to go to the big school,' she had said, hiccuping into everyone's ear. Gemma had just hoped that, for Brian's sake, Oliver and his weak bladder would mature at Big School.

Sometimes Gemma wished she could pick up all the parents and roll them into one so they came out with each other's pluses and minuses. Fussy Mum could give some of her worry to Couldn't Care Less Mum. Pushy Mum who had been going on at her about extra counting lessons after school could lose some of her pushiness to Forgetful Mum who had forgotten, again, to bring in her emergency contact form. And Helpful Mum ('Are you sure you don't want me to stay and help you put everything away?') could be balanced with Untidy Mum who had left a trail of chewing gum and dirty tissues on her way out.

'I've done the register and everyone's here,' said Jean importantly, coming up to her.

'See you later, Danny,' the American woman was saying.

'Poor thing,' whispered Jean. 'Did you see how our new boy didn't even give his mum a second look? Just like my lot when they went off to college.'

Bella sniffed. 'Better than yelling for their mums if you ask me. Now, bags I don't go on messy corner this morning. I'm still trying to get green jelly off my new bootlegs. By the way, have you seen what Lily is wearing? I'm sure I saw that silk dress in *Junior Vogue*.'

Gemma sighed. Bella was definitely in the wrong job. Anyone who wore new clothes to a nursery shouldn't complain if they got ruined.

Gemma clapped her hands, giving Bella a sharp look. 'Time to practise Puddleducks songs, I think, everyone!'

Sienna pouted. 'Why?'

'That's a good question,' said Gemma, ignoring Bella's rolling eyes. So what if Sienna was always asking 'why'? It was normal at this age. 'It's because singing is fun! Right, everyone. I'd like all the Puddleducks who were here last term to help the new ones with the words. Clemmie, can you stand next to Danny? Lovely. Off we go then.'

Gemma was rather proud of her Puddleducks songs, which she herself had made up. Singing was a great way of releasing emotions and also of helping children to learn how to do things. She was pleased to see Danny, his eyes bright and excited, nudging Lily in enthusiasm.

Automatically, Gemma's hand went up to her neck to touch her silver chain in the way she often did when feeling emotional. But a cold chill struck through her. It wasn't there.

Chapter 9

'Has anyone seen my silver necklace?' Gemma heard her own voice come out with a panicky edge as she crouched down on all fours, looking to see if it could be anywhere on the floor.

'What does it look like?' asked Bella in an interested tone.

Gemma tried to get her head straight. 'It's a chain.'

'With a pendant or without?' asked Jean soothingly.

'Without,' she said, almost in tears.

'Oh.' Bella's disappointed voice clearly suggested that in that case, there wasn't much to get excited about.

Bella, Jean and all the children tried to find it, but without any luck. Together they searched the messy corner, the quiet corner, the Wendy house and the playground. Nothing.

Gemma's neck felt naked and there was a lump in her throat which threatened to choke her. Was it a sign?

'Did someone special give it to you?' asked Bella in a knowing voice.

Gemma pretended not to hear the question, not trusting herself to give a coherent reply. Meanwhile, she was in charge of twenty small people for the morning, and she simply had to put her personal pain behind her to concentrate on their needs rather than hers.

It didn't help when there was a scrap over the sandpit, thanks to Freddie deciding it would be fun to flick sand at anyone who passed. Jean had handled it brilliantly, bless her.

'Freddie,' she'd begun, 'can you put a bit of sand in your hand and move it around with your finger like this? Good. It feels sharp, doesn't it? That's what it's like for someone if they get some of your sand in their eyes. So shall we stop?'

'I catched it,' called out Matthew, who was playing softball.

'*Caught,*' groaned Bella, rolling her eyes exaggeratedly. 'Not catched. And watch what you're doing with those play scissors, Billy. It's not nice to cut off people's noses.'

It was amazing, thought Gemma as she helped Clemmie to cut playdough shapes into quarters (four quarters make a whole – see?) how you could almost tell what kind of adults they would become. Clemmie, who always wore the princess costume and would only eat her mid-morning snack off a pink spotty plate, might well end up as a fashion designer. Freddie, who was very organised – just look at him lining up the cars in the play garage – might be an engineer.

Molly, who had a permanently runny nose, wanted to work with animals like her mother. And as for Billy, who was leaping up and down in his seat at Bella's paper-cutting table, who knew what Billy would do? Prime Minister? Young Offender? Either was possible.

Meanwhile, Gemma was keeping her eyes peeled for the silver chain. If only she had time to look! But then Johnnie bumped his head on the corner of the sandpit during Messy Play and had to go down in the Accident Book, although there wasn't even a bruise to be seen. 'No problem,' said Lars his au pair smoothly when he arrived fifteen minutes late to pick up his charge. 'I will sext my boss.'

It was all Gemma could do to keep a straight face. No wonder Johnnie's command of the English language was rather sketchy!

'Come on then,' Bella said as they started tidying up the art corner, otherwise known as fart corner thanks to Toby whose inability to keep smells in, regardless of whether he was on antibiotics or not, was legendary. She nudged Gemma. 'You can tell me now they've gone. Lily's surname isn't her name at all, is it? She's the daughter of . . .'

'Shhhhhh!' Gemma gave her a warning look as their new cleaner, a rather ferocious-looking young woman who, judging from her accent and yellowy-white complexion, came from an Eastern European country, clanged by with her bucket and broom.

'Anna's all right. She hardly speaks so she probably doesn't understand much English. Go on. You can tell me.'

Gemma thought back to her conversation with Beryl during the summer holidays and last night's chat with Joe Balls. Privacy was everything. It was one of the reasons why Dilly Dalung, one of the most famous female rock singers in Britain, had chosen to send her daughter Lily to a state playgroup rather than a high-profile society pre-prep or nursery school.

Certainly she could have afforded the latter. It was no secret that, much to the locals' excitement, Ms Dalung had bought a mansion on the other side of Hazelwood after her very bitter divorce, during which she'd accused her husband of some pretty awful things. Gemma, like many women in the country, had been unable to prevent herself from following the case in detail.

The fact that she had chosen to send her daughter to Puddleducks was, as Joe had pointed out unnecessarily, a huge compliment to the playgroup. Now it was up to Gemma and her staff to ensure they all rose to the challenge. If Dilly Dalung was impressed by the care and education they prided themselves on offering, it might help in saving their skins.

They also had an obligation to look after the child. Of course, they did that with *all* their Puddleducks, but after what Dilly Dalung had told Beryl about her ex, Gemma couldn't help feeling a special concern for Lily.

'Sorry,' she said, sounding primmer than she'd meant to. 'I can't say. Now, if you mop up that puddle over there, I'll prise the glue off the cupboard door.'

Bella gave the puddle a doubtful glance. 'Is that soapy water from Messy Play or Honey leakage again?'

Could be either! Despite her worry over her necklace, Gemma felt like laughing at her assistant who was now putting on her own pair of rubber gloves with black fur trim (which she always carried in her bag) and reluctantly mopping up the spillage before washing her hands thoroughly at the sink. 'I'll be off now, if that's all right.' She sniffed. 'Honestly, at times I wonder why we do this.'

Because, thought Gemma, taking a palette knife to the cupboard, we love it. Because there was nothing like seeing the relieved look on the face of a new, worried mother, like the American woman when she came to collect her son yesterday and he not only gave her a big warm hug, but was also jumping up and down with excitement to show her the papier-mâché football he had made. Or the look on Daisy's mother's face when she'd arrived this morning, complete with twin slings, to see her daughter shooting off to the sandpit.

'Miss Merryfield?'

Joe's deep voice made her jump. She hadn't even heard him pressing the security buttons. She tried to hold his gaze to show she wasn't intimidated by him, but it was difficult. His eyes, which were strangely mesmeric, had that intense expression which reminded her of a former university tutor who was never happy with his students' performance, even if they achieved top grades.

'Thought I'd come down to see how your day went.'

His voice had that tough, let's-go-forward edge, and Gemma suspected that this man was more into power talking than power walking.

'My day? Great, thanks.'

'Great?' he repeated.

'Is that the wrong answer?' She hadn't meant to retort so sharply, but she'd always wished she'd stood up more to that tutor, and now this northern Mr Grumpy, as Di in the school office rather naughtily called him, was bringing out some of her past resentment.

He gave her a steely look. 'What do you mean by that?'

'Well,' she said, taking a deep breath, 'I can't help thinking that whatever I say is wrong. If I say I had a great day, are you thinking that I am being too self-congratulatory? What I really mean is that over the last two days, I persuaded one child to leave her mother's ankles with the help of Mouse's baby, who was also feeling homesick. I also stopped a rather lively Puddleduck from shearing someone's hair and turned his attention to writing letter outlines instead. Together with my team, we got through Music Mania without bursting any eardrums, and we've also had our first rehearsal for Pyjama Drama.'

Was that a smile curling on Joe Balls's lips? It almost made him look friendly.

'May I enquire what Pyjama Drama involves?'

She pointed to a pile of neatly folded pjs on the side. 'Everyone dresses up in them and we write our own play about a family of pyjamas. This term the storyline is about Mr and Mrs Pyjama teaching their children to fold themselves up properly.'

It *was* a smile!

'And this baby mouse? Where does he come in?'

Quick as a flash, Gemma pulled out a spare baby from her skirt pocket. Tucking her index finger into his body, she made him do a quick bow. 'Pleased to meet you, sir,' she said in a squeaky voice. 'You can take me home if you like.'

Instantly, Joe's face tightened. 'I don't have children.'

Really? Somehow she'd assumed that at his age – he must be in his mid-thirties, surely? – he'd be married with a family of his own. Too late, Gemma realised she'd put her foot in it again. She herself always felt slightly inadequate when new parents asked if she had children herself, and now she'd made Joe feel awkward too.

'Sorry. How about nieces or nephews?'

Her keenness to make amends was making her gabble.

'Godchildren. Two.'

She thrust Mouse Baby Mark One at him. 'Then please, do give him as a present. I've made plenty more.'

Looking decidedly amused (a good sign, surely?), the new head of Reception shoved the poor mouse in his trouser pocket. Then he spoke with a lower voice so that she had to go nearer to hear him. Their proximity made her feel slightly awkward: she could even smell something lemony which might or might not be his aftershave. 'I also came down to find out how Lily has been getting on.'

Gemma glanced around to check that everyone else had left. The coast was clear apart from the cleaner who was clanging away in the downstairs loo, far enough away to be out of earshot.

'Great. Fine. I mean, she settled in without any trouble.' She paused. 'Her mother dropped her off yesterday.'

'Really?' Joe's very dark blue, almost black, eyes

flickered with interest. Nice to see he was human, deep down, thought Gemma. Talk had been rife amongst the staff, and she'd had to warn Bella to keep off the topic. Now it seemed that Joe was as curious as the rest of them.

'She looked very elegant.' Gemma couldn't help it. After all, it wasn't as though she could share this juicy piece of information with anyone else. 'Just like the magazine pictures, if you read that sort of thing.'

'I don't.'

'Me neither, apart from old copies,' she added hastily. 'Anyway, we only spoke briefly. Lily's nanny picked her up as arranged and brought her in today.'

Joe nodded. 'I can't tell you how important it is that a) this is kept private, and b) you make sure that no one picks up that child apart from the designated carer.'

As and Bs? What kind of a man spoke like that?

'Of course!' Gemma felt righteously indignant. 'We are always careful about security, regardless of whether a child's mother is famous or not. By the way, I thought you might be interested to know that Lily's very bright – got a great ear for language. She was incredibly quick in our French game this morning.'

'French?' He raised his eyebrows. 'I didn't realise you started so young here.'

Was that criticism or praise? It was so hard to tell with this man, who seemed approachable one minute and almost hostile the next. 'We just count to ten and do hello and thank you,' she said casually, making to put away a clutch of crayons that had sprawled over the desk. 'That sort of thing.'

'I see.' His tone was grudgingly admiring. 'By the

81

way, have you got any ideas for the banking competition?'

Give her a chance! 'I've given out the handouts but it's early days.'

Joe's head was nodding. 'Of course.' His hand was in his pocket, as though fiddling with the mouse gift. Gemma only hoped her stitching would survive. 'Listen, I didn't mean to sound prickly early on. I wonder . . . would you like to have a quick cup of coffee down the road?'

Not another work meeting! 'Sorry. But I've got a date.'

He was nodding again. 'Of course you have. Well, thanks for the update. You look as though you're doing a pretty good job.'

How condescending! 'Thanks.' Gemma returned his look. 'Brian always used to think so.'

'Ah yes, Brian.'

A silence hung between them. 'The thing is, Gemma,' said her boss in the voice he had used before suggesting a working coffee, 'things are very different from Brian's day. And the sooner we get to accept it, the better.'

He put his hand in his pocket again. 'By the way, I spotted this by the gate as I came in. Maybe one of the mums has lost it.'

Gemma's heart soared as she saw her silver chain lying in the palm of Joe Balls's hand.

'It's mine,' she cried. 'Thank you.'

For a minute she felt like hugging the man, but stopped herself just in time. Instead, she started to fasten the chain around her neck.

'Want me to help you?' asked Joe, his tone indicating that he would really rather not and was only issuing the invitation out of politeness.

'It's all right thank you.' Gemma wanted to burst into song, but at the same time she couldn't help wondering why she was so happy. Didn't the chain stand for everything that she had given up? 'I can do it myself.'

If only Joe had known that her date was with a can of baked beans and a baked potato, thought Gemma lightly as she flew up the stairs, looking forward to getting into her cosy bedsit at the top of Joyce's warm Victorian terrace home.

'Had a good day, love?' called up her landlady from the kitchen. Joyce, who always enjoyed a natter (rather too much of one, at times), made a habit of keeping her kitchen door open so she could have a chat with her lodgers. At the moment, Gemma was the only one left on the top floor now the woman next to her had saved up enough money for her own deposit, and so far no one had responded to the ad that Joyce had put in the local newsagent.

'Yes thanks.'

Joyce's smiley face popped out from behind the door. She was a woman in her early fifties who looked much younger, and she happened to have a son who was working abroad at the moment but was coming home in a month. It was clear from the way she always spoke about him that she thought he and Gemma would make a perfect couple. If only she knew!

'Had another postcard from Barry, I did. Want to see it?'

Not wishing to disappoint her landlady, Gemma made admiring noises at the picture and appropriate noises as she read the scrawled message about diving in South America, where Joyce's son had just spent some of his leave from the army.

'Sure you don't want a bite with me, love? I've made more than enough macaroni cheese.'

'No thanks.' Gemma thought with longing of the packet of chocolate raisins she had treated herself to on the way home and the romantic DVD she'd borrowed from the library to play on her laptop after she'd done her lesson-planning for tomorrow. 'It's really kind of you but I've got some work to do.'

Joyce shook her head as Gemma departed to her bedsit on the top floor. 'I don't know, dear. All work and no play. You teachers work so hard, even nursery teachers.'

Talk about damning with faint praise! Slipping out of her skirt and into a nice comfy pair of jeans, Gemma became aware of her phone bleeping with a text message or as Johnnie's au pair would have said, 'sext message'.

'How did it go?'

The text popped up just as she lay down on her bed, allowing herself to stretch out and finally relax. Dear Kitty! The two of them had met on the first day of uni. 'I'm going to be a singer or actress,' her new friend had announced. 'Not sure which, yet.'

When she had, after a rather chequered career, got to the semi-final of *Britain's Best Talent*, Gemma hadn't been at all surprised. Kitty was always doing crazy things, and appearing on a reality show in an evening dress, a bright scarlet bow in her hair and a recorder that she managed to play like a flute, was exactly what she'd have expected of her. The only pity was that she hadn't been selected to go through to the final. Still, it had led to all kinds of bookings, including a stint at Puddleducks Playgroup which she'd kindly promised to do without charging.

It was typical of her that even with all her showbiz commitments, Kitty hadn't forgotten Gemma's troubles.

'*OK,*' Gemma texted back.

'*Did u get that stuff done?*'

'*Still wtng.*'

Gemma shivered. Kitty was the only one who knew her secret. The only one aware how important this December was to her.

Sometimes she wondered if she was doing the right thing. On the other hand, surely she'd waited long enough? It was time to finally accept that there was no hope. The only way forward was to move on.

Chapter 10

Nancy sat in her car outside the playgroup. This was the fourth day she'd been keeping watch all morning to make sure that Danny didn't escape.

Frankly, it was getting boring.

A woman with her dog had been giving her odd looks. I'm not one of those perverts, she wanted to say. I'm making sure my son is safe. Danny was all she had left. If anything happened to him, she just couldn't cope. Oh dear. Now she could feel her eyes filling all over again.

'Nancy!' Someone was knocking on the car window. 'Blimey, Nancy, are you all right?'

Lifting her head off the steering wheel, she gazed through the blur at a short, smiley mother wearing clear braces. Brigid. A chill ran through her as she recalled the last time they'd met, when she'd run out of the coffee shop without picking up the check. This was awful.

'Got a bit of a cold,' she sniffed, gesticulating through the closed window.

'I can't hear you!' Brigid was mouthing back.

Reluctantly, Nancy wound down the window. 'I said I've got a bit of a cold. Look, I'm sorry about the other day. I didn't mean to be rude.' She sniffed again. 'It's just that I was feeling a bit low.'

Rummaging in her handbag, she found a five-pound note. 'I think I owe you this.'

'Nonsense,' said Brigid crisply. 'I bawled my eyes out, believe it or not, when Billy started playgroup, even though he can be a real pain in the you-know-what. It's a weird feeling going back to the house and not having anyone there, isn't it?'

Her unexpected kindness made the tears well up in Nancy's eyes again.

'But it's not for long!' Brigid was patting Nancy's arm as it rested on the window. 'You'll be collecting him in a few hours' time and then before you know it, your bloke will be back and you won't have had time to cook tea – at least you won't if you're like me. Nancy? What on earth is wrong?'

It was no good. No good pretending that Sam's cool email messages were normal, or that she believed him when he said it wasn't always easy to ring because the phone lines could be dodgy. No good pretending that she could cope by cleaning the house from top to bottom just as her own mother had done when Dad had left, in order to have control over *something*.

'I think,' said Brigid quietly when she'd finished listening to all this, 'you'd better come with us to the coffee shop again. Don't worry. It will only be me and Annie.' She grinned. 'And it goes without saying, that coffee is on you!'

For two pins, she'd have made an excuse and shot back home. But Brigid's kind insistence made it impossible, and somehow Nancy found herself sitting at a round table in the café. Break and Flake was full of other parents whose faces she vaguely recognised from the playgroup. Brigid and Annie were ordering lattes at the counter, and the former was doubtless filling the latter in on what had happened in the car park.

So embarrassing! Yet when they came back and sat down opposite her, it seemed comforting that she too, like all the other customers, had 'friends' to talk to.

'It can't be easy being so far from home,' began Annie with a concerned look on her face. 'Where did you say your mother-in-law lives again?'

'Norwich. But I don't think she likes me much. She's very horsey and doesn't seem to think very much of her son having married an American. Apparently Sam had a girlfriend before me whom she got on really well with, and I just don't match up.'

Brigid's brace seemed to glint with sympathy. 'My mother wanted me to marry my first boyfriend too. Took her ages to warm to my partner, but now she thinks he's great.'

She raised her voice to be heard above the grind of the coffee machine on the other side of the counter. Nancy was actually grateful for the noise; together with that and the crescendo of chatter all round them, there was more privacy. 'What's this about Sam leaving you, then?'

Nancy stiffened. 'He hasn't left me!'

Annie tutted in disapproval. 'Don't mind Brigid. She says what she thinks and we all know that isn't always publishable, especially in the Puddleducks newsletter!'

The two women smiled at each other and Nancy felt the pang of being an outsider.

'He might not have left you, Nancy, but it didn't sound great from what I've heard. What was it he said again? Something about giving you space for you both to think?'

Nancy shot Brigid a look of accusation.

'Hope you don't think I've betrayed your confidence,' said Brigid briskly, 'but Annie's a good person to run things past. Blimey, she was halfway through her counsellor's course before she got preggers again.'

Annie nodded ruefully at the sleeping bundle in the sling round her neck. 'Worth every waking night, she is, and as soon as she's old enough for Puddleducks I'm finishing the course. Well, probably anyway, although I'm also rather interested in photography.' She beamed. 'Who knows?'

Brigid took a slurp of latte, leaving a large white moustache on her upper lip. 'Meanwhile, she's practising on the rest of us. That's both the counselling and the pornography. OK. That's a joke. You know what I meant.'

She leaned forward as though about to spill another confidence. 'You see, Nancy, you're not the only one to wonder what's left when our kids go to playgroup and then school. There are loads of us in the same boat. I wanted to be a dentist. In the end, I trained as a dental assistant but as soon as my kids are at full-time school, I'm going to think of something else. Not sure what exactly, but I'll work it out. Maybe when you have more time, you'll be able to pick up your science career. Meanwhile, we're all sort of casting around for something that fits in between the hours of 9 and 11.30 a.m. The question is, what *can* we do?'

Annie was nodding madly. 'She's right. In fact, I've just had a brilliant idea. You know, when we were up there ordering lattes and Bridge was filling me in on your life – sorry about that – I saw this poster on the wall. Look over there.'

They all looked.

'Can't read it,' grumbled Brigid. 'Forgot my new reading glasses again.'

Annie grinned. 'Sign of approaching middle age. Well, I can read it and I'm only a year younger than you. Can you read it, Nancy?'

She could.

Taster creative courses at Church House. Not sure if you want to do Hatha Yoga; T'ai Chi; Handbag Design; Sew and Crow; Mosaic Marvels; or Early Morning Tango? Then investigate our taster courses. You can try them out and then sign up for whichever one takes your fancy.

Brigid's and Annie's faces were shining. 'Remember us saying we were looking for a course? These sound great, don't you think?' smiled Annie.

Nancy hesitated. Sam was always saying she ought to do more but somehow, with everything going on, it seemed too self-indulgent.

'Come on,' chorused the girls. 'Register now with us before you change your mind.'

Chapter 11

In the end, Nancy had gone along with them. By general agreement, they all signed up for Handbag Design and a few other taster courses. Somehow, by the time they'd finished, it was almost picking-up time. 'Our lot love Puddleducks so much that they're going to be staying two afternoons a week,' said Brigid casually as they left Church House. 'Billy even goes to the After-School club at the main school. It's good preparation for next year when he goes up.'

Annie giggled as she unlocked her bike with a bucket seat on the back that looked, to Nancy, highly unstable. 'Bet you send him even more now that that dishy first-year head has taken over. Have you seen him? A slightly stocky northerner with definite attitude. Gorgeous! Take a good look, Nancy. If he's like dear old Brian he'll be coming down quite regularly to Puddleducks, so the children have a familiar face when they go up to his year.'

Nancy felt awkward, as she always did when she heard women admire other men who weren't their husband. Sam had been her first real boyfriend, which had possibly accounted for Danny's rapid conception only a few months after they'd met.

The others were peeling off now. 'There's a great second-hand designer shop down that street, Nancy.

Want to check it out? We've got at least five minutes before pick-up time.'

No way was she being late! Instead, she walked briskly up to the playgroup, crunching through the yellow and gold leaves that Danny liked to toss up in the air when she allowed him out of his pushchair to stretch his legs.

She'd intended to be early but she was bang on time. To her shame, there were four other parents in front of her, which meant she wasn't first through the security door which one of the helpers was holding open.

Heart thumping, Nancy searched the circle of bright-faced children in blue Puddleduck sweatshirts, sitting cross-legged on the carpet which had – oh dear – some glue stains on it. There was Danny, holding hands on one side with an exquisite little girl, like a china doll with jet-black hair and a flower-like pale complexion. Danny had a girlfriend already?

Next to him, Brigid's Billy was wriggling around with what the British called ants in his pants. Then he picked up a plastic hammer which had been lying on the floor and began banging his own shoe. Danny and that lovely child were giggling as though they thought it was funny, but surely he might hurt someone?

'Calm down, Billy,' said Gemma. Nancy had to admit that she did have an authoritative edge to her voice, which was good.

'What *is* wrong with that child?' demanded one of the other mothers in piercing tones.

Exactly what she, Nancy had been thinking. Poor Brigid, who was just arriving now, clutching a carrier bag from the designer shop and muttering something about being caught up. She must be so embarrassed. But no. She was saying something now. Really loudly, as if it was the other woman who had a problem and not her.

'That's my son Billy you're talking about. He's just lively, and there's nothing any of us can do about it. It's like being born with different-coloured eyes or,' her eyes narrowed as she stared at the woman, 'with your kind of red hair.'

Nancy could hardly believe her ears. Gemma looked as though she was about to try and smooth things over, but before she could say anything a very tall, elegant woman, wearing a pashmina draped over her shoulder and part of her head, swooped in. Without saying a word, she nodded graciously at the group of parents, including Toby's dad whose jaw had virtually reached the neck of his egg-stained T-shirt, picked up the china doll with the jet-black hair and pale complexion, and glided out again.

'Could someone please tell me,' said Toby's dad with a catch in his voice, 'if that was who I think it was?'

That afternoon, Nancy took Danny to the park. It was a ritual. They had always done this before playgroup had started and now they went in the afternoons. The roundabout first. Then the swings. And then the slide – she made sure that she always stood near the middle of it, so she could grab her son if he showed any sign of getting into trouble.

Not that he ever did. Danny was far more agile than she had been as a child. Sam had indicated that he had been quite sporty, but they hadn't really known each other long enough to have gone through the 'these are my old school photos' stage.

But today Danny didn't want to go on the roundabout or the swing or the slide. 'Want Billy and Lily,' he kept saying, looking around the park wistfully as though they might appear from the clump of trees at the side (where Nancy had always thought unsavoury characters might lurk), or from the dog-walking field at the top which led to a large housing estate.

By the seventh time he had said this, Nancy was beginning to feel somewhat irritated. She'd had enough of all the parenting chatter that had started up after the tall, elegant mother had left. She'd never been one for celebrity magazines, so when Dog Dad, as she privately called him on account of the poo bags that were always spilling out of his pockets, told them all that if that wasn't Dilly Dalung he would eat his hat (another weird English expression), she hadn't known who he was talking about.

As for Brigid's son, well, clearly he wasn't a suitable play date for Danny. According to her American parenting magazine, behaviour like that could be catching.

No. Danny would have to make do with her. Besides, he was all she had until Sam came back. Nancy's eyes began to mist over as she encouraged her son to try the roundabout just once. Gangly Annie and Brigid the Brace clearly thought she was being naïve in expecting her husband to return.

Now, as she took Danny's sticky hand firmly in hers to go home, only to find that he tried to shake it off as they waited to cross the road, she began to wonder herself about Sam. He hadn't phoned last night. He had merely sent her a short text instead, saying that he was going off to a business dinner and would give her a call later that week.

It didn't feel good.

That night, for the very first time since he'd been born, Danny fell asleep immediately after his bath and story. When Nancy woke with a start at 4 a.m., realising that her son hadn't sneaked into her bed as usual, she leaped up and ran to his room. He was sleeping evenly and calmly, to her relief.

Playgroup had clearly worn him out. How ironic, thought Nancy as she padded back to her own empty bed, that he should do this while Sam was not here. If only her husband hadn't had to go away, they could have cuddled up and then . . .

Nancy couldn't help smiling at the memory of how Sam's cuddles, and then his deep kisses, had utterly melted her soon after they had met. The physical attraction between them had been mutual; she could tell that, despite her inexperience, from the way he had held her and run his hands over the back of her head, pulling her towards him.

If they had had a bit longer together before Danny was born, would he have tired of her so easily? Because judging from the lack of phone calls or texts tonight, that was exactly what he had done. And now Danny was at playgroup and would, within a year, go up to Big School, where on earth would that leave her?

Chapter 12

'Shhhh! He's coming!'

Joe could hear the whispers before he even went into the classroom. It was as though word had got around that the new head of Reception was an ogre, and that everyone – children and staff – were terrified of him just because he wasn't laid-back and avuncular, like poor old Brian Hughes with his Bourbon creams.

But, as he'd tried to tell himself, he'd been brought in for a reason. The headmistress, Beryl, knew that. 'We need more people like you,' she'd told him during one of their meetings at the beginning of term. 'The teaching profession is changing. We are lucky enough now to be "invaded" by people from other professions, such as yours, or accountancy or even journalism. It all makes for a much richer environment. Of course you are going to come across people who don't agree with that, but just keep going. As you know, maths was our weak point in the latest report, so if you can help us there, that would be invaluable.'

He was making an effort, thought Joe now as he walked into his Reception class. But it wasn't easy. For a start, the children didn't even seem to know their tables. In his day they had learned them by rote, just as they had held the door open for teacher or said 'please' and 'thank you'. But this lot looked blankly at him when he asked them what three times two was. 'We didn't do that at Puddleducks,' one boy with ginger freckles had volunteered.

Why not? He'd have to have another word with the giddy Gemma Merryfield, whose very name suggested she was more interested in frivolity than maths. In the meantime, it was up to him to make maths *fun* for these kids, who clearly viewed numbers with the same suspicion that he still viewed semolina, with memories of school lunches. 'You see,' he could just imagine Ed saying, 'not everything was good in the old days!'

No. Not now. He'd taught himself to think about Ed only between eleven and twelve at night. Otherwise, he would think of nothing else. He had a job to do. And he was bloody well going to do it.

'Good morning, everyone!'

After they had replied, Joe surveyed the rows of faces before him. Thirty children in the class was currently meant to be the maximum, but somehow they had acquired one more. That was his fault, if that was the right word. There had been a last-minute application by a family who had just moved into the area after a very chequered history which involved a Third World country, complications at immigration and a series of transitional homes. Their story had moved Joe, and somehow he had persuaded Beryl that they could take on one more.

Now, as he looked at Juan's shining face in the front row, Joe was glad he had. The boy was the only one who was any good at adding up. If it wasn't for his trusting expression as he waited for Joe to throw him a titbit of learning, Joe might have wondered if he was in the right profession. When Mike had suggested teaching, he had to admit that he'd seen it as a sort of 'moving out to pastures'. Then, when he'd started at the inner-city school, he'd realised how tough it was, but he had proved himself there, just as he had proved himself at the bank.

A primary school in a backwater like Hazelwood would, he had told himself, be a doddle. But it wasn't! In some ways he preferred the devil-may-care attitude of some of the hard-faced kids in London. This lot, many of them pampered by their parents to an amazing degree, just didn't have the attitude. And attitude, as Ed always used to say, was what divided the flyers from the sinkers.

'Did you all do your homework?'

The sea of faces in front of him merged into waves of unsure nodding, blank stares and a few giggles. Only Juan was putting his hand up. 'I did, I did.'

'Great!'

Joe beamed, even though he knew he had to remember the magic word 'differentiation' which had been drummed into him during his teacher training. It was typical of many of the words and phrases in his course which sounded complicated, but which really meant something very basic. Differentiation was simply ensuring that you made allowances for kids like Elsie, who was sitting in the back row comparing designer pencil cases with the girl in front of her.

'Elsie! Would you like to come out here at the front, together with that rather lovely pencil case of yours?'

Reluctantly, the girl made her way to his desk. 'Would you care to put your pencil case down for a minute?'

Joe knew he was sounding tough, but he couldn't help it. If Gemma Merryfield wasn't preparing the children in the way she should be, it was his job to put matters straight.

'Now if everyone in the class had one of your pencil cases, how many would there be?'

Elsie's eyes flew along the rows of desks, trying to count them. 'Twenty-nine,' she managed.

The child couldn't even count what was before her eyes. She'd been in Puddleducks for two whole years. What had she been doing there?

'Thirty-one, actually. Now supposing I gave everyone in the class another pencil case each. How many would there be altogether?'

Elsie started counting frantically on her fingers. Meanwhile, the boy who'd been sitting next to her was waving his hand.

'Yes, Oliver?'

'I need the toilet!'

Not again. That child either had a seriously weak bladder or was skiving.

'OK but don't be long. Someone else give me the answer, please. Yes, Melissa?'

'Sixty-two.'

Joe felt a beam of warmth flowing through him. That was extraordinary! Yesterday the girl couldn't even add ten and twelve.

''Snot fair.' Elsie's eyes were glaring. 'She could only do that cos she's got a calculator sewn on the top of her new pencil case.'

Joe felt a heaviness in his chest. 'Is that true?'

The others around Melissa nodded.

'Sir! Sir!'

Joe looked down at the boy with brown skin. 'I am sorry to correct you, sir, but I do not think you are correct when you say that we should have a total of sixty-two pencil cases in the class.'

Not him as well!

'It depends, you see, sir, on whether someone has already left the class to sell them.' Juan's eyes were gleaming. 'If they are all special pencil cases with calculators on, they would be worth a lot of money. So it would be easy for someone to run out of the door and sell them at the market.'

A ripple of giggles moved through the class. 'It is not funny, sir.' Juan looked hurt. 'In my country, sixty-two pencil cases like that would feed a family for several weeks.'

Suddenly a picture of the apartment in Hampstead that he and Ed had shared flashed into Joe's head. Their salaries, combined, meant that they had wanted for nothing. There had been the widescreen TV; the David Linley dining-room table; the huge pale oak bed . . . Even now, his more modest apartment in Notting Hill was more luxurious than this boy could ever imagine.

'Juan's right!' His voice rang round the classroom, extinguishing the giggles. There was something to be said for a tone acquired during boardroom infighting.

'In fact, instead of maths this morning, I think we might do geography instead. No, you don't need to get out your exercise book. Instead, I'd like Juan to come up here and tell us a bit about his country.'

OK. So he'd got the idea from Gemma's habit of inviting zookeepers and curry-powder makers into the playgroup. But he had incorporated some facts and figures into his own adaptation and it had worked! It had really worked!

Joe couldn't help feeling somewhat apologetic towards Gemma, yet also excited, as he tidied up the classroom at the end of the day. Juan's early childhood, living in South America in a family of ten, had provided a vivid and fascinating geography lesson for the children, and a few maths games had been slipped in as well.

How many fish did Juan's family catch a day? Maybe five if they were lucky. So he had got five children to stand in a corner of the room pretending to be fish. How many might they catch in two days? He had asked five more to spread their arms as though they were swimming, and then go and stand with the original group. And so on!

Joe could feel an exclamation mark occasionally creeping into his thoughts, which had never been there before. Indeed he wasn't sure that it had any right to be there, except there was no escaping the 'I've got it' light that had suddenly gone on in Elsie's eyes when she announced, still clutching her precious pencil case, that she could 'see now'.

Not only was this approach imaginative, he told

himself as he walked down the path through the autumn leaves to Puddleducks for his arranged meeting with Gemma, but it also fitted in with the National Curriculum, which was more than Gemma seemed to be achieving. Pre-schools and playgroups were meant to meet Early Years Goals. Surely the simple task of learning one's tables should be included?

'Hi, Mr Balls!' Gemma smiled at him as she let him in.

Hi? Joe wanted to say. *This isn't another car park run-in, you know.* 'Hello.' He followed her into the main room and stood stiffly.

'Would you like to sit down?'

The girl was actually offering him a child-sized chair, and bright red at that, while she took her own chair. 'No, thank you, I'd rather stand.'

Gemma nodded. 'May I start by asking you something?'

How dare she act as though she was in charge of the show?

'I'd like to know more about the strategies in place for dealing with a celebrity child at Puddleducks.'

Her question – exactly the one he had put to Beryl – took the wind out of his sails.

'I'm getting questions from the parents who saw . . .' she hesitated. 'Who saw Lily's mother when she came into playgroup today. What am I meant to say?'

Deflect the question. That had been Joe's motto back at the bank. 'What *did* you say to them?'

'That I hoped very much that they would not discuss private issues about *any* parents with others.'

Joe nodded, relieved. 'Couldn't have put it better myself.'

Her surprise at his approval was obvious, and Lynette's words came back to him. *Don't be too sharp, Joe. Let this new school see the real you. The kind but efficient one that we know.*

'But I still don't get it. Why would . . .' Gemma paused, glancing around as though someone might be listening, before continuing in a quieter voice. 'Why would Dilly Dalung choose Puddleducks and not one of the private playgroups?'

Frankly, Joe wished the singer had done just that. It would have been simpler for all of them. After all, it surely wouldn't be long until some sniffling rat from a tabloid found out, and then they'd get all kinds of unwanted publicity. 'Perhaps she wanted her daughter to have a simple childhood. One that didn't involve learning her tables.'

Gemma frowned. 'What do you mean by that?'

Well done, Joe, he told himself. You've done it again with that tongue of yours. No excuse apart from the fact that he was feeling out of his comfort zone here, in a slightly draughty village hall with a distinct smell of disinfectant that probably masked the whiff of pee.

Just for a second, he had a very slight twinge of regret for his old office, with the desk overlooking High Holborn and the secretary who had respect for him. 'I mean that I am surprised to find myself with a large number of children in my Reception class who appear not to know their tables.'

Gemma's expression suddenly sharpened. 'Learning

tables is not in the Early Years Goals. Brian never used to complain.'

'Well, I'm not happy. See that you do something about the next lot, can you, before they come up to me. Try counting bubbles or something.'

Immediately he could see he'd gone too far again by speaking before thinking. Gemma's face showed him that, clear as day. Say something conciliatory, he told himself, and fast. 'By the way, I asked one of my boys to give a talk about his life in South America. I've got you to thank for that.' He tried to keep it light. 'Your zookeeper mother inspired me. Thank you.'

She nodded. 'Glad to see that not all our ideas are hopeless in your eyes.'

'I didn't say they were hopeless.' Joe heard himself sounding brisk again. 'I just said they needed to be relevant, which was why I added some numeric values to the exercise. By the way, have you had any ideas on the playgroup competition?'

'No.' Her face was completely unsmiling now. 'What about you? I gather there's a similar competition for Reception.'

As if he didn't know! He'd been trying desperately to think of a suitably dazzling entry. Something that would impress his former bosses, whom he'd had to persuade to offer the award in the first place.

In a way, this was a test for him too. The bank would take a keen interest in the entry that Joe Balls, who'd chucked away a six-figure-job, sent in. He needed to prove, both to them and himself, that he'd been right to throw in the towel on the fourteenth floor, and this was one way of doing it.

'I'm still working on it,' he said.

'Fine.' Gemma shot him a look that said she didn't care for his presence any longer. 'And I'll keep working on counting those bubbles. By the way, I hear you're not too happy about the new friendship circle we're building in our outdoor play area.'

'I don't think it's necessary.'

'It's for children to stand in if they don't have anyone to play with.' Gemma's eyes flashed. 'And it's staying. That was decided before you came here. OK?'

Chapter 13

The conversation with Gemma troubled him all the way down to Lyme Regis that weekend. It almost affected his concentration at one point, as he swerved in and out of the traffic on his bike down the motorway. Maybe, he thought, as he parked outside Mermaid's Nook and took off his helmet, casting a glance at the mirror to see his tousled hair and flushed face, he was getting a touch too old to ride a Harley.

'Uncle Joe, Uncle Joe!'

Fraser and Charlie fell on him as soon as he clicked the bike stand into place and looked around. Mike and Lynette lived in one of those lovely stone three-up, three-down, wisteria-clad fishermen's cottages that sat slightly precariously on the hills leading down to the sea. When they had first bought their seaside home, they had made it clear that he and Ed were to see it as a retreat whenever they needed time off from their crazy city life. And they had. Now it was just him.

'Can we have a ride? Can we have a ride?'

'Boys!' Lynette appeared at the doorway, looking gorgeous in skinny jeans and a white T-shirt. 'It's "may", not "can". I've told you before. Anyone *can* ride a bike – well, most people. But you are only allowed to if someone says so. And I say you may not, because you're not old enough.'

Ed laughed. Lynette was an English teacher and a stickler for grammar, but somehow the boys always took her on-the-spot lessons in good heart, and also managed to lead healthy lives on Facebook. He liked to think he might have been that sort of parent.

'Now come on in.' Lynette draped an arm round him briefly and took him into the kitchen. 'Mike will be back soon after his staff meeting. You look as though you could do with a drink. OK, boys. Uncle Joe will be outside in a few minutes and then we can all go down to the beach.'

The seaside was definitely the place to bring up kids, thought Joe, as he walked along the shingle with his godsons and their hyperactive red setter. It wasn't just that they learned so much about rock formations and tides and moons; they were healthy and enthusiastic and not world-weary or phone-crazy, like so many of 'his' London kids had been.

He and Mike had played football with them in the surf and then Lynette had hung back with him and, in her usual quiet way, asked him about what was going on in his life. Somehow he'd found himself telling her that perhaps he'd been a bit sharp with Gemma, the acting head of the playgroup, and that some of the kids in his class were really pretty dim. Then he told her about the bright South American boy who had revolutionised his lesson the other day.

'Sounds like you taught on your feet,' commented Lynette, tossing her hair back in the wind. 'Mike always said you'd be a good teacher.'

Joe felt a lump in his throat. 'Actually, I'm not sure

that I am. My predecessor seems to have been such a hero in everyone's eyes that I don't think I stand a chance of matching up to him.'

Lynette's eyes softened. 'I can see that. But unless I'm mistaken, there's something else wrong as well, isn't there?'

His friends knew him so well: at times it comforted him, and at others, it made him feel vulnerable. 'You're right.' He kicked a pebble in front of him. 'Much as I hate to admit it, I feel knackered all the time. It's not just the teaching, which, as you two have always pointed out, is much more exhausting than many people realise. It's the commuting too. My journey's a real killer.'

So then Lynette made two suggestions. The first – renting a flat nearer school during the week – seemed to make quite good sense. As for the second, he'd just have to think about it.

Later that night, after a delicious supper of spaghetti bolognese around the kitchen table, Joe flopped down on the ancient, oh-so-cosy duck-blue Laura Ashley sofa with its slightly worn arms which somehow seemed comforting rather than shabby, while Mike and Lynette put the boys to bed. His eyes fell on one of the last pictures of him and Ed, still sitting on the pine dresser next to the photos of them all at different stages of their lives, from uni onwards.

'Are you two still in touch?' Mike's voice cut in suddenly as he came down the stairs.

Quickly Joe looked away from the photo. 'Only about practicalities. What about you?'

Mike shrugged. 'We've had a couple of phone calls.'

Joe wanted to ask what about, but pride prevented him.

'Does this new life of yours,' asked Mike, leaning forward confidentially, 'help to ease the pain now? Does it make you feel stronger about whatever lies ahead?'

The last thing he wished to talk about was the dreaded F word. F for Future. But Mike's question, which brought a lump to his throat, forced him to recall everything he had lost; so precious that it could never be recovered.

Then, for no reason at all, he suddenly recalled the girl with the designer pencil case who had finally 'got it', and the South American boy who had experienced so many difficulties in his short life. 'Sometimes,' he said quietly. 'Sometimes.'

There was a shout from upstairs. 'Uncle Joe, Uncle Joe. Are you going to come up now and read a bedtime story?'

Both men grinned at each other. 'See you later,' said Joe.

Mike nodded, and Joe was glad that he and Lynette were the only ones who knew his secret. The last thing he wanted was pity from people who didn't know him properly.

'I'll have a large glass of red waiting.'

Joe shot his friend a grateful look. 'That would be great.' Goodness. He'd nearly forgotten. Leaping up, he headed for his overnight backpack, which contained Fraser's birthday present. 'Think he'll like this?'

Anxiously, he watched Mike examine the computer game and the pencil case with its Kool Calculator.

'Wow. These are all the rage at school.' He raised his eyebrows. 'But I thought you said that children needed to add up for themselves instead of relying on gadgets.'

Joe shrugged. 'Let's just say that I'm having to be a bit more flexible than I used to be.' Ed flashed into his head and he attempted unsuccessfully to blank the image. 'I'm trying, Mike. I really am. But it's hard to get rid of old habits. Really hard.'

Chapter 14

The weekend, Joe told himself on the following Monday morning, had been just what he needed. He wasn't so sure it had been that great for Lynette, though. Even though he'd offered to help, she had insisted on giving him 'boy time', as she'd put it, with Mike, while she ran around after the boys and arranged the birthday beachcombing party for five of Fraser's schoolfriends.

She was, thought Joe, exactly the kind of wife he would have liked if things had been different.

Meanwhile, today was a big one. The older class at Puddleducks was coming up to visit Reception and sit in on the school assembly. Under Brian's regime, these visits hadn't happened until the end of term, but in Joe's opinion, this was too late. The pre-school needed regular visits in order to feel familiar with the school if their parents were going to be persuaded to send them there.

And here they came right now, headed – not by Gemma, he was relieved to see – but by some girl in black leggings and a rather low-cut T-shirt, who introduced herself as Bella in a decidedly plush accent. Joe noticed an engagement ring on her finger, next to the one it would normally be worn on. Maybe that accounted for her rather fed-up expression.

There were a couple of mothers too, from the looks of things. Let me do anything, one of them was saying. Anything at all to help.

'We needed some volunteers to make up the required staff ratio,' Bella whispered. 'Watch out for . . .'

Too late. A tallish, very thin woman, with a spiky elfin haircut and great cheekbones, was already heading his way. 'Mr Balls?' She spoke in one of those twangy American accents he was familiar with from his New York meetings. 'I'm Nancy Carter Wright. My son is coming up to your class next year. I just wondered if you had any illness in the school.'

Had he heard her correctly?

'I'm concerned that Danny might fall sick with all these children in a rather confined space.'

One of the other Puddleducks mothers whom he already knew, as her elder daughter was in his class, began to giggle. Instantly, Joe felt sorry for and strangely protective of this owl-like woman, who was clearly distressed. Indicating that they should move away from the group, he spoke quietly. 'Mrs Wright, may I ask if Daniel is your first child?'

'It's not Wright. It's Carter Wright without a hyphen.'

'I do apologise.'

She nodded as if in acknowledgement. 'Yes, Danny is my first child but the reason for my question is not because I am a neurotic mother.'

Of course not.

'It's because I am a scientist . . . or rather I used to be. So I know about the dangers of germs spreading when you have large masses of people.'

A flash of recognition shot through Joe. An intelligent mother. Not an arty-farty one. 'I thought of becoming a scientist myself,' he said quietly, 'but chose to read pure maths instead.'

Immediately he spotted a similar light of recognition in her eyes. 'Really?'

'Really. So, as a mathemetician, let me tell you that statistically speaking, your son is far more likely to be protected against illness by being with other children than if he was wrapped in a bubble.'

The woman nodded nervously. 'That's what my parenting magazine says, but I still can't help worrying.'

Joe smiled. 'I'd feel the same if I didn't remind myself of the numbers. You're a scientist. You know the value of numbers. Every time you feel worried, remind yourself of the statistics.'

'Thank you.' The woman looked less tense. 'That really helps.'

Joe felt a warm glow inside. 'Not at all. Now, are we going to be seeing you at the Parents' Social at the end of the month?' He glanced down at her left hand, which bore a shiny wedding ring. 'Fathers are invited too.'

The woman flushed. 'My husband is working away at the moment but yes, I will be there.'

Working away? In the inner-city school that had frequently been a euphemism for being in prison, but out here it was more likely to mean that a father was earning megabucks in Dubai. Poor woman. Money was nothing compared with the important things in life, as he'd tried, on numerous occasions in the past, to explain to Ed.

'Then I'll look forward to chatting to you then.' There was an irritating snort of laughter from the silly woman with the daughter in Year Two, who was saying something loud about 'the new year head chatting up Danny's mother'. He only hoped the American woman hadn't heard. 'Meanwhile, it looks as though assembly is about to start. Shall we take our seats?'

The assembly went well. Most of the Puddleducks children behaved themselves, apart from one excited puddle on the floor. A couple of mothers came up with ideas for the Top Ten Playgroup competition but, as he pointed out, a sponsored bowling evening didn't really have that *X Factor* ring.

Later that evening, remembering Lynette's advice, he rang up a woman who had advertised a bedsit in the local newsagent. He went to see it briefly and agreed to take it from Sunday. 'I'll only be there during the week,' he'd said to the landlady, who didn't even ask for references. Similarly he hadn't volunteered any information on his job; if he'd said he taught at the school, she'd be bound to have a grandchild there or know someone who did, and frankly, he could do with some peace during the week. That was part of the point. As Lynette and Mike had said, it would mean that he could work a bit later and then have a bed close to hand without risking life and limb on the motorway back to London at the end of the day.

Then at the weekends, he could go back to Notting Hill and 'our' old haunts, as Ed used to call them. *Ours*. It had, he thought, to be one of the most difficult words in the English language to erase when you were no longer a couple. He could spend Saturday mornings mooching through the charity bookshops and browsing round the Portobello market. Saturday lunchtimes, he could pore over the papers in 'their' favourite deli; the one where you could get broccoli and Stilton soup or wraps and find a spot, hopefully in the corner, safe in the knowledge that you had your own privacy without being lonely, given the noisy chatter all around.

In the afternoons, maybe an art gallery – the Royal Academy had a new Pre-Raphaelite exhibition he wanted to see – and then perhaps a DVD or a film in Leicester Square.

In other words, all the things he used to do with Ed, except that now, he was slowly getting accustomed to doing them on his own. Meanwhile, he still had the rest of the evening to kill. Maybe this was the time to take up Lynette's second suggestion.

Two hours later, Joe found himself parking his bike against the railings of a pretty semi-detached Victorian villa on one of the side roads on the way out of Hazelwood.

When he'd made the phone call on the spur of the moment, an hour ago, he'd been surprised when the cheery-sounding voice at the other end had invited him round.

'Tonight?' he had questioned.

'No time like the present,' the voice had replied. 'I've learned to live in the moment, lad. Got the directions now? Good. You can't miss us. There's a large *Beware of the Missus* sign on the front gate. Watch out for the dodgy hinge that needs fixing.'

Joe didn't know if he was joking or not about the sign, but now as he opened the creaky gate, clutching a gift-wrapped packet of Bourbon biscuits and bottle of whisky, he could see that it did indeed exist, although a stray piece of ivy was covering the 'Beware' part. The front door was at the top of a small flight of steps and he could see, through the front window, the flicker of a television screen and a maroon outline sitting on the sofa. Maroon was not a colour that Joe cared for; it reminded him of his uniform at his old school years ago, where he had shone at maths but been unable to master what was known as 'composition'.

Did the front doorbell work? If so, it wasn't audible. He tried the knocker instead but it made an ineffectual hollow noise. Perhaps a tap on the window? He tried that. This time, the maroon shape jumped up as though it had been shot. Oh God, thought Joe, I've startled him. Wishing now that he'd just waited patiently, he heard the shuffling of feet along the hall and the door opened.

Joe's first impression was of a man who wasn't as old as his shuffle had indicated. Although he was almost bald, he had a surprisingly youthful laugh and twinkly eyes to match, rather like a small boy who had been caught out doing something naughty. He also looked as though he had been somewhere warm from the slight tan on his cheeks, although Joe knew that was more likely to be a residue from the jaundice infection that had set in after the heart attack which could, apparently, have killed him but somehow hadn't.

'Joe Balls,' the man in the maroon cardigan said, pumping his hand. 'Nice to meet you at last. I've heard a lot about you.'

Joe wondered why he felt nervous. 'All good, I hope.'

The man put his head on one side as though considering the question. 'That depends,' he replied.

That depends? Joe suddenly felt uneasy. Was this really, he wondered, as he followed Brian Hughes into his small front room with rather grubby lace curtains, such a good idea?

'Thanks for the gift,' said Brian, indicating the bottle and biscuits that Joe was still clutching. He'd forgotten about those for a minute, but clearly the older man hadn't. 'Very good, very good,' he was nodding now approvingly. 'Might not be what the doctor ordered but like the wife always used to say, a bit of what you fancy and all that!' He twinkled again and Joe could begin to see why Brian had been so popular at school. He exuded warmth but, so Joe suspected, he could be firm when it was necessary.

'They'd given me up for dead, you know,' said Brian cheerily, settling himself into the larger pale blue wing chair with the cream antimacassar.

Joe had once had an uncle who had survived three strokes and was continually reminding everyone of how lucky he had been. He detected the same sort of triumph in Brian's voice, but now he was older than he was when his uncle had been boasting, he could understand Brian's pride. Cheating death was no mean feat, and Brian had certainly done that.

'I could have gone back to school.' Brian was eyeing

him challengingly. 'I told them that, even though my right side is still a bit awkward. But there was only another six months before retirement and what with Mavis having passed away two Christmases ago, I felt it was time to let a new pair of hands take over.'

He nodded in the direction of Joe's hands, which he'd thrust into his pockets, partly because that was what he tended to do when faced with a strange situation, and partly because his chair didn't seem very clean.

'Mavis?' asked Joe tentatively, wondering if this referred to a cat.

'The wife.'

'But the sign on the gate . . .' He felt his voice tailing away.

'Been there for years, it has. Mavis bought it me for our twenty-fifth. Didn't see much point in taking it down after she passed on.'

Joe searched for something to say but fortunately Brian was talking again. 'Now, let's get this right. You've not come here to pay a courtesy visit, have you, lad? No, don't protest.' His eye fell on the bottle of whisky that now sat between them on the old-fashioned oak table with its barley-twist legs. 'I mean, I appreciate the booze and all that, but something tells me that a man with your background – banking, wasn't it? – doesn't just visit an old teacher put out to grass without some kind of ulterior motive.'

This man, maroon cardigan or not, was more insightful than he'd thought. Joe looked around the room, at its 1930s dark oak mirror over the fireplace, and the row of photographs of Brian and presumably

Mavis holding a small child who was probably a granddaughter. He looked at the television which stood on a rocky-looking stand, and at the sideboard which reminded him of one owned by his grandparents. And he thought that you could have so many gadgets and so many ideas to push the world forward, yet there were some things like experience that could only be bought with time, not money or bright ideas.

'A friend of mine,' he began, thinking back to his long talk with Lynette as they'd walked along the beach, 'a friend of mine suggested that you might be able to help me.'

The greeny-brown eyes twinkled. 'And how exactly might I be able to do that?'

Joe took a deep breath. 'I think I might have got off to a wrong start with certain people at school and . . . and at the playgroup. There are also some things that I think I'm good at and some things that I'm not. So I wondered if you would be my mentor.'

There was a silence, punctuated only by the faint drone of *Coronation Street* from the television, which was turned down low. Brian was unwrapping the packet of Bourbons and after offering one to him, took one himself, devouring it rapidly regardless of the stray crumbs it left on his chin.

'You have the experience, sir.' To his surprise, Joe found his palms were sweating. 'I'm just the new boy. So would you help me? Please?'

The following weekend Joe packed his motorbike carrier with essential clothes for his new weekly life. He'd get the other stuff – cushions and maybe a new duvet cover – in the town. It seemed odd turning up at Hazelwood on a Sunday night. As he let himself into his room with the key that his landlady had given him, he felt slightly homesick for Notting Hill until he reminded himself that when he woke up the next morning, he wouldn't have to worry about commuting into work.

There was the sound of the door next to his slamming shut, and some footsteps running down the stairs. His new landlady had said she rented out two other rooms, only one of which was occupied. She'd wondered if he knew anyone else who might want the third and he'd promised to give it some thought, although he didn't like to say that at his age, most of his friends had at least one house of their own.

Maybe, thought Joe, he'd unpack a few bits and pieces and then go for a walk through town. It was at this point that his right pocket began to vibrate. Probably Mike or Lynette checking up that he really had done the sensible thing and rented somewhere nearer school.

'Hello,' he answered.

'Joe?'

The shock of hearing the voice almost made him drop his mobile.

'Hello,' the voice said urgently. 'Please don't hang up, Joe. It's me. Ed.'

IMPORTANT NOTICE FOR ALL PARENTS AND CARERS!

You'll be glad to know that rehearsals for the end-of-term concert/nativity play are going well. Thank you so much for practising the songs at home – it's been a big help. Below is another rhyme we have added to our repertoire. If possible, could you please have a go at this one too! Maybe you could do it at bathtime and before meals!

THE PUDDLEDUCKS WASH-
YOUR-HANDS SONG

We are the little Puddleducks
We always wash our hands
To keep those nasty germs away
That come from Baddy Land!

Chapter 15

Sometimes, thought Gemma, looking around the room wondering where to start, it was just as well that the parents weren't here during Puddleducks working hours to see what was going on. This morning it looked less like a pre-school and more like a cross between a zoo and a jelly factory. The washing-up bowls containing green jelly had been Bella's idea, and certainly fitted the Early Years Goals by providing children with texture, measurement ideas, colour and – although they weren't meant to eat it – taste!

Why was it that everything nowadays had to be classified into goals and objectives? What was wrong, as her grandmother used to say, with good old-fashioned play? Still, at least she was managing to include that as well. At the moment they were working on a project called Significant People, all about well-known figures in history. Joe Balls had actually liked that idea and agreed to her suggestion that they held a joint assembly where the Puddleducks would dress up (providing the parents got their costume act together) and they'd all troop off to Reception, who would be similarly dressed up.

'The staff do it too,' she had warned Joe. It had been worth making this up just to see his face.

'What should I go as?' he blurted out, clearly thrown by her suggestion.

Henry VIII, she felt like saying. Or the Black Death? No, that wasn't fair, especially as he had found her precious necklace for her. In fact, she owed him one. If it had been anyone else, she would have offered to take him out for a drink to thank him for spotting her chain but then again, she didn't want him thinking she was making a pass. Even with her limited experience, Gemma couldn't help feeling that Joe was just the kind of good-looking, single and slightly arrogant man who thought every woman in the office (or school) was after him.

'I'm going to be Queen Elizabeth I,' she volunteered. 'I'm sure you'll come up with something.'

Now, as she walked around checking everyone was doing roughly what they were meant to be doing, she regretted the Elizabeth I bit. The only possible outfit was the dress at the back of her wardrobe, which she had sworn never to wear again. Yet somehow she had never been able to throw it away, just like the silver chain which she still wore every day for a reason she couldn't explain, even to herself.

'Mrs Merryfield, Mrs Merryfield!'

'Yes, Mikey?' said Gemma, noting that he didn't have a pinny (lost again?).

A pair of bright blue eyes stared up at her mournfully. 'It's my go on the cornflakes modelling table but Billy won't let me.'

What *were* they going to do about Billy? The doctor had apparently suggested that his mother cut out additives to see if that helped.

'Let him try keeping Billy out of the kitchen cupboards,' his mother had snorted. 'That child can sniff an E number from miles away!'

Meanwhile, Billy had started jumping up and down. Oh no! Now he was shoving Mikey's head into a model of a cornflake dinosaur. Where was Bella, or Jean, who combined her role as helper with that of nursery manager, sorting out fees with those mothers who wanted more hours than the nursery vouchers provided?

'Billy, don't do that!' She pulled the offender away from the victim, who was spluttering madly. 'Are you all right, sweetheart?' *Now* what was Billy doing? Jumping up and down on the cornflakes, crunching them into the ground. Yet at times, this was the boy who screamed violently if anyone moved his possessions because they had to be exactly as he placed them on the table.

At last here was Bella returning from the loo *again*, muttering something about 'this time of the month', which added up to at least three periods every twenty-eight days. Clearly it was her way of having a quick break from the masses. Well, the girl could jolly well take poor Mikey to the green-jelly pit while she had a word with the cornflakes aggressor.

'Billy, you really can't behave like this,' she began. And then stopped. Because somehow Danny and Lily had got there first. Lily, who had hardly said a word since she'd started, was holding Billy's hand while Danny was quietly speaking to him. Gemma tried to listen without being obvious. 'Don't do that to people,' the boy with those lovely long fair lashes was saying solemnly. 'It's not nice.'

How sweet! Maybe this was what his mother said to him when he did something wrong.

'Danny's right, you know,' said Gemma firmly but kindly. 'You could hurt someone. Now how about saying sorry to Mikey?'

Billy scrunched up his face. She knew from past experience that pushing for an apology could make you look weak if you didn't get one. 'Tell you what,' smiled Gemma. 'Supposing you make Mikey a corn-flake model now with Bella, and give it to him as a sorry present.'

There was a quiet groan from Bella's direction at the thought of model-making with Billy. 'Look,' he was saying now. 'You've dropped something.'

Flushing, Bella tried to pick up the packet that had fallen out of her pocket, but Mikey had got there first. Unfortunately for her, he was one of their best readers. 'C . . . a . . . n . . .' he began. He beamed up at her. 'Are those sweeties?'

Bella was getting redder. 'No,' she snapped. 'It's something called Canny Sten. It's a sort of tooth-paste.'

She shot a challenging look at Gemma.

'May I suggest you keep your . . . er . . . toothpaste out of reach in the staff lockers, Bella?' Gemma said.

'Whatever.'

Oh dear, thought Gemma, heading towards the Adopt a Word corner. Now she'd have a sulky Bella to deal with on top of the terrible three, as Jean called them. 'Terrible' was a bit strong, but they were definitely a concern. There was Lily, who hardly spoke and spent most of her time covering anything from tables to toys with her soft pink comfort blanket. During her training, Gemma had come across a theory, which suggested that children who did this were often attempting to make things safe, because they needed to feel safe themselves. Was that how Lily felt? She'd have to keep an eye on that.

Then there was Billy, who was either jumping about, thumping people for touching his things or taking everything very literally: he'd got very excited recently when she'd said it was raining cats and dogs. And of course Danny, who'd really come out of his shell now and had had to be reprimanded gently the other day for jumping up on one of the tables and pretending he could fly, before curling up on the beanbag in the sleepy corner and having a nap.

Yet the three of them seemed to have formed a rather sweet trio. How funny it was, the way children chose each other as friends. Rather like she had teamed up with Kitty at university as well as . . .

No. She wouldn't think about that now. 'Right, everyone,' she beamed at the group of children who were sitting round the wall display waiting for her to start. 'Which word are we going to adopt this week?'

It had been an idea she'd got from one of the weekend newspaper supplements. Apparently there was a trend now for the expensive nursery schools in Britain to pay money to a charity in order to adopt a word. They would then use that word as often as they could in order to increase their vocabulary.

Gemma had adapted the idea so that they did the same, but without asking parents to fork out. Although there were some families, like Danny's and Sienna's, with plenty of cash, judging from the four-by-fours and Harrods labels, there were also children like Billy, who came from the council estate round the corner and wore the same cherry-red anorak winter in and summer out.

'Here we are!' Gemma handed round a bag of words that she'd spent the previous night writing on card, which she'd then laminated before cutting the words out. 'Whose turn is it to choose one today?' She pretended to think. 'I know. It's Lucy, isn't it?'

Lucy was one of those children who did nothing wrong. If they were all like her, thought Gemma as she watched the girl with the blonde plaits dipping her hand into the word bag, life would be very easy. On the other hand, that was not why she had entered this profession.

'Magic!' beamed Lucy, having pulled out the word.

Sienna pouted. 'Why? Why does magic happen?'

Over to you, said Bella's rolling eyes.

'Good question! Actually, some people believe in magic and others don't, because no one really knows how it works.'

Cop-out, she could hear Bella muttering. Ignoring her, Gemma clapped her hands. 'Let's write our new Adopt a Word on the whiteboard, shall we, for everyone to learn. Can you see how it's spelt? M . . . a . . .'

'Mrs Merryfield, Mrs Merryfield!'

Darren, who was more than ready for Big School

128

now, was jumping up and tugging at her shoulder, almost catching her silver chain.

'Darren, don't do that. You might hurt someone.'

'But Mrs Merryfield, Mrs Merryfield, I want to say something.' Darren's face had a serious look on it that wasn't normally there, and something caught in Gemma's throat. Suddenly she had a bad feeling about what he did want to say. 'Can I choose a word too?'

Gemma bit her lip. 'That depends on what it is, sweetheart.'

He nodded. 'Can we have Div Orse? Cos that's what my mum and dad are going to do when I get big.' His face crumpled. 'How do you spell that, Mrs Merryfield?'

It always happened, of course. Statistically, it was bound to do so. Every year, if not every term, there was at least one parent who would come up with a worried look on their face, asking if he or she could have a word. And Gemma, whose own parents had somehow rumbled along together, despite her father's moods, and seemed reasonably happy, possibly because they had produced five children, always floundered for the right thing to say.

It was all very well reading books on the subject, or talking to Brian, who had always been very kind but equally ignorant of the messy lives people could lead since his own marriage had been perfectly content until poor Mavis's death, but there were no easy answers. And somehow, Gemma got the feeling that it wasn't worth asking advice from the tough Joe Balls.

In the meantime, she sat Darren down quietly, wondering if this was why he'd been clingy at the start of term, and read a book with him about a boy whose parents lived in separate houses but who each loved their son very much. Then, when Darren's mother arrived to collect him at the end of the day, asking if she could have a private chat with Gemma, she was able to explain that she *did* know about the situation on account of the Adopt a Word table.

Chapter 16

The week continued much as it had begun. On Tuesday, there was an outbreak of nits, which meant Gemma had had to run up to Corrybank's office at lunchtime to print out a 'Please check your child's head' letter to go out at the end of the day.

On Wednesday, four-year-old Megan, who had Down's syndrome and was as bright as a button, came up, tugging her arm and leading her to the hamster cage, explaining earnestly that she thought Hammie, who had been curled up in a corner since yesterday apparently, was 'poorly'.

This meant a visit to the vet's after school. Had someone given him something to eat that they shouldn't have? asked the vet. Gemma thought of all the children at Puddleducks who were always poking their fingers through Hammie's bars, and of all the different snack boxes that came in and out, containing anything from processed cheese and jam sandwiches to smoked salmon with fromage frais.

She couldn't be certain, she admitted. In that case, suggested the vet, it might be a plan for Gemma to take Hammie home with her for a few days, just to keep an eye on him.

And then on Thursday, there was a rather nasty scrap between a pair of so-called best friends who fell out over their mobile phones. Mobiles weren't allowed at Puddleducks – not for the children, anyway – but somehow these two had smuggled theirs into their shoebags and then had a big row over whose was 'better'.

Ridiculous, as Bella said during their quick lunch hour, when they munched sandwiches in the kitchen while the cleaner crashed her way round the hall to clean before the afternoon intake. 'Remember that craze over sparkly shoes last year?'

They nodded, recalling the group of girls who had excluded a newcomer because she hadn't had the same shoes as them; the ones with the sparkly heels that flashed as they walked.

Children could be so cruel! And yet, thought Gemma, remembering how Lily and Danny and Billy looked after each other, they could also restore your faith in humanity. What would we do without them?

Gemma had planned to visit Brian on Thursday evening, but had felt so exhausted by toddler politics that she decided to put it off until Friday or maybe the weekend. It wasn't, after all, as though she had told him she was coming, although she'd written 'I'll be round soon' on his get-well card. Amazing, really, that he had survived when everyone had said it was unlikely.

It was also strange, she thought, as she walked back to Joyce's house and made her way up the stairs to her room, how she had got used to comfortable old Brian, with his penchant for maroon jumpers and biscuits, *not* being there. It wasn't that she was slowly warming to Joe, his replacement; it was difficult to do that in view of his critical manner.

But she could also see, rather reluctantly, that he was much more efficient at his job than poor Brian had been. And when she'd popped into Reception the other day, she'd been really impressed by the maths games involving pictures of iPhones and computer screens which were still on the whiteboard from a previous lesson. If they'd taught maths like that in her day, she might be better at it now herself!

'Hello, Hammie,' she said, coming into her room and closing the door behind her. 'How are you doing then?'

On the mend, or so it seemed. The creature sat happily in the palm of her hand, gazing up at her with bright beady eyes as if it knew exactly what she was thinking. Gemma hoped not. Despite the nit alert and the mobile phone drama, not to mention the divorce chat, she hadn't been able to squash some of the private thoughts which kept coming into her head during the week. No prizes for guessing why. It would be half-term before long, and then it would only be another two and a half months to go.

'What are you going to do then?' Kitty had asked when she'd rung up to talk about the *Britain's Best Talent* event at school tomorrow.

'Not sure.' Gemma's voice had sounded hesitant, even to her.

'We'll discuss it when I come round,' Kitty had said reassuringly. 'By the way, it is all right if I stay on your floor, isn't it? Just for the night. It will save me having to go back up to town that night and besides, we can have a good old girly chat. Catch up, just like the old times!'

Gemma couldn't wait, and Hammie seemed to sense her excitement from the way he jumped off her hand and on to the bed. Quickly she managed to scoop him up in her palm and pop him back in his cage.

At the same time, she heard the door next to her bang. Joyce, who had gone away for the week to visit her daughter, had left her a note to say that she'd let the room next door, without giving details of the new incumbent. Whoever it was must leave very early and come back late, because she hadn't seen him or her. In fact, this was the first night she had even heard the door go.

Maybe she'd give him or her a knock and suggest coffee? It would, after all, be only friendly. Checking her reflection in the mirror – slightly smudged mascara but on the whole not too bad – Gemma opened her own door and, as she did so, spotted a very beautiful, glamorous redhead gliding up the stairs, wearing a stylishly cut black silk skirt and short boxy scarlet jacket. Kitty, who was also auburn, was the only redhead she had ever known until now who could get away with wearing scarlet, but this woman made even Kitty look like an amateur when it came to style.

Gemma was about to ask if she was looking for someone, but the woman with long ten-denier legs up to her armpits merely nodded in her direction, and then knocked on the door next to hers. Gosh! That perfume, which she could smell from here, was definitely of the expensive variety!

The door opened and Gemma went back into her

room, otherwise it would have looked nosy. 'Darling,' she heard the woman purr. 'How are you, darling?'

'Very well, Ed.' The voice, dark and deep, jolted Gemma so that she almost fell against the hamster cage. 'And I can see that you are too. You'd better come in.'

Surely not? Gemma didn't know whether to laugh or drill a hole through to next door just to make sure. Unless she was very much mistaken, the other voice belonged to Joe Balls. Her new neighbour. And immediate boss.

Chapter 17

Now what should she do? Gemma sat on the ground with her back to the wall and the hamster in her lap, which was nibbling the treats she'd scattered around her jeans zip. She'd have, at some point, to tell Joe she was living next to him.

How awful! Joyce's house was her refuge from school. Much as she loved Puddleducks, she needed an escape at the end of the day, and her room, which she'd come to see as 'hers' despite the weekly rent, was the only space she could call her own.

Over the last three years she had customised it with the antique patchwork throw from the bring-and-buy sale in town; a cornflower-blue lampshade from Heals that Mum had bought her one Christmas; a charming Victorian pine chest of drawers with white china handles that she'd picked up from a house clearance advertised in the local paper, and of course her books. Rows and rows of them on the shelves which Joyce had allowed her to put up.

Joe Balls didn't seem like the type to have romances, either Victorian or contemporary, on his shelves. In fact, the man who'd always made it clear that numbers were his 'thing' probably had an array of calculators on show.

There was a murmur of voices through the wall which Gemma could feel reverberating through her back, and the sound of heels click-clacking across the landing to the bathroom and then back again. Oh no! She'd have to share the bathroom with him too! That would be so embarrassing. Mentally Gemma did a quick check of all her personals which she'd kept in the bathroom cabinet even though it had been shared with the previous next-door lodger, a girl who worked at an employment agency with whom she'd got on really well.

They'd had some fun girly chats and even swapped bath stuff sometimes. But now she was going to have that awful situation where she might actually bump into Joe Balls as she or he came in and out of the bathroom, unless one of them got up really early. If he'd been someone else at school, like Di perhaps or even that quiet young man who was in charge of Year Three, she might have coped, but Joe with his grumpy, gruff manner was a different matter. He was just the kind of person who would complain about ring stains. That was a thought! How embarrassing would it be to share a bath – at different times, of course!

No. This wouldn't do at all. How could Joyce have done this without consulting her? Surely her landlady must have realised they worked together. On the other hand, she'd been in a terrible rush to get away to see her daughter, who was having her first baby. Maybe she hadn't been as thorough as she usually was when quizzing prospective lodgers.

Meanwhile, Joe Balls – dark horse! – was entertaining this extremely glamorous woman next door. So much for Bella's furtive speculation about his love life. 'I reckon he must be gay,' she had said only the other week. 'After all, he never mentions a girlfriend.'

Gay? Privately, Gemma thought she was being unfair. Perhaps he simply hadn't found the right one. Yet that embrace at the door, which she'd heard rather than seen, had sounded pretty intense on the redhead's part with that rather breathy 'Darling'.

Ed, he had called her. Probably short for Edwina. That would fit with the well-bred voice and the gorgeous clothes.

'Perhaps,' she whispered to Hammie, who was looking up at her with his cute, knowing black eyes, 'I should just pop next door when she's gone and tell him I'm his new neighbour.'

Just saying it out loud made her feel that this was the right thing to do. She only hoped that the glamorous auburn girlfriend wouldn't stay the night.

When, an hour later, there was the sound of the door opening and shutting again, Gemma still didn't know what to do. Did that mean Ed had gone out, or both of them? Would it look intrusive if she knocked on his door and she was still there?

Oh blow it. The sooner done, the sooner over, as her grandmother used to say. Popping Hammie gently back into his playball, Gemma ran her hands through her hair and tentatively knocked on Joe Balls's door. Had he heard her? She knocked again, louder this time.

'Coming,' called a deep voice, and Gemma's heart quickened as footsteps came towards the closed door. This was ridiculous. She had as much right to live next door to him as he did to her, so why did she feel awkward?

'Gemma!' His surprised look removed any chance

that he might have known the identity of his fellow lodger. 'Is anything wrong?'

She felt an embarrassed flush crawl up her neck, deepening when she saw that he was wearing just a pair of shorts. He had a towel slung around his shoulders as though he'd just stepped out of a shower, even though his room didn't have one. This was excruciating! 'No. Not exactly. I just thought you ought to know that I live next door.'

His eyebrows rose. 'To this house?'

'No. To you.' She indicated the door next to him. 'I've rented a room here for ages. Obviously Joyce didn't tell you.'

He put the towel more firmly round his shoulders, but not before she'd glimpsed the rather unexpected crop of black hairs on his chest. 'She was in a rush.'

'Her daughter's having a baby.'

They both spoke at the same time and then each paused, uncertain whether to speak next or to give way. Gemma gave way.

'So,' he mused, as though digesting the information. 'We're neighbours. At least, during the week. I still intend to go home to London at the weekends.'

She nodded. 'Don't worry. I'm not the type to cadge tea bags. Just the odd spoonful of hot chocolate.'

He smiled, and for a minute he looked like a different man, thought Gemma. Perhaps, she felt like telling him, he ought to smile more. It certainly made her feel more at ease with him. Then, unable to contain her curiosity, she took a sneak peep behind him. His room was smaller than hers, and as far as she could see there was no one else there, unless she was under the bed.

'Does your girlfriend live here too?'

She could see from his eyes that she'd been too nosy.

'My girlfriend? No. She's . . . What the hell is that?'

His eyes went behind her towards the floor at the same time as she felt something hard brush her ankles.

'Oh my God,' squealed Gemma. 'Hammie!'

She ran towards the top step, but it was too late. Horrified, she watched the ball bump down first one step and then another and another . . .

'Stop him,' she screamed, and Joe, to give him credit, seemed to take in the situation and ran past her, scooping the ball off the bottom step.

'What's inside?' he asked, handing it to her.

Gemma could hardly speak. 'The hamster. The playgroup hamster.' Her hands trembled. 'Oh God. Is it dead? I can't bear to look.'

She shook with fear as Joe peered inside. 'It's breathing but it is lying on its side. There's a spot of blood too on the sawdust. Look, I think we ought to take it to the vet. *Is* there one in this place?'

It was after hours, but what was an emergency if it wasn't a hamster who had fallen down the stairs in its playball? Yes, the duty vet was prepared to come in to the satellite surgery just out of town, but they would need to be there within the half-hour.

'My car's being serviced,' wailed Gemma.

'Then I'll give you a lift.' Joe strode up the stairs. 'Just give me a second to put something on and get the bike keys.'

Five minutes later, Gemma found herself clutching the back of Ed's leather jacket – so weirdly intimate

140

to have her arms around his back! – and flying through town on a Harley-Davidson, with Hammie wedged into the bike box on the back. Joe had said he'd take it slowly on account of their precious cargo, but it still felt fast to her. Would Hammie still be alive when they got there? And how could she have been so stupid as to leave her bedroom door ajar?

'He's sitting up!' said Joe when they got there, in a voice that didn't sound like Joe Balls at school. 'Look!'

The vet didn't seem surprised. 'You'd be amazed what animals survive,' she said. 'Ouch. Don't bite, you little rascal.'

Together Gemma and Joe marvelled as the vet very carefully felt each miniature joint. It was incredible how she could do an examination on such a tiny creature.

'I think its right arm looks broken,' said the vet at last.

Gemma gasped with horror.

'But it's not a problem. I had one in last week, exactly the same. We'll just pop a miniature splint on it and providing it has plenty of rest – you'll need to leave him here overnight – your Hammie should make a full recovery.' She smiled at them. 'Just don't let the children play with him for at least three weeks.'

She thinks we're a couple, realised Gemma with embarrassment but if Joe thought the same, he didn't put the vet right. Instead, he just gave Gemma a look that said, clear as day, 'that's a relief', and drove her back. Without the excuse of a mercy dash as there had been on the outward journey, it now felt really awkward to put her arms around his waist and feel the heat of his body under the leather jacket.

'Thanks,' said Gemma when he parked outside Joyce's. She stared down at the ground, wondering about the correct procedure for dismounting. In the end, she swung her leg over the seat – so high! – and almost fell on to the pavement in a most inelegant fashion.

Righting herself, she wondered if she should ask him in for a coffee. Then again, she'd just run out, and after what she'd said about not cadging tea bags, it didn't seem the right thing. In silence, they walked side by side up the stairs to their respective rooms.

'I'll say goodnight then.' He made as though to shake her hand but then stopped.

'See you tomorrow at your *Britain's Best Talent* gig.' His mouth curled slightly as though he was trying to smile. 'My class is looking forward to it.'

'Us too,' Gemma heard herself saying. 'And thanks once more. I don't know what I'd have done without you. I really don't.'

Instantly he stopped his attempt at a smile. 'It was nothing. Anyone would have done it.'

Oh dear. Now he thought she was being too friendly. As if he was her type! Gemma walked back to her room, telling herself that with some men, you just couldn't win.

Kitty, it had to be said, was absolutely brilliant. She arrived in a bright pink shirt dress with sparkling black trainers and a purple hair bow that made her look like Minnie Mouse. Even at uni, she'd been the one who had dressed eccentrically with leggings that had clashed intentionally with the rest of her, and a different hair colour every month. She might not have got through to the final of *Britain's Best Talent*, but she had done well enough for a record company to offer her a contract.

The children were so excited, as they nattered to Kitty while walking up to Reception, that Gemma and her helpers could hardly keep them in line.

But if she'd hoped that the hamster episode might have thawed Joe Balls's attitude to her at school, she was mistaken. The entire drama, from her boss's distant expression, might as well not have happened.

'Very good of you to make time to visit us,' he'd said stiffly before introducing Kitty to his own class. The idea was that the children did their own acts after hers. The Puddleducks sang the toothpaste song which she had written especially for them to encourage them to clean their teeth at night, while Joe's class did a variety of songs, and performed a play about a wizard who was also a mathematician. Boring, boring.

Some of the mothers were there, and there was a big round of applause afterwards.

Gemma had arranged to meet Kitty in one of the wine bars in town after work. 'He's gorgeous,' gushed Kitty before Gemma could say anything. 'Just like Colin Firth but slightly more rounded, with attitude. I've always had a thing about northerners.'

Not Kitty too!

'Joe Balls can be very rude and besides, he's got a girlfriend,' said Gemma quickly. 'An extremely glamorous one with a voice like slub silk and legs up to her doubtless perfectly waxed armpits. Besides, have you forgotten about . . .'

'Don't even say that man's name.' Kitty laid a hand on her arm. 'Listen, I'm sorry I can't stay the night but like I said, I've got this gig. As for that other thing we talked about, in my opinion, the sooner you take the plunge the better. Gemma, are you listening to me?'

The last part of this conversation haunted Gemma all through the weekend. Usually, she enjoyed her weekends. On Saturdays she went to a t'ai chi class and often she went on a cycle ride along the canal. 'You ought to get out more and see people your age,' Joyce was always telling her, but Gemma would laugh and say she was happy as she was. Sometimes she met up with friends in London and they went to a play or the cinema, but when they suggested clubbing, she always made an excuse.

Meanwhile, she needed to see Brian, and Sunday was just the day to do it. 'You were lucky to catch me, young lady,' he said when she arrived at about midday. 'Only just got back from church, I have. Didn't used to go but when you've survived something like I have, it makes you count your blessings.'

She stood in the kitchen, watching him check the roast in the oven. 'Fancy a bite?'

She automatically started to make an excuse, but then she stopped. When news of Brian's heart attack first got out, the rumour was that he might not survive but here he was, bright as a daisy, despite moving rather more slowly than she remembered. Dear Brian, who had been so kind to her when she had been a new girl at Puddleducks. She owed him some time, thought Gemma, especially as he didn't have his adored Mavis around any more.

'A bite to eat?' she repeated. 'That would be lovely. Thanks. I would have brought a bottle of wine if I'd known.'

His eyes twinkled. 'Don't you worry about that. My successor presented me with some whisky and my favourite biscuits the other day. I've polished off the last ones but I have some wine.'

'Joe Balls came to visit?'

'He did,' said Brian, carefully stirring flour into the gravy. Gemma briefly considered offering to help, but had a feeling that his pride wouldn't let him agree. 'And the man's not the ogre that everyone makes out. In fact, he could do with a bit of help.'

Help?

'It's not easy for the poor bloke.' Brian poured the gravy into a jug, slopping it slightly with his shaking hand on to the yellow-and-black-flecked Formica worktop. 'He might have the business background but three years at a tough school in London isn't enough, in my opinion, to weave your way into the hearts of Corrybank and Puddleducks. The man's got other issues too. Things that he told me in confidence that clearly I can't share. But let's have our lunch, shall we? And then I'm going to tell you how you can help him.'

It was ridiculous, thought Gemma walking home. Help Joe Balls? The problem with him, as she'd tried explaining to Brian, was that he was one of those people who always thought he was right. In fact . . .

What was that?

Her eye fell on a newspaper placard outside the garage. This one, with a tabloid name above it, stood out far beyond the others.

Singer Dilly Dalung secretly sends tot to state playgroup!

Gemma felt sick as she bought a copy and quickly scanned the article. It contained all kinds of details, like the type of snack box which Lily took to playgroup and the kind of car that dropped her off – details that only an insider could have provided. There was even a picture of the Puddleducks building.

How on earth did they get that? It was such an invasion of privacy!

On the other hand, it was inevitable that one of the other parents would eventually say something to a newspaper. Some of them had already asked her if Dilly Dalung really was Lily's mother, and although she'd explained she couldn't comment, it was clear from their expressions that they knew what was going on. Maybe Beryl had been wrong when she'd vetoed Joe's idea to discuss the situation with the other parents. Personally, Gemma had thought that everyone concerned should know the truth.

On the other hand, maybe it had been a member of staff who had provided this 'Exclusive'. Someone who wanted the money that the paper had no doubt paid. A picture of Bella with yet another new pair of shoes flashed into her mind, making her shiver with apprehension. Bella wasn't an ideal playgroup assistant, it was true. But surely she wouldn't stoop to something as low as this?

Just at that moment, her mobile rang. 'Gemma?' It was Joe's voice. The old, gravelly, distant voice before the hamster incident. 'I expect you've seen the newspapers. Beryl wants us both into school first thing Tuesday morning, for an urgent meeting.'

'OK,' said Gemma tightly, wondering why she always got the feeling that she had done something wrong when Joe talked to her.

'By the way,' he added, 'I wonder if . . .'

The line went dead. Bother. Her battery had gone. Now Joe might think she had cut him off! With a heavy, sinking feeling, Gemma found herself making her way towards Puddleducks. Something made her wonder if the scummy journalist who had broken the story might just be having another look right now when no one was around.

Yes! There were three of them, each with their cameras taking a picture of the giant blue and white Puddleducks sign. 'Oi,' she heard herself yell. 'You lot there! Clear off! Do you hear me? This is private property.'

Whipping out her mobile – they weren't to know that her battery was dead – she pretended to talk down the phone. 'Is that the police? I'd like to report some intruders at . . .'

That did it! They were off, leaping over the fence and legging it down the road. Gemma felt a combination of shock (she hadn't realised she could get so angry) and a sense of achievement. It just went to show what she could do when she really tried. If only she could have got angry like that in her personal life, she might not be in the mess she was in right now.

Chapter 18

Handbag Design had been her first choice, but that was full so she needed to put down an alternative. What should it be? Belly Dancing? Hatha Yoga? Mosaic Marvels?

Nancy leafed through the brochure as she stood in her spacious hall (one reason why they had bought this nice bright airy town house), waiting for Danny to 'Finish, Mum!' in the loo.

Since starting Puddleducks, he'd become much more vocal and demanding. 'Want Lily, want Billy,' was all he would say when he was on his own. So she'd given in and enrolled him for two whole days a week instead of just five mornings.

As a result, he was bored silly at weekends unless she did something energetic with him, like taking him out in the park with a football. Exactly the sort of thing that needed a father's input.

She'd said as much to Sam on the phone when he had rung yesterday to see how they were doing, as he put it, but either the line had been bad again or he'd chosen to ignore the heavy hints. Soon afterwards he'd asked to be put on to Danny. Instead of falling silent as he always did on the phone to her mother in Connecticut, their son began chattering away about his new friends and jelly pools and messy corners and that woman who sang on TV who had come into Puddleducks the other week.

'Sounds like he's enjoying playgroup or pre-school or whatever they call it nowadays,' Sam had said in an 'I told you so' voice.

Nancy knew just what he was thinking. She should have sent Danny when he was rising three and not nearly four.

'He's settling in well because he's at the right age,' she said in a sharper tone than she'd intended. 'Where were you the other night when I rang, by the way?'

'Out at another meeting, I expect.' He sounded irritated. 'I can't always pick up the mobile and the time difference doesn't help.'

Well, she had a meeting too, she wanted to say. The next morning, in fact. 'I'm starting a belly-dancing class tomorrow.'

'Jelly dancing?'

'No. Belly . . .'

Too late. The phone went dead. It did that all the time. Since the war, in which her mother had lost a distant cousin, Vietnam had apparently been desperately trying to claw its way up to Westernised standards. But from what Sam had told her, it had a long way to go. It had been much easier to keep in touch when he'd been in Hong Kong.

December! She had to wait until then for his return. If last night's terse phone call had been anything to go by, they both had a lot of making up to do if they were going to make this work. And she had to. She would not – hear this, Nancy Carter Wright! – would not allow Danny to grow up in a fatherless family, as both his parents had done.

Now, Nancy glanced in the mirror, shaking her head. If that *Britain's Best Talent* girl could have so much confidence with a nose like that, why couldn't she? Maybe if she got her hair tinted a slightly different colour and perhaps if she played around with a bit of eye make-up like Annie, she might be more like the girl that Sam wanted her to be.

Yet that wasn't her. Besides, did she really need to be someone else in order to woo her husband? And if so, did that mean they weren't really suited?

'Heard about the article in the paper?' gabbled Brigid excitedly. When she spoke fast, her tongue seemed to get stuck at the back of her mouth, but her 'you've got to hear this' voice demanded that Nancy and Annie really needed to listen to her.

'There was a big piece in one of the tabloids on Sunday all about . . .' here Brigid lowered her voice as they were queuing up for their class, 'Dilly Dalung.'

Nancy frowned. 'Who?'

Annie nudged her in the ribs. 'You know. Dilly Dalung.'

'Shhhh.'

'All right, Bridge, but Nancy must be the only one in this building who doesn't know. She's a famous British pop singer and she's having this really dirty custody battle with the father of her child even though . . .'

Brigid groaned. 'Get to the point. We're about to go in. Her daughter is the new one. Lily. The one that looks like a Chinese doll but with very white skin. You must know who we're talking about. She's a friend of your Danny.' She preened slightly. 'And our Billy too.'

Danny had a celebrity friend? Nancy didn't like the sound of that. Celebrities in her view were totally unreliable, always leaving one partner for another. Not the kind of family group she wanted Danny to associate with.

Then she remembered. 'But I've asked her on a play date tonight along with Billy. Danny insisted.'

Annie snorted with laughter. 'Bridge's wild kid and Lily Who Doesn't Talk. Great combination. Sorry, Bridge, but he is a case, isn't he? All I can say is, Nance, don't expect Lily to turn up. Not after yesterday's article. My Kevin saw Gemma on Sunday when he was going to fetch the papers. Shouting at some photographers she was, who were hanging around trying to get a story about the playgroup. She was great, he said. Difficult to imagine, don't you think? I always thought she was so quiet!'

Nancy didn't like the sound of all this. She thought back to the note she'd sent into playgroup addressed to 'Lily's mother'. A written invitation had seemed rather formal but she wasn't sure how else to do it, as neither Lily's mother nor the nanny seemed to be around when the children were dropped off at the beginning of the day. Lily would be already sitting in the story corner with a book. Similarly, when she collected Danny, Lily had usually gone.

A note had come back in Danny's bag the following day, written in violet ink with loops and flourishes, to say that Lily would love to come to tea at Danny's house and would be dropped off at 4 p.m.

Nancy related this to the girls, adding, 'I thought it was a bit odd that her mother didn't want her to come back with us after playgroup.'

Brigid shrugged. 'I suppose people like that live in a different world. They have to be careful about their privacy. Great! Look! Class is starting.' She wiggled her hips, laughing in a deep infectious roar. Nancy couldn't help joining in. 'Now, are you ready, girls?'

One hour later, Nancy knew that belly dancing simply wasn't for her. It wasn't just the fact that she was wearing tight jeans and everyone else was in loose jogging bottoms or, in a couple of cases, harem-type pants. No. It was that she simply couldn't let go of her limbs, let alone her inhibitions, to do the slinky, side-to-side movements that Fatima, born and bred in Croydon, demonstrated.

Annie, on the other hand, was a natural! She moved with apparent ease from one side of the room to the other, following her hands with her eyes just as Fatima did, and at the same time shaking her hips in that snakelike movement their teacher had shown them at the beginning of class. She'd even bought a 'money belt' off the Internet, consisting of a scarf belt adorned with gold metal bits, to make the right noises as she swished around.

'Wish I could do that,' breathed Brigid. 'It's all I can do to get my feet to move in the right direction, let alone my hip bones!'

Thank goodness Nancy wasn't the only one! Maybe it was Annie's height that helped, or perhaps it was that amazing ingrained confidence, which the *Britain's Best Talent* girl had had too. Confidence! She suddenly realised how important that was to instil in your child. Her own mother, presumably unaware of this, had always criticised her as a child and continued to do so now by email.

'Coming on to t'ai chi now?' Brigid asked, interrupting her thoughts. The idea was that this was a full 'taster' day, so there were two classes in the morning and two in the afternoon. If you liked the look of one, you could stay on for the day. If not, you moved on until hopefully you found a class you enjoyed.

Nancy began to feel twitchy as she always did midmorning, in case Danny suddenly needed her. Even though he had taken to pre-school like a duck to water (a joke that was rather common at Puddleducks), she still couldn't help fretting, especially as she'd had to turn her phone off during class. Quickly she turned it on and checked. No messages.

'Come on,' urged Brigid. 'Or we'll miss the beginning. Someone told me that t'ai chi is deceptively complicated.'

She wasn't kidding! Nancy had been secretly enthusiastic about this one, having gemmed up on the scientific benefits of improving your health through moving certain parts of your body. It made sense! Yet now, as she watched the teacher – a young guy who looked not much older than Mrs Merryfield – she wondered if her body might have the physical equivalent of dyslexia. It simply wouldn't move the way that everyone else's would. Even worse, it transpired that if you put your foot just the smallest degree out of line with everyone else's, the lithe young man would glide over and, in front of the entire class, loudly explain how you needed to place it just a millimetre this way instead of that.

At the end Nancy was supporting an imaginary ball with both hands (something about holding the world in your hands apparently) in the wrong direction, so that she was facing the rest of the group.

'You've got to see the funny side,' said Brigid, who declared that her insides felt purified after the class.

'I feel utterly confused,' replied Nancy, who suspected that Brigid's enthusiasm had more to do with the supple young man running the class. Brigid had already casually mentioned that her 'partner' was only twenty-four, which meant that he'd probably been a freshman when he'd fathered Billy, if indeed he was the father. The British made such a big deal of being traditionalists, but since she'd been here she'd been struck by their lack of morals. Where was the England she had read about, with its crumpets for tea and good manners?

Meanwhile, she was beginning to feel left behind, now Brigid and Annie had found their niches. If the other two classes didn't work out, she'd have to find something 'realistic' to do with her life. Her mother had told her that in no uncertain terms when she'd confessed, during a recent Skype date, about Sam going away until Christmas.

'OK.' Both Annie and Brigid were looking at her now. 'Enough daydreaming over your sandwich. Lunch over. We're back to our classes and you're off to Sew and Crow!'

Sew and Crow? It was, explained the girls, a group where you learned to sew and also chat, although 'crow' suggested something that sounded like boasting.

Nancy had never been very good at Homecraft during high school, so she wasn't particularly surprised when she found herself unable to thread a needle either manually or on the machine that was put in front of her. It reminded her of the quilting circle that her mother had belonged to. The members would come over to her house once a week and bitch about their exes, while Nancy would pore over her homework in the adjoining kitchen and promise herself that her own life would be very different.

'Sorry,' Nancy announced at the end. 'Not for me, I'm afraid!'

She was getting rather good at this goodbye business, she told herself. Just one more taster session, and then she could say she'd given it a go. It would even be something to tell Sam about when – if – he rang that night. Anything would be better than the 'not much' when he asked her what she'd been doing.

'Hi, everyone! My name's Doug.'

A tall, bearded man beamed at her as she walked in with two other women, one of whom looked about four months pregnant without a wedding ring. Automatically, Nancy glanced down at her own slim band of gold, bought with haste when the pregnancy test had been positive.

'Afraid there's been a change of plan. The tutor for Bead Jewellery has been taken ill so you have me instead.' He smiled warmly in Nancy's direction and she automatically looked around to see who was behind her. No one.

'Any of you done mosaics before?'

Instantly, Nancy thought of the wonderful Roman

villa that Sam had taken her to in Italy when she had been so sick every morning with pregnancy nausea.

'No, but I visited some in Pompeii!' She glowed as she remembered how she'd spent ages admiring the way that craftsmen had painstakingly arranged the brightly coloured pieces of stone into patterns. It had seemed to her the perfect mixture of science and imagination, and even Sam had been entranced.

'I see we have someone from the United States. Connecticut, if I'm not mistaken.'

Nancy felt a thrill that came from being recognised in a country where most people asked if she was American or Canadian.

She beamed at this bearded man who was taking off his glasses, polishing them and putting them back on as though he too was feeling shy like her.

'Do you know it?'

'Spent three years of my life there, teaching at Westport College.'

Wow! 'I was at high school there before Harvard.'

'We must chat about that later. Right, everyone. Now, today we are going to make a mosaic frame for a mirror. It might sound ambitious but that's what mosaics are all about. They seem tiny but they're part of a bigger picture. Don't worry. You'll soon see.'

For the next hour, Nancy watched with fascination as Doug, the tutor, showed them how to break up small pieces of glass and arrange them in patterns in the cement that they learned to smooth on in thin layers round the mirror frame.

Her original thoughts about the mosaics in the Roman villa were right. This was a mixture of science and aesthetics. In a way, it reminded her of tessellations at high school, because you had to move the shapes so they fitted just so.

The result wasn't as finished as she had hoped. In fact, to be honest, it wasn't that dissimilar from some of the 'Look what I've made' objects that Danny brought back from Puddleducks. But it wasn't just that she had made something. It was that unlike the previous courses, this one had flown by.

'What did you think?' asked the pregnant, ringless woman as they gathered up their things.

'Loved it!' Nancy heard her voice sparkle. 'I'm going to sign up for the whole course.'

The tutor's voice boomed next to her. 'I'm so glad. Once you get into mosaics, you'll find a world you haven't ever seen before. There are variations, too. Instead of glass, you could use pebbles or seashells to create murals. It's quite complicated, of course, and requires a certain amount of measuring as well as artistic skill.'

Murals! Something snapped in the back of Nancy's mind. Gemma at Puddleducks had been urgently asking them for weeks now to think of something that could be entered for this playgroup award. What about a mural on the wall outside the nursery? She'd seen one before in somewhere called Gloucestershire (which was confusingly pronounced in a different way from the one it was spelt) when they'd been house-hunting. It had been like a map of the village, but in stones that had been set in such a way that it looked more like a picture.

She and the other mums at Puddleducks might, with

some help, do something like that. Their mural could be a map of Hazelwood with its church, its canal, its shops, its school and of course its pre-school. It had to have a community flavour, Gemma had said. That was it! They might even be able to get some of the local businesses to sponsor their firm being on the map.

'You look as though you've just thought of something,' said the pregnant mum.

'I think I have.' No point in saying anything until she'd had a word with Gemma.

'Don't I know you from somewhere?' persisted the woman. 'You've got a son at Puddleducks, haven't you, like me?'

Nancy nodded, glancing enviously at her companion's stomach. 'When are you due?'

'Due?' The woman frowned. 'What do you mean?'

Oh no. Too late, Nancy realised she'd made a mistake. 'I'm sorry. I just thought . . .'

Her voice tailed off miserably.

'This,' said the woman stiffly, glancing down at her stomach, which did indeed look as though it was four months gone, 'is left over from Tracy.' She glared at Nancy. 'He's now three.'

I'm sorry, Nancy wanted to say again, but it was too late. The woman had flounced off. Please don't let her sign up for mosaics too, she prayed. Somehow, she had a nasty feeling that she'd just made an unexpected enemy. A woman who called her son 'Tracy' was definitely a force to be reckoned with.

Chapter 19

In view of what the girls had said, Nancy fully expected that Lily would fail to turn up for tea after the article in the paper. Brigid, on the other hand, had been almost indecently keen to palm her son off, an expression which Nancy had heard more than once at playgroup.

It always amazed her that some parents would ask others in a casual way if they'd 'mind having' one of their children after the session had finished. Toby's dad with the puppies, she'd noticed, was frequently being asked this by Honey's mum, who'd gone back to work full-time and was always running late.

But anyway, here was Billy playing happily with Danny in the kitchen, where she'd set out some of that play clay stuff. OK, so Danny was making it into a football and chucking it around while Billy was banging his head every now and then into the sticky mess which was consequently sticking to his hair, but so what?

Sometimes Nancy found herself alarmed at her new casual approach to parenting, which was definitely a result of hanging around with Annie and Brigid. But it also helped to know that she didn't have to get everything tidied up by 8 p.m. when Sam would come back. In fact, she found herself getting equally alarmed by the thought that would cross her mind every now and then. The thought that actually it was sometimes easier without Sam around . . .

Just as this thought was crossing her mind yet again, Nancy heard the doorbell go. There, on the doorstep, stood Lily, looking every inch the perfect white Chinese doll. Behind her was a big black car. Someone wearing large glasses and a headscarf was at the wheel, waiting without waving or giving any indication that this was a parent dropping off a child.

Hang on! Lily had a note in her hand in the same elegant writing as the acceptance note. *Thank you for having me. I will be collected at 6 p.m.*

How odd! Nancy waved at the uniformed driver to show she had received the note and then smilingly welcomed the girl, who looked at her when she spoke but said nothing. The child was holding a pale lavender silk bag containing indoor slippers which, even now, she was slipping into, leaving her other shoes by the door. How thoughtful!

'Come inside,' said Nancy warmly, wondering if she might ever have a daughter like this. 'Billy and Danny are playing with clay in the kitchen and I'm doing something called a mosaic . . . Oh no!'

Horrified, she stared at the kitchen. There were shapes where clay bits had clearly been thrown at the walls. On the floor was broken glass from her mosaic 'homework' for class, which she had – foolishly – been doing on the side counter. And out in the garden, through the kitchen windows, she could see Billy and Danny climbing the blue frame that she'd had delivered from Kids And Toys last month.

How could they? Her immediate instinct was to march out into the garden and yell at the pair of them. But then she recalled her own mother going ballistic once when she had brought home a new schoolfriend and together they had left dirty footprints on the carpet. She'd been really embarrassed at the time, and the friend had never asked her back to her house after that. No, Nancy told herself, she couldn't do that to her son. Not when he seemed so happy playing out there.

'Do you want to join them?' she asked Lily. Their guest didn't need a second invitation. She was off! For the next hour, all three seemed to play in their own way. Lily would just stand and watch while Danny and Billy hurled themselves around. It was too much of a girl-stereotype thing, perhaps, but they all seemed perfectly happy like that.

Maybe Lily would talk when it was teatime. But no. Instead, she ate delicately while the boys chomped their way through cold sausages followed by jelly beans, a menu that Danny had specifically requested. OK, it might not be that healthy but it wouldn't hurt for a special occasion.

And then it happened. Nancy had seen Billy behave oddly before. Everyone had. He would go a bit wild, it was said, if things didn't go his way. But she was totally unprepared for what happened next. 'Finished, Billy dear?' she asked, her hand out to pick up his plate.

Billy's face turned red. 'Don't touch that!' he screamed and slammed his head on the table so loudly that he simply had to have knocked himself out. Nancy felt sick. 'Billy, Billy, what are you doing?'

161

He was lifting up his head now and roaring, throwing the empty plate at the cooker. It splintered into large bits which flew back across the room, narrowly missing Lily.

'Are you all right?' screamed Nancy, wondering if the boy was having a fit. Billy rushed out of the kitchen.

Lily shook her head. 'The plate,' she said quietly and slowly. 'Do not touch. Billy not like it.'

There was another crash. This time from next door. He had gone for the stereo. Sam's stereo! Horrified, Nancy watched this small dervish tearing round the room, hurling whatever he could on to the floor in a blind fury. For someone who didn't like his own stuff being touched, he didn't seem to care about ruining everyone else's.

Danny, who seemed to think this was a fantastic game, joined in, despite her pleas to stop. Somewhere in the midst of all this, Nancy could dimly hear the doorbell ringing but there was no way she could take her eyes off this lot.

'Please, stop,' she began.

'What on earth is going on, Billy?'

Nancy whipped round to see Brigid standing behind her. Lily must have opened the door.

'Blimey, Nance, what has he had to eat?'

Desperately, she tried to think. 'Sausages. Jelly beans . . .'

'You're joking?' Brigid groaned. 'Didn't you find the note?'

'Note?'

'The one in the bottom of his bag. Look. There!'

162

She flourished the sheet of paper in front of Nancy.

Thank you for inviting me to tea. My behaviour may seem strange at times because I don't like it when people touch my things because I have put them in a special order. If you want me to do something, please look at my face when talking or I may not bother listening to you. It can be useful to repeat instructions at least twice. The good news is that my mum has put me on a new diet that might help! Please do not give me any of the following . . .

Below were listed several foods including sausages, sweets and anything containing artificial colours.

'It's a standard printout that I give to everyone who is brave enough to have Billy,' explained Brigid. 'It was Gemma's idea. Sorry. I thought I'd pointed it out to you.'

'No,' said Nancy, feeling the anger welling up inside her. 'And I have to say, Brigid, if Danny was allergic to all these foods, I would darn well tell another parent about it instead of leaving them to find a note, or rather not find one.'

She hadn't meant to sound angry, but it was all pouring out now. Somehow all the hurt over Sam, coupled with this awful mess around them, was making her act in a way that she never had before. Even as a child, her mother used to say, she'd been remarkably placid.

'Flip, Nancy, I'm sorry.' Brigid got down on her knees and began to pick up the shards of china and glass and goodness knows what else that had got broken.

'No! Leave it. I just want you to go now.'

Brigid's face was a picture of repentance. 'I'm really, really sorry, Nancy. It was my fault. I should have thought.' She lowered her voice. 'To be honest, I was so grateful for a bit of time to myself without Billy that I forgot to tell you about the food thing.'

Something clicked in Nancy's head when she heard this. It couldn't be easy to look after a kid like Billy. She was lucky with Danny, who usually did what he was told and rarely gave her any trouble.

'It's OK,' she said, trying to breathe deeply to calm herself down. 'It's just that I have so much on my plate at the moment. Honestly, you go.'

'Really?' Brigid bit her lip. 'I've got to pick up my daughter from her friend and I'm already running late but I'll make it up to you, Nancy, I really will. Come on, Billy.'

'No. Don't want to go.' Billy's arms lashed out at his mother, who deftly caught one before it hit her, as though she was practised. Appalled, Nancy watched Brigid frogmarch her son down the path. What a child!

Meanwhile, Billy's departure seemed to bring a sense of calm to the house. 'Want to watch a DVD?' she asked Danny and Lily who were standing in the kitchen, looking at her and holding hands (so cute!). They both nodded silently. Thank heavens for that. It would give her some time to clear up this mess before . . . Was that the doorbell already? Nancy glanced at her watch. Six o'clock! It would be Lily's mother or maybe nanny to pick her up. Quickly she glanced at her small guest, who was now sitting on a beanbag in front of the screen. Apart from some mud on her blue silk skirt and a large dab of ketchup on her face (another thing on Billy's no-no list) she seemed more or less in good shape.

'This way, Lily. Time to go home.'

It was like leading a doll. Nancy opened the door but – how weird! – there was no one standing there. But there was the large black car outside and the driver, still in her black glasses even though it was a cold autumn day with hardly any sun now, seemed to be waiting. Nancy watched while the little girl glided down the path towards the car until the door opened and she got in.

How odd. How very, very odd.

Nancy went back into the house. It looked like a battlefield. Broken shards of plates were everywhere. The cooker had a large dent on the front. And Danny was dozing in front of the television, his right hand working its way up and down the inside of his trousers. Obviously practising for adult male life.

Clearly the boys had been into Sam's study, because there was a pile of papers on the floor that had *Private* written on the top one, as well as a folder containing some photographs. Unable to stop herself, Nancy drew them out. There was Sam, clearly in his late teens or maybe early twenties, with a slim, pretty girl in front of a billboard that said, *Welcome to the Grand Canyon!*

She hadn't known that Sam had ever been there. Was the girlfriend, if that's what she was, American or British? How odd! Someone had blanked out her face with a pen as though they were angry or maybe hurt, or because they didn't want her identity known.

Who was she? Of course it was crazy to think Sam hadn't had any history before they got together – he was, after all, older than her. But even so, the picture disturbed her.

Oh God. The doorbell again. Brigid had probably left something behind. Hopefully it wasn't Billy.

'Hello again . . . Patricia?'

Nancy stared in horror at the tall woman with a thin, haughty, bird-like face, large hooded eyes and a brown suitcase by her side.

'Nancy!'

Sam's mother's clipped aloof voice still had the power to make her quake in her shoes.

'I wasn't expecting you.' Too late, she realised that sounded rude, but then again, so was turning up unannounced. In the books she had read about England as a child, people left calling cards if a visit wasn't convenient.

Patricia had already swept into the house, taking in the chaos around her with tightened lips. 'I came as soon as I heard.'

'Heard what?' Nancy's heart quickened. Had something happened to Sam? Suddenly all those things she'd been thinking earlier, about not caring if he didn't come back, disappeared. She needed Sam. Of course she did. And now he'd been hurt in some accident or God forbid, a terrorist attack, because otherwise why else would his mother be here?

'I came,' announced Patricia, 'because I heard you were on your own now Sam has decided to walk away until Christmas.'

Patricia's voice was even more imperious than usual.

166

Sam had warned her before they'd met that the shock of his father leaving had resulted in his mother sometimes using the wrong words or mispronouncing them, and that it was best to ignore them. Privately, Nancy thought Patricia's verbal mistakes were deliberate, in order to sound posh, as Brigid would say.

'Sam hasn't walked away. He's working away.'

Patricia's eyes glinted dangerously. 'That's what I said.' Her gaze fixed on the broken plates, and then on her. 'If you don't mind me saying so, it's obvious I was right to come down. I have to say, Nancy, that I do think you have got yourself into a terrible mess. It's not even as though Sam is your husband.'

There was a noise behind them. 'Excuse me?' It was Brigid, who had come through the French windows into the kitchen. 'Sorry. Didn't think you'd heard the bell so I came in the back way. I've brought you these.' She held out a pot of tired-looking grey chrysanthemums: a speciality from the local garage. 'It's to say sorry for Billy's behaviour and for me forgetting to tell you about the list. Oh and by the way, I think I might have forgotten Billy's plastic hammer. He's a nightmare without it.'

Patricia's eyebrows rose. 'Did you say hammer? Is that suitable?'

Nancy felt hot with embarrassment, and not just because of what her mother-in-law was saying right now. It was the bit before . . . Silently, she picked up Billy's hammer from the floor and held it out.

Brigid smiled at Patricia. 'It's all right. I take your point but it keeps him quiet, which is something. No one can understand what it's like unless they have a son like Billy, but I wouldn't swap him for the world. Bye then, Nancy. Thanks for the hammer and sorry once more. See you on Monday.'

She'd gone! Too late to explain, thought Nancy desperately. Too late to ask her not to tell anyone that she and Sam weren't actually married. Not that that would really matter in this day and age.

But what did matter, at least to her, was *why* Sam had always declined to marry her even though, to make things easier, she had taken his name with hers and referred to him as her husband. There was something else, too. Why, she wondered, as she watched Patricia take off her coat and begin to clear up without being asked, did she have that funny niggling feeling that that photo with the crossed-out face might have something to do with Sam's refusal?

Chapter 20

Joe Balls got up early for the morning meeting. Very early. Anything so as to get into work without being seen.

There was no doubt about it, he told himself, tiptoeing down the stairs in order not to wake the rest of the house, it was awkward. Extremely awkward. Joe hadn't believed his eyes when Gemma had turned up at his door, claiming to live in the room next to him.

Then, before he could take it in, there had been the hamster incident, which had had Lynette and Mike in stitches when he'd described it. It had surprised him: somehow, the mercy dash to the vet had made him see a completely new side to himself. Who would have thought he could have got so worried about a tiny creature?

But when the vet had made that embarrassing assumption that he and Gemma were a couple, he had realised that it would be impossible to carry on living next door to each other. It simply wasn't professional, which was why he had felt obliged to be rather cool with Gemma when they were back at school the next day.

How, he wondered, as he got on to his bike, parked in Joyce's garage, could he possibly share a bathroom with a colleague? And how could he have a serious staff meeting with Gemma if they'd both seen each other that morning in their dressing gowns? Hers had been a rather pretty pink one, down just below her knee. His was navy blue paisley silk, a present from Ed a few Christmases ago, which covered more of him than Gemma's had of her. Even so, she had looked aghast at him as though he was virtually naked.

By the time he arrived at school, he had decided the whole situation was untenable. He would definitely have to find another room to rent. Meanwhile, he needed to concentrate on this morning's security meeting after that horrendous newspaper report on Lily Dalung, which had led to some extremely terse emails between him, Gemma, Beryl the headmistress, Dilly Dalung and the school governors.

The meeting was meant to have taken place in the main school but Beryl had changed the venue to Puddleducks, declaring she wanted to walk round the pre-school building and check for any possible security lapses on site. What did she expect? Holes through the walls where the paparazzi could poke their cameras? Beryl, like so many of the staff out here in the sticks, was so parochial!

Now, as he let himself into Puddleducks early, thanks to Gemma and the bathroom issue, Joe's stomach churned, although not with apprehension. The takeaway he'd had last night from that place on the high street hadn't settled, but he'd felt unable to do anything about it in the lodgers' bathroom, knowing that Gemma might try to turn the handle on the other side at any minute.

It reminded him of life on the fourteenth floor, where some bright spark had decided to combine the Ladies and Gents to form unisex loos in order to create space for a new office. The younger lads had immediately brightened at the thought of 'new mating ground', but Joe had found it excruciatingly embarrassing to perform in a cubicle containing machines for Tampax.

Consequently he had often 'hung on' as his mother used to say, which was just what he was doing right now. But the urge was increasing – it always did that in times of stress – and dammit, he simply had to go.

Wildly, Joe looked around for the staff loos. Snatching open a door hopefully, he groaned at the sight of the broom cupboard with a stack of metal buckets and mops. Still, he might just need them if he couldn't find the real thing.

In desperation, he tried another door. With relief, he found it led to a row of loos all right, but then his heart sank again. They were built for Snow White's dwarfs with miniature seats and slatted doors that had huge gaps both at the top and the bottom, presumably so staff could check that the occupants were all right.

Joe's stomach gurgled once more. Groaning, he flung himself in, shut the door behind him – no locks! – and closed his eyes in relief, even though it was like sitting on an egg cup.

Bloody hell. A noise! A female noise! Gemma and Beryl were outside in the hall and he, stupidly, had left the main door to the loos ajar so he could hear snatches of their conversation.

'Can't understand how it could have happened.'

'None of the staff would have done anything like that.'

'Mind you, since I called the police the other day, we haven't had any other trouble.'

'Probably found another story to chase by now.'

Quietly, Joe pulled down the lavatory roll. What was this? Each square had a printed letter of the alphabet on it, with a picture of an object starting with that letter. At the moment, he had D for Drum in his sweating hands.

Now he was in a quandary. If he pulled the chain, they would hear him. But if he didn't . . . No. That didn't bear thinking about.

'What's that?'

Joe froze. It was Gemma's voice.

'Hang on. The door's open. Someone's in there. I can see feet.' She was whispering, but he could still hear her. '*Men's* feet.'

One man, he wanted to shout out. Just me.

Desperately, he put himself together and stood against the door so she couldn't get in.

'Be careful,' called Beryl's voice.

There was the sound of something being scraped along the floor. No! Someone was carrying a stool and was about to stand on it to look over the top!

There was no other option now. 'It's me.' His voice came out cracked with embarrassment. 'Joe. Joe Balls. I got caught short, so to speak. I'll be out in one minute.'

The shocked silence, followed by more whispers and a definite suppressed giggle, was everything he had feared. Pulling the chain (well, what else could he do?) he came out, washed his hands with the tiny bar of pink soap and shook them dry, not fancying the look of the towel, which clearly hadn't been changed from the day before.

'Sorry about that.' He sheepishly waved his hand about as though he made a habit of sitting on miniature loos every morning. 'Thought I'd test out the er, "facilities" as part of the security check.'

Beryl's face, which reminded him of a crinkled King Charles spaniel at the best of times, exploded into tears of laughter. 'Get a life, lad. You needed to *go*, didn't you! Nothing wrong with that. It's happened to us all.' Her expression grew serious again. 'Now, we need to talk about this situation. Luckily, Dilly Dalung has said she still wants to keep her daughter at Puddleducks.'

'Really?' Joe could hardly believe it.

'That's down to Miss Merryfield here.' Beryl flashed a warm smile of approval at Gemma, which made Joe feel like the least favourite child. 'The parents, including Miss Dalung, say she's a real gem.'

Turning back to Joe, she sniffed, making it clear she didn't feel the same way about him. 'Not that that means we should be complacent. I want to take a look around and see if anyone could have got in without us knowing. I'm absolutely certain that none of the staff would pull a stunt like this, and several parents have approached us promising that none of them would have done anything to jeopardise a child's safety by talking to the press.'

Joe cleared his throat. 'If you don't mind me saying, all this is very naïve. Most people would do anything for money.'

Beryl shot him a sharp look. 'Not in Hazelwood, they wouldn't.'

He exchanged a glance with Gemma, finding, with a surprised flash of relief, that her face confirmed exactly what he was thinking. Beryl wasn't living in the real world.

'There are some oddballs out there,' began Gemma tentatively.

Joe nodded gratefully. 'She's right and I do think, if you don't mind me saying, Beryl, that we should have talked to the parents more formally about the situation.'

Ignoring Beryl's hostile expression, he reached into his pocket for the notes he had made earlier. 'Now I've got a few suggestions.'

They spent the next half an hour putting forward various ideas, which included Joe's proposal to write to the Press Complaints Commission about the invasion of a child's privacy. As Gemma pointed out, they couldn't afford to have photographers peering over the fence like the ones she'd sorted out the other day. He had to hand it to her: she had guts! Pity he hadn't been there to see it.

'Right,' said Beryl at the end of the meeting. 'All that sounds good. Better be getting back now, hadn't we, before school starts.'

He turned to say goodbye. 'See you tonight then,' he said to Gemma.

Beryl raised her eyebrows.

'We live in the same house,' explained Gemma, flushing.

'Not like that,' added Joe, but Beryl was already clucking something about it was none of her business but she was glad to see that they were getting on so well. She then bustled off, leaving Joe to shuffle from one foot to the other in front of Gemma, feeling that he ought to say something. On the fourteenth floor, when you needed to get out of an awkward situation, the best plan had been to surprise the opponent with an unexpected comment.

'Nice loo paper, by the way.'

Gemma's face relaxed. 'Thanks. I ordered it from this new educational supply company to improve my children's spelling.'

Big mistake. They were never 'your' children: he'd learned that in the inner city, where he'd seen too many teachers trying to help kids who then spat in their faces afterwards.

'Pity you can't do the same with their maths.' The comment slid out of his mouth before he could stop it and, too late, he could see he'd hurt her.

'We're working on it. The numbered loo paper is coming in next week.'

'I'll look forward to seeing it.' There was a pause. 'Not, I mean, that I intend to make a habit of sitting on Puddleduck loos.'

They both laughed, and Joe felt a sense of relief that he had saved the situation. It had been surprisingly nice just now, when they'd been working together rather than against each other.

'Just one thing.' She was moving towards her desk

as she spoke, and her authoritative tone made him feel as though he was the junior and not her. Something inside him bristled.

'I hope you don't feel,' she said smoothly, 'that you have to find another room to rent, just because of me. I'm sure it will work out if we don't get in each other's way.' She coloured again. 'I mean, what I'm trying to say is that I'm a very private person. In fact I was thinking. Suppose you use the bathroom before, say, seven, and I use it at seven thirty. Does that give you enough time?'

There was something in that. After all, it would be a pain finding somewhere else to live right now. Maybe he and Gemma could make it work just until Christmas and then he'd start flat-hunting. 'I prefer to get up earlier. How about six thirty and seven?'

She seemed amused at this. 'I'll find my kitchen timer.'

Was she poking fun at him? Ed had always teased him about his strict timekeeping.

'By the way, what are you going as on Wednesday?'

'Going as?'

'For the assembly. You know, the Significant Figures.'

'Oh that.' He tried to sound as though he hadn't forgotten about it. 'I'm still making up my mind about that one. Are you still going as the first Queen Liz?'

He'd tried to phrase this casually, but somehow it came out in an awful pseudy way.

'No. I decided my dress wasn't right.'

Her voice had a slight edge to it. Women were so odd about clothes! In his experience, you never knew how you were meant to react. Was she expecting him to assure her that the dress would be perfect, even though he hadn't seen it? That would have been just what Ed would have required.

'At the moment,' she continued more brightly, 'it's a toss-up between Mother Teresa, because that's quite easy with a double sheet, or Peter Pan, because I've still got my old green school tunic.' She flushed. 'You never know when that sort of thing will come in handy, do you?'

Suddenly he had a mental vision of Gemma in tights. Where on earth had that come from? 'I'm sure you'll find something. Is that the time? I must be getting back to the main school. See you later. As for the security lapse, I don't need to remind you that as Beryl said, this simply can't happen again.'

Chapter 21

Joe came away from the meeting knowing that he'd confused Gemma with his blow hot, blow cold approach. *He* felt confused too, and not just by the girl. It was this place! Corrybank and Puddleducks and Hazelwood, all rolled into one. Somehow, teaching had seemed much simpler in the inner-city school, even though they'd had a community police car outside all day, in case a pupil or parent whipped out a knife.

Yet the issues here in this suburban town were just as challenging in their own subtle way and, to be frank, he didn't always know how to deal with them.

'Explain more,' Mike said when he rang that night for a general chat.

Joe tried but it wasn't easy sitting on his bed with his back to the wall, knowing that Gemma might or might not be listening on the other side. Even though this was a Victorian house, the walls weren't all as thick as one might think. He had definitely heard her laughing on her mobile the other evening, and had felt awkward in case it was at him. 'Everyone here seems more sensitive, somehow,' he attempted.

Mike roared with laughter. 'You mean they're offended by the famous Joe Balls waspish comments?'

Joe shifted uncomfortably. 'Something like that. But

there's something else too. You'll never believe who turned up at my door the other evening.'

Mike whistled. 'Not Ed?'

'Incredible, isn't it, after everything she said.'

'I don't believe it! How did she know where to find you?'

'I was hoping you might tell me,' Joe said quietly.

'You think Lynette might have given her your address?' Mike's voice sounded reflective at the other end. 'If she did, mate, it would only be because she's worried you're lonely.'

Joe's throat tightened. They had all been such good friends at uni, the four of them. They'd been a striking four, too: two tall, strapping lads each with attractive auburn-haired girlfriends. In some ways, the girls looked quite alike, but their personalities couldn't have been more different. 'But Lynette knows why Ed and I split up. Why would she have done such a thing?'

'Point taken. I'll ask her. Meanwhile, how did you feel when she turned up like that?'

He'd been asking himself the same question. 'Confused. It doesn't help that she's started leaving messages on my answerphone, asking if I feel like a drink sometime.'

There was a groan from Mike's end. 'You're not going to fall for all this, are you?'

'No, I'm not.' He tried to sound firmer than he felt. Of course Ed had done something he could never forgive, but it was still difficult to move on when you'd shared so much history. 'There's something else too.'

'Don't tell me! You've got another woman after you. Honestly Joe, I don't know how you do it. How many proposals did you get at your last place? Six, or was it seven?'

Joe couldn't help feeling a slight flush of pride. 'Nine and a half actually, but before you ask how I worked out the half, the issue I was talking about was what I'm going to dress up as tomorrow.'

There was the sound of crashing from Mike's end, which no doubt came from one of the boys. 'Sorry, Joe, can you repeat that? For a minute I thought you were into cross-dressing.'

'Very funny. I've got to dress up as something tomorrow for Significant Figures. Nothing to do with maths. It's a project to teach the children about people who meant something in history, and staff have to do it too.'

There was another crashing sound and then Lynette's voice chipped in. 'Hi, Joe. Sorry to take over but Mike's needed to sort out the troops.'

Joe felt a flash of envy. Usually he managed to keep that part under control, but he had a sudden picture in his head of himself as a dad with two small boys and he began to wonder, yet again, if that was ever going to happen. He told Lynette about his costume problem.

'Have you got a spare sheet and pillowcase?' Lynette's voice had taken on a professional edge. 'Because if so, you could go as . . .'

'Mother Teresa?'

'Only if you want a sex change. I was thinking more of the Dalai Lama. And by the way, I couldn't help overhearing. It wasn't *me* who gave Ed your address. I wouldn't do that. Must go. The boys are flooding the bathroom again. Byeeee.'

Lynette hadn't given Ed his address? Then how had she found him? The only person who knew his new rented address, apart from his friends, was the school secretary. Ed's mouth tightened. If Diana-but-call-me-Di had given that out without permission, he truly would have an axe to wield. Meanwhile . . .

Within minutes, he found himself standing at the door of Gemma's bedsit. Too late, he wished he'd been a bit nicer at their last meeting, which might possibly account for the cold look she was giving him now. 'Sorry to bother you. I'm not actually after tea bags but I did wonder if you had a spare sheet and a pillowcase. My spares are all in London.'

Her frostiness melted. 'I take it you're going as the Dalai Lama?'

He was astonished. 'How did you know?'

She shrugged, and he observed for the first time that she had rather pretty shoulders under that skinny top. 'It's one of the easier dressing-up options. You can always tell from someone's linen cupboard if they've got kids in school plays because there'll be at least two pillowcases with a half-circle cut out of the side.'

She was already bending down, getting something out of a small pine chest of drawers and revealing, presumably unintentionally, a rather attractive band of brown flesh between the top of her jeans and the bottom of her top.

Joe tried to look away but found himself inexplicably

drawn to her bottom, which was exactly as he liked them: not too small but not obvious either.

'Will these do?' She suddenly turned round to catch him staring.

'Perfect,' he stammered, which was a complete first for him. He'd never, even when Ed had been at her worst, stammered. 'Thank you.' Then grabbing the not-so-neatly folded offerings from her hand, he almost bolted back into his own bedsit, feeling like a spotty, gauche sixth-former all over again.

Chapter 22

The following day, Joe got up before his 6.30 a.m. time slot to give himself enough time to sort out his outfit in his office. Now how exactly had Lynette suggested that he twisted those sheets?

'Morning, Mr Balls,' said a breathy voice.

Joe glanced at Di in yet another of her too-tight skirts. Just the person he needed to talk to! 'May I have a word?'

'Certainly.' She stood in front of him, her bottom lip quivering as she stared at his costume. Joe felt his old irritation rise to the surface and, remembering Lynette's advice, tried to imagine how the Dalai Lama might have reacted when faced with a school secretary who might or might not be in the wrong.

'Di, can you tell me if you've given out my address to anyone?'

Instantly, the woman went a deep shade of red. 'Only to your wife, sir. She rang the other day.'

So Ed had called the school! His ex-wife's effrontery was astounding, but it didn't excuse a severe lapse of security on the part of the school. He took a deep breath. It would be so easy to lose his temper, but that wouldn't help. 'Didn't it occur to you, Di, that if the caller *had* been my wife, she would have had my address anyway?'

Another deep flush. 'It did, but it's none of my business, sir, and she *did* say it was urgent.'

'Exactly. It wasn't your business. Especially as, whatever you were told, she isn't my wife. Not any more.' He gave her one of his famous fourteenth-floor stares. 'I don't need to tell you, Di, that after the recent security scare at the pre-school, it is imperative, absolutely imperative, that this sort of thing doesn't happen again. Do I make myself clear?'

Presumably the answer to that was yes, since the woman then scuttled back to her office, leaving Joe to go back to his classroom where Gemma and her helpers were already arriving for the Significant Figures joint assembly. Slightly disappointedly, he saw that she'd gone for the Mother Teresa look. Meanwhile, there was an assortment of loud, highly restless small Supermen, a couple of popes, John Lennon, Princess Diana, Henry VIII and, rather alarmingly, a miniature panda. Clearly, the parents had some imaginative interpretations of significant figures in history.

At his inner-city school, there had been no place for middle-class dressing up. Joe could hardly believe how much trouble parents had gone to here. There had clearly been a run on pillowcases and sheets, but there was also a fair smattering of quite professional-looking papier-mâché hats and face paints. One mother could be heard confessing that she'd hired her child's Winston Churchill costume, complete with mock cigar.

Inwardly, Joe groaned. As he'd tried telling Gemma on more than one occasion, it was maths that was really important in life. Anyone could dress up or play pretend games.

'Mr Balls, could I have a word?'

Help. It was Eco Mum. Joe had heard one of the other mothers call her that, and it had been so apt that it had stuck in his head. 'My daughter was in Puddleducks last year,' she began, 'and they did two recycling projects in the space of nine months.'

It had provided a project during her last pregnancy, presumably.

'I had rather hoped that by now, Mr Balls, Jemima would have done something similar, but so far nothing has happened.' Her forehead, gleaming with some ghastly and doubtless recycled cleanser stuff, thrust itself forward in indignation. 'Our children are our only hope in saving the world.'

Please! Of course recycling was important, although he had to admit that the 'Recycled' label on loo paper always made him recoil. But the woman was over-stating her case.

'So I thought,' continued Eco Mum urgently, standing in what looked like home-knitted Yeti boots, 'that we could enter an eco project for that bank award.'

Boring! Boring!

'I think you'll find,' began Joe carefully, 'that we might need something more cutting-edge.'

Gemma touched his arm. 'I agree,' she said quietly. 'In fact, one of my mums has just come up with an amazing idea. Mrs Carter Wright, would you like to tell Mr Balls about it?'

It was the quiet American woman with the short urchin haircut whose son was always kicking balls round the classroom, just as he was doing now. 'Danny, stop it,' ordered his mother in a resigned twang that suggested she'd said that more than once already. 'I've just started doing a mosaics class, and the tutor said he could help us build a mural on the playground wall in Puddleducks. It would be a picture of the whole town, and we could get some of the businesses and shops and churches and other groups to help us.'

Gemma's face was beaming. 'Great idea, isn't it?'

In principle, perhaps, but just think of the practicalities! 'Who owns the playground wall?'

Gemma shrugged. 'I presumed it belonged to school.'

'Might be a party wall. How much is it going to cost?'

'We've got to check, but . . .'

'And how long will it take? We've only got until December.'

Both the American and Gemma looked deflated, as well they might.

'I suggest you do a bit of forward planning before we decide.' He tried to move away but his foot slipped on his sheet. Bugger! To his horror, he found himself on his bottom, splayed on the floor and – even worse – with his underpants showing! He knew he should have worn trousers under that bloody sheet. That wretched Bella girl, who was dressed up as Princess Kate, was openly sniggering, and some of the children were laughing too.

'Mr Balls!' A tall, pretty blonde woman, whose husband had left her six weeks ago and had already been in twice to tell him about it in great detail, was at his side immediately. 'Mr Balls, are you all right?'

His right ankle was throbbing mercilessly where

he'd caught it on the table leg, but he wasn't going to say so. 'Fine, thank you.' Picking himself up with as much dignity as possible, he limped towards his desk. 'Right. Let's begin, shall we?'

After the Significant Figures assembly, during which each one gave a brief account of his or her life and why they had been important in history, Joe and his throbbing ankle had spent the rest of the week submerging his class in arithmetic. Of course, under the National Curriculum, he had to make sure that other subjects were covered too, but since it was maths that they were woefully weak in, he considered himself justified in pinching some lesson time from wishy-washy areas like story-writing.

It was such a relief to zoom back to Notting Hill on the Friday night and park his bike outside his own flat, where he didn't have to worry about getting up early for his bathroom slot.

It was also a relief to find that there weren't the usual messages from Ed, either on his mobile or the home answerphone. Nor, as it turned out, did she appear unannounced at the flat over the weekend. Ed was so unpredictable! You never knew what she was going to do next.

The following week, the office was in a fever of excitement about the imminent Parents' Social on Thursday. The parents were just as bad, chattering about what they were going to wear and did anyone fancy going out to the new pizza place afterwards?

Meanwhile, he'd managed to avoid his fellow lodger by getting up early, and putting in extra hours in classroom preparation so that he came back late. At some point he'd need to make time to see a doctor about this wretched ankle, which was still puffed up.

'Everything all right?' trilled Joyce when he'd left his monthly rent on the kitchen table. 'Sorry I haven't been around much, but my daughter had a baby. My first grandchild, you know!'

No. He didn't know and frankly he didn't want to. Not where babies were concerned. And he couldn't wait for tonight's event to be over with so he could get on with his real job of drumming facts into heads, and also trying to think of a stand-out entry for the bank's competition.

On the night of the social, Joe groaned inwardly as the parents began trooping in, headed by the blonde newly single mum who was making a beeline straight for him. Even Di gave him a sympathetic look, handing him a glass of cheap wine.

Despite his earlier intentions to avoid the stuff, Joe took a swig. Disgusting. But it numbed the pain. A bit.

'So I told him that if he was going to talk like that . . .'

'It's not right for children to hear their father say such things, don't you think?'

'The trouble is that there aren't many places where single people like us can go, are there?'

'I say like us, Joe – I can call you that, can't I? – because I can see from your left hand that you don't wear a wedding ring . . .'

The room was getting slightly blurry.

'Joe,' said a familiar voice. No. It sounded like

Gemma's, but softer somehow. 'You look a bit pale. Are you all right?'

At the same time, Joe realised that the throbbing in his head was being overtaken by the throbbing in his right ankle.

'I do feel a bit odd,' he began and then stopped. Things must be really bad if he could imagine that Ed was striding across the room towards him in an impossibly tall pair of black heels and one of her beautifully tailored business suits, which revealed her chest (which he'd always admired) to perfection.

'Joe, darling!' The image that pretended to be Ed flashed a smile at Single Mum, who was now looking decidedly put out. 'So sorry I'm late.'

Late?

'Your landlady told me I'd find you here.' Ed flashed another smile at Single Mum. 'We live in London, you see, so my poor husband has to live out here during the week.'

We? Husband?

Gemma and Single Mum both seemed to take a backward step, as though they didn't want anything more to do with him. Too late, Joe wished he hadn't drunk that cheap wine. It had made his head go horribly fuzzy. Maybe he shouldn't have taken a double dose of painkillers before leaving the bedsit, either.

'This woman,' he managed to gasp out before collapsing on a chair, his ankle now throbbing in white pain, 'is not my wife. She's . . .'

And then it all went black.

THE PUDDLEDUCKS PLAYGROUP NEWSLETTER OCTOBER ISSUE

Yes! Another month has already passed and we're into October already! Please remember to put the following dates in your diary:

Parents' Evening on October 15

Half-term on October 20

Halloween Dressing-Up Day on October 28

We'd also like to give you advance notice of:

Fireworks Night (sparklers only) on November 5

Shoebox Day on November 12. For those of you who are new, this is when we ask you to fill shoeboxes with suitable Christmas gifts for children abroad who are not as fortunate as ours. They will then be distributed by the Shoebox Charity.

Christmas Bring and Buy Sale on December 9

And of course, the Nativity Play on December 14.

Finally, if your little Puddleduck is allergic to dogs, please let us know immediately.

PS. Below is another Puddleducks song. As usual, we'd be really grateful if you could practise it at home. Thank you.

THE PUDDLEDUCKS POLITE SONG

We are the little Puddleducks
We try to be polite.
To say 'yes please' and 'thank you'
From morning through to night!

Chapter 23

'Mrs Merryfield, Mrs Merryfield! They're coming. The puppies are coming!'

Danny was hopping up and down in front of her, his eyes wide with the pure excitement that you only really saw in the under-fives. When they went to Big School, some of them gradually lost their sparkle, Gemma noticed, because a teacher had told them that they weren't good at a particular subject. Then bang went that natural confidence, possibly for the rest of their lives.

Others became arrogant, as though to provide a protective layer between themselves and outside critics. A sudden flash of a small Joe in school uniform came into her head for some reason. Was that what had happened to him at school, or later in life, and explained his difficult manner?

If, on the other hand, you could make a child feel good at something, they took that certainty into adulthood. And that was why she loved her job so much, just as her grandmother had done before her. 'Teachers can make the difference,' she had told Gemma when she was growing up, 'between a happy adult and a discontented one.'

Now, as Gemma bent down and held Danny's hot hands in hers, she wanted to bottle his excitement and squirt it out at some adults she knew – no names mentioned! – who could do with a large dollop of imagination and spontaneity not to mention integrity.

Some people, she thought, couldn't help distorting the truth, just like Joe had at the school social. 'We've split up,' he had kept muttering when his glamorous companion had helped him into the ambulance en route for A&E. As Single Mum had remarked acidly after his departure, 'There goes one more married man pretending to be single so he can have a good time.'

Her words had made Gemma shiver. All she wanted was a simple life with a husband and three, maybe four children who looked just like Danny, with those shiny eyes and that earthy smell. She'd always thought it would happen by her thirtieth birthday, but time was running out.

'Here they are!' Danny's excitement had mounted to fever pitch, and she could see a small trickle of yellow dribble down the inside of his leg.

'Danny, I think you might need to go somewhere first!'

Bella, helpful for once, cut in. 'I'll take him. Darren needs to go too.' Her eyes met Gemma's pointedly. 'He had two breakfasts this morning apparently. One with Mummy and then one with Daddy.'

Why did divorcing parents do this sort of thing? Meanwhile, Toby's dad was coming in, carrying a large box. At his side was a beautiful elegant dog that was so clearly feminine, her udders still swollen from feeding her puppies, that she might as well have had a Chanel dog jacket on.

'Do come in,' said Gemma. 'That's right, children, sit down in a nice circle. Now what do we say?'

'Morning, Toby's dad,' chorused the group.

She had taught them to say Mr Thomas, but clearly they'd forgotten. Never mind. Greeting people socially was all part of the playgroup curriculum; she'd have a word with them later.

Now Toby's dad was explaining how long Millie, the beautiful black pointer who was sitting quietly next to Gemma, had carried her puppies for, and how they had been born in what looked like plastic bags.

'Like H&M or Topshop?' demanded Clemmie keenly, but before Gemma could answer Sienna had her hand up, straining urgently.

'Why do dogs come out in bags?'

'Good question,' said Toby's dad enthusiastically. 'It's to keep them safe when they are being born, rather like wrapping up a fragile parcel.'

It was a great lesson which managed to roll biology, parental care and hygiene all in one. Afterwards, the questions were endless.

'Mrs Merryfield! Do dogs have arty fishal in cement Asian too? That's how my mummy got me!'

'Toby's dad! How do the puppies get out of their plastic bags when they are born?'

'What if you don't like them? Can you take them back to the shop? My mum does that.'

'Why does that puppy have a funny tail?'

The last one came from Danny, who was sitting almost nose to nose with the smallest one in the litter. Gemma's heart melted and when she looked across at Bella she could see her assistant mouthing, 'Sweet!'

Wow, if the pair had melted Bella's heart, they definitely must be cute!

Toby's dad put a large gentle hand out and stroked the puppy's back. 'Each one of us is different in life, you see. Some of us are born with two arms and some with one.' He glanced at Gemma to see if he was stepping out of line, but she nodded in encouragement. No doubt this would lead to more questions later, but that was why they had talks like this.

'Pongo here has a kink, which means he might not be so valuable when the puppies are old enough to be sold. But to us he's as special as all the others, because we love him.'

Pongo gazed up at his master with a look that clearly said 'thank you'. Gemma felt her eyes fill with tears. This was happening more and more recently: something that was to do either with her impatient hormones, or the official letter that had arrived in the post that morning.

Toby's dad – such a nice man! – stayed for over an hour, and was still there when the mums arrived to collect their offspring.

'You won't prise Danny away very easily,' Gemma warned the quiet American woman whom she was beginning to warm to. They might only be five weeks into term but already she'd noticed that Nancy Carter Wright was much calmer. She loved it when that happened. It meant that she, Gemma, and her team were doing their job in helping not only the Puddleducks to grow, but also their parents to start letting go.

Together they looked at Danny, who was sitting

now with Pongo in his lap while Toby's dad carefully supervised. 'He's head over heels in love with that gorgeous puppy.'

'Head over heels in love,' repeated the American softly. 'I was that once.'

Gemma glanced at the woman's damp eyes. 'Is there anything you'd like to talk about?' she asked quietly.

The woman shook her head. 'I'm going through some stuff at the moment.'

Gemma's heart sank. Not another, after Darren's parents? Children are resilient, she tried to tell herself, but her experience at Puddleducks had shown that wasn't always true.

'Let me know if I can do anything.'

The woman nodded. 'Thanks.'

'Mummy, Mummy!' Danny was calling out to her. 'Look. This is Pongo! Can we have him? Pleeeease!'

The American woman laughed, but it wasn't a happy laugh. It was an 'are you kidding on top of everything else that I've got to cope with' laugh. Gemma had learned to recognise those, over the years.

'Sorry, sweetheart. But a dog wouldn't be right for us at the moment.'

Danny's face was crestfallen. 'Why not, Mummy? Pleease.'

Toby's dad was talking now, softly but in an authoritative manner. 'Puppies need someone to be at home with them all day.'

'But my mummy is!'

'They also need lots of care and attention.'

'I can do that!' Danny's voice was getting more tearful. 'If Daddy was home, he'd let me have a puppy.'

196

There was a hushed silence. 'You know that Daddy will be home by Christmas,' said the American woman quietly. 'We'll see then.'

Danny's voice rose in a wail. 'But Pongo might have gone to someone else then.'

'That's enough, Danny. Besides, someone would have to pick up his . . . pick up his business and we know that means nasty germs, don't we?'

Toby's dad shot Gemma a shocked look.

'Come on, Danny.' Mrs Carter Wright's voice was rising now with impatience. 'We need to go back now. Granny's waiting.'

'Hate Granny. She's a bossy boobs.'

The American mother gave a sad smile. Poor, poor thing. 'All things must pass,' whispered Gemma to her. 'It's an old saying, but true. Difficult times don't go on for ever.'

Danny's mother bent her head in acknowledgement. 'Thank you.'

'And by the way.' She'd almost forgotten. 'Your mural idea. We've got the go-ahead from the head. So if you can organise a team of parent volunteers, we're on!'

The woman's face lit up. 'That's great. Really great.'

Whoops! Johnnie and Sienna had got their hands on the paints and were face-painting each other ('The brush just jumped up, Miss Merryfield!'). And Bella was half-heartedly washing up the orange, blue and pink plates from elevenses so she could get to an 'appointment' somewhere. Gemma had a feeling that the various appointments Bella had had recently were not with the doctor or optician, as she had claimed, but were job interviews.

Maybe it would be only kind to help. 'What's happened to the shopkeeper?' she teased as she bent down to collect the plastic apples and pears which had rolled on to the floor. 'Honestly, you just can't get service like you used to! By the way, Bella, thanks for cleaning the sink. Great lemony smell!'

Bella shot her a filthy look. 'That's my new perfume.'

Oh dear. Still, in this job you won some and you lost some. A bit like life, really. A memory came into Gemma's head of the appointment she had had in town on the day that she'd accidentally reversed into Joe's bike. That reminded her. She needed to make a phone call or two. Just to make sure that everything was still on track for Christmas.

Chapter 24

By the end of the following week, Gemma was exhausted. She loved Puddleducks – oh how she loved it – but unless you were in a classroom from 7.30 a.m. to gone 7 p.m. on some nights, it was impossible to imagine what it was like.

Sometimes she felt like a mini United Nations. ('It's nice to share, Kyle. Why don't you swap your spade for Lucy's sand bucket?') At other times, it was like being on a junior version of *University Challenge*, answering a constant barrage of on-the-spot crazy and not-so-crazy questions from the children.

Take Harry, who still sucked a dummy at the age of three and wanted to know how 'they' got glass in windowpanes. Maybe she should get someone in from the local glaziers to talk about that?

Then, before she'd had a chance to reply, he'd asked if the window hurt when the glass got put in and that was why it was in pain.

So Gemma had written both 'pain' and 'pane' on the whiteboard and explained the difference. Harry might be glued to his dummy but he was a strong reader, and this was just the thing to help.

Then Kyle had clobbered his spade rival and although no one was hurt, it had led to tears. 'Naughty,' reproved Clemmie in such an adult voice that, for a moment, she'd thought it was the child's mother speaking.

'My mum's naughty too,' Clemmie added.

Gemma wasn't sure she wanted to hear this. Some of the children came out with howlers about their parents that could never be repeated.

Clemmie, however, whose vocal skills were far above the average age, was clearly bent on telling her. 'She's always on the computer when I'm in bed. I can hear her on the keyboard.'

Was that all? Thank goodness for that.

Then one of the mothers had flown into the playgroup after the morning session, in floods of tears. 'I've locked Dillon in the car by mistake!' she'd yelled. 'I put him in and then came back to get something but I must have left my keys inside and it locks automatically.'

Easily done, Gemma told her, Jean rushed off to ring the AA and Gemma went out to try and pacify Dillon, who had started at the same time as Danny and Lily.

'Want out,' he had said plaintively from his toddler seat in the back.

How did you tell a child that he needed to wait until help arrived? 'I know!' Gemma clapped her hands. 'We'll sing a Puddleducks song.' So she did, while Dillon mouthed the words back through the window. Lily, who was staying on for the afternoon session, solemnly stood next to her.

'OK, Dillon, OK,' Lily had said in a soothing tone and sure enough, when the AA man arrived in record time and released the poor child, she was the first to give him a big hug. Children were so affectionate to each other sometimes, thought Gemma. It always brought a lump to her throat when she watched them holding hands in a queue or very gently stroking their faces, like Lily was doing now to Dillon.

'You need a break,' commented Kitty when Gemma filled her in on all this during one of their catch-up mobile chats. 'Come up to town for the weekend.'

'Town' in Kitty language meant London. She'd heard Joe use the same expression. It was tempting.

'Come on,' urged Kitty. 'I don't understand why you won't let your hair down every now and then.'

'Yes you do.'

'All right. But I still think you should put the past behind you now. When's your next appointment, by the way?'

'After half-term.'

'Which is when?'

Sometimes Gemma forgot that Kitty's world – now made up of recording sessions and trips to New York – was so different from hers.

'Third week in October but I've got Parents' Evening before then and mid-term reports, and you wouldn't believe the paperwork . . .'

'Right. Then this Saturday it is. We'll go clubbing and you can meet some of my friends.'

Gemma hesitated. Clubbing really wasn't her thing but if she wasn't careful, she'd end up like some spinster schoolteacher without any friends. 'That would be great. Thanks.'

Gemma couldn't wait to get home. She'd tried. She'd really tried to be interested in what this tall, aquiline-nosed actor friend of Kitty's was saying about the new ad he'd just been asked to do for skincare. He was clearly expecting a compliment but even if she could have forced one out, he wouldn't have heard her anyway. The noise was too loud! She'd also drunk more than usual, partly because it gave her something to do and partly because the aquiline-nosed actor kept topping her up without asking.

'Not my type, I'm afraid,' she confided to Kitty as they both headed for the Ladies about elevenish, which was way past her usual bedtime.

Kitty eyed her in the mirror. 'Know your trouble? You're still holding a candle for that man. It's about time you woke up and remembered that he's gone.' She clicked her fingers. 'Vanished. Poomf! Maybe when you've done the necessary, you'll be able to convince yourself of that.' She patted Gemma's shoulder kindly. 'Now go on. I can see you'd really rather go home. No, it's all right – honestly. Give me a ring next week.'

The aquiline-nosed young man got her a taxi to Marylebone and even saw her on to the train before kissing her goodbye on both cheeks, very close to her mouth. As she watched him push his way back through the barrier, Gemma almost wished she *could* feel something for this well-mannered actor who would undoubtedly meet with her parents' approval.

'Excuse me?' An incredibly tall, smooth-shaven, good-looking man with piercing blue eyes, who looked as though he was the rugby-playing type, leaped on the train just as the whistle was blowing. 'Do you know if this is the right train for Hazelwood?'

Gemma nodded, taking in the army kitbag. From his clean-shaven face and short haircut, not to mention the smartly pressed beige trousers and navy jacket, he was possibly in the services like her younger brother Tom. Every time she rang home, the phone would be answered by her mother whose voice would immediately soften in relief when she knew it was Gemma and not someone bringing bad news. Yet at the same time, they were all so proud of him.

'Have you come far?' She hadn't meant to engage in conversation but the wine had loosened her up. Besides, you never knew with the army; people often knew each other. By some coincidence, Tom was serving with a cousin of one of the parents at Sunnyside. Maybe this gorgeous-looking man with the kitbag might have come across her brother too.

'The Middle East and then a few weeks of training down in the West Country.' He gave her a broad smile that lit up his eyes, unlike Joe Balls's smiles, which were few and far between and never got any further than the edge of his mouth. 'I'm in the services.'

Just as she'd thought!

'The paratroopers?'

His broad face nodded. 'You have someone there?'

No. Tom was in another division and it turned out that the stranger on the train didn't know him, but did know several of the places that her brother had been to. So they spent a very pleasant hour discussing all kinds of things, from world security to the funny things that children say. By then she'd already told him what she did, taking care not to mention any names or divulge parental antics. You never knew who was on the train!

'I'm on leave until January so I thought I'd spend it with family, especially as my sister's just had a baby.' He patted the large carrier bag from Hamleys that was sitting next to his kitbag. 'My mother's on cloud nine at being a granny. She's already been at my sister's for a week but can't stay away!'

Baby? Mother away for a week? No. It would be too much of a coincidence if this was Joyce's son. She'd look awfully silly if she asked him, and he wasn't.

'Looks like we're here!' He had seen the sign before her. 'Please. Let me help you.'

Gently he took her bag even though it was light compared with his, which he had hoisted on his back before cupping her elbow and helping her off the train. The touch of his hand made her skin tingle, as though she had grazed her funny bone.

'Thank you.'

'Not at all. May I walk you back? I don't like to see a lady going home on her own.'

No, really, she was about to say. It was very kind but she didn't want to put him out. Besides, she was always telling the children not to talk to strangers. So why on earth was she now telling him where she lived? Too late, she wished she hadn't had those three glasses of wine at the club. This really wasn't like her; not like her at all!

'Hazel Road?' He grinned. 'It's where I'm going too. My mother lives at number 43.'

So she was right! 'I rent a room at the top of your mother's house.'

His face beamed in recognition. 'Then you must be Jane . . . Jean . . .'

'Gemma,' she corrected him.

'I know we've never met but I feel as though we have. My mother's always talking about you.' He put out his hand. 'I'm Barry.'

I know, she almost said. Your mother's always talking about you too, although she didn't say you looked more like a Daniel Craig than a Barry.

'Tell you what,' he continued, 'as we're going in the same direction, let's get a taxi. I insist. My treat.'

Taxis were a luxury she could ill afford on a teacher's salary. How nice to be treated and looked after for a change!

'Evening, Gemma!'

Her heart plummeted as she spotted Joe Balls at the head of the queue, still with the one crutch he'd been using since being taken to hospital after passing out at the Parents' Social. Blast! Judging from the disappointed look on Barry's face, her new companion obviously thought that Joe was a boyfriend. Somehow she felt the urgent need to put him straight.

'Barry, this is Joe Balls, my boss at school.' She accentuated the last few words so the relationship was quite clear. 'He also rents a room from your mother during the week.'

Joe gave a sharp, short nod which could hardly be described as friendly. Typical!

Barry nodded at the crutch in an almost reverent way. 'Been in the wars, have you?'

Joe looked uncomfortable. 'Just a fall.' He shot a

look at Gemma that seemed to beg her not to tell him what had really happened.

She almost felt sorry for him, but not quite. 'I hope your wife is looking after you,' she couldn't help slipping in.

He frowned and to her surprise, she saw a look of hurt flitting across his face. 'Ed is my ex-wife actually. We've been divorced for a couple of years now but we still keep up contact.'

Clearly! 'Been to see her, have you?' She couldn't help slipping that one in.

'No. I was actually staying at my flat in London this weekend.'

'Want to share a taxi?' Barry was saying. 'Makes sense, doesn't it, if we're all going to the same place? Here's one now.' He stepped ahead of them smartly and held out the door. 'After you, Gemma.'

She took her seat, feeling a tingle running through her. Barry wasn't just devastatingly good-looking. He had excellent manners, too, which fitted in with the nice things his mother was always saying about him. Things finally seemed to be looking up!

Chapter 25

When Gemma woke the next morning, she felt an unusual lightness in her chest. Then she remembered the previous evening. Don't be so silly, she told herself. Just because Barry made polite conversation and gave you a taxi ride home, it doesn't mean he fancies you. Besides, he's in the army, which means he will go away. And did she really want to play the waiting game all over again?

'Gemma!'

Joyce stood at her door, beaming.

'Hope I didn't disturb you, dear, but I just wondered if you were going to be around today? I believe you met my Barry on the train. Such a coincidence, isn't it? Anyway, I thought you might like to join us for lunch. Nothing fancy. Just a roast.'

Gemma hid her smile! Joyce's attempts at matchmaking were so obvious as to be worthy of Mrs Bennet, but she felt it would be rude to refuse. Besides, she really wanted to see Barry again!

'*Guess who I've met?*' she texted Kitty. '*Joyce's son. The one she's always going on about. He's v dishy and I've been invited to lunch 2day!*'

Kitty's reply came back almost immediately. '*Is this variation on boy next door? Wear smthing nice. Not 2 casual bt not over top either!*'

She had a point! Gemma rifled through her wardrobe looking for something that wasn't too dull (like that grey knee-length skirt) or too revealing (like one of Kitty's cast-off tops). In the end, she settled for a crisp white shirt and pale blue designer jeans that she'd bought in the sales, plus a pair of soft brown ankle boots. Somewhat nervously, she walked down the stairs and knocked on Joyce's door, feeling as though she should be there to pay her rent instead of arriving for Sunday lunch.

'My dear girl, come on in!'

Joyce, joined by Barry, ushered her in, past the kitchen, to the rest of the house where the tenants never went. She hadn't seen this part before. 'What a lovely sitting room,' she exclaimed, admiring the beautiful French windows that led out on to the garden.

'Thank you, dear. Now Barry, do get Gemma a drink.'

Joyce waved her hand towards a cocktail cabinet in the corner that reminded Gemma of an almost identical one owned by her parents. Its surface, like every other piece of furniture in the room, was covered with photographs of Barry and certificates ranging from those for school swimming to the Duke of Edinburgh Gold Award. 'What would you like to drink, sweetie? Gin, vodka, Pernod? Just name it and my Barry will sort you out.'

She gave Gemma a wink. 'Men in uniform know how to pour a girl a drink, I expect, and much more! Besides, we all deserve a celebration drink to welcome back my boy.'

Not sure whether to feel amused or embarrassed, Gemma watched as the diminutive Joyce tried to put her arm around her son's enormous waist. 'Our men in the forces are so brave. So very brave.'

'Mum!'

Clearly poor Barry didn't know where to look. 'I've only been diving in South America.'

'Yes, darling, but before that you were in that terrible place. Now what was it called again?'

He gave her an affectionate squeeze and then disentangled himself. 'Let's not talk about that now, shall we. I'd much rather hear about Gemma's work at her nursery school.'

If that had been Joe, Gemma found herself thinking, he would be asking her *why* she did pyjama drama at Puddleducks or what was the point of making hedgehogs out of baked potatoes and matchsticks, but Barry seemed genuinely impressed.

However, by the time they all sat down at the dining-room table, laid with gleaming silver cutlery and sparkling crystal, Gemma had run out of small talk and so, she suspected, had Barry. She needn't have worried. Joyce was more than happy to take over.

'One slice or two, Gemma? You need building up, sweetie. You girls are so thin nowadays. Needn't ask how many slices for my boy, need I? Just look at him, Gemma. He eats like a horse but never puts on an ounce.' She winked again across the table. 'It's all those exercises they make him do. Up at 5 a.m., my Barry is, even when he's home, to do his press-ups.'

Barry gave her an 'I'm sorry about this' look across the table, and she tried to make a reciprocal face to show that she understood.

'Sprouts, Gemma, or broccoli, or both? Barry, pass

her the gravy, would you? By the way, that girl round the corner rang this morning to see if you were back yet.' Joyce sighed. 'She's one of many broken hearts that Barry has left behind over the years. Of course, it was a long time ago but they don't forget, these girls, and it's not surprising when you look at how handsome and brave he is.'

'Mum!'

This time there was a warning in Barry's voice that startled Gemma and actually managed to stop Joyce in her tracks. 'Sorry, dear. I can't help it.' She gave a shrug. 'There's nothing quite like the bond between mother and son, you know, Gemma. You'll find out that for yourself one day if you have one. I can't wait to see little Ashley again next week. You're going to adore him, Barry. In fact, he looks a bit like you. I think it's the ears. Wouldn't be surprised if it got you broody at last. Now, more wine anyone? By the way, dear, do you have a special man in your life?'

The last question, coming on the heels of all the previous gabble, took Gemma by surprise. 'No. Not now. I mean, I did but . . .'

Her voice tailed away and she felt herself colouring up. Joyce, however, was beaming. 'Isn't that a coincidence? Barry's single too. Poor dear, I do worry that he doesn't have enough time to relax in between his assignments. In fact, I was wondering if . . .'

'Mum.' Barry laid a hand on his mother's. It was a large hand, Gemma couldn't help noticing: the type with black sprouty hairs in between the fingers. 'Why don't you tell me about your flower-arranging class that you mentioned in your last letter? It sounded absolutely riveting.'

Joyce made a face. 'Well, it's all right, dear. But frankly, it's nothing more than something for me to do until you come back on leave. Now, Gemma, I do hope you have room for trifle. Barry helped me make it. He's a man of several talents, you know!'

Afterwards, feeling bloated with food and the sheer volume of conversation, Gemma thanked Joyce and explained that she really had to go in order to get ready for school the next day. 'But you must let me help you clear away and wash up first.'

'Nonsense, my dear, I won't hear of it. Now if you must get back, Barry will walk you.' Joyce spoke as though she had miles to go instead of a flight of stairs.

'Of course.'

Immediately he was at her side, helping her into her cardigan which she had brought in case it was cold (no need, since Joyce's part of the house was absolutely baking, with the radiators turned up high). 'I'm sorry about my mother,' he said as they walked up towards her bedsit. 'She does get carried away at times and with my father dead and my sister safely married, she does tend to focus all her energies on me.'

Gemma gave him an understanding smile. Poor man. He must have felt awful. 'I totally understand. My mother is always asking me if I've met Mr Right yet. They don't understand that these days, we don't all get married at twenty like they did.'

Barry put his head slightly to one side as though considering it. 'Mind you,' he said while she was fishing for her key in her bag, which needed a bit of a clear-out, 'if you find the right person, there's nothing wrong with that, is there?' He touched her lightly on the arm as she finally managed to open the door. 'I really enjoyed your company at lunch. Thank you. I do hope I see you again soon, Gemma. Actually . . .'

He stopped.

'Yes?' asked Gemma.

'It's just that . . .' Barry appeared to be hesitating. 'Well, if you don't think it's too forward after my mother's rather pointed suggestions, I wondered if you'd like to come for a walk along the canal with me.'

It was on the tip of her tongue to say that she really ought to be getting on with her lesson preparation for tomorrow, but it was a lovely bright crisp day outside and somehow she found herself saying yes.

'Don't you just love it here?' Gemma said as they walked down the hill towards the canal. 'Just look at those boats!' She pointed to one which had the name *Valiant Sailor* painted in a gold scroll on its side.

'They have such magical names, don't they?' agreed Barry.

'Exactly!' Her eyes shone. 'I talked to one of the owners the other day. She used to run a shop and then she threw it all up to spend her life on the Grand Union.'

'Brave,' smiled Barry. 'I like the way you can look through the window and see them brewing up tea in those galley kitchens.'

Gemma pointed to the flower pots on the roof of

another boat, which were spilling over with herbs and geraniums left over from the summer. 'Wouldn't you just love a garden like that?'

He nodded and as he did so, accidentally brushed against her. 'Sorry.' He moved away. 'I've always rather liked the idea of living in a boat like that, actually.'

'Me too.'

'Really?' He looked at her as though surprised by this. 'I thought most women dreamed of bricks and mortar.'

'I'm not like most women,' she said before she could stop herself, but he was nodding again.

'I can see that.'

His hand brushed hers as he spoke. Somehow, that didn't feel like as much of an accident as the way he had bumped into her before.

'Mrs Merryfield, Mrs Merryfield!'

A tot with bunches on either side beamed up at her from her tricycle. Jogging towards them was a rather frazzled mother in a blue and white tracksuit and no sign of the usual twin baby slings on her chest.

'Hello, Daisy!' Gemma knelt down. 'Is this the new bike you were telling me about? What a beauty!'

The Puddleduck nodded solemnly and looked up at Barry. 'Is this your husband?'

Hot and cold flushes of embarrassment surged through her. 'No. This is Barry. He's a friend.'

'But friends can get married, can't they, Mummy?' Daisy was looking up at her mother, who had arrived now, puffing and panting. Gemma remembered that she belonged to a slimming and exercise circle that some of the other mums went to as well. 'You were friends with Daddy first, weren't you?'

Help me, Gemma wanted to cry, and the mum nodded as though she immediately took in the situation.

'Yes, Daisy, I was, but that doesn't mean that all friends get married. Now come on and let's leave your poor teacher in peace until tomorrow! Bye!'

Gemma didn't know what to say as they continued walking along the towpath. 'I'm sorry,' was all she could manage.

Barry was grinning. 'I'm flattered actually, although I am a bit worried about the Mrs Merryfield bit. I didn't realise you were married!'

'The children call everyone Mrs, regardless of whether they're married or not.'

This time, she could swear, Barry's brush of her hand was not accidental. 'Theirs is a simpler world, isn't it?'

'At times.'

The warmth of his touch had made her feel slightly dizzy.

'I'm here until the new year. And I'd like to think,' he added, his hand now firmly holding hers, 'that we'll get to know each other a bit better over that time. What do you think?'

Gemma's voice came out as though someone else was speaking. 'I'd like that too.'

Kitty's voice could surely be heard through the wall next to which Joe was probably sitting. 'That's fantastic. He sounds fantastic too. Oooh, Gemma, that's so romantic.'

'Maybe, but the fact remains that . . .'

'Don't start that all over again. Oooh, Gemma, you will tell me what happens, won't you?'

Yes and no. There were some things that were private. All she did know was that every time she'd been out with Barry that week, to the wine bar or to the pizza place or the cinema, she'd felt a definite funny-bone tingle. He was amusing and entertaining, not to mention a good son. While she'd been at work he'd taken his mother to visit his sister, and come back bursting with pride at being an uncle. 'I love babies, don't you?' he had said and Gemma had nodded and said that yes, she loved children too, while Joyce smiled her approval across the kitchen.

If only they knew.

Meanwhile, she had Parents' Evening to think about. Even as a child she had worried about them, although she'd always been so conscientious at school. It had been her brother Tom who was the tearaway. So she understood why the Puddleducks parents now worried about their children's progress, especially as in today's world so much was expected of kids.

It was even more complicated these days, with everything having to have an Aim or an Objective, which needed to be measurable. Learning had to be both physical and emotional, which was why they had to focus on sensory activities like the feel of cornflour and water ('No, Billy, you mustn't eat that – it's for touching') and construction ('If we put two blocks on the pile, Lily, how many will we have altogether?')

and writing, even if it was just making a mark on the sand. Then there were role plays, which in her day had been called dressing up, and Small World activities, like doll's houses, all of which required feedback both on paper and across the table at Parents' Evening.

Gemma found it awkward telling the mother in doggy slippers and a badge saying *Kyle's mum* that her son's role play, which invariably involved the only soldier's outfit in the box, wasn't always socially acceptable. It wasn't the outfit, although that had caused some fighting due to its rarity; it was the dialogue that went with it.

'Sometimes,' explained Gemma nervously, 'Kyle comes out with some unacceptable sentences.'

'Like what?'

'I'm going to kill you, you . . .'

Gemma stopped, unwilling to fill in the three-word expletive. The woman's slippers shifted uncomfortably. 'I don't say stuff like that. Is that what you're accusing me of?'

Gemma tried to keep her voice even. 'No. I'm not. But I've explained to Kyle that we can't use words like that, and it would help if you could do the same.'

She gave the woman a firm but reasonably friendly look. Such a fine line to tread! There had been a horrible case recently in the papers about a child who had role-played a scene of domestic abuse. When the pre-school leader had approached the parent, the latter had turned the tables and accused the pre-school leader of committing the abuse. The teacher had to be suspended until the case could be investigated. It was ascertained that the parent was indeed guilty, and the poor child had to go into care. The pre-school leader was reinstated, but her career had clearly been damaged.

This woman in slippers, thought Gemma as she watched her walk huffily out, with all five of her children in tow because she 'couldn't afford a sitter like', might be exactly the sort of parent who could have sold the story about Lily to the papers.

No. She mustn't think like that. It wasn't fair. She had absolutely no proof. She had heard some of the mothers whispering and wondering if Dilly Dalung might turn up for Parents' Evening, and many of them had got dressed up for it. Clemmie's mum's plunging neckline, Gemma thought, was probably in aid of the promised visit by the so-called 'dishy' Reception head.

'That was his *ex*-wife, you know,' she heard her say. 'Yes, he's definitely single.'

Bella, who was handling Sienna's mum ('I have to tell you that I am *not* happy about the parking arrangements every morning'), rolled her eyes at Gemma across the room. Gemma had just finished speaking to Poppy's mum.

Yes, she *had* read the report that one in five children can't write their own name when they reach the age of five, but Poppy was doing very well with her outlines – honestly! – and really didn't need any extra homework. Playgroup was meant to be fun.

Then an extremely tall woman with bird-like features and a haughty demeanour sailed up, wearing a badge saying *Danny's grandmother*.

'Good evening. My daughter-in-law wasn't able to attend because Danny has a cold, but . . .'

She stopped.

Gemma did a double take. No. It couldn't be. Not *her*.

'I thought you were meant to be *Mrs* Merryfield,' said the tall lady faintly as she sank heavily down on the child-size red plastic chair, almost missing it altogether.

Gemma felt the room close in on her. It was difficult to breathe, and the silver chain around her neck seemed to tighten. At the same time, her throat began to pulse and her ears felt as though they were popping underwater when she tried to speak. 'The children call *everyone* Mrs.'

Patricia's mouth tightened. 'What are you doing *here*, my dear? Please tell me you are a figment of my emancipation.'

Imagination, Gemma wanted to say. It's imagination. 'I work here!' She felt her lips move as though someone else was manipulating them, rather as she manipulated the finger puppets. 'I'm the playgroup leader. May I ask why *you* are here?'

But even as she spoke, she had a horrible feeling that she already knew the answer.

'You can see why.' The bird-faced woman with hooded eyes pointed to the name badge on the stately bosom which preceded her. 'I'm Danny's grandmother. Nancy and Sam moved here because it was within commuting reach of London and . . .'

Danny's grandmother? Then . . .

'Yes! That's tight.'

Gemma had forgotten Patricia's habit of coming out with the wrong words every now and then.

The older woman was leaning forward now, clutching Gemma's wrist. 'Danny,' she hissed, 'is Sam's son.'

But he couldn't be! Sam hadn't wanted children! That had been the whole reason for splitting up. He'd made his feelings clear, but not until it had all been too late.

'And he's still holding a candle for you! He told me.' The woman was glancing over her shoulder now. That's why he hates discussing marriage with Nancy.'

Gemma's head was reeling. 'Does she know about me?'

Patricia gave her a scornful look. 'Don't be silly, dear.'

Gemma was trying to make sense of it all. 'If Sam still feels something, why hasn't he tried to contact me?'

There was a heavy sigh. 'Wish I knew, dear. You young people are so difficult to pin down. I was married at your age with a five-year-old son!'

Something didn't add up. 'But I've been searching for him on Facebook and everywhere I could think of.'

Sam's mother's lips tightened. 'He dropped part of his name, silly boy. Thought it sounded too grand, even though it's been in the family for at least two generations. Then he went to the States and New Zealand before finally seeing sense and coming home. He's got a very good job, you know. Travels all over the place. And he's very highly regarded by his company.'

It was as though his mother was trying to sell him, but it was the name bit that threw her. Sam's name was Fortnum-Wright but he had dropped the first bit, which explained why she couldn't find him on Facebook. But why was Danny, whose lovely long fair eyelashes and brilliant blue eyes were so like Sam's, now she came to think of it, called Carter Wright without the hyphen? She asked Patricia to explain.

Patricia's lips tightened. 'The Carter name comes from *her*. She insisted that if he wouldn't marry her, they should combine their names.'

No guesses as to who the 'she' was!

'It's too long ago now,' said Gemma faintly, horribly conscious that the next parent in the queue was now hovering. It was Tracy's mum, who had been lobbying some of the Puddleducks mothers to join a slimming group she'd started. Gemma dropped her voice to a whisper. 'Besides, he has a son. I couldn't break up a family. That's not me.'

Patricia's grip on Gemma's wrist grew tighter. 'Nonsense, dear. I still don't know what happened between you. But I do know that he's not happy with Nancy. Shall I give you his mobile number, dear? Not his work one. The private one.'

Chapter 26

'Listen,' Nancy had said to Brigid at the first opportunity after her friend had walked in on her and Patricia, 'please don't tell anyone that Sam and I aren't married.' She had been worrying that Brigid might have heard Patricia's words to that effect.

'Blimey, Nance, what are you going on about?'

Awkwardly, Nancy explained that she and Sam weren't legally married, although she saw him as her husband and wore a ring because otherwise it would be a bit embarrassing.

Brigid waved her hand dismissively. 'Nonsense! Loads of people aren't married at Puddleducks, including me and that stupid moaning cow, Sienna's mother. But if you're worried about it, of course I won't mention it to anyone else.'

Meanwhile, if it wasn't for the mosaics course to distract her, Nancy would have gone mad. At first she'd thought Patricia would only be here for a few days, but now it seemed as though she had no firm departure date in mind.

'I can't think why you didn't tell me about your problems, dear,' Patricia announced one evening after insisting on cooking Beef Wellington – a dish that the British seemed to regard as a treat, although how anyone could enjoy the combination of heavy

221

pastry and meat, Nancy simply couldn't understand.

Nancy, who had managed to get Danny to bed early partly because he was exhausted by pre-school, poured herself a large slug of wine to shut out Patricia's voice. The bottle had been a sympathy present from 'the girls' as she now called Brigid and Annie, both of whom had been appalled by her tales of the 'mother-in-law' from hell.

Stand up to her, they both said. Nancy was trying. 'Sam and I don't have problems, Patricia.'

'My dear child, it's obvious! No, I won't have one, thank you. I don't believe in drinking. Did you know that alcohol is more dangerous than rugs?'

Drugs, Nancy wanted to say. It's drugs.

'Besides, you'll be setting Danny a bad example. If children grow up watching their adults condone a habit like alcohol, they'll do the same. It's exactly like marriage or, as in your case, living together. If you two continue to squabble, Danny will think that all parents do this.'

Patricia paused for a sigh-breath and Nancy seized the opportunity to leap in. 'We don't squabble all the time, but Sam has found it difficult to adjust to parenthood.' Simply saying the words out loud made her feel they were true. And, she reflected, weren't British men meant to be rather reserved with their emotions?

Patricia nodded briskly. 'Exactly like his own father. But my dear, you haven't helped, have you? The way you fuss around that child is totally unnecessary! Always fretting when he gets a cold, or leaving messages on the phone for that nice Miss Merryfield at playgroup, to check that the security lock is working. Yes – I heard you the other day when we both went to pick up Danny. You ought to take a leaf out of her book. She's got all those children to look after, yet never once have I seen her flap!'

Nancy drained her glass. 'That's because she isn't a mother herself.'

Patricia looked peeved. 'There's no need to snap, dear.'

'I'm not.'

'I think you are, dear. I'm only trying to help. That's why I've been tidying up. You haven't happened to spot my hysterical novel, have you? I'd almost got to the last chapter and now I can't find it.'

'Historical,' said Nancy tightly. 'Don't you mean your historical novel?'

'That's what I said, dear. Do pay attention. Anyway, as I was saying, I'm doing my best. That's why I picked up Danny today so you could carry on with your muriel and that's why I'm cooking dinner, even though I have to say that I think it might be a good idea if you have a bit of a cupboard sort-out.'

Mural! It's a mural. Nancy's thoughts drifted to the collection of large paving stones which she, Doug and some of the other mums were working on. The picture really was taking shape!

Annie and Brigid had been roped in too, despite their commitment to belly dancing, t'ai chi and photography classes. 'We'll find you some great pebbles during our canal walks with the kids, won't we, Brigid!' Annie nudged Nancy. 'Provided we haven't let them fall in first. Don't worry – only joking.'

Meanwhile, they were all learning fast from Doug, who was a clear, patient teacher. 'There are all kinds of ways to make murals,' he explained as they crouched down on the floor, looking at the outline he had sketched on the paving slabs. 'But I've found this one works well. The trick is to smooth the concrete on very lightly – great, Nancy! – and then press in your different-coloured stones and pebbles.'

It was really coming on! Of course, they couldn't do it without Doug's help, but already Nancy could see the outline of Puddleducks rising out of one of the slabs, and Corrybank Primary on the one next to it.

Toby, the dog dad, had created part of the park, and someone else was working on the church. Tracy's mum, whom she'd mistakenly taken to be expecting, had glared when Nancy had invited her on to the Puddleducks mural team, saying frostily that she had other things to do.

It wasn't easy, because murals took time and time was what none of them had. Yet somehow, partly because of non-mural parents who offered to babysit, the picture was coming together and might, with any luck, be ready for the deadline.

'And another thing,' snorted Patricia, bringing her back to the present. 'If you don't mind me saying, you're becoming slightly obsessed with this muriel business. It's only a competition, my dear.'

One more glass of red. And, hell, why not, maybe a third. Otherwise, how on earth was she going to get through half-term with her mother-in-law? The prospect of a whole week stretching out in front of her without Puddleducks or Gemma Merryfield, whose lovely warm smile made her feel that she wasn't the neurotic mother that Sam and his mother thought she was, filled Nancy with panic.

'Just one more thing, my dear.'

Again?

'Have you considered doing a course on CBT for your problems? I've been doing one myself. It stands for Controlling Behaviour Therapy, you know. In fact, I do believe I have the number in my address book. I'll just nip up and get it. By the way, is that your phone ringing?'

She picked it up. Nothing. Then it rang again and there was a brief period of silence before someone spoke.

'Nancy?' Sam's voice seemed a very long way off. 'Is that you? You sound different.'

Of course she sounded different. She'd had two glasses of wine when normally she had one a week, if that. She told Sam so.

'Three glasses?' She almost heard him smiling. 'Is my mother that bad?'

'That bad? She's driving me nuts with her muriels and her hysterical and her search for non-existent suet and her insistence on hot-water bottles even though it's not that cold.'

'I get the picture.'

The sympathetic tone in his voice made her feel a bit better.

'Listen,' he said soothingly. 'I know this might sound like a silly idea and I'm pretty certain you won't leave Danny, but I just wondered. Do you fancy coming out here for a few days? My mother could babysit and it's such an amazing place.' His voice dropped. 'I've missed you, Nancy. More than I realised, and I think I've been a bit unfair to you. Please don't say no. Just think about it.'

Chapter 27

Of course it was out of the question! How could Nancy leave her son? How would he sleep if he wasn't curled up against her all night? How would she manage without him? On the other hand, was Patricia right when she'd said Nancy wasn't doing her son any good by being such a neurotic mother? She was beginning to think she might have a point.

They were in Doug's studio, working on the outline of the pretty church with that lovely spire at the top of the high street while the children were at playgroup. But it was difficult to concentrate after Sam's phone call the night before, and somehow she'd found herself telling the others about it.

'You must go,' insisted both Annie and Brigid in one breath as they crouched side by side, sifting through an assortment of stones and broken glass from old wine and beer bottles.

'She's his grandmother,' added Annie. 'Pass me that pebble, will you? No, not the grey one. The blueylooking one. It will be good for them to have time together. And you need to see Sam. Molly's mother's husband, the first one, wanted her to move up nearer to his job in Stockport, but she didn't want to disrupt the kids.'

Nancy didn't like the sound of this. 'What happened?'

she asked, carefully pressing a piece of blue glass on to the top of the church tower, where the cement was still damp.

Annie made a face. 'Don't ask. But suffice it to say that's why he became the first husband. Mind you, Vietnam beats Stockport in my book, any day.' She touched Nancy's arm lightly, and the clock tower nearly wobbled. 'It's a bit odd, don't you think, that suddenly your man wants you out there when he was being all off before. Do you think something's happened to make him realise how much you mean to him? By the way, how about a new hairdo before you go? I've got a great hairdresser. Pink streaks might suit you too!'

She thinks I've got competition, thought Nancy. Annie reckons Sam might be having an affair and now wants to check out his options back home.

It wasn't as though she hadn't considered the possibility. If Sam did fall for someone else, she'd decided, she would just let him go. But now it seemed like it might have happened, she realised she wanted him. The old Sam, that was. The one who had loved her properly before Danny had been born.

Danny! 'I can't just leave him. I'm not sure I trust Patricia. Supposing she leaves the front door open and he wanders out? And what if she leaves her bottle of indigestion tablets out and he helps himself?'

Doug's kind, firm voice cut in. 'You know, Nancy, I couldn't help overhearing. Would it help if I said that in former times grandparents played an extensive role in bringing up their grandchildren, and that all the generations involved benefited from this?'

He gave her a reassuring pat on the arm that felt

friendly rather than a come-on. 'If I were you, I'd listen to your friends. I'm sure they'll keep an eye on your mother-in-law. And don't worry about letting us down on the mural or muriel as she refers to it, although I have to say that I suspect these malapropisms might be an affectation on her part to gain attention. We'll work extra hard, won't we girls, and we'll be looking forward to having you back.'

She couldn't go! She couldn't! Yet if she didn't, Sam and she might really be over and then Danny wouldn't have two parents. She and Sam had both had this disadvantage, and clearly it hadn't done either of them any favours in life. In the end, it was that which made her decide that she needed to go out to join Sam. A child needed two parents in an ideal world, and she had a duty to do everything to make that possible.

Even so, the terrors of leaving her son tormented her for the next week. When it came to saying goodbye to Danny, Nancy felt as though her heart was being cut out with the new set of kitchen knives that Patricia had insisted on buying ('If you don't mind me saying, dear, yours are frightfully blunt').

'Mummy loves you very much, darling.'

Danny had given her a quick hug. He smelt of baked beans and earth where he'd been digging outside; something, she was ashamed to say, that she wouldn't have allowed before he'd started playgroup. 'Mummy, can we go to Devon like Mrs Merryfield when you get back? She's going to make castles on the beach.'

Nancy felt another stab of guilt. She should be there, doing things with her son instead of jetting off to the other side of the world to patch things up with a man who had no idea what parenthood was really about. 'Maybe another time, poppet.'

And then she was off, with Annie driving her to the airport because, as she said, she wouldn't put it past Nancy to chicken out at Departures. She, Annie, would jump at the chance to go to Vietnam, if only for a sixteen-hour nap on the plane away from the kids.

It all felt very strange, thought Nancy, who couldn't stop herself from putting her hand up to the side of her face and tentatively feeling the unfamiliar layers that Annie's hairdresser had created. She'd said a firm no to the pink-streak idea, luckily, and found herself asking for blonde highlights instead like Gemma's, which were probably natural and which she'd always admired.

Now, as Nancy pulled down the sunscreen mirror to check her make-up after a few tears, it was as though another person was looking back at her. One who was brave or foolish enough to leave her son and go to the other side of the world.

After saying goodbye to Annie and checking in, Nancy found a seat in Departures next to a family of five who all seemed to be laughing and joking and arguing in a good-natured way. She'd wanted to take Danny, but Sam had said it wasn't a good idea and that besides, his jabs might not be up to date. Anyway, with his mother at home, it was an ideal opportunity for her and Sam to have some time alone as a couple.

Then her flight was called. It wasn't too late to go back, Nancy told herself as she presented her boarding pass at the gate. She could be back with Danny within a couple of hours; already she was missing the smell of his downy head and his constant chatter like the small boy in the family in front of her. But if she did that, Sam would give up on her. She knew he would. So somehow, feeling as though another person was moving her legs down the long tube of a corridor leading to the plane, she found herself taking a window seat near the emergency exit.

When the plane, an enormous thing with three flights of stairs, took off, Nancy felt as though she was going to be sick. Supposing it crashed? Who would bring up Danny? Patricia with her stuffy British mannerisms, or her own self-help-obsessed mother who was equally crazy?

Nancy eyed the air stewardesses sitting in their chairs. They looked relaxed, which was surely a good sign, even though the seat-belt sign was still on. Yet the further the plane rose in the sky, the more breathless she felt. She'd never been this far from Danny before. From the minute he had taken his first breath she had been with him, apart from his time at Puddleducks.

'He'll be fine,' Gemma Merryfield had assured her when she'd explained where she was going. 'You go and enjoy yourself. It's important for parents to have some time together. By the way, I like your new hairdo. Those blonde streaks suit you, and the feathered layers are really soft.'

But she had said all this in a voice that sounded a bit different from her usual cheery tone, so it was obvious that even she thought Nancy was being neglectful.

What was she doing?

PING!

'May I help you?' The pretty Singaporean stewardess in a beautiful peacock-blue silk outfit was at her side in a moment.

'Is it possible to make a phone call?' Nancy knew she was overreacting, but couldn't help it. 'I've just left my son for the first time and I need to check he's all right.'

It was expensive and a bit of a fiddle, as Patricia would have said, as the stewardess showed her how to pull out the screen and dial her home number. 'Patricia? It's me. Yes, I'm on the plane. Yes, I know it's costing a lot but I wanted to know if Danny's all right. Good. Thanks. Yes, I know I'm worrying unnecessarily and I'm sure you'll call Sam's phone if you need us.'

After that, Nancy slept: a long deep sleep, despite the odd bout of turbulence. The stress of the previous months, coupled with the knowledge that now there really was no going back, completely knocked her out until it was time to change planes at Singapore and get on the last leg to Ho Chi Minh City, a place that a few weeks ago she hadn't, to be honest, even been able to spell correctly.

It was, she thought, helping another mother with all her baby stuff through to Arrivals, like being someone else.

Someone who wasn't Danny's mum.

Someone who was just Nancy.

Chapter 28

It was so busy and noisy! Nancy had to wait half an hour at the visa window where someone who hardly spoke English eventually stamped the forms she had brought with her, and she was finally allowed through passport control into the sea of small brown faces, some holding up sheets of papers with names on them. Hers wasn't there.

Sam hadn't been sure he could get away from a meeting but if he couldn't, he'd promised, he'd send someone to collect her; someone from the office. If he had, that person wasn't obvious. And then she saw him! Taller and blonder than anyone else around him, striding through the crowd, doing a double take at her new look and pulling her into his arms.

It wasn't a kiss – how long since they had done that properly? – but it was a lovely warm cuddle that made her feel that yes, she was right to come out even though part of her body felt missing without Danny's small hand in hers.

Finally Sam released her and a small brown wizened woman nearby, wearing one of the pointed Vietnamese hats Nancy had seen on television, clucked her approval and said something she couldn't understand. Sam said something back that made the woman cluck again and laugh with a gummy mouth.

'You speak Vietnamese already?' she asked in wonder.

'Just a few words.' He laughed, slightly embarrassed. 'She says that we make a nice couple.'

Not if she knew our problems, thought Nancy, turning back to give the old woman a quick smile. Meanwhile, Sam was taking her hand and leading her through the crowds to find a taxi. 'How was your flight? You must be exhausted.' He glanced down at her hair. 'I like the zigzaggy blonde bits. They suit you.'

As he spoke, a fleet of motorbikes shot by, making her jump. The air was dusty, making it hard to breathe, and the roar of the traffic and the constant, very fast talk around them was like four Puddleducks playgroups put together.

'I know this is all going to seem very strange to you, especially as Ho Chi Minh is so noisy. It takes a lot of getting used to at first, and the traffic is manic. So I thought we'd have a day in the city and then I've booked a week-long trip down the Mekong Delta.'

She listened to Sam talk away and watched astounded through the window as the taxi made its way through the city. Motorbikes wove in and out like bluebottles, with total disregard of traffic lights or the few pedestrian crossings. Crossing the road, Sam was telling her, required a leap of faith, rather like crossing the M25. You simply had to walk at an even speed and somehow the traffic would usually make its way round you.

He went on like this, filling her in on the sights. 'That's a famous hotel where journalists holed up during the war writing their dispatches, and that's the town hall with its French architecture because the French were here before you Americans. There's the former presidential palace with the famous North Vietnamese tank that broke through when the South finally lost, and look, do you see that man crouching down at the side of that building, showering himself? Incredible, isn't it, how you get hotels next to places that are literally falling down?'

But it wasn't until they got to District Seven, where the litter and the ramshackle shops and shacks on the main streets gave way to a crop of smart restaurants and an HSBC bank just round the corner from Danny's tenth-floor apartment, that she realised. Sam hadn't even asked how their son was. Nor, when she cuddled up to his back in bed, did he suggest doing anything else. Instead, he fell asleep before her, leaving her wide awake from jet lag after having slept on the plane.

The following morning, Sam had an unexpected meeting. Would she be all right waiting in the apartment for him? No, she decided, feeling an unaccustomed rush of independence. It would be unadventurous not to explore in a new place, especially as she was there for such a short time. But first, she needed to call home.

The ringing tone seemed to take ages to kick in and when it did, it took several rings before it was answered. The sound of her mother-in-law's breezy voice brought back all the old anxiety she'd had before leaving.

'Patricia? It's me. Is everything all right?'

'Not really, dear.'

Nancy's heart quickened. 'Why?'

'I've looked everywhere but I simply can't find it.'

'Find what?'

'The sage, dear.' She spoke as though the subject had already been mentioned. 'Where on earth do you keep it? It's absolutely essential for my power surges.'

Her *what*?

'Sage leaves, eaten whole, are absolutely vital for the menopause. You'll find that out when you get there. In fact, it probably won't be long – you Americans always like to get to places before anyone else.'

She was speaking so fast that before Nancy had fully absorbed the rudeness of the last remark, her mother-in-law had moved on. 'As for Danny, he's as happy as a sandboy. You really ought to calm down a bit, dear, like that lovely Gemma Merryfield. We saw her in town today, you know. Danny absolutely loves her toothpaste song. Such a good idea! It makes him really enthusiastic about cleaning his teeth and in fact I had to stop him the other night, as his gums were bleeding. Isn't that sweet? Gemma says that . . .'

At that point, the phone cut off, proving that Sam hadn't been telling white lies when he'd said that communication could be difficult at times. Nancy wasn't sorry. To be constantly compared unfavourably with the pre-school leader who seemed, at times, too good to be true, was becoming really rather irritating. Even Brigid and Annie agreed that if Gemma Merryfield had children of her own, she'd be as stressed and disorganised as the rest of them.

Afterwards, Nancy simply had to get out of the apartment for some fresh air, as well as the exploration she'd promised herself. However, judging from the masks which everyone wore and the hordes of motorbikes which shot by (often six or seven abreast), fresh air was in short supply. At one point Nancy crossed the road, but it was terrifying. No one seemed to stop for anyone, not even at the so-called pedestrian lights.

Glancing up through the crowds, she spotted an indoor market that seemed to offer a haven from the chaos of the road. How wrong she was! As soon as she entered the market, she found herself besieged by small brown-skinned men and women keen to sell her their silks and small wooden knick-knacks. It was all a little overwhelming, so she made a swift exit, pausing to look around her.

She saw a crowd of people gathered around a uniformed Vietnamese man. He was obviously a tour guide, just what she needed. She'd never see anything if she wandered about on her own like this. He glanced her way, smiled and asked if she wanted to join. When she nodded with relief, he carried on.

Nancy spent the rest of the day visiting the sights of Ho Chi Minh: she cried at the War Remnants Museum, walked through Chinatown and visited the most beautiful post office she had ever seen.

Afterwards she made her way back to the apartment. In her absence, it appeared that the maid had been in. Breakfast had been washed up in the compact kitchen and everything else, including the streamlined beech furniture, was polished and beautifully neat and tidy. She could do with someone like that at home! No wonder, as Sam had told her, many expats found they couldn't come back to England unless they were as well off as Lily's mother, with her nanny and driver and goodness knows who else.

Nancy poured herself a gin and tonic while waiting for Sam, and stood looking out through the window at the view below of other apartments and a park.

When he returned, not long afterwards, Nancy had forgotten her earlier resentment and now felt flushed and exhilarated, bursting with stories to tell him.

'Really?' he said with genuine interest at regular intervals while she was recounting her day. It made such a change having something to talk about! When he'd been at home, he would come back in the evening and dutifully ask what she had done during his absence. She had usually replied, 'Not much,' and their conversation had then disintegrated amidst Danny's demands and Sam's commuter exhaustion.

'We've got an early start for our trip,' he now said excitedly when she'd finished. 'Looking forward to it?'

She nodded, waiting for him to suggest that he might phone their son before leaving. But no. The thought didn't even seem to occur to him. That night, when he moved towards her, she began to go through the motions mechanically, but then found herself strangely aroused. It was, she thought afterwards when Sam had fallen asleep and she was lying listening to the constant hooting of the motorbikes and cars outside, almost as though they were a couple on their own all over again.

For the first time in her life, Nancy found herself wondering if what Sam had said right at the beginning – about not particularly wanting children – meant that they would have been happier as a couple without Danny.

Nancy shivered. How could she live without her son? If it came to making a decision between him and Sam, she knew which one she'd choose.

Chapter 29

The following day, a guide turned up to take them on their trip. Many of Sam's contemporaries were taking time off, since it was a national holiday, and they were all going on one-to-one guided tours. It sounded so luxurious, but Nancy soon found that despite the individual attention, the word 'luxury' had different connotations in Vietnam.

And thank goodness it did! She hadn't wanted a five-star trip, Nancy thought, as the guide drove them to a small port where they were helped on to a boat with rickety cane seats for four people. She wanted to see the country as it really was, and this was exactly what they were doing.

'Look!' Sam pointed to another boat going past with a group of Vietnamese waving and smiling. 'They're coming back from the paddy fields after starting work at 3 a.m. And over there is a floating market.'

She gazed riveted at these boats, one of which actually had a television on board and a line of washing. The guide explained, in English that was more enthusiastic than accurate, that the market was for local people rather than tourists. The floating shops sold essentials such as washing powder and oil.

'Tonight,' the guide announced, 'we go to home-stay.'

This, Sam explained, was a bed and breakfast run by a Vietnamese family from their house on the river. Nancy gasped when they arrived and clambered from the boat on to their landing stage. The house, painted a faded turquoise, was charmingly quaint, with a wooden verandah at the front and miniature wooden doves. A smiling Vietnamese woman met them, bowing and ushering them into a room with a row of beds like a dormitory, each one with a blue mosquito net.

'Are we staying with other people?' Nancy asked, and the guide laughed. 'No, this is just for you. When you are ready, we eat.'

They dined on a sort of wooden deck, overlooking the river.

'Look,' instructed the guide excitedly, and suddenly the tree outside lit up like a Christmas tree. 'Fireflies,' he explained and sure enough, Nancy could see lots of little lights hovering and moving around.

Dinner was a stuffed fish standing upright, with carrots coming out of its mouth. Nancy didn't feel keen, but took a mouthful so as not to offend their hosts. Delicious! Afterwards, they swayed in hammocks on the verandah. So strange, thought Nancy, before dropping off into a postprandial stupor. She missed Danny, yet because there wasn't any mobile-phone reception she had stopped worrying so much about him, because there was nothing she could do if something had gone wrong.

Besides, she had a feeling that nothing would. The girls had been right when they'd said she needed to get away for a break. It put everything in perspective, somehow. And hadn't they both promised to call in on her mother-in-law to check everything was all right?

That night, after using the outdoor loo and 'shower', which was no more than a hose coming out of the wall and a bucket, Nancy was astonished to find that her body did things with her husband that it hadn't done since they had first met. She knew it sounded crazy, but her new hairdo had given her a confidence that she hadn't had for years, if ever. Maybe, like her parenting psychology magazine said on its Relationships page, if *you* feel attractive, your partner will think so too.

'That was amazing,' gasped Sam. 'I've missed you so much.'

She waited for her heart to stop its post-coital thudding before replying. 'And have you missed Danny too?'

There. She had said it.

'Of course I have.'

His tone was hurt, reproachful. Suddenly all the warmth from their lovemaking drained away. But the new Nancy, with the hairstyle that made men turn their heads in the street – Sam had noticed that too – felt stronger and more certain of herself. She could hold her own in this conversation.

'Then why don't you talk about him?'

'Why don't *you*?'

Their words were like bullets of anger under the blue mosquito net.

'Because I was waiting for you to start, Sam.'

'I didn't mention him in case it upset you. I knew it took a lot to leave him.'

She was silent for a minute. 'We've changed since we had Danny.'

In the half-light streaming through the shutters from the moon outside, she could see him nodding. 'I know.'

'You didn't want a child. You said that at the beginning.'

He turned away from her. 'What are you trying to say, Nancy?'

'I feel that you put up with me and Danny and that you don't love us any more, if indeed you ever really did. It's not as though we had much time together before I got pregnant. My mother was right. It was too much, too soon.'

'That's not true,' he said quietly, 'but I did tell you right at the beginning that I didn't want children. My parents split up, as you know.' His voice faltered. 'My mother once told me that if it hadn't been for me, they might have been all right.'

She hadn't known that before. 'But that's awful.'

'Awful perhaps, but maybe also true.'

'Danny and I need you.' She was crying now. 'Have you thought about the family who live here? They lead a simple life, but they're happy. Everywhere, on the walls, are pictures of their children. The mother looks after her niece's baby. They make the family work. They aren't selfish.'

'Selfish? Who's being selfish?'

'You are,' she cried. 'You just think about yourself all the time. You don't get up in the night when our son wakes, although now he's at pre-school he doesn't do that any more. And you don't understand that parenthood frightens me.' She tried to control her sobs. 'It

243

scares me because, unlike my work, I don't know what I'm doing. I'm worried that if I do something wrong, Danny will get hurt. In fact one of the reasons I came out here is that I didn't feel I was doing him any good by being there for him because I'm so neurotic.'

'Ssh.' Sam was soothing her. 'You're not neurotic. You just worry, that's all. But neither of us is perfect.' He hesitated fractionally. 'Maybe I've been selfish, both as a father and a husband. But being out here has made me realise how much I love and miss you, Nancy. And Danny too, of course. Do you know why I asked you to come here?'

He paused, and Nancy's heart beat so loudly she could almost hear it in her ears. Not an affair, she begged silently. Please, not an affair.

'It was a test.' He had turned back to face her now. 'I'm not proud of myself but that's how I saw it. I thought that if you really loved me, you would leave Danny just for a few days and spend some time with me instead.'

Her heart plummeted. Back home she had wondered if Sam had been using this trip as a test of her feelings for him, and now she knew it was true, she felt deeply disappointed.

'How very childish of you,' she said coolly.

'I can see that now.' Sam looked away. 'But I can also see that you were much braver than I gave you credit for. Not every woman would come out here on her own and get down to basics, like this.' He waved his hand round the room – it was still possible in the moonlight to see the small black insects crawling up the wooden walls. 'It's no five-star hotel, is it?'

244

That wasn't the point. 'It's a family home, Sam. And that's what makes it special. It's full of love, with a husband and a wife working together instead of against each other, or setting silly tests. And have you seen how the father here spends so much time with his children?'

He had the grace to sound ashamed. 'When we get back, I promise I'll be more involved. It will be different.' He stroked her arm.

'Honestly?' Should she now mention something else that had been on her mind? Not the thing about the girl in the photograph in his study, because, after all, the past was the past, and Sam had made it clear that he loved her. But the other thing. 'Do you think . . . I mean . . . is there any chance of us having another child?'

She felt his stroking stop. 'I'm not sure, Nancy. I wish I could say I'm ready, but I'm not. Can't we just sort out this stage of our lives and enjoy the rest of this trip?'

It was a deal. The following few days were, thought Nancy, more like the honeymoon they'd never had. After going down the river, they ended up in a beautiful hotel bungalow overlooking the beach on an island with an unpronounceable name. The first thing Nancy did was to make a call home from the hotel room, but the lines were down, the reception told her, due to a storm last week.

A few weeks ago, this would have sent her into a panic attack, but she was amazed to find herself receiving the news quite calmly. If something had happened, surely someone would have found a way to have got hold of her?

By the time it came to flying back from the island to Ho Chi Minh on the tiny sixteen-seater plane, she felt totally and utterly relaxed. Just as important, she and Sam had never felt closer.

'Do you think he'll like this?' asked Sam, holding out a small football which he'd bought at Duty Free.

Nancy nodded. 'Definitely, although what he'd really like is you to play with him instead of putting up with me kicking a ball around the park.'

She gave him a tough look; a look which she wouldn't have been strong enough to have given before. Sam smiled. 'Point taken. I will spend more time with him, even if it means having extra time off work.' He reached out for her hand. 'I can't wait to see him again and talk to him.'

She felt a tingle of anticipation. Soon they would be back in a city and communication would finally be possible. She couldn't wait to hear her son's voice, either.

Her mobile finally swung into action when they got off the plane at Ho Chi Minh, planning to get a taxi back to their apartment. Sam asked if he could speak first. It was a good sign.

Smiling, Nancy watched his face. 'Mum, it's me. Yes I know, our phones didn't work but we've had a great time. How about . . . what?'

He turned to look at her with an expression that she'd never seen before. And as Nancy gazed at her husband's stricken face, she realised that all her worst fears had finally come true.

Chapter 30

He was more than ready for half-term, thought Joe as he sorted out his desk, placing a copy of his email reply to Gemma about the nativity play in his *Finished* file. In comparison with Di's desk in the office next door, his own looked smugly neat and tidy.

Almost *too* neat and tidy, he thought suddenly. Di's desk, with her own special mug bearing a flowery D initial and her tin of Highland shortbread biscuits, was certainly more inviting than his own, with its neatly stacked files and sharpened pencils in the brown plastic container.

Joe felt a sense of unease crawl through him. He hadn't been himself since last month's Parents' Social, and the thought of Ed turning up out of the blue like that – not to mention his fainting fit – still brought him out in a cold sweat. He'd have liked to think that everyone had forgotten about it by now, but something told him that in a school where even the minutiae such as skimmed-milk sell-by dates were examined in detail, the arrival of a glamorous ex-wife would not be bypassed in a hurry.

'Joe?' Beryl put her head round the door. 'May I have a word before you go?'

His initial reaction was to tell her that actually this wasn't very convenient. After all, he'd brought his weekend bag in this morning, intending to take advantage of school ending at lunchtime so he could shoot straight off to Mike and Lynette's immediately school finished. But then he remembered Brian's advice. 'Go with them, lad. They've been there longer than you and they don't all talk rubbish. Some of them – yes. But not all.'

So, forcing himself to look as though a meeting after hours with the head was exactly what he wanted, he followed Beryl into her office.

'Please.' Beryl indicated the seat on the other side of her desk, which bore a cluster of photographs showing her with a small child of about three. Joe looked away, feeling the usual chill that ran down his spine whenever he saw pictures of kids who were that age.

Meanwhile, Beryl was taking off her spectacles, wiping them on her pale blue cardigan and then putting them on again. She seemed nervous. What was up?

'This isn't going to be easy, Joe,' she said softly.

A spark of alarm went through him. That was exactly the phrase he used to start off with at the bank when he'd had to let someone go.

With difficulty, he flashed her one of the smiles that he'd been working on in front of the bathroom mirror ever since Brian had suggested that a grin or two might make him seem less severe in the classroom.

'What's the problem, Beryl?'

He used her first name intentionally, just as he'd been taught by Psychology Management on the fourteenth floor. It made the speaker seem more in control, because he had ownership of the other person's name.

Beryl sighed. 'You see this photograph?'

There was no getting out of it.

Clenching his fists by his sides, Joe made himself look at the blond boy cuddling up to Beryl in the frame. The kid had a challenging look on his face, as though teasing Joe for not owning something that everyone else seemed to possess.

'That's my grandson. He's three.'

Don't think about what might have been, he told himself. Don't think about it.

'Do you know what he loves at this time of the year?' Beryl was eyeballing him now, without her glasses, and he had a sudden feeling that she wouldn't have been out of place on the fourteenth floor herself.

'He loves Halloween and nativity plays.' Beryl paused, looking down at the papers in front of her. Joe was aware of a horrible heavy feeling filling the pit of his stomach.

'Gemma sent me copies of your recent email correspondence on the subject of both the planned Halloween dressing-up day and the nativity play. I gather that you consider the first to be "outmoded and irrelevant to society today", while the second is "politically incorrect in view of today's varied religious beliefs". Is that true?'

Joe felt an unfamiliar cold trickle of nervous sweat run down his chest. 'When I was in my previous school, we banned both events for exactly those reasons.'

There was a nod, as though Beryl had thought he might say something like that. 'That was in a tough inner London area, wasn't it? I think you'll find that things are different out here. We do, of course, include plenty of learning and play about other religions, in accordance with the Early Years curriculum. But the nativity play is a tradition, Joe. If we got rid of that, we would be destroying our heritage and would probably cause a riot amongst the parents as well.'

There was the glimmer of a smile, as though she was trying to soften the blow of what was coming next. Joe knew the signals all too well. He had followed a similar pattern at the bank except that then, he hadn't been on the receiving end. 'I'm afraid that's not all, Joe. We have received various complaints about you from both members of staff and parents.'

'Complaints?' He stiffened in a mixture of anger and alarm. 'What about?'

Beryl's voice took on an authoritative edge he hadn't heard before. 'One parent who wrote in said she was deeply concerned about your emphasis on maths at the expense of, as she put it, "story riting", spelt without the "w".'

Beryl gave another half-smile. 'You can see that if a parent can't spell correctly, it is even more essential that we help their children to do so.'

This wasn't fair! 'I follow the guidelines on writing but I have to say, Beryl, that some of the Puddleducks children have arrived woefully inadequate in terms of mathematical skills, and I am only doing my best to correct it.'

There was a sigh from the other side of the desk. 'Ah, yes. Puddleducks. That's another thing. I gather from Gemma that you have been rather critical of the joint assemblies.' She gave him a reproachful look.

'I have to say that she's been rather hurt by your behaviour.'

Nonsense! Well, not nonsense about the hurt bit, obviously, because women's emotions were a mystery unto themselves. But Gemma's complaint about his attitude to their assemblies was nonsensical. 'I simply feel that the appearance by a failed *Britain's Best Talent* participant, who also happened to be a friend of Miss Merryfield, didn't seem particularly pertinent.'

'Really?' Beryl's glasses were eyeing him coldly. 'You don't think it's an example of how someone can get to the finals – even if she didn't win – and then go on to make a success out of her life?'

Joe shifted from side to side in his seat. When she put it that way, it did indeed seem reasonable.

'Then there was the unfortunate matter of the Parents' Social when you had a little too much to drink, which presumably triggered that rather unfortunate scene between you and your wife.'

'Ex-wife,' he said weakly. 'Ed's my ex-wife. I keep telling people that but no one will believe me.'

Beryl's face showed that she was one of the disbelievers too. 'Your personal life is your own affair, Joe, provided you don't let it interfere with your professional one, which sadly is exactly what happened. All in all, I'm afraid that so far, your first term hasn't been what we'd all hoped. I need to write my staff reports this half-term and I am afraid, Joe, that I will be suggesting in yours that you might like to consider your position.'

Had he heard her correctly?

'I can see from your face that this has come as a shock.' Beryl's voice was oozing with sympathy, which made him feel worse. 'Maybe I have been a bit hard. Supposing you and I have another talk about your teaching skills at Christmas. Perhaps that will give you more time to get used to our ways out here in Hazelwood.'

Consider his position? Joe was still seething as he leaped on to his bike. Thank God he'd been able to give up the crutches so he could ride again.

Another talk about his teaching skills?

Did Beryl know what she was on about?

He, Joe Balls, had more experience of the real world than any of them put together. And that was exactly what they needed! A good dollop of the real world to prepare children for what was out there. That was why he had got on so well at the inner-city primary, and that was why he had been asked to come here.

How dare they?

Joe's anger propelled him down the motorway towards Lyme Regis in almost half the time it usually took. Not because he broke the speed limit, because he couldn't have coped if he was responsible for killing someone. There had been enough of that already. No. He got there when it was just about light because he was too angry to have his usual halfway break.

'Uncle Joe, Uncle Joe!'

Fraser and Charlie were sitting on the stone wall outside Mermaid's Nook, waiting for him.

'Are you coming to the beach with us?'

'We've got a whole week off school!'

'Fraser broke the kite you gave us in the summer.'

'No I didn't.'

'Ouch. That hurt. Have you brought us a present?'

'Boys!' Lynette's clear voice sang out of the front door as she came to greet him. 'That's so rude. Joe, I'm sorry.'

She brushed his cheek and he got a lovely whiff of her perfume, which reminded him of a scent his mother used to wear.

'Come on in and take your gear off. Boys, give Uncle Joe a bit of time before we head down to the beach for an evening walk. He looks exhausted!' She took Joe's arm in the old familiar way. 'Mike's doing a bit of extra teaching.' Dropping her voice, Lynette added, 'We could do with some extra money, to be honest.' Then she spoke more normally. 'But Dad will be back by supper and then I thought we'd have a game of charades.'

Boring, boring, thought Joe.

'Boring, boring,' chorused the boys.

Lynette laughed. 'Thought you might say that. OK, the option is an extra half-hour on Facebook while Dad and I catch up with your godfather.' She spoke softly again to him. 'Not to mention a large glass of wine. I meant it when I said you look all in. What on earth has happened? It's not Ed again, is it?'

Joe had always been able to talk to Lynette. At times he could kick himself for not having got in there at university before Mike had made his move, but this wasn't a thought he was proud of. Anyway, the sort of platonic friendship he had with Lynette was the type that lasted longer than many marriages, which was why he found it so easy to tell her about his conversation with Beryl as they walked down to the beach.

'Joe, that's awful.' Lynette squeezed his arm. 'You must be really upset.'

He nodded, watching the boys skim pebbles into the sea as they walked along the shore. It was so peaceful here. So far removed from everything.

'Do you think, however, that Beryl has a point?' continued Lynette gently. 'Don't get me wrong but you have always been, well, rather politically correct, wouldn't you say?' She pinched his arm playfully. 'Don't put on your grumpy look! We admire you, Mike and I. But to try and ban two traditions that have been very important to this pre-school, well, that's a pretty big thing, isn't it? Especially when you're only in the first term of your job.'

Joe felt a stirring of unease. Now she put it that way, he didn't feel quite so sure of himself.

'I'm beginning to wonder,' he said in a voice that came out all cracked, as though he had sand in his throat, 'if I'm cut out for teaching after all. To be honest, I was getting itchy feet even at the other school, but I don't know if I could go back to banking.'

'Know what I'd do?' Lynette took his arm again. 'It might sound a bit crazy, but hear me out. In my view, there are three things you could do.'

When she'd finished, it seemed like such a good, sensible plan that he was filled with even more affection for her, and for Mike and the boys, the latter by now specks on the beach far ahead.

'Thank you.' He bent down to give her a warm

cuddle but somehow as he aimed for her cheek, their mouths touched. Hers was so soft. So warm. So comforting. Exactly as he had imagined back in their university days.

Lynette pulled away immediately, and too late he could see from the flush on her face that he should have done the same.

'I'm sorry.' He was covered in confusion. 'I didn't mean that.'

'I know.' Lynette's flush had developed into a bright red spot on either cheek, and she was smoothing down her beautiful hair which was so like his ex-wife's. 'It's OK. I think we ought to head back.' She began walking briskly on ahead. 'Mike should be home by now.'

Chapter 31

Stupid, stupid, stupid, Joe told himself as he sped home at the end of the weekend. Lynette had been courteously distant during his stay, while Mike had been his usual jolly self.

What should he do? Lynette was bound to say something to her husband after he'd gone: they always said they didn't keep anything from each other. Should he come clean and tell Mike that he hadn't meant to kiss his wife in that way, and that it was merely to show gratitude?

Or should he pretend it had never happened?

Either way, he was in deep shit as Ed would say, both in his personal life and at work. Still, Lynette's suggestions, all three of them, were good ones, so he might as well start with the first. After all, half-term wasn't over yet so he had enough time, despite the amount of planning and marking that awaited him.

It was merely academic though. Because he'd decided now. He'd hand in his notice at Christmas. And then he'd think about his future outside the classroom.

The following day he still didn't feel any better. What was wrong with him? he asked himself. Why was he having so many problems with people? Gemma, whom he'd succeeded in rubbing up the wrong way. Beryl, who clearly didn't rate him any more (although inexplicably, it was Gemma whom he felt more upset about). Ed, whom he couldn't seem to move on from. And now his best friends Lynette and Mike. He'd really screwed up there and no mistake.

You need to talk to someone, urged a voice in his head. But who? There was only one person he thought might understand. How sad that after all these years, he had to go to an old man whom he barely knew for comfort.

After a quick phone call, Joe found himself knocking on Brian's door clutching the mandatory bottle of whisky and packet of Bourbon biscuits.

'Come on in, lad,' Brian said, waving away Joe's apologies. 'It's good to see someone. This early-retirement stuff is getting a bit dull, I don't mind telling you. I could do with the company.'

Following him in, Joe sat down in the chair opposite Brian's and found himself spilling it all out. 'So you can see my problem,' he said when he'd finished. He hadn't meant to include the Lynette business, but had found it coming out along with everything else. Brian was a good listener. There was something about him which enabled one to ignore the maroon jumper with holes in the elbows and the creased cream antimacassar on the back of his chair, which actually looked as though it had been washed since his last visit. Brian had a presence which, thought Joe ashamedly, he hadn't given the bloke credit for when they'd first met.

'Mmmm.' Brian took a draw of his pipe. Smoking had been banned from the fourteenth floor for so long that Joe had been astounded when Brian had started smoking in front of him without asking his permission first, but now he was feeling strangely drawn to it himself. The tobacco had a fragrant woody smell that reminded him of his father's factory. He had loved to squat on the floor there during the rare occasions he was allowed in, and play banking while his father did something hot and steamy with machines.

'I can see what you're up against. Mind you, I do think Beryl needs taking down a peg or two. Always was too big for her boots. Needs to see the bigger picture, if you ask me.' He took another draw. 'She applied for the headship at the same time as me, but I reckon they gave it to her because they hadn't had a woman before.' Another draw. 'Political correctness, eh?'

Joe was beginning to feel dizzy from the smoke.

'You know that modern idea about not sweating the small stuff? How parents should ignore minor bad behaviour and concentrate on what's really worth making a stand for? I reckon that's what you need to do here. If you really feel that Halloween is outmoded and irrelevant rather than a bit of silly fun, ban the dressing-up assembly. Good luck with doing the same for the nativity play, mind you. On the other hand, you have a point with the maths. Puddleducks do need a bit more help if you ask me, even though they're meant to learn through play. Has its pros and cons in my book. And they need someone who's good with figures.' He winked. 'I used to be, but not that kind.'

Joe was clearly expected to laugh then. Brian had already suggested that before marriage to Mavis, he'd been a bit of a 'ladies' man'. So he obliged with a quick smile.

'I also reckon,' continued Brian, puffing happily, 'that your friend's ideas are good ones. Gems, in fact. Might be just the ticket to put life in perspective. As for the lady herself, know what I'd do?'

In some ways, this was the worst dilemma of all. Joe didn't know what he'd do without his two best friends. They meant more to him than Ed ever had. 'Keep mum, that's what I'd do.' Brian was tapping the side of his blue-veined nose in a gesture that suggested they were in the secret service instead of his front room with its dusty china ornaments on the mantelpiece, and the television which had seen better days. 'I don't reckon she'll say anything to her husband in case he thinks she gave you the come-on.'

Joe couldn't help feeling impressed. 'You sound remarkably knowledgeable on such matters, if you don't mind me saying!'

'I am, lad, I am. What do you think I do with all my spare time?' He indicated a women's magazine on the dusty pile next to him. 'Belonged to my wife, these did. She used to keep them; never was one for throwing stuff out. Now I reckon I know more about women's minds than I ever did.' He gave Joe another wink, but one that wasn't quite so sparkly. 'Only wish I'd done it when she was alive. Might have understood her better. By the way, come up with an idea for that bank competition yet?'

Joe shook his head. 'Puddleducks are doing some kind of mural, but I'm still trying to think of something cutting-edge for Reception.'

Brian nodded in a satisfied way. 'Thought as much.

So happens that I had a bit of an idea the other night when I couldn't sleep. What do you think of this?'

No doubt about it, Joe told himself excitedly as he got out at Embankment. It was a corker. Their book, Brian had explained, would be a compendium of advice from both the old Reception head and the new one. They could write alternate chapters or maybe, as Joe had chipped in, make it more readable for certain parents by having one gem of wisdom on each page-length section.

Then they'd both got the next idea almost at the same time. They could ask parents and children to add their pennyworth. The result would be a book called *MY SKOOL!* Joe himself hadn't been so keen on the intentional misspelling or the exclamation mark, but Brian insisted it made it more contemporary. For his part, Joe knew of some websites which could print the book at a reasonable cost, and after the competition they could sell copies to raise money for school equipment.

Joe's spine began to tingle in the way it had when he'd first entered a classroom as a newly qualified mature teacher. He had wanted to start work on the book then and there in Brian's front room. If nothing else, it would prove to that headmistress that he was capable of working as a team.

On the other hand, he still couldn't get rid of that horrible voice in his head that kept asking him if he really was cut out to be a teacher. There were, as Lynette had told him, two ways to find out, and he was standing in front of the first right now.

Joe came to a halt outside the huge blue-glass building that housed thousands of two-legged ants, each chained to their computer and New York hours, not to mention whopping mortgages. They'd changed the doors since he had worked here. They were revolving now, rather like his head.

'Name?'

They'd also changed the receptionist, but of course they would have done. It had been four years since he'd thrown in the towel, much to everyone's surprise, and joined the mature graduate teacher-training scheme that was being advertised in *The Times*.

What a hero he'd felt at the time! It made Joe crawl with embarrassment to think of the self-congratulatory way in which he'd announced to Ed and his colleagues that he was giving up a six-figure salary to do something meaningful. The fact that this came just after he'd discovered Ed's betrayal was something, he had told himself, that was pure coincidence.

Now, as Joe pressed the button for the fourteenth floor, he felt a flutter of excitement. Garth, his old boss, had been surprised to hear from him, and clearly curious. Curious enough, in fact, to look up from his desk instead of talking with his eyes still on the screen.

'Joe! Great to see you.'

This was Garth? Joe nearly hadn't recognised him. Rather as Blair had aged during his years in power, so had Garth, with hair that was almost completely grey instead of being merely peppered. His face had sagged, too, and he had huge pools of soft-looking flesh under his eyes.

'I would suggest lunch, but it's been mad here.' He

glanced at the other occupants of the sixty-odd desks around him, each one speaking loudly and urgently into their headphones or stabbing their keyboard.

'You probably heard about the Footsie. Tokyo's gone mad. Stark raving mad. Listen mate, I don't want to be rude but I've got about . . .' He checked his watch. 'Roughly 2.78 minutes. How are you doing?'

Fine, thanks. Better than you lot, Joe wanted to add. How could he possibly have spent ten years in this place? Why hadn't he gone stark raving mad too? Nothing, not even the Audi convertible, the bonus, the Savile Row shirts (which he'd had to have sent in by taxi sometimes when he'd been working too hard to get home at night) could ever compensate for this hamster wheel.

The thought of hamsters made him smile as he recalled that trip to the vet with Gemma's arms around his waist. He'd felt a strange thrill then, not because of her arms of course, but because he had been doing something different, almost knight-like.

'Don't regret your decision then?' said Garth, his eyes moving back to his screen. 'Listen, if you want to hang around for a bit, I might be able to get out for ten minutes or so for a bite.'

'How long might that be?'

'Say three to four hours? I might have a window then, although that does depend on New York and San Francisco.'

Clever woman, this Lynette, Brian had said admiringly when Joe had told him that a trip to the fourteenth floor had been her idea. 'Sometimes,' she had said, 'we need a trip down memory lane to remind us that what we think we've missed isn't worth missing at all.'

The question was, would he feel the same way about BlackEnd Primary, his first and only school before Corrybank? Joe's first impression, as he picked his way through the used condoms and discarded matchboxes towards the reception, was that there wasn't a community police car outside any more.

There were three.

The police presence in his day had been necessary when the kids started threatening each other. On more than one occasion, this had involved knives, and not just in the classroom. There had been one Parents' Evening when a mother had been escorted out in handcuffs.

'Fuck off!'

A boy who could be no more than eight or nine pushed past him, knocking him against the glass door that led to the reception. At first Joe thought the expletive was directed at him, but then he realised that it had been hurled at Tim, the French teacher who had also been a mature graduate.

Tim did a double take. 'Joe? Good to see you.' His face was red and covered in perspiration. 'Heard you were paying us a visit.' He was panting, clearly with the effort of having chased the child, who had now probably legged it through the council estate next door. Joe had had several such chases himself. How could he have forgotten?

'What did he do?'

'Jason? Nicked someone's dinner money again.

Apparently he was feeling peckish because there wasn't any breakfast in the house, or dinner last night either. No point telling the men outside in blue uniform. I'd rather save it for something more important. Anyway, come on in, mate. You've come at a good time. The canteen should be open.' He rolled his eyes. 'We have to share it now with the kids. Cutbacks, you know.'

Since starting at Corrybank, Joe had told Beryl on several occasions that they ought to have a canteen instead of having to eat their sandwiches in the staffroom. Now, as he picked his way through a small piece of battered, plastic-tasting fish in a room which reverberated with noise from both teachers and pupils alike, he had a sudden yearning for the quiet polite chit-chat of Corrybank staffroom.

'Bloody hell.' Tim's language had become much more colourful since he'd last seen him. 'Don't say O'Riley is back? Thought he'd been packed off to the primary school equivalent of 'Young Offenders'.

A woman whom Joe vaguely recognised leaned towards them. 'He was, but he's out now. Not for long, I shouldn't think. Oi. O'Riley. Watch what you're doing with that fork!'

How old was he? Nine or ten at the most? The boys of his age at Corrybank were more likely to be fishing in the canal than stabbing someone with a fork, which was why O'Riley had previously been in trouble.

'I admire you,' Joe told Tim, pushing his fish to one side. 'You're doing a great job.'

Tim gave a short laugh. 'That's what I thought when I started. Now I know better. You know, Joe, there are some people who can take this kind of life and others who can't. I've decided I'm one of the latter. Between you and me, I'm applying for something quieter, a bit like your place. Somewhere that's not too far from London but just far enough for us to bring up the kids in a nice calm environment.'

But what about all their ideas of contributing to society? Fiery ideas which he and Tim had shared when they had come here?

Tim gritted his teeth as a couple of girls went past, pushing his chair with sarcastic Sorreee Sirs. 'I think you were right to bail out.'

Bail out? Was that what everyone had thought when he'd taken the job at Corrybank? Had he really gone soft? That wasn't Joe Balls. That wasn't the man who was proud of what Ed had unkindly referred to as 'ridiculously outdated morals'.

Joe's mouth tightened as he walked back past the community police cars and towards the Tube. That was it then. He'd hand in his notice at Christmas and apply to a school like this.

Some things, like Puddleducks and all its issues, just weren't worth the effort. Not like kids who knew no better than fighting with forks, until someone helped them see the light.

And maybe, just maybe, that person might be him.

THE PUDDLEDUCKS PLAYGROUP NEWSLETTER NOVEMBER ISSUE

Thanks to everyone for making the Halloween Dressing-Up Day such a great success!

We hope everyone will be able to join us for our sparkler tea party on November 5th, which will be held in conjunction with Reception year.

On November 27th, there will be a combined trip with Reception to a local farm. Please provide a packed lunch for your Puddleduck.

Please note that the Nativity Play will be going ahead, despite rumours that it might be cancelled. If anyone has any spare pillowcases that they don't want back, please contact either Gemma or Bella.

Thank you, everyone!

Finally, here's one more song to practise.

THE PUDDLEDUCKS TIDYING-UP SONG

We are the little Puddleducks
Sometimes we make a mess!
We spill things on our trousers
Or make marks on a dress.
But that really doesn't matter
So long as we tidy up.
We always put our toys away
And wash up every cup!

Chapter 32

It was amazing she could still function after what she'd learned about Danny and his American mother, whom she'd felt so sorry for at the beginning of term.

Now, to her shame, Gemma found she was jealous of this quiet, unassuming woman with the twangy American accent and plainish face, despite her new, softer hairstyle.

This Nancy Carter Wright had achieved what Gemma hadn't been able to. She'd persuaded Sam to give her a baby! And that hurt. Really hurt.

Automatically Gemma touched the silver chain round her neck that Sam had given her all those years ago, and watched the November Puddleducks newsletter flying into cyberspace ready for term next week. She'd already posted copies to the few parents who weren't online, grudgingly conceding to herself that Joe's email suggestion had indeed saved money.

Meanwhile, it was still half-term and try as she had to divert her thoughts about Sam with the newsletter, there was something else niggling away at the back of her mind. Something that she had seen with her own eyes, just a few days ago.

It was Joe – Joe kissing a tall, pretty woman with long, flowing auburn hair, on the beach, even though she had seen him, only last week, walking along Hazelwood high street with the tall, red-haired, legs-up-to-her-armpits wife or ex-wife (depending on whose gossip you listened to in the staffroom) clinging on to his arm and talking urgently.

What a rat!

Part of her hadn't been surprised to see him on the beach. Hadn't she heard him tell someone that he was going to visit great friends in Lyme Regis, or, as she and the other locals called it, Lyme?

Strictly speaking, Gemma wasn't that local. Her seaside home town was about forty minutes away, and it would have been simpler, when she was driving back for that half-term duty family visit, to have stayed on the motorway. But then the petrol light on Granny's Morris Minor came on, even though the fuel indicator had cheerily promised that she had at least a quarter of a tank left. So, not wanting to take risks, she had come off and filled up.

Then, because she'd been missing the sea for so long (the canal in Hazelwood simply wasn't the same), she'd decided to take the coastal route home. Nothing at all, she told herself firmly, to do with wondering if she might see Joe. Nothing to do with the fact that she was slightly curious to see what he was like out of school, and whether his friends were as stuck-up and aloof and set in their ways as he was.

And that was when she'd spotted them. Her first thought had been that the woman was really pretty, and nearer Joe's age than hers. At least ten years older than her, anyway, although why she was even bothering to compare ages, she really didn't know.

Then two children had come running back along the beach, and her heart had done a funny acrobatic dance. Joe was dating a single mother! Or maybe she was still married and he was having an affair. From the way those boys were dancing around him, pulling him down to the shore to skim pebbles, they certainly liked him.

Goodness, thought Gemma, pulling in without meaning to, and looking at the scene from a safe distance, Joe Balls, he of the stern 'nativity plays are politically incorrect' school, was actually laughing and cavorting around like they did during Pyjama Drama!

Starting the engine, Gemma's eyes pricked with tears. Everyone else had children in their lives. How did she, who had wanted kids for as long as she could remember, get to the grand old age of almost twenty-seven without a baby?

Clearly this was a topic that had been on her parents' minds. Almost as soon as she got through the front door of the tall white semi-detached Regency villa where she had grown up, only a ten-minute walk from the sea, the polite questioning began.

'So lovely to see you, darling.' Her mother's arms enveloped her, and Gemma felt a rush of love and nostalgia for Granny, who had been so like her daughter, Gemma's mother. 'You didn't bring anyone with you, then?'

Every time she came down, her mother would ask the same question, as though Gemma could somehow magic someone from out of the air.

She could almost see it now. Actually, she would say, I've brought Sam. Remember him? The love of

270

my life who just happens to be married, or as good as, to the mother of a child in my class at Puddleducks. That would certainly stop the questions!

Dinner wasn't too bad, with Gemma trying to steer the conversation towards her job rather than her personal goings-on, and her parents telling her all about her older sister Patsy out in Sydney who was expecting again.

'Isn't that wonderful?' enthused her mother, who then actually got up in the middle of the meal (something which had always been a no-no when she'd lived at home) to find the latest photograph of Patsy, looking so serenely pregnant that Gemma found herself feeling horribly jealous.

Even her father, who rarely showed emotion, was nodding as he tucked into his apple pie. 'We're going out to see them in the summer. Did we tell you?' He gave her mother an affectionate look. 'Yes, I know I've always said I wouldn't go on a long flight, but someone in this room twisted my arm. It will be so lovely to see them all again.'

'It doesn't seem so long ago since we were all sitting round the table as a family,' said her mother with a catch in her voice. She tried to smile. 'It's so difficult to get you lot to do that nowadays.'

Her father cut in. 'Fiona and David are at medical school, dear, not a kindergarten. They don't have time to come home.'

Gemma stiffened. 'Puddleducks isn't a kindergarten, Dad. It's a playgroup, and it's actually not that easy for me to get back here either.'

Her mother gave her an anxious 'please don't annoy

him' look. 'We know that, darling, and we're so thrilled to see you, especially now Tom has been posted so far away. Every time I listen to the news I get a funny feeling, and it's always such a relief when it gets to the end and they haven't reported something horrible. When you were young I used to think I was going to go mad with all the noise, especially after the twins were born, but now I'd give anything to have those years back again. The house seems so quiet now, doesn't it, dear?'

For a minute, the table fell silent. Gemma knew exactly what her mother meant. It had been wonderful growing up in a lively noisy family: in fact, it had been another reason why she had chosen to work with young children. But Mum was right. Everything *had* changed now.

Gemma watched her father's hand reach out for her mother's and squeeze it. The unusually caring gesture made her feel quite lonely. Tom was her brother too, and she worried about him as well. Suddenly wanting to make her mother feel better, she took a deep breath. 'Talking of Tom, I've met someone,' she said casually.

Her mother's head jerked up with a keen, almost bird-like interest, and immediately Gemma knew she should have stayed quiet. Now it would lead to the grand inquisition!

'Another teacher?' Her mother's eyes were positively ablaze with curiosity. 'Is it that man Joe whom you've mentioned in your calls?'

'No.' Gemma felt a flash of annoyance. 'He's called Barry and he's in the paratroopers.'

Her mother looked as though she was going to leap out of her chair with excitement. 'That's wonderful news. Isn't it, Dick?'

Don't start talking wedding bells yet, Gemma wanted to say. 'He's the son of my landlady and he's home for a few weeks.'

Her father, who still wore a suit at dinner even though he was retired, nodded gravely. 'I presume he can't tell you where he's going.'

'No.' Gemma took a large slug of red in preparation for the next predictable question. Was it worth committing yourself to someone who was away a lot? That was what her mother would ask.

'Darling?'

'Mmmm.'

'I was wondering. Please don't think I'm interfering. But is it worth committing yourself to someone who is away a lot? I just don't want to see you hurt again, that's all. I know how long it's taken you to get over . . .'

That was it. She couldn't bear to hear his name mentioned. It wasn't fair. It just wasn't fair. There she was, having searched, although not very hard it had to be admitted, for her teenage sweetheart, only to find that his partner and child had turned up on her doorstep.

'I'm sorry, Gemmie.' Her mother put a comforting hand across the table. 'We didn't mean to upset you, did we, Dick?'

Her father was still looking grave and had actually put down his pudding spoon. Not a good sign. 'I have to say, Gemma, that I do think your life might have turned out differently if you had followed my advice after university. You got a First, my dear. Surely you can do better than working in a playgroup?'

Her mother made the sort of sound she used to make when they'd been young and her father had been overstrict. 'I don't think that's very fair, Dick.'

Too right. Gemma stood up. 'I'm sorry you feel like that, Dad. I happen to love my job. And as for finding Mr Right, maybe I never will. Perhaps I'll hook up with a turkey baster instead.'

And with that, she flounced out of the room up to her bedroom to write the nativity script, feeling like a child about to do her homework.

Chapter 33

All that was four days ago, but the memories were still as fresh and hurtful as they had been then. Gemma had made up with her mother on the phone, but as for her father, she felt it was up to him to apologise.

Now, back in her own room at Joyce's (how lovely to feel safe with her own bits around her, especially as the rat next door was away for half-term), she continued working on the nativity script. After Joe's constant criticisms of everything she did at Puddleducks, she was determined that this year's performance should be particularly good.

'Gemma?' There was a knock on the door.

Even though she had told herself not to be too hopeful, her heart leaped.

'It's me. Barry. Have you got a minute?'

Hastily running a hand through her hair, she glanced in the mirror. Panda eyes! She always got them when she was working, thanks to her habit of rubbing her eyes when she was trying to concentrate. Too bad. He'd have to take her as he found her.

'Hi.' She opened the door a crack.

His eyes went straight to her smudged mascara. 'You weren't having an early night, were you?'

She laughed. 'I wish. Actually I was trying to work out how three small stars, three not-so-wise men including one who won't remove his dummy, a hyper-active ox and a plastic Baby Jesus could manage to last for thirty minutes on stage without having an argument or forgetting their lines.'

Barry grinned. He had a nice grin, she decided. One that was warm and crinkly and friendly. 'Is it possible for the scriptwriter to take an hour off? Because if so, I've arranged a bit of a last-minute surprise.'

'A surprise?' She felt that mixture of excitement and panic when someone threw something at you out of the blue. 'But I'm not dressed for it!'

'You don't know what it is yet,' pointed out Barry. 'Just wear something warm.' He glanced down at her blue spotted pyjamas which she always wore when she was working on the bed because it was comfort-able. 'Those will do, if you want.'

Was he joking?

'OK.' She'd take him at her word. Any man who seriously didn't mind a woman with panda eyes and a duffle coat over her jim-jams had to be special. Sam, she remembered, had always liked it when she'd dressed up. A fat lot of good that had done her.

'Where are we going?' she asked as they went down the stairs.

'You'll see.' Barry took her hand and it felt nice. 'It's only a short walk.'

It looked as though they were heading for the canal, past the evening dog-walkers including Toby's dad, who gave her a cheery 'Good evening', and glanced with curiosity at her companion. He thought Barry was her date! Gemma felt a thrill go through her. Well, maybe he was.

They reached the towpath and began to walk past the canal boats, some of them lit up inside with warm cosy kitchens glowing through the windows. Now the clocks had changed, making the evenings earlier, the visible interiors of the boats seemed even more attractive in the dark. One couple were sitting opposite each other at a small table, eating, and Gemma's heart leaped again in envy. It would be so cosy to have someone to be with; someone to talk to. Even the grumpy Joe had a wife or ex-wife or whatever she was, who was clearly still keen to share his company.

As on her previous walk here with Barry, she enjoyed looking at the boats' names. *Miranda's Boy* sounded almost mermaid-like, the boat itself painted turquoise, with gold scrolls. There were two children's bikes propped up outside, and inside she could see a small girl doing a jigsaw with her brother. Maybe they were away on an end-of-half-term holiday. A pang of longing for the old, noisy days of her own childhood passed through her. She'd give almost anything, thought Gemma, to recreate that with children of her own.

'Here we are!' Barry stood next to a small red canal boat with *Wanderlust* painted on it in flamboyant midnight-blue lettering. He held out a firm, steady hand. 'Let me welcome you aboard!'

She stood in wonder, staring at it. 'It's yours?'

'Not exactly.' He grinned as though pleased at her stunned reaction. 'Belongs to a friend of mine from round here. He's lent it to me. Mmm.' He pretended to sniff the air. 'Smells like dinner's ready.'

Pinching herself, Gemma jumped on board. Inside

was a galley kitchen with two plates of smoked salmon, out-of-season new potatoes and asparagus with hollandaise sauce, on a table already laid for two.

'Who cooked the meal?' she asked, looking around.

Barry handed her a glass of something sparkly. 'I'd like to say that it's one I prepared earlier but actually it's a certain supermarket's finest, courtesy of the microwave.'

'This is amazing!' Looking around, she could hardly believe it. It was like one of those films where the heroine just happened to step into an empty boat and find a banquet, not to mention a handsome hero. Then she felt a twinge of regret. 'If only I'd known we were going out to dinner, I'd have dressed up!'

'Nonsense.' Barry was eyeing her approvingly. 'You look lovely as you are. In fact, one of the things I like so much about you, Gemma, is that you just don't realise how lovely you are.'

Help! Kitty had always accused her of not being able to handle compliments, and she was right.

Sensing her awkwardness, Barry invited her to sit down. He raised his glass. 'Here's to us,' he said. 'And may there be many more evenings like this.' His face became serious. 'I like being with you, Gemma. I really do.'

His words made her tingle with expectation. This was so romantic! It had been so long since she'd gone on a date (partly through her own choice and partly through the lack of opportunity) that she wasn't sure if she was acting in the right way. 'Don't be too eager,' Kitty had always said, but she couldn't help it.

'I like being with you too, Barry.' Then she took a

huge slug of wine to try and hide the fact that she was blushing all over her face and goodness knows where else.

After dinner, during which they talked non-stop about his life in the paratroopers, Puddleducks, his family and hers, where they had gone to school and uni, Barry suggested they sat outside. As she stepped over the bit that led up to the deck, he held out his hand so she wouldn't fall. The touch of his skin made her tingle all over again. It was so nice to feel looked after for a change!

He also insisted on draping a large brown rug over both of them as they sat sipping coffee outside the boat, watching others walk by. She'd always felt envious of boat owners in the evening, sitting there so cosily: a silent fleet who could, if they wished, set sail the next day. And now she was one of them! It made her feel special and for a moment, she was reminded of the princess outfit at Puddleducks.

'Does your friend take his boat out on trips?' she asked, trailing a finger in the water as a swan glided by with its downy cygnets.

Barry nodded. 'He said he'd lend it to us next summer if we want.' His eyes seemed to be searching hers carefully for a reaction. 'That's how long I'm going to be away for, you see. I won't be back until at least June, so I would understand if you felt that was too long to wait.'

Gemma shivered with something she hadn't felt for so long that she almost didn't recognise it. It was that delicious mixture of apprehension and excitement because the person you liked also clearly liked you back.

But it was no good. Tell him, tell him, insisted the voice in her head. Granny had always been a stickler for the truth. You can't go on until you tell him. It wouldn't be fair.

'I'd love to go on a trip with you,' she said slowly, 'but it would definitely have to be after Christmas.' She took a deep breath. 'In fact, there's something I have to tell you.'

His eyes flickered and she recognised the feeling behind them. Apprehension. Fear. Just what she had felt nearly five years ago.

'If you'd asked me to go away with you right now, I would have had to say no. In fact, I nearly said no to tonight.'

Another flicker. 'Why?'

'Because,' said Gemma, looking out across the canal to the church with its tall spire piercing the night sky, 'because I'm a married woman.'

Chapter 34

Barry's shocked face instantly made her wish she hadn't said anything. If only she had waited a bit until they'd got to know each other better, he might have understood. Now, as she tried to explain about Sam, stumbling and repeating her words in her confusion, she told herself that she'd blown it.

Every now and then, while listening to her story, Barry nodded sharply, or looked away as though silently condemning her role in it all. It made her voice shake even more and it struck her that although she'd been so keen to criticise Joe about his ex-wife, she was in no position to do so. Hadn't she, too, given others the wrong impression about her own marital situation?

'So that,' she said finally after what seemed like an age, 'is how I ended up in the position I am in now.'

Barry looked at her in a way that made her determined not to turn away, in case he thought she was hiding any more unpalatable truths. 'I still don't understand some of this stuff. Why did you break up so soon after getting married? Did you have a row about something?'

She could see him trying to smile, and her heart leaped at the thought that maybe there was still hope, if he was still talking to her.

'A row? You could say that.' Her mouth had turned horribly dry, so her voice sounded cracked. What had turned out to be the perfect evening now looked as though it was going to be ruined, and it was all her fault. 'I told you that we continued backpacking through America after the wedding.'

He nodded.

'Well . . .' She faltered, making herself push out the words. 'By the time we reached San Francisco, I realised I was late.'

'Late?'

'*Late*,' repeated Gemma, emphasising the word. 'You know.' She looked away, embarrassed to be talking about something so personal with a man she had only known for a few weeks. 'I thought I was pregnant. Sam utterly freaked out. Said he'd never wanted kids and that I'd tricked him.'

Barry frowned. 'But you must have talked about having children before you got married?'

Exactly what Kitty had said at the time.

'Not really. I just presumed he'd want them. Doesn't everyone? Besides, like I said, we did it – got married, that is – on the spur of the moment, without talking things through like most couples do.'

Barry squeezed her hand. 'I won't think any the worse of you if you tell me that you had an . . .'

'Abortion?' Gemma felt a cold shaft shoot through her. 'I wouldn't do that. I can understand why some women do but personally, it's not for me.'

The lump in her chest got bigger. 'I had a late period a few days later. Afterwards, I was told it might have been a very early miscarriage. We had a terrible argument and then I walked out of our hotel room. I flew back home and never heard from him again. In fact, I didn't know where he was until a few weeks ago.'

Barry's eyebrows knitted in disapproval. 'Didn't he come after you to check you were all right?'

If only! Hadn't she spent weeks at Kitty's flat, hoping Sam would do exactly that? 'I managed by throwing myself into my teacher training. I didn't tell anyone, apart from my friend Kitty, that Sam and I had actually got married, because I felt so stupid. My family, well, Dad anyway, simply wouldn't have understood. The longer I left it, the harder it would have been to have said, hey, guess what, I got married a few years ago. Of course, I tried to get in touch with him to get a divorce through the university, but when I wrote to the forwarding address they gave me, it came back with a *Not Known Here* stamp.'

'What about his mother?'

Gemma thought of Patricia with the bird-like face and gimlet hooded eyes, who had observed her use the cutlery in the right way during a holiday visit in her second year and, rather surprisingly, announced her approval of their relationship before it had all gone wrong.

'I wrote to her, asking if she knew where Sam was, but she didn't. Apparently he was still backpacking. In fact, she had hoped I had news of him. He wasn't even on Facebook.'

Barry gave her the sort of look she gave to one of the children when they denied doing something they shouldn't have done. 'Nowadays, it's possible to find almost anyone. I suspect you let it slide because you were still partly in love with him and hoped he might come back of his own accord, declaring he was ready to start a family.'

How was it possible for someone she hardly knew to understand her so well?

'I fell in love with someone once who decided that our plans weren't a level playing field,' Barry went on quietly. 'For years I hoped she might change her mind, but she didn't.' His eyes took on a faraway expression for a minute, and then flickered back to her. 'There's one thing I still don't understand. You said earlier that you might come on a trip with me next summer, but you couldn't before Christmas. Why?'

'Because that's when I can get a divorce.' Gemma heard her voice rising in excitement. 'I've seen a lawyer in town and he said that even if I couldn't find Sam, I can start proceedings after five years. We're nearly there now. My decree nisi should be sorted by Christmas.'

A couple of dog walkers strolled past, and they paused until they'd gone. It was easy to forget, out here in the dark air, that there was anyone else around. Barry gave a big sigh. 'You mentioned his mother. How come you've seen her again?'

Gemma bit her lip. 'That's the other thing. Sam's son is in my class.'

'His son? But he said he didn't want children.'

'Exactly.' Her voice came out cracked, and she had to fight back the tears of betrayal. 'That's what was so awful. I left him because he'd said he didn't want children. But he *did*! He's got this lovely son with an American woman whom I like. Well, sort of like. Her surname is a mixture of her maiden name and Sam's surname. But according to his mother, they're not married even though she pretends they are.'

'Isn't that a bit odd?' He was frowning as though doubting her.

'Not really. Lots of women take their partner's surname when they have children, even today; I suppose it makes it easier.'

He didn't look convinced. 'And what about you? Do you still have feelings for Sam?'

He said the name in a voice heavy with disdain. He was jealous! Despite the awkwardness of it all, Gemma found herself feeling flattered.

'No,' she said, automatically reaching up and twisting her silver chain nervously. It felt cold to her touch, even though it had been next to her skin all day. 'And even if I did, I could never break up a family.'

He seemed to be weighing all this up in his mind. 'So you're sure you're over him?'

Gemma nodded tightly. Of course she was, she told herself. Those small stabs of doubt were natural. Everyone (well, most people) had the odd twinge when they finally broke out of a relationship. Her so-called marriage to Sam had been dead for years; as Kitty said, it was time she finally let it go.

'And how does *he* feel?'

Barry was clearly determined to know everything about the situation.

It was the question that Gemma had been asking

herself. 'I don't know. I haven't seen him. I only know about him now because his mother told me at Parents' Evening when she came instead of Nancy – that's Sam's wife, or rather not-wife.'

She stopped. For some reason, it gave her a funny taste in her mouth to say Nancy's name. Something told her that now was not the time to repeat what Patricia had said about Sam 'still holding a candle' for her.

Just at that moment, a heron swooped past them very low on the canal, landing on the water with a splash and breaking the silence which had descended on them.

'Wow.' Barry leaned back in his chair. 'What a story.'

Gemma nodded. Her mouth was dry from all the talking, but she felt lighter than she had for a very long time after releasing the secret that had been troubling her for years.

He reached out for her hand. 'I'm flattered you chose to confide in me.'

She flushed. 'I also needed to explain why I haven't allowed myself to have a meaningful relationship until now.'

Barry's face lit up. 'Until now? Does that mean you might consider it now?'

She paused. Barry was so kind! She felt a tingle every time he touched her. Yet he was going away. It would be another 'waiting' relationship, except that this time, he would be coming home. Providing he didn't get injured, that was.

'We don't really know each other yet,' she said, 'but . . .'

He leaned towards her. 'Let me finish that sentence for you. We don't really know each other yet, but one day we might have more time to do exactly that.'

One day, thought Gemma. One day. Is that really such a good idea?

But then he kissed her.

When Gemma went back to the playgroup after half-term, she was still reeling. 'You look wonderful,' remarked Clemmie's mother enviously. 'Have you been to a spa? I used to be a model for this really lovely one in Hertfordshire.'

A spa? Better than that, she wanted to say, thinking of the long evenings she and Barry had spent together after that incredible night on the boat. Once, when he got too close, she had reluctantly stopped him.

'Not until you're unmarried?' he had said in a quiet teasing tone, and she had nodded while feeling slightly silly. It wasn't just that she was not divorced yet. She had only known Barry for a short time and, even though he seemed almost too good to be true (so courteous, thoughtful, good-looking and steady), it didn't seem right to jump into bed with him. Not yet, anyway.

Meanwhile, she'd returned the necessary documents to the crisp woman solicitor in town whom she'd met on the day that she'd collided with Joe's bike. By the end of next January the degree absolute would be through, and then she'd be a free woman.

Thank goodness Sam was still abroad and she wouldn't have to see him. Thank goodness too for the second half of term at Puddleducks to distract her.

The first morning was almost as hectic as the first morning back in September. 'Mrs Merryfield, Mrs Merryfield, can I be a sheep in the nativity play? I can bleat really well. Listen. I've been practising.'

'Mrs Merryfield, Mrs Merryfield, my mum says it's silly just having sparklers. Can't we have rockets too for the firework tea party?'

'Mrs Merryfield, Mrs Merryfield, will there be chickens on the farm visit? Cos my mum says I'm allergic to eggs.'

'Mrs Merryfield, why do eggs go hard when you boil them?' (Good question, Sienna. Things often change when they are heated up.)

'Mrs Merryfield, have you heard about Danny?' asked Billy's mother, who usually wore clear braces on her teeth, although now they were noticeable by their absence. 'No Billy, not now. I'm talking.'

Heard about Danny? Gemma's heart froze. 'What's happened?'

'Billy, I'm telling you one more time. Stop it. He's got something called aplastic anaemia, poor mite. Not good. He's in hospital and his dad's flown back to be with him.'

Chapter 35

It was so quiet on the children's ward. Nancy sat in the chair by the side of Danny's bed and listened to the quiet rustling sounds as the night nurses glided about, speaking in hushed tones to the patients who needed something. A glass of water here. A painkiller there. Quiet words of reassurance for both a child who was whimpering and a parent whose low urgent questions punctured the darkness.

Danny lay fast asleep in his favourite Thomas the Tank Engine pyjamas, his chest rising and falling gently. He seemed so small, so pale, so fragile. So reliant on this place.

Why, Nancy asked herself, wasn't she freaking out? She'd always been such a panicker, yet when Patricia had told Sam on the phone she'd called the GP because Danny kept falling asleep on his feet, she had felt a calm sense of unreality descending on her. She was the one who had taken the phone and grasped the mechanics of the situation, while Sam had gone to pieces.

She was the one who had sat calmly considering the facts and their implications on the seventeen-hour flight home. Sam, in the seat next to her, had kept asking her to go over her subsequent conversation with the doctor.

Danny had aplastic anaemia. It was a serious condition,

resulting from his bone marrow and stem cells not producing enough blood cells. Also known as bone marrow failure, it could develop over a long period of time or, as in Danny's case, suddenly and acutely.

Nancy repeated all this off pat. In a way, reciting the facts made her feel calmer, just as it had when she'd been revising for her high-school science exams.

Symptoms of aplastic anaemia, she'd explained to Sam, included bleeding gums. Poor Patricia had put that one down to Danny being overenthusiastic with the toothbrush song actions. Tiredness was another symptom, although she'd attributed that to Danny's new-found interest in football and also being exhausted after playgroup.

Nancy's tone became even more matter of fact when she continued to go through the facts. If she didn't pretend this was a case study in a textbook she would fall to bits, and then where would that leave Danny? Sam, by contrast, was gripping her arm and hanging on her every word as though recognising that this time, she was in charge.

Danny's illness could be treated by drugs and blood transfusions. If that didn't work, bone marrow transplants were the only hope. Usually the best matches were from parents or close relatives.

One of the first things they did, after arriving at the hospital where the GP had sent their son, was to get tested for suitability as donors. They were still waiting for the results. Nancy's mother was flying in from the States at the end of the week to be with them, and to be tested herself. 'I want to help, dear,' she'd said on the phone, her voice quivering.

So did everyone. As Nancy sat by her son's side in the hospital, she counted once more the huge number of colourful get-well cards which the little Puddleducks had made. There was even one from Tracy's mum (which was generous, given her unfortunate mistake over the 'bump') as well as Doug the mosaics tutor, all dwarfed by the giant teddy that Patricia, who seemed to be blaming herself, had brought in.

'I thought he was just a bit run-down dear, after his first half-term at playgroup. So I didn't take much notice when he kept falling asleep on the sofa.'

Nancy had reassured her, promising that she didn't hold her responsible in any way. If anything, she said, it had been her who should have noticed.

Still, there was no point in blaming herself or others. They needed to concentrate on the here and now. Right at this moment, that meant waiting to see if the recent transfusion was having any effect.

The consultant, a lovely bear of a man in his fifties who was, Sam kept saying as though to reassure himself, old enough to be experienced but young enough to be aware of new developments, hoped that they might know how the treatment was progressing by the end of the week.

Meanwhile, she couldn't bear to leave Danny's side. Nor could Sam. Nancy's doubts about her 'husband's' commitment to parenthood had been put to one side when watching him cradling his boy in his arms and telling him to imagine that his body was a fort containing lots of big brave soldiers.

'Imagine that they are fighting an army of evil monster germs in your blood,' he had said in a voice that had wobbled. 'Your soldiers are going to win. Trust me, Danny. They will.'

'Oh no.' Danny's face crumpled.

It was as though he was frightened that his father was going to tell him off, remembering Sam snapping at him for splashing water on the floor during his bath or not staying in his own bed at night.

'Monster germs!' He looked panic-stricken. 'Mum said I'd get them if I didn't wash my hands.'

No, Nancy had tried to explain, realising too late that she had fussed too much about insignificant stuff. It wasn't anything to do with washing hands. It was . . . what? One of those things? How did you explain a random, terrible illness to a child?

Now, as Nancy tried to get comfortable in the chair, she wondered how she and Sam would cope if anything happened to Danny. Her son was everything to her. More than Sam, if she was to be honest.

'Mummy?' Danny's long eyelashes flickered as his eyes slowly opened. He sounded so sleepy that she could barely hear him. Carefully, so as not to knock him, she pulled back the corner of the duvet and slid into bed with him, wrapping her arm around his thin shoulders.

'Yes, darling?'

His voice came out all breathy. 'Do people eat cornflakes in heaven for breakfast?'

Nancy's chest felt as though it was going to cave in on itself.

'Why, darling?'

His warm hand crept out and squeezed hers. 'Cos Granny said if I didn't eat my cornflakes, I wouldn't grow big and strong. Is that why I might go to heaven? Cos I'm not going to be big and strong?'

Nancy bit her lip. Sometimes a parent had to be economical with the truth. 'Of course not. Now, why don't I tell you a story?'

Danny nodded. 'A story about a dog. A black dog with a kink in its tail.'

Nancy hugged him gently. How ironic. She had texted Toby's dad only that morning to see if Pongo the kinky-tailed puppy was still available. If so, she would have bought him there and then. Anything to see Danny smile again. But he had been sold to a couple who had apparently been looking for a dog just like him, kinky tail and all.

'OK, then,' she began. 'Once upon a time, there was a dog with a funny bend in its tail.'

Danny moved under the covers. 'Not *its* tail. *His* tail. Pongo's a boy, like me.'

Nancy smiled in the half-light spreading out from the nurses' office at the end of the ward. 'OK. With a funny bend in his tail.'

Danny's voice was sleepy but firm. 'No, Mummy. Start again. Begin with "Once upon a time."'

Before this, Nancy would have got irritated. Now she couldn't help admiring her son for his preciseness. She had been exactly the same as a child, according to her mother. Maybe it was a sign that he was going to be a scientist too when he grew up.

If he grew up.

'Once upon a time,' she began again, 'there was a black dog with a kink in his tail. And do you know how he got that kink?'

No answer.

Nancy felt her heart lurch. Was he still breathing? His chest was only just rising and falling, but there was a definite low steady warm breath on her arms. She held him gently, protecting him from whatever evil she could.

'Do you know why Pongo had a kink in his tail?' she repeated.

Still no answer. Danny had fallen asleep again. Nancy felt a sickening realisation. His earlier chit-chat about cornflakes and dogs with kinks in their tails had fooled her into thinking that he was getting better. But he wasn't. He was sleeping more and more. As she watched his chest rise and fall so slightly that she had to rest her hand on his body to feel it, fear encompassed her, and a line of sweat trickled down her back.

What would they do if, one day, he simply didn't wake up?

Chapter 36

By the end of the week, they had fallen into a routine that made Nancy feel they had always lived this way. It struck her that she had led a very privileged and lucky life until now, not thinking what it was like for families with sick children, living in a sterile environment often far from home, while hanging on to every thread of hope that was offered to them. And now she was one of them.

Their days were all much the same. She would sleep by Danny's bed at night and Sam, who had been given compassionate leave from work, would arrive in the morning after getting the train in from Hazelwood. It would have been much easier if Danny had been at the big local hospital, but the consultant had explained that he was better off here in this specialist London teaching hospital.

Danny would doze on and off during the day, the hours punctuated with breakfast, lunch and supper, most of which he rejected, saying he wasn't hungry. The consultant would arrive once a day, sometimes with a small gathering of medical students. Nancy didn't like this, but appreciated that if it helped them enlarge their experience, she could hardly say no.

In the afternoon they were allowed visitors. Patricia came up nearly every day, but it was a different

Patricia from the one Nancy had known before. This one was humble, suggesting, instead of insisting, that Nancy might like to have a break in the canteen with Sam while she sat with Danny.

Brigid had come up – so kind – and also Annie, along with their kids. The nurses had given permission, since no one on the ward had anything contagious. She hadn't even thought of that, Nancy realised. It proved how far she had come in her efforts to be less fussy and panicky. How ironic that she should only calm down now there really was something to worry about.

'We've brought some sparklers,' hissed Brigid, patting her sequinned cross-shoulder bag in a conspiratorial manner. 'Do you think the nurses would let us light them on the balcony outside? It might make up for Danny missing the sparkler tea party at Puddleducks. Do you like my teeth, by the way? Look, no braces! I've always wanted straight gnashers and now I've got them. It's part of the new me. By the way, Nance, all this is going to make you stronger, even though you might not believe it yet.'

Amazingly, one of the junior nurses had said that they could light the sparklers on the balcony, just for a few minutes. 'Cool,' breathed Danny as they wheeled him out in his chair to take part. Some of the other children on the ward whose parents Nancy had bonded with, especially during the night watches, also came out in their pyjamas and dressing gowns.

'Wow,' whispered one small girl without any hair, whose father held a sparkler for her as she didn't have the strength to do it herself.

Everyone, thought Nancy, after her friends had gone, had been very thoughtful, including Mrs Merryfield, who had sent a card. Apparently Puddle-ducks was arranging a parent-and-child disco to raise money for the aplastic anaemia charity. 'We all wanted to do something to help,' Annie had said, giving her a big warm hug that had brought a lump to her throat.

And then, about a week after they'd been here, her mother arrived. Nancy heard her before seeing her.

'What do you mean, visiting hours are almost over? I've flown in all the way from the United States of America and I am not, do you hear, *not* going to be turned away. My grandson is very seriously ill.'

Sam, who was there at the time, flashed Nancy a wry smile, the first since all this had started. 'Sounds like she's going to be more than a match for my mother,' he whispered.

'What's funny, Mummy?' said Danny, looking slightly brighter. Was it her imagination or did he have more colour in his face today? 'Why are you laughing, Daddy?'

Sam stopped abruptly. 'It's good to laugh, poppet.'

'Yes, but you don't usually . . .'

'There he is!'

A large shape in a violet velvet cape carrying a huge tapestry knitting bag over her arm, out of which was poking a book called *The Meaning of Now*, advanced towards them. 'There's my Danny. Look what Grandma has brought you!'

Nancy watched speechless as her mother pulled a giant teddy wearing a Stars and Stripes outfit out of the bag. 'He's going to make you feel much, much better. Now let me give your poor momma a hug. Goodness dear, you've changed your hair. You look quite pretty!'

She glanced at Sam as though he was something that one of her cats had brought in. 'I see that you've managed to get back from wherever you were.'

Another voice, almost as loud as her mother's but crisper and more formal, cut in. 'Actually, my son was away working in order to provide for his family. It's Christabel, isn't it? My name is Patricia.' As if on cue, Sam's mother materialised beside them.

Nancy's mother took Patricia's hand and pumped it furiously. 'Nice to meet you, Patty. I had hoped we would have met up at the wedding but there you are. If these young people hadn't gone and done it their way on the quiet, we might have had a good family occasion.'

Nancy shot Sam a warning look which she hoped he would interpret correctly as 'Remember she doesn't know we're not actually married.'

'But they're not . . .' began Patricia until Sam nudged her. 'I mean, they had hoped to introduce us at some point.' Her voice quietened as she looked down at Danny, who had snuggled up with American Ted under one arm and British Ted under the other before going back to sleep again. 'If you don't mind me saying so, it's such a shame that we're meeting in such an unfortunate situation. And by the way, it's Patricia. Not Patty. And Danny's already got a new bear. From me.'

'Is that so?'

Oh dear. It might have been a year since Nancy had last seen her mother, but she could still read the 'prepare for battle' signs.

'I know we don't know each other very well yet, Patricia, but I wonder if you'd like to borrow this wonderful book I'm reading. It's all about letting go of anger and the past.'

'How very kind of you, Christabel. As you say, we don't know each other yet but since we're almost related, I'm sure you won't take offence if I give you the name of my colonic irritation specialist.'

Patricia cast a pitying look at Nancy's mother's ample silhouette. 'He does wonders in reducing one's waistline. All my friends say so.'

Christabel's face, which had been crestfallen until the last sentence, suddenly beamed. 'How lovely of you, Patty, to count me as one of your friends. I know we've only just met but already I'm beginning to feel we've known each other for ever. Don't you agree?'

Chapter 37

By the end of the second week in November, it was clear that Danny wasn't improving, despite having had an increase in his medication. That change of colouring which Nancy thought she had noticed had reverted to a deathly white.

'The next step,' said the consultant, who spoke in a tone that made Nancy feel everything was going to be all right, despite the statistics he had just run through, 'is to find a bone marrow match. I'm afraid that yours and your husband's aren't suitable.'

Nancy started up out of her chair. Sam, while squeezing her hand, began to stammer, something she had never heard him do before. 'But we're his parents. Why aren't we suitable?'

The consultant nodded solemnly as though he understood Sam's disbelief. 'In my experience, the best matches come from siblings, although even then there's just no guarantee it will work. However, since Danny doesn't have any brothers or sisters, we need to spread the net. I believe that both your mothers have offered to be tested, but it is also possible for unrelated donors to be a match. This is known as MUD BMT which stands for Matched Unrelated Donor Bone Marrow Transplant. We have a wide network of willing donors, and my staff are currently trying to find a possible pairing.'

They were talking to the consultant in the side room while nearby their respective mothers were sitting on either side of their grandson's bed, vying for his attention. Usually this provided some sort of light relief for Nancy and Sam, but now, as they left the consultant, Nancy ignored the competing grannies and felt her anger rising. 'I told you we should have had another baby. I kept saying it wasn't right for Danny to be an only child. But oh no. You wouldn't have it, would you? You hadn't even wanted Danny. In fact, you even suggested that I had an abortion.'

'Stop!' Sam was white-faced as he tried to put his arms around her. Neatly, she sidestepped away.

'I was wrong, Nancy. Do you hear me? OK, so I hadn't felt ready for fatherhood when you got pregnant, but nor do lots of men. I love our little boy.' His eyes were wet with tears. 'If anything happens to him, I don't know how I'll cope. I really don't.'

She stood away from him, not wanting to be any closer than she had to be. 'If anything happens to Danny,' she said quietly, 'we're finished. Do you hear that? Finished. Now why don't you get back to your precious mother? I'm going outside to get some air.'

Shaking, Nancy took the lift down to the main reception and almost collided with a couple coming in.

'Mrs Wright! I mean Mrs Carter Wright.'

Nancy wiped away the tears from her eyes as she took in Gemma Merryfield and, gracious, Mr Balls, the head of Reception.

'I do hope this is still convenient,' said Gemma, unobtrusively handing her a tissue which appeared as

301

though by magic from the young woman's handbag. 'We can go away if you like.'

Too late, Nancy remembered that Gemma had texted to see if she and Mr Balls could visit as representatives from Puddleducks and the school. 'Of course.' She blew her nose on the tissue. 'I've just come down to get some air, that's all. But do go up. My husband is on the ward and also my mother and his mother.'

Gemma seemed to hesitate. 'Maybe it might be best if we came back another time, when Danny doesn't have so many visitors.'

'No, really, it's fine.' It would probably help to lessen the tension around Danny's bed, thought Nancy. 'I'll be up shortly. I just need a break.'

Joe gave her a kind, caring look; the sort, she thought bitterly, that her own husband ought to give her. 'Why don't I get you a cup of coffee over the road? We can catch up with Gemma in a few minutes.'

'Actually, Joe, I'll stay with Mrs Carter Wright.'

'No. Please.' Why did everyone have to argue about the slightest thing? 'You go up, Mrs Merryfield. I just know that Danny would love to see you, and you'll be able to meet my husband too.'

Chapter 38

I can't do this, thought Gemma, waiting in reception for the lift, her chest thumping with fear. I can't go into a hospital ward where a grief-stricken father is sitting by his son and say, 'Hey! Remember me? We were married nearly five years ago and by some crazy coincidence, your kid is now in my class.'

Perhaps, instead, she could hang around for a bit here and then join Nancy and Joe in the coffee shop. She could pretend that Danny had been asleep and that she hadn't wanted to wake him up. Anything rather than face Sam in a situation like this. Yes. That was what she'd do. OK, it was chickening out, but better that than cause some sort of dramatic upheaval, with dangerously ill children all around.

How ironic, she thought, crossing the road towards the café, that a few months ago she'd have given anything to see Sam again, if only to tidy everything up. Now it was her worst nightmare. What would he say? What would she say? And what would she tell Barry? Even though he'd been very understanding about all this, it would only be natural for him to be jealous.

'Back already?' asked Joe, his eyebrows raised questioningly as she walked in and joined them at a corner table by the window.

She nodded, hating herself for her deception.

'Was Danny asleep?' asked Nancy with a note of alarm in her voice.

Gemma nodded again.

'He's almost always asleep.' Nancy was standing up now, gathering up her bag. 'I'm sorry, Joe – may I call you that? – but I need to get back to my son. Was my husband there?'

Gemma felt a knot in her throat. 'I didn't see him.' That was true enough.

'Then I'd definitely better be getting back. Thanks.' She looked for a minute as though she was going to hug them both, and then held out her hand instead. It felt cool to Gemma's touch. 'I'm really grateful to you both for coming up.' Her eyes filled with tears. 'I didn't expect you all to be so caring. I'm so sorry for fussing earlier when Danny started, and for doubting some of the things you did.'

Gemma couldn't bear any more of this. 'Please don't beat yourself up,' she said, taking Nancy's hands in hers. 'It's natural for new parents to worry.'

Nancy made a rueful face. 'Maybe, but I worried about the wrong things, didn't I? I never thought this would happen.'

Together they watched her leave the café. After a pause, Gemma felt Joe's gaze on her. To her surprise, he looked concerned instead of his usual critical self, which was surprisingly comforting. It seemed odd to see him in his casual jeans and jacket, away from school. That checked shirt suited him, she couldn't help noticing. It made his eyes look blue, rather than scary black.

'I think you might need a strong cup of tea,' he

said gently. 'I know how much you care for your Puddleducks. This can't be easy for you.'

She gulped as he poured her a cup from the pot already on the table. Part of her almost wanted to tell Joe that it wasn't easy because of something he knew nothing about, although she was desperately worried about Danny, of course.

'If we find it difficult,' she said, shaking, 'how must it feel for a real parent?'

Joe made a strange noise and, for a moment, she thought he had choked on his tea. 'Are you all right?' she asked and then he looked at her with such pain in his eyes that she realised he wasn't all right; not at all.

'Joe,' she said softly. 'What's wrong?'

He started to say something, and then stopped.

'It's OK,' she whispered, taking his hand almost without realising it. 'You can tell me. I won't tell anyone.'

She sat and watched him struggle to come to terms with his emotions. Eventually, he raised his head and she could see that his eyes were red. 'You might be aware,' said Joe slowly, 'that I used to work for a major bank.'

Everyone knew that! It was partly why some of the staff were rather in awe of him, and why others thought he wasn't suited to a classroom.

'I was married,' he continued in a voice that sounded unusually deadpan and flat, 'to a very bright woman. A lawyer. Together we earned a considerable amount of money and had the kind of lifestyle that many would dream of.'

She couldn't help cutting in. 'I met her. At the Social.'

Joe nodded and there was a brief flash of humour in his eyes. 'Of course. How could I forget? Ed has always specialised in making entrances.'

Then his voice went flat again. 'I wanted children but my wife kept delaying it. She wished to concentrate on her career. By the time we reached our early thirties, I grew impatient and, one night, we had a row about it.'

Gemma was filled with a sudden need to tell him that this was understandable, but before she could say anything, he continued.

'Don't get me wrong. I'm not the kind of man to become violent. But when my wife, who is now my ex, told me something during the row, I walked out of the flat and never came back.'

Gemma's mouth went dry. 'She must have told you something pretty dreadful for you to do that.'

Joe nodded slowly. 'She did. She told me that four months earlier she had indeed got pregnant, but by mistake.'

Gemma could hardly breathe. 'With someone else's child?'

'No.' Joe shook his head. 'In some ways, I wish it had been. It would have been easier. It had been my child. But without telling me, she had had an abortion.'

Tears were now openly rolling down his face. Joe Balls, the super-tough head of Reception, was crying! Poor man. Gemma wanted to weep with him. What a terrible thing for his wife to have done.

'If she had kept our baby, it would have been Danny's age by now. That's why I find it hard to go down to Puddleducks. That's why the picture of the headmistress's grandson on her desk makes my chest ache. That's why, as you've implied in the past, I am hard and unfeeling, because I have had to erect a steel wall around my emotions in order to function as a human being.'

But you're not hard, Gemma wanted to cry. You're just hurting inside. She almost felt like telling him about what had happened to her, but that wouldn't have been right. There were some things that had to be kept private.

'I'm so sorry,' she whispered. 'So very, very sorry.' Then she remembered something. 'But why *did* your ex-wife turn up at the Parents' Social if you've split up?'

Joe's mouth tightened. 'Because she now wants us to start again. Can you believe that? We divorced within a year of me finding out about . . . about my baby. It made me reassess my life, which is why I threw in my job and turned to teaching. Now she is getting older and most of her friends have children, she likes the idea of a baby.'

'And she wishes you hadn't got divorced?'

'Apparently so. As far as I'm concerned, it's too late. But Ed is a strong woman. She doesn't take no for an answer. And maybe, maybe I've been too weak with her.' As he looked at her, she could see raw pain in his eyes. 'But it isn't easy to walk away from the past, even when someone has hurt you. You keep thinking that they might change and that somehow you might be able to make it all right again.'

307

She nodded. He had put into words the feelings she had been secretly harbouring for the past five years. 'I know what you mean,' she said softly.

They sat for a moment in silence. All kinds of thoughts were whirling round in Gemma's head. She'd misjudged the man – and badly. If she had known what terrible pain he'd been suffering, she wouldn't have been upset by some of his remarks.

Eventually, Joe spoke in a more normal voice. 'Do you think we ought to go back now? I'm sure you've had enough of hearing about my problems. After all, it's Danny we're both here for.'

As he spoke, he looked down at her hand, which was on top of his. When had she put it there? Judging from the flush on his face, he was as surprised and embarrassed as she was.

Feeling really stupid, she waited while he placed some money on the plate for the bill, and then lightly put his hand on the small of her back to steer her towards the door. That was all right then. He clearly wasn't cross with her for that spot of sympathetic hand-holding. 'I'm sure it goes without saying,' he said in a low voice, 'that this conversation is confidential.'

Gemma nodded. 'Of course.' She smiled up at him. 'I'm very flattered that you chose to confide in me.'

He gave a curt nod. 'You're a very good listener. Thank you.'

Chapter 39

By the time she got back to the ward, Danny had fallen asleep. Sam apparently had, just this second, nipped out to make a call to the office. Before this had happened, Nancy knew she'd have been cross about him leaving Danny alone as both grannies had gone home. But not now. He'd already shown how committed he was to them by outlining the situation to his boss and explaining that he needed to spend every day by his boy's bedside. Perhaps she shouldn't have been so hard on him earlier on. It was all so complicated.

That night, Sam was very quiet; something she was grateful for, since she didn't feel like talking either. Truth to tell, as Patricia would say, she could have done without any more hospital visitors, but the following day, Billy and his mother arrived again.

Danny's eyes lit up when he saw his friend.

'Hope you didn't mind us coming up again, but Billy kept going on about it,' said Brigid, ignoring the fact that her son was tearing round the ward, playing imaginary cars. 'Sorry my bone marrow didn't match but on the bright side, just imagine the effect on Danny if he inherited Billy's wild ways! Mind you, I'm sure it's my ex-husband's genes and not mine. His mum says he was a terrible kid, so with any luck our

Billy will grow out of it by the time he's thirty-five. By the way, Lily's mother sent this into Puddleducks.'

Nancy opened the beautifully wrapped parcel. It was a kite! A lovely red and blue kite with a picture of a duck on it. Attached to it was a note in adult handwriting that said, 'When Danny is better, maybe we can all fly this together.' Then came a childish scribble: 'Love from Lily'.

Such a shame Danny will be missing the Puddleducks day out to the farm, Brigid was saying amidst all her Billy-directed reprimands. Then again, she continued, there would be other trips when Danny got better. Wouldn't there?

The following day the consultant arrived with a grey face and no bevy of medical students, to invite them into his office for a talk. Neither Nancy's mother nor her mother-in-law were a good match, he told them in a voice that didn't have the same confidence as in previous weeks. So far, none of the donors on the list matched either.

'We'll keep looking,' he told her and Sam. 'But I have to be honest. Danny's blood count is getting worse.' His voice dropped. 'I suppose what I am trying to say, in the kindest way possible, is that time is running out.'

Chapter 40

Joe sat at his desk poring over the contributions to the *MY SKOOL!* book that he and Brian were trying to put together.

Quite a few parents and children had come up with thoughts about why they liked school, and there were some real howlers.

I like school but only wen its holydays.

Brian had suggested that they kept that one exactly as it was.

School is better than it was in my day. You can use Google to help you cheat with your homework.

This one was from a father who was, thought Joe, being sarcastic. He had a point, however.

I like Corrybank because we can play football outside. We don't have a garden at home.

That contributor had beautiful handwriting.

I like school because my teacher loves me. She puts kisses next to my sums.

Joe groaned. Such an old joke, and it came from yet another single mum who also had a sprog at Puddleducks and kept telling him how much she was looking forward to the parent-and-child disco in aid of the aplastic anaemia charity.

Joe had been trying to block out his conversation with Gemma, but it was no good. What on earth had come over him, confiding in her like that? So unprofessional! Yet she'd been a good listener.

Opening a drawer and reaching for a Bourbon biscuit (Brian's habits had become strangely comforting), his mind drifted back to last week when he had suggested to Gemma that they both visited the Danny in hospital. It was, as he'd pointed out, surely their duty to represent the school and playgroup. Gemma had been strangely cool about the idea, probably wishing she could stay at home with Barry, who for some reason really irritated him with his crisp manner and authoritative air. Joe knew Gemma was spending many of her evenings with him.

Then, when she'd made that comment in the coffee shop about neither of them being parents, all his pent-up grief had come pouring out, which was why he'd found himself telling Gemma his own sorry story. He'd even confessed that he intended to leave Corrybank and go back to inner-city teaching. 'That's a shame,' she had said in a voice that sounded as though she really meant it. 'I've enjoyed working with you.'

So had he, he had almost added, despite their differences.

There were footsteps outside, interrupting his thoughts. Di put her head round the door.

'Heard the news, have you?'

Just as she spoke, there was a loud noise from next door. Gemma must be using that classroom for her After-School club. What a racket with all those xylophones and tambourines! Gemma might have been a good listener in the coffee shop, but that still didn't mean he agreed with her teaching methods. It was a pity she didn't push times tables as heavily as music or dough craft or whatever it was called.

'The news?' he repeated. 'What news?'

Di's face had the pained look of someone who was bursting to tell but was, at the same time, aware that the content was not good. 'Danny Carter Wright has been given weeks to live unless they find a bone marrow match. Gemma's just told me. They've tested all the relatives and the donors on the hospital list and now they're asking friends to go for blood screening.'

Di's face was shining with self-congratulation. 'The girls and I are going up tomorrow to see if we are any good.'

Joe's mind swung into action. He had enough contacts over the years, surely, to find someone who could help. Forget the competition to find the top ten playgroups. Forget the *MY SKOOL!* book. This was far more important. This was life or death. Turning his computer on again, Joe began typing.

DESPERATELY NEEDED! A BONE MARROW MATCH FOR THREE-YEAR-OLD DANNY WHO IS CRITICALLY ILL.

TESTS HAVE SHOWN THAT HIS RELATIVES AREN'T SUITABLE, SO CORRYBANKS SCHOOL AND PUDDLE-DUCKS PLAYGROUP, WHERE DANNY IS A PUPIL, ARE ASKING YOU, A COMPLETE STRANGER, TO HELP.

ALL YOU HAVE TO DO IS GIVE A SMALL AMOUNT OF BLOOD SO IT CAN BE CHECKED TO SEE IF IT MAKES A MATCH. PLEASE HELP US TO MAKE SURE THAT DANNY SEES HIS FOURTH BIRTHDAY.

He'd run the wording past Danny's parents, of course, and then, if they agreed, he would email, Twitter and text it to everyone he knew.

Joe gripped his fist in resolve. Someone out there had got to be able to help.

'By the way, Mr Balls.' Di was still there. Her face reminded Joe of a pug dog that an uncle of his had once had, who was constantly pinching food from the kitchen and then assuming an 'I'm terribly sorry' expression. 'I was terribly sorry to hear about your resignation.'

Was nothing confidential around here?

'I mean, I hope that we did everything to make you feel at home here.'

The woman was going red and stammering. The Joe who had arrived here in September would have snapped something back.

'Are you referring to your comment about me being a cross between a paunchy northern Colin Firth with attitude and Mr Grumpy?'

Di's face crumpled. 'I'm so sorry . . . I didn't mean . . .'

Joe put up his hand. 'Actually, I was quite flattered. About the Mr Man bit, that was.'

He paused, waiting for her to laugh. Oh dear. He'd frightened her too much. Immediately he felt repentant. 'It wasn't you, Di. It was me. I'm not that great with small children, to be honest. In my previous school, I was teaching Years Five and Six in a much tougher environment.'

She nodded. 'I've heard about places like that in London. Wouldn't suit me, I must say. I couldn't possibly live there, let alone work there. Going back to the same school, are you?'

He hoped so, but his application was still being considered. Mike and Lynette had thought he was crazy to hand in his notice before having a job to go to, but he'd needed to make that decision in order to move on. Besides, he had enough savings to keep going until the following September, or even the year after that, if he didn't get his old job back.

Meanwhile, he needed to get on with his SAVE DANNY CARTER WRIGHT campaign. Whipping out his mobile, he began to text Nancy on the number she had given him. He had had an idea which might just help her and that husband of hers.

Yes, texted back Nancy Carter Wright in very correct language with capital letters and no abbreviations. Anything that could help would be wonderful. And as for Mr Balls's other offer, to let them stay in his Notting Hill apartment, that would be absolutely amazing. It would mean one of them could get a good night's sleep while the other stayed by Danny's bed.

'That's really good of you,' said Gemma when she came up for a meeting about the charity disco which was being hastily organised for next week. 'Danny's grandmother told me what you'd done.'

Joe shrugged. 'Means you'll have me as a permanent neighbour until Christmas.'

'Yes.' She seemed to hesitate. 'So you're definitely going, then?'

He nodded, not trusting himself to speak. It seemed

safer to change the subject. 'How many disco tickets have we sold so far?'

Gemma checked her list. 'Nearly ninety. That's about as many as we can take. And I've got some good news. The local paper is going to be running a big piece on the bone marrow campaign to encourage others to get tested.'

Great. However, Joe reminded himself that it was easy to get so caught up in the organising of campaigns and fund-raising discos that you almost forgot the pain behind the cause. 'Did Danny's grandmother say anything about how they were all doing?'

Gemma's voice sounded strained. 'Patricia says they're being very brave. Danny's such a lovely boy. I just can't believe this is happening.' Her eyes grew moist and Joe, hardly realising what he was doing, reached out and touched her shoulder very briefly in what was meant to be a comforting manner.

She seemed surprised and immediately Joe moved away, trying to pretend it hadn't happened. 'Now,' he said in a brisker tone, 'let's go over the details for the disco again, shall we? And after that, I need to talk about the farm trip to make sure we've got everything covered.'

Chapter 41

'Work,' said Brian, during one of their regular chats over a bottle of malt whisky in his predecessor's sitting room, where Joe was even getting used to the dusty mantelpiece and antimacassars, 'is the best way to cope when life gets tough.'

He gave Joe a knowing look. 'Sorry you're leaving, son. Still, it was good of you to bring me this. Always fancied a laptop, I did.' He winked. 'Not the dancing kind though; my Mavis wouldn't approve of that.'

Joe gave the required smile. 'I had a spare at home, and I thought it might help with the editing of the *MY SKOOL!* book.'

Already Brian's thick old fingers were moving at quite a speed over the keyboard. 'You're a good lad, Joe. Mind you, I've got to confess that at the beginning I had my doubts along with everyone else, but now – where did they put that Q? – I reckon that Corrybank and Puddleducks need someone like you.'

He let out a cry of triumph. 'There it is. The Q. Forgot it was right up there on the left. What a daft place to put it. By the way, did I tell you that I went along to get my bone marrow tested for that lad at playgroup?' He snorted. 'My innards are probably ancient enough to belong to the Natural History Museum, especially after my heart attack, but any road, I wasn't suitable, more's the pity. Still, thought I'd do my bit, as it were.'

He stood up to refill Joe's glass. 'I'd have liked to have helped the little lad. Still, I intend to do my bit by coming along to that disco of yours tonight. No, don't look like that. I've checked with my doctor and she says it's quite all right.' The old man winked at him. 'Reckon there'll be any hot totty there, do you?'

Joe laughed. 'You'll get to meet my ex-wife. She's considered pretty hot.'

Brian frowned. 'What do you want to bring her along for, after everything you've told me about her?'

Considering he had only let slip the odd fact during their friendship and that Brian didn't know the full story, this was strong stuff indeed.

'She wanted to come over and drop off some of my things she'd discovered while having a clear-out. I said I'd be out and when I explained why, she asked herself along.'

Brian nodded knowingly. 'I reckon you're just bringing her along so everyone thinks you've got a girlfriend and you can't be gay. Not that there's anything wrong with batting for the other side, mind. My nephew's just gone out.'

Come out, Joe wanted to say. But as he gave a wry smile, he couldn't help thinking that Brian was smarter than he seemed. He did want to bring along a woman, but not for the reason Brian had suggested.

Ridiculous as it sounded, he didn't want to be the only one to leave Joyce's house without a date. Over the last few weeks he'd had to get used to the sound of whispers and giggles on the other side of the wall

318

between him and Gemma Merryfield. It had had a strange effect on him that he couldn't quite define.

Meanwhile, he needed to get on with the campaign and the book and all his other work. He didn't want anyone to accuse him of not bothering just because he was leaving. Hell, he had even helped out with that mural which Nancy's friends and mosaics teacher had taken over now Nancy was spending all her time in the hospital. There was so much to do! And that was the only way to shut out the constant thoughts of a rosy-cheeked boy (he had been so sure his baby would have been a son) who would have resembled him, or Ed, or both of them.

The disco was a great success. Even Ed said so, but then again, she would. All eyes were on his ex-wife as she arrived on his arm, wearing a slinky black dress that wasn't too short, but showed off her legs to perfection.

As Joe watched her make small talk with the parents, including Clemmie's mum whose face had fallen when they'd walked in, he began to wonder if this was the same person who had taken herself off for an abortion without even consulting him. She seemed so much softer now, so understanding. When he'd explained that Corrybank wasn't for him and that he'd handed in his notice, he'd expected her to say, 'I told you so'. But instead, she had merely nodded and said that he needed to make these decisions for himself and that wherever he ended up, whether it was in a school or back in business, his employer would be lucky to have him.

What had come over her? A huge lump rose in his throat as he watched her bend down and talk to some of the children. At one point, she had looked up at him and he knew, he just knew, that finally she felt remorse at what she had done.

'Mr Balls, Mr Balls, is that your wife?'

'Mr Balls, did you bring your children?'

'Mr Balls, would you like to dance with me and my friends?'

Yes, everyone said the disco was a great success. But not for him. It was hurting too much. Mike had been right when he'd doubted Joe's decision to bring Ed as his partner. He'd been wrong in hoping that he might be able to forget the past.

'Hi, Joe.' There was a tap on his shoulder and there stood Gemma, but not the Gemma he knew. This one was wearing a slinky black dress too, but because he usually saw the owner in work clothes, it took him a second to take in the make-up, the sheer tights and the shiny black high heels.

'You look amazing,' he said before he could stop himself.

'Doesn't she just!' said Barry, who was beaming with pompous pride as he slid his arm around Gemma's sparkly bare shoulders. For some reason that he couldn't pin down, Joe still couldn't warm to him, even though he was always pleasant to him when passing on the stairs in Joyce's house.

'You're not leaving, are you?' Gemma asked, glancing at Joe's coat, which he'd been about to put on.

'Just slipping out for some air.'

'Why don't you two have a dance?' Barry gave Gemma's shoulders a quick familiar squeeze. 'I'll get the drinks. Orange or lemonade?'

Joe put down his coat and smiled at Gemma. He could hardly refuse to dance with her. He glanced across the room to where Ed was dancing with a small boy who came up to her knees. She waved at him but then her eyes hardened as she spotted him taking to the floor with Gemma.

The music was changing now to a slow beat, leaving him no option but to put his hands awkwardly on her waist and shuffle round in a circle. Dancing had never been his thing.

Gemma seemed similarly embarrassed, and once or twice bumped her head against his chest, partly because he was so much taller than her. She smelt nice; not of the expensive heavy stuff that Ed favoured, but something soft without being too sweet.

'Sorry,' he grimaced when he trod on her toes yet again. 'I'm not great at this. Ed always says that . . .'

A clear, cool, amused voice cut in. 'Ed always says that I have many strengths but dancing isn't one of them.'

They both looked round to see Ed standing there. 'Aren't you going to introduce me then, darling?'

What right had she to call him darling? Surely she wasn't jealous? 'Gemma, this is Ed. My ex-wife.'

He emphasised the 'ex', so there should be no mistake.

'Ed, this is Gemma, the pre-school leader who also happens to rent a room next to mine.'

Ed's beautifully waxed eyebrows rose in surprise.

'I didn't realise you two lived so close. You're practically bedfellows!'

How could she? Poor Gemma was virtually puce with embarrassment. 'Excuse me.' She had pulled a mobile phone out of her tiny evening purse. 'I've just seen a text message that I need to reply to.'

In the event, Joe and Ed stayed to the end, helping to clear up along with Danny's two grandmothers, who had come to lend support, and had both been flirting mercilessly with Brian.

'Looks like I haven't lost the touch after all,' he beamed, flicking some biscuit crumbs off his maroon jumper. 'By the way, Gemma left me a message to pass on to you. She had to go early.'

I'll bet she did, thought Joe. Back to bed with lover boy.

'Aren't you going to ask me to yours for a coffee?' pouted Ed when he ordered a cab to take her back to London.

'Sorry.' He brushed her cheek. 'I've got work to do.'

She waggled a finger in front of him, half-mocking. 'I know. Balls Law. All work and no play makes Joe a rich boy. At least it used to.'

He shook his head. 'That's changed now. Like me. And like us. I'm sorry, Ed, but there's no point pretending. And that includes pretending about us too.'

Her face crumpled, and he could have sworn he saw a tear threaten to mar that flawless make-up. 'Then why did you ask me here?'

'I didn't. You asked yourself.'

'But you didn't say no.'

True. But as he'd said before to both Mike and Lynette and himself, it wasn't that simple to forget an ex. Even irritating habits were comforting, simply because they were familiar.

He patted her shoulder, but the very touch made him want to take his hand away. 'I'm sorry, Ed. Maybe for a minute, I thought we could turn the clock back. But every time I think about our baby, I feel sick. It's over. Really over. We both need to move on and the sooner we accept that, the better.'

Chapter 42

Life might have been hectic on the fourteenth floor but it was pretty hectic here at Corrybank too, especially now it was the day for Reception's farm trip with Puddleducks.

Joe and Gemma had gone over the arrangements again and again. Parental consent slips had been signed. Five parents had volunteered to come with them, so they were over and above the required adult/child ratio. The coach was due any second. And Gemma wasn't here.

'Haven't you heard?' said Bella, checking her cuticles.

Joe was getting a bit fed up with this 'Haven't you heard?' phrase. It always signified trouble. 'Now what?'

'Gemma can't come so Miriam is taking her place.'

'Miriam?'

'I forgot.' Bella was opening her handbag now, producing a bottle and dabbing something on a nail as though she was in a beauty salon instead of at work. 'You haven't met, have you? She used to run the playgroup and Gemma's covering for her now she's on maternity leave. Her mother's looking after the kid so she can help us.'

'Yes, yes, yes. But why isn't Gemma here?' Joe couldn't help feeling cross. If she'd taken a day off to be with lover boy while he was on leave, he'd have something to say.

'That's what I was trying to tell you.' Bella, now seemingly satisfied with the nail, was putting the bottle back in her bag. 'Gemma got a text on Saturday night at the disco. It seems that her bone marrow is a perfect match. She's in hospital right now.'

Joe tried to keep calm and rational on the coach journey. People donated bone marrow every day of the year. It had to be safe, otherwise they wouldn't do it. On the other hand, all surgery carried a certain risk. Gemma must know that. She was a good woman. And brave, too.

'Mr Balls, Mr Balls, Billy is kicking the back of my seat!'

'Mr Balls, are you going to marry the princess from the disco and have babies?'

'Mr Balls, will there be elephants cos my mum thinks I'm allergic to them.'

'Mr Balls, I've forgotten my packed lunch.'

'Mr Balls, where's Mrs Merryfield?'

'Mr Balls, I want to buy something for Danny from the gift shop.'

This last was from the lovely white-skinned daughter of that stunning singer Dilly Dalung. Lily was one of Danny's friends: he knew that from one of the early joint assemblies, where they had sat hand in hand. Even then, it had struck him as being sweet. It was so hard for children when their friends got ill, or worse.

'I'm sure you can, Lily,' he said, getting up as the

coach stopped to make sure that he was out first to do the head count. He nodded at Bella and a woman he took to be Miriam, who was, astoundingly, carrying her baby in one of those stripy slings. 'Who's this?'

Miriam flushed. 'This is Nicolas. That's Nicolas without an "h", by the way. Sorry, I tell everyone that as people keep getting it wrong. Mum was meant to be having him but she's got this bug that's going around, so I thought it would be all right if I brought him.' She beamed as though expecting him to fawn over this incredibly ugly, square-faced baby with three chins and a distinct smell emanating from a brown patch on the sling.

No, it wasn't all right, but it was a bit late now. 'OK, everyone,' said Joe to the adults. 'You know which children you are in charge of. Follow me, please.'

The day had been planned carefully. First they were to have a short tour round the hen house, and then visit the shed where eggs were incubated.

'Mr Balls, how does the chicken get the sperm through the shell?'

That one came from a boy in his own year. He'd explain later in biology.

Next they were taken to see the sheep pen.

'Mr Balls, my mum says that Dad is a sheep.'

They moved on to the pigsties.

'Mr Balls. Why do pigs make that noise?'

Joe was just about to explain the mystery of swine nasal passages when Bella, who was rounding the corner with her group, cut in. 'Stupid question, Sienna. They just *do*.'

Her eyes fell on Beth, who was lagging behind, clutching her puffa. 'Actually, I've got a riddle for Beth, which she ought to get since her mum says she's allergic to everything. What do you get from pigs? Don't know? It's a rash-er. Get it?'

That was cruel. Joe was about to say so when Miriam flustered up, still in her maternity dress despite having given birth three months ago. 'Has anyone seen Lily?'

'What?'

'Oh dear.' She was handing him her list. 'I thought Lily was on your list of children to look after but I've just realised that she's actually on mine. I'm so sorry. My mind's all over the place after having this one.'

Joe snatched the list, which stated quite clearly that Lily was in the group headed by Miriam. 'When did you last see her?' he asked quietly.

Miriam bit her lip. 'Not since the chicken house. Nearly an hour ago. I know it was then because I had to stop off for a bit and feed this one.'

His first thought was that Lily had gone to the gift shop to find a present for Danny. But no. She wasn't there. An exhaustive search by staff, parents and children revealed that Lily had completely vanished.

Joe felt sicker than he had on the day that one of his team had lost twenty million pounds on the stock exchange. Money was one thing, but a child was irreplaceable.

'We'll have to phone the police.' Numbly, he felt in his pocket for his mobile. 'And her mother.'

THE PUDDLEDUCKS FRIENDSHIP SONG

We are the little Puddleducks
We care about each other.
If someone's hurt, we'll comfort them
Just like a little mother!

Chapter 43

'Gemm-a. *Gem*ma.'

The voice seemed to be coming at her from a distance, but she didn't want to reply. It was as though she'd had a lovely deep sleep from which she was now slowly, very slowly, waking up. How rested she felt! Apart, that was, from a strange sensation in her right arm.

'Gemma! Can you hear me?'

She didn't know the chirpy voice but it sounded as though it knew her.

'You're coming round from your operation now and you're in the recovery room. Everything is all right.'

Everything was all right? Then it all began to come back to her. The text from the hospital when she'd been at the disco. The news that by some incredible stroke of luck, her bone marrow matched Danny's even though they weren't related. Barry's face when she'd pulled him to one side and explained what had happened.

'But that means you'll be saving the life of the child whose father is actually your husband,' he said slowly.

She put her finger to her lips. 'I've got to do this. You do understand, don't you?'

Why did his eyes look so uncertain? 'For Sam or for Danny?'

Surely he got it? 'For Danny, of course. I don't feel anything for Sam any more.'

Barry was looking at her in that suspicious way she was beginning to recognise. 'Did you see him in the hospital?'

She stepped away from him. 'No, only Nancy. Look Barry, this is silly. I've got to get going. The hospital want me there tonight so they can do the operation tomorrow. I'll only be in for a night. Two at the most.' She tried to make light of it, although her heart was beating wildly. It was all so sudden, and she'd hated hospitals ever since Granny had died. Just hated them.

Barry reached for his jacket. 'I'll drive you there. No, honestly. I insist.'

That had been last night. At least she thought it was. Which meant that today was Sunday. Maybe Danny was having his operation right now. Gemma didn't often pray, but she found her lips moving. Please God. Please make Danny live. Please make him well again.

The words seemed to have a soporific effect. How heavy her eyes felt! 'Just taking you back to the ward now, Gemma,' said a cheery voice and she drifted back to sleep while, at the same time, being vaguely aware of someone wheeling her bed along a hospital corridor.

The next morning she woke feeling much brighter, in a smallish ward with five other women, two of whom had their curtains closed around them. Her first thought was Danny. Had he had his operation? Was he all right?

The nurse who was bringing breakfast round on a trolley didn't know, but promised to find out. Gemma wasn't hungry. She felt restless with uncertainty. The sun was shining through the windows of the ward, so it would be a perfect day for the farm trip. Luckily, she'd managed to text Bella on the way into hospital to explain the situation. She only hoped that her assistant would remember to pass on the message to Joe and find an extra parent or member of staff to make up the adult/child ratio.

Joe! Gemma's arm began to throb slightly where the drip had been inserted. She just couldn't get the measure of him. First he was married. Then he wasn't. He lent his flat to the Carter Wrights, showing that he was a better man than she'd thought. Then he brought his glamorous ex along to the disco. And he'd told her all that terrible stuff about Ed having an abortion.

Her eyes felt heavy again. How weird it was that Joe could be preying on her mind when the only thing that really mattered was Danny.

And Sam.

Had she really meant it when she'd told Barry that she was doing this for Danny? Of course she wanted to save the boy's life but wasn't there, as Kitty had suggested when she'd rung her at the hospital just before the op, a small part of her that also wanted to punish Sam? 'It will be a terrible shock to see you if his mother hasn't told him,' her friend had pointed out. 'I wouldn't fancy being in his shoes.'

When Gemma woke up again, it seemed to be lunchtime. This time she did feel like having a small bowl of tomato soup, and she was able to pad along in her dressing gown and slippers to the loo, which, the nurses told her, was a very good sign.

'You've got a visitor,' said one of them when she'd cleared away lunch.

Barry! He'd promised to be back as soon as this was permitted. Gemma whipped out her mirror from the handbag in her locker and ran a hand through her hair before trying to get the last of her mascara out of a nearly empty bottle. Inside the locker sat her silver chain, which she'd had to take off for the operation. Somehow, despite knowing about Sam and Nancy, she couldn't bear not to wear it any more. It had been part of her body for so long: a symbol of hope that he might come back, saying he'd made a mistake and that he loved her, enough to have their children. Slowly, she fastened the chain around her neck.

'Gemma?'

Her blood froze. That wasn't Barry's voice.

She looked up as the tall, blond man who was standing awkwardly in front of her sat down on the chair next to her bed. It was Sam, all right. An older Sam, who had put on a bit more weight and grown a moustache. It suited him. His eyes, still the same stunning periwinkle blue, held hers uncertainly. 'I couldn't believe it when Nancy said you'd volunteered to be a donor. I don't know what to say.' His voice had a catch in it.

'Don't know what to say?' repeated Gemma. The anger lashed out of her mouth, and the woman in the bed next to hers looked across curiously. 'Are you talking about my bone marrow, which, by the way, I would have given to any needy child? Or are you talking about breaking my heart by declaring that you didn't want children, although you didn't mind having them with someone else? Perhaps we are talking about you going off and not leaving a forwarding address? Or maybe you don't know what to say about leaving your "wife" and son to "find yourself" during an extended business trip. I think those were the words that poor Nancy used when she was crying on my shoulder not long ago.'

Sam reached out to touch her arm but she moved away. 'Don't.'

He shook his head. 'I'm sorry. Sorry for all those things you've just listed, although actually I didn't go off and leave you. You left me.'

'Yes. Because you couldn't cope when you thought I was pregnant.' She was crying softly now. 'I loved you, Sam. I loved you so much.'

He took her hand, the one that hadn't had the drip in it. 'I felt the same. I even went through all our photographs and blanked out your face in an attempt to get over you. Part of me wanted to come back and say I'd made a mistake, but I was too proud.' His voice faltered slightly. 'You're still wearing my chain.'

She nodded, trembling, remembering how he had bought it for her as a wedding present from some tacky souvenir shop in Vegas.

'There's something I've got to tell you,' he continued unsteadily. 'I met Nancy on the rebound. It was very soon after you and I split.' His eyes refused to meet hers. 'I told her I didn't want to get married or have children. I know I should have told her I *couldn't* get married, but then things happened so fast. We'd only been dating for a few months when she got pregnant.'

How horribly, horribly ironic!

He glanced behind him nervously but there was only a nurse at the far end, talking to a patient. 'Danny was an accident.'

Gemma tried to pull her hand back. 'He's a lovely little boy.'

At least Sam had the grace to look embarrassed. 'I know he is, but the truth is that he wasn't planned. I had to think really hard about whether I could make myself do the right thing and stay with Nancy. But I did, Gemma. I did because I felt so guilty about not having stood by *you* when you thought you were pregnant.'

Congratulations! Did he expect her to clap?

Sam's story was pouring out of him now. 'We stayed in the States for a bit and then came back to London because of my work. I have to admit that I suggested living in Hazelwood partly because it was easy to commute, but also because I remembered that your grandmother lived there.'

Gemma's eyes smarted with tears. '*Used* to. She died. But that was one reason why I took the job at the playgroup. It was near the nursery she ran, years ago.'

Sam shook his head bemusedly. 'Neither of us expected to find the other through your Puddles playgroup.'

'Puddleducks,' she corrected him, 'although Puddles isn't a bad name, considering the odd leakages that occur now and then.'

Hang on. What were they doing talking about this, when the only really important thing was Danny? 'How is Danny doing? Has he had the operation?'

Sam nodded. 'That's why I'm here. He's still in the recovery room but the nurses say he's come round. It's too early to tell yet if he's going to . . .'

His eyes filled with tears. This time it was Gemma's turn to reach out to him. 'He'll be all right, Sam. I just feel it.'

Awkwardly she watched him struggling and trying to talk while holding back tears. 'I hope so, Gemma. I really do.' His eyes searched hers again and she could see the pain in them. 'But I can't help thinking that Danny might be taken away from us as my punishment for not being a good enough husband. To either of you.' He put his head in his hands. 'Nancy doesn't know about me being married. I just told her that I wasn't ready to get married to *her* yet. What a mess.'

She almost felt sorry for him. 'Listen,' she said, squeezing his hand. 'What really matters at the moment is Danny. OK, you might not have got off to the best start as a dad. But you can make up for it now. It's not too late. So go and be with him, as soon as they let you. Sit by his side. Stroke his brow. Tell him how much you love him.'

Sam raised his head again, and this time his eyes were more hopeful. 'You're a lovely woman, you know that?'

'And so is Nancy,' said Gemma quickly. 'You've got a family, Sam. You're a very lucky man.'

Suddenly she realised he didn't know something: something so important that she couldn't understand why she hadn't mentioned it before. 'The divorce,' she said urgently. 'Our decree nisi. It's about to come through.'

He looked shocked. 'How did you manage to sort that out when you hadn't got my permission?'

'I saw a lawyer and she told me that in the case of a missing person, as she put it, I had to wait five years and then I could file for a divorce without your signature. But now you might as well sign the papers.' She opened her handbag and began rustling through. 'Here they are.' She gave a short sigh. 'Crazy as it sounds, I carry them around with me for reassurance. The address to send them to is at the bottom.'

Gemma watched as he took them with that wry smile that she used to know so well, and which still, dammit, gave her a slight pang.

'You're quite a girl, you know that, Gemma?' He leaned towards her, brushing her cheek. 'Some man out there is going to be a very lucky bloke some day.'

Then, with an enormous lump in her throat, she watched him leave, walking across the ward with his head bowed. It was clear he had a huge weight on his shoulders, yet the weird thing was that she felt as though her own weight had lifted. She had done her best to save Danny's life. She had found Sam and started to put that part of her life behind her.

There was Barry, too: a kind, steady man who showered her with love and presents and for whom nothing was too much trouble. And there was Puddleducks, and her wonderful Puddleducks children, who would, even as she lay there, be tramping through the farm in their brightly coloured wellies, asking all kinds of funny questions.

'Blow me,' said a voice from the bed next to hers.

'That was some story from your ex. Sorry, I wasn't really eavesdropping but I couldn't help it.'

Gemma was so mortified she didn't know what to say.

'It's OK, love. I'm not going to tell anyone. But I watch a lot of those soaps and you know what? They couldn't write a better storyline themselves. Just think. You wanted his baby. He didn't want kids. Then he goes and has one with someone else. And you give his kid your bone marrow. That means this Danny boy is sort of yours now, doesn't it?'

Chapter 44

Later that afternoon, Nancy came to see her. The poor woman looked drawn and weary, as though she hadn't had any sleep, but she was smiling. 'Danny's come round fine and he's talking quite a lot! You can see he's got more energy. I know it's early days, as everyone keeps telling me, and we've got to stay in hospital for a few weeks apparently, but we're so grateful, Gemma. We really are. I sent Sam round to meet you. I hope he said thank you. He can be a bit reticent at times but he really is as grateful as I am. We don't know how we can repay you.'

Gemma squeezed her hand, thankful that her nosy neighbour had her curtains drawn round her again. Despite their short acquaintance, she wouldn't put it past the woman to leap in and add her pennyworth. 'You've repaid me already by telling me that Danny is chattering away.'

Nancy bent down and brushed Gemma's cheek. 'Do you feel all right?'

'Fine.' A bit tired but there was no need to tell Nancy that. 'They're letting me out tomorrow.'

'That's wonderful. Then in that case, I wonder if you'd mind seeing my mother-in-law? She insists on coming to thank you herself. Says she has something really important to tell you.'

Someone's got a lot of visitors, one of the nurses remarked to Gemma. Yes, and not all were wanted. Gemma braced herself as Patricia sailed in, wearing a very large skirt that swished along the floor like that of a Victorian matriarch. 'Ah, Gemma. There you are.'

As if she would be anywhere else!

'I'd like to thank you for what you've done for my grandson.' Her voice dropped. 'About that other thing. You know. The thing we were talking about last month.'

'Do you mean our conversation about Sam?'

Patricia put her finger to her lips. 'Shhh. Walls have fears. I mean ears. Yes, of course I do. Do be a bit quicker, dear. If you don't mind me saying, it would be a shame if either of us told Nancy the truth, don't you think? Just imagine the effect on Danny.'

Gemma nodded. Suddenly the chain around her neck felt hot and itchy, as though it was telling her to take it off. But for some reason, she couldn't. She just couldn't.

'I quite agree. Sam has undertaken to sign the relevant papers. Don't worry about Nancy. We will both be free soon after Christmas.'

One of the nurses came up behind them. 'Goodness, Gemma, I've never known anything like it. You've got another visitor now.' She gave Gemma a 'this one is special' look. 'If you don't want him, I'll have him myself!'

Patricia wobbled to her feet. 'Must go now, dear. I'm expecting a call from Brian – such an attentive man, don't you think? – and of course I want to get back to Danny. So glad you see things my way. Bye!'

She and Barry almost bumped into each other. It was difficult to see him through the huge bouquet of red roses he was carrying.

'How are you feeling?' He bent down and kissed her. Not on her cheek, but a proper one that made the nearby nurse sigh with admiration. Gemma was embarrassed, but Barry beamed. 'I won't stay long, my lovely girl. I'm so proud of you for doing this.'

She felt a rush of relief. 'Thank you for understanding. Not everyone would.'

He began arranging the flowers for her in the vase next to the bed. 'They say you can come out tomorrow morning. I'll be here on the dot to take you back. Mum says you're not to worry about cooking or looking after yourself. We'll do that for you.'

'Sorry,' said Gemma. She could feel herself drifting. 'Please don't think I'm being rude but I just have to go to sleep.'

'Wow,' said a voice through the curtains after Barry had said his goodbyes. 'He was a looker – no mistake. Whatever was in that drip of yours, I'll have some!'

The next morning, when Gemma woke up, her first thought was that she needed to see Nancy before being discharged, to check how Danny was doing. But first she needed to get to the loo. It still felt odd swinging her legs out of bed and waddling along to the cubicle at the end but it was easier than yesterday. She had thought it would be more difficult to be a bone marrow donor, so it was a relief to feel almost normal.

'Want to borrow my newspaper, love?' asked her neighbour on the way back.

It wasn't a paper which she normally read but even so, she could get quite used to this. Lying in bed and reading after nine in the morning, when she was usually at the playgroup. But what was this all over the front page?

MISSING! DAUGHTER OF CELEBRITY DILLY DALUNG HAS GONE MISSING DURING A PLAYGROUP TRIP TO A FARM IN BEDFORDSHIRE. HER FATHER, WHO IS ESTRANGED FROM THE SINGER AND IS IN THE MIDDLE OF A FIERCE CUSTODY BATTLE, IS CURRENTLY BEING QUESTIONED.

Gemma felt hot and cold, and at the same time she wanted to be sick. Why wasn't her mobile working? She began to shake so hard that it was difficult even to ring the bell for the nurse.

'Please.' Gemma could hardly get her words out. 'Please. I need to make an urgent phone call. Something awful's happened.'

Lily lay very still. Don't make a noise. That was what her mother always said in the evenings when she was sewing in the dim light of their bedroom. Be a good girl.

Her mother spoke in the language Lily felt comfortable with. Not the strange language that they all spoke at playgroup, which she had made herself learn just like Mama had told her to.

You must not get found out, her mother had said. If you do, we will all be in trouble. Big trouble. Then, Lily knew, they would have to go back to that cold place where her tummy made funny noises because it was empty inside.

But if she played the game, as her mother called it, they could move out of this place and have their own palace just like the lovely lady in the sunglasses.

Lily shivered. It was cold and her coat wasn't thick enough. Her mother would be worried about her. But if she came out from here, she might be angry too.

All she had wanted was to get something for Danny. Lily opened her right hand, which contained a blue and pink stripy rubber in the shape of a cow. She had bought it from the farm gift shop with the pocket money that the lovely lady in the sunglasses had given her for the trip.

And now she needed to get it to Danny.

Chapter 45

So far, Danny's body hadn't rejected the new blood cells. It was early days, mind you, warned Deirdre, the warm, gently rounded Irish nurse who had three of her own at home.

Early days, she repeated as she bustled round the bed, tucking Danny in and checking his temperature. Was Nancy sure she didn't want another cup of tea? She didn't mind her calling her Nancy, did she? Only she, Deirdre, always felt that her mums, as she called them, were more like friends than patients by the time they left.

'Sisters, even,' she said as she handed Nancy the cup of tea she had at first turned down but which she found strangely comforting, even though she didn't usually take sugar. 'That's why I'm not going to lie to you, Nancy.' She glanced down at Danny, who was still asleep. 'I know the poor mite seems to have more life in him – he had a great time with that electronic game your husband brought in, didn't he? – but you just can't tell at this stage. All we can do is say our prayers and be positive.'

'I'm *trying* to pray,' Nancy whispered, although she hadn't done so since her father had left. 'But does it count when I've lapsed for so long? Isn't it cheating?

'Not in my book, love,' retorted Deirdre, who wore,

Nancy had noticed, a gold cross around her neck. 'Oooh look. Someone's waking up. Morning, Danny boy. How are you doing then?'

Nancy bent down to kiss her son good morning, thinking how children and adults differed in the way they woke up. How, instead of stretching and yawning and checking the alarm clock to make sure that really was the time, children just opened their eyes and were wide awake, ready to start the day. Maybe that was enough of a prayer: just say a silent thank you (to whoever was out there) for the day itself, because you never knew how it was going to end.

'Is Billy here yet, Mum?'

It might be early days, but his voice definitely sounded brighter and his speech clearer.

'Not yet, poppet.' She lowered her voice while making an aside to the nurse. 'I'd better warn you. Billy is a bit of a handful.'

Danny's indignant tones shrilled out. 'No he's not. He's a one. That's what Mrs Merryfield says.'

Deirdre wiped the tears of mirth from her face. 'They come out with some good ones, don't they? Mind you, if you're talking about the big mite I saw the other day, your teacher might be right. Was he the kid who was testing that plastic hammer of his on the walls?'

Nancy groaned at the thought, although she was looking forward to seeing Brigid. 'I've got a surprise for you,' she said, stroking Danny's warm hand. 'Billy's mum might be bringing Lily too, if her mum agrees.'

'Lily?' Danny's eyes lit up. 'Cool.'

Deirdre clucked her approval. 'Is she your girlfriend, Danny boy? Oooh, look who's gone all red!'

Danny had slid underneath the covers so his voice came out all muffled. 'She's my princess and when I'm big, I'm going to marry her.'

Nancy couldn't bear to look at Deirdre. When he was big. *If* he ever got big. A firm hand stretched across and squeezed hers. 'Remember.' The quiet Irish lilt was remarkably soothing. 'Be positive. It's the only way.'

Brigid had texted to say they'd be in after lunch so Billy could go to Puddleducks first. '*Owise I will go mad*,' she had said. A few weeks ago, Nancy would have understood that. Now she didn't care if Danny hit everything in sight with a rubber hammer, providing he lived.

The weird thing was that Sam probably felt the same. He had changed so much! He was devoted to their son in a way she'd never seen before. 'No,' he'd insisted the other evening at the hospital. 'You go back to Joe's apartment to get a few hours' sleep. I'll spend the night next to Danny.'

When she'd looked back, before leaving the ward, her chest had tightened with love and other kinds of emotions at the sight of him stroking their boy's forehead tenderly and speaking softly to him.

Of course she hadn't been able to sleep much in a strange place away from Danny, even though Joe's place was very comfortable in a bachelor-like way with its deep squashy black sofa which reclined at the touch of a switch, shelves of CDs in strict alphabetical order, which was the way she had her books at home, and the massive bed which took up most of the bedroom, with its large geometric print in red and black acrylic over the head.

No. She hadn't been able to sleep because she needed to be near her boy. To feel the warmth of his hand and the determined heartbeat through his new blue cotton pyjamas that her mother had brought from the States. To be there if he woke and called out 'Mummy'.

But she also knew that Danny deserved some daddy time with Sam. So when she came back in the morning and found Sam fast asleep on the edge of the bed with Danny in his arms and a Thomas the Tank Engine book lodged between the two of them, she knew she had done the right thing.

She had persuaded Sam not only to go back to Joe's apartment for a sleep last night, but also to go into work for the day. He could see them in the evening, she had assured him, knowing how concerned Sam was about the office. Compassionate leave could only go on for so long, and as the doctors said, this was not a battle that could be fought in a few days. Meanwhile, could Sam just pop into a florist on his way back from the office and send Danny's playgroup leader a big bunch of flowers? Stargazers, maybe. A small token to show how much they appreciated what Gemma had done for them. 'She's been so lovely,' she'd told Sam tearfully. 'I do hope you get to know her, if Danny gets better.'

'When,' Sam had corrected her. 'We've got to be positive.' But his voice wasn't as certain as his words.

It was later, just after lunch, which, like so many hospital meals, seemed to come at least three hours earlier than meals in the real, outside world, that she heard the shouting.

'Danny! Danny!'

No mistaking Billy's voice or that of Brigid, running after him.

One of the other mothers groaned. 'Please don't tell me that's that crazy kid again. The one who tried to beat up the ward last week? Why can't his mother control him?'

Nancy felt a rush of sympathy for her friend. Besides, she didn't care much for the woman in the cropped sports leggings and pink slippers whose daughter had been brought in with bruising all down her legs. Not the small bruises which Danny had had, along with the bleeding gums, but massive purple ones which, judging from the overheard conversations between mother and doctor through the curtains, were similar to those seen on the child only three months ago.

'She can't help it,' Nancy hissed back. 'Billy's just lively.'

The woman sniffed and wiped her nose with the back of her hand. 'No manners. Needs a good smack if you ask me.'

'Danny!'

With one bound, Billy was on Danny's bed, grabbing the new console that Sam had brought the other day.

'Not there,' puffed Brigid. 'On the chair next to him. And share, will you?' Her eyes rolled. 'I'm sorry,

Nancy. He beat me to it as usual. Listen, I need to tell you something.' She glanced around. 'Is there anyone who can keep an eye on those two?'

The woman in the pink slippers sniffed. 'I will if you want.'

No thanks, Nancy was about to say, but Brigid was already whisking her out of the ward into the corridor. They stood by the handwash bottle on the wall. 'I've got to tell you something that the kids mustn't hear.' Her eyes feverish, she grabbed Nancy's hand. 'Have you seen the papers?'

'Danny's notes?'

'No, the newspapers. It's Lily. She's gone missing. And they think her father has got her now he's out of rehab.'

Missing? Lily's father? Dimly Nancy remembered the rumours that had been circulating in what she now called the Before Danny Got Sick days, when life had been normal even though she hadn't realised it. Lily's father was a well-known actor who had been married several times. Nancy wasn't one to read celebrity magazines, but even she had heard of him. He and the singer Dilly Dalung had split up last year and there was an ongoing fierce battle for custody of their daughter. The story had sent shivers down Nancy's spine at the time, making her wonder how on earth she would manage if she and Sam split up and he fought her for Danny.

Now, as she listened to Brigid's hurried account of what had happened during the farm trip, her heart went out to Dilly. How awful! She'd never liked the idea of school trips in case something happened to

Danny. It was like all her fears come true, except that this time it had happened to another child.

'How come the staff didn't realise she was missing for so long?' she demanded.

Brigid looked nervously at a nurse who was pushing a clanking trolley of medicines into the ward and was giving them curious looks. 'Shhh. We reckon it was because Miriam was there instead of Gemma Merryfield. I forgot. You don't know Miriam, do you? She's really the pre-school leader but she's off on maternity leave.' Brigid rolled her eyes again. 'She's not familiar with the new kids and I know that shouldn't be an excuse, but somehow she lost sight of Lily, who was in her group. It was only for a few minutes.'

Only for a few minutes? Nancy felt physically sick. That's all it took. Everyone knew that. The Keep Your Child Safe column in her American magazine was always saying that.

'There's something else.' Brigid's voice suggested that this was more than a small something else. 'Don't tell anyone, whatever you do, as this bit isn't in the papers yet. The canal runs up past the farm shop. And they're dragging it this morning.'

Chapter 46

Nancy was still trying to take in Brigid's news when they walked slowly back towards Danny's bed. Amazingly, the two boys were hiding under the covers, playing some game, while Danny's electronic handset sat abandoned on the bedside cabinet.

'No hammers? No murder on ward nine?' asked Brigid incredulously.

The woman with pink slippers smiled smugly.

'Good as gold, they were. Your boy did start up a bit but I had a word. A firm hand. That's all that's needed.'

Poor Brigid! This wasn't the first time that a mum had suggested that Billy's behaviour was down to bad parenting. Nancy shot her friend an 'ignore her' look.

'I told them,' continued Pink Slippers, 'that if they couldn't share that expensive toy, neither of them could have it. So I suggested they made up their own game instead.'

They all looked at the bedcover, which was moving in what appeared to be giant ripples, with giggles underneath. 'Please no,' said Brigid faintly. 'Bella at Puddleducks said Billy wouldn't stop playing with what she calls his nether regions during the nativity rehearsal the other day. Did I tell you that he's landed the role of the front half of the ox? Sienna's mum was furious because Sienna's only the back feet.'

Nancy, still distraught at Lily's plight, wasn't really listening. Besides, masturbating was, according to her American parenting magazine, quite normal at this age.

'Boys, what are you doing?'

Danny poked his head out. His face was hot and sweaty. Surely this wasn't good for him? On the other hand, he had a lovely rosy flush, unless . . . please no . . . was that a temperature?

'Playing boats.'

'Playing boats?'

'It's Lily's favourite game. We always play boats cos she lives on one, but that's a secret so don't tell anyone.' Danny's face beamed at her. 'Is she coming soon? Cos we've made her a special place.'

The women looked at each other. 'What do you reckon?' asked Brigid, dragging Nancy off to the side again. 'Fact or friction? I'm not joking. You never know with this lot. Billy's always making stuff up to cause trouble. On the other hand, probably there *was* a canal at the back of the farm, so maybe there are some boats to hide in.'

Nancy dropped her voice. 'But surely they'd have checked, wouldn't they?'

Brigid shrugged. 'You'd think so. But I think I might just make a phone call. You OK with those two for a bit?'

The boat drama under the bedcover kept the boys distracted for a good half-hour. Nancy would have thanked the mother in pink slippers but one of the other doctors had arrived, a tall serious grey-haired man, and the curtains had been drawn round the bed occupied by the woman's daughter. Behind them, she could hear low urgent whispers.

When Brigid came back she seemed flustered, pulling Nancy to one side again so the children didn't hear. 'I rang Corrybank but Mr Balls was in some kind of meeting, so I left a message with the school secretary and then I rang the police. Yes, I know that sounds a bit extreme and believe me, I felt a right twat at first when I told them what the boys had said about Lily living on a boat. But then this really nice policewoman said that they were following up all leads and we agreed that kids were usually much better at telling the truth than adults.'

She leaned against the wall, fanning herself with a leaflet asking if she was willing to donate blood. 'Phew, it's hot in here. By the way, on a lighter note, I hear that your mother-in-law and mother were both making a play for Brian at the disco. Do you know him? He used to be the head of Reception. He's a really nice man. Oh no, look at those two! Billy!'

Nancy felt embarrassed at the way her friend was yelling across the ward, as though they were back in the Puddleducks playground.

'Stop banging the hammer on Danny's bed. You'll bend it. And the hammer too.'

It was almost a relief when Brigid went. Danny was sleepy again and Nancy wanted to find a nurse to check that his rosy face was just a sign that he'd been having a great time with his play date.

The lovely warm Irish nurse had gone off duty to be, no doubt, with her husband and their three children. Nancy felt a twinge of jealousy at the thought of them cosily snuggled up in front of the television with their supper trays, a scene which Deirdre had described on more than one occasion. That wasn't the sort of thing which she and Sam had ever allowed in their house, but maybe when they got back they might do things differently.

Meanwhile, several of the nurses had gone behind the curtain around the bed of the child whose mother wore pink slippers. The voices were still low and urgent and, if she wasn't mistaken, she could hear tears. Still, as Patricia had said when she'd visited yesterday and seen the bruises on the child's legs, parents like that ought to be punished. Nancy felt a sudden chill. If it hadn't been for Brigid being so insistent, she would never have left the boys with Pink Slippers. Still, they had been on the ward and she had kept her eye on them all the time through the glass in the door.

'No! No!'

The woman's anguished cries rang out. One of the nurses emerged from behind the curtain and came towards Nancy. 'I'm sorry about this,' she whispered. 'We'll be moving her soon.'

'You're charging her mother?' asked Nancy.

The nurse looked shocked. 'No. Her daughter is going to a side ward.' She began to whisper. 'I shouldn't be saying this, but your neighbour has just had some bad news. The tests have shown the child has leukaemia.'

Chapter 47

It was getting dark outside now. Lily knew that from looking out through the crack in the door of the store cupboard. This would be her second night. One. Two. She counted on her fingers, just as they did in the bed game at playgroup.

A funny gurgle came from her tummy. Lily had eaten her way through the packet of stale biscuits in the cupboard and now there were no more left. It was cold, so she'd snuggled up to the soft pink blanket that she'd had since she was a baby, even though those oil marks on it made it smell nasty.

When it got really dark, she would go out on the top and look for Mama like she had last night.

'Lily! Lily!'

Lily pulled the store-cupboard door shut and wrapped her pink blanket around herself to keep safe.

She'd heard the same voices yesterday and earlier today. Voices that she didn't recognise, which called out this name that wasn't her name at all.

It belonged to another girl, Mama had explained in their own private language that no one else understood. 'You have to pretend you are her. It's like the dressing-up game you play at Puddleducks. Remember, if you play it well, the lady in sunglasses will give us more money so we can live in a proper house. But if you don't, they will take Mama away and she won't see you for a long, long time.'

That prospect was so terrible that Lily would have done anything to prevent it happening. But she needed to see Danny in his London hospital. When she'd left that lady called Miriam, who smelt like funny cheese, to go to the gift shop, she had spotted the boat on the canal. It was like the one she and Mama were living on, except this one was green. And it was about to move!

Maybe, she thought, as she hid in the cupboard, it might take her to London. Then she could give Danny his present. But it had been going very slowly. It could take ages. Almost as long as it had taken her and Mama to get here in that big lorry all the way from their homeland.

'Lily! Lily!'

The voices were coming closer. She could hear people talking. The same people who were driving the boat. Lily had learned many English words from playing with Billy and Danny. She could pick up some now.

There were other phrases that she didn't understand. What did 'Just come from the south?' mean. She needed to find out. Mama said she had a good ear for language. It would take them far.

Footsteps! She could hear people coming down the steps into the boat. The voices were now right outside her cupboard home! Lily's throat tightened as though someone had put a rope round it, which is what Mama had said might happen if they were caught in the lorry.

'No! No!' she cried out.

But the doors were opening and there was a woman standing there with a black hat on and a black coat.

No, she screamed again. And then she started singing. Singing the song they'd learned at nursery because even though she didn't understand all the words, they made her feel better. Besides, when Dillon had got locked in the car, they had sung the song with Mrs Merryfield and then a nice man had come along and let him out.

'We are the little Puddleducks . . .'

'It's all right, Lily,' said the strange voice. 'I'm a policewoman, dear. You're safe now.'

Lily looked up at her in disgust. For some reason, now they were face to face, the fear had gone. Be brave, her mother had said. Always be brave, especially if the people in black uniform found them.

'My name is not Lily.' She spat on the ground as if to prove her point. 'My name is Natasha.'

Chapter 48

It had been *his* fault. He had been the leader in charge of the school trip. Although Lily's disappearance wasn't directly attributable to him, he, Joe, had to carry the can. Just like he'd had to when his team had lost all those millions, which had been another reason, truth to tell, why he'd quit banking.

'It could have happened to anyone, lad,' said Brian, topping up his whisky glass. Joe thought about declining, but leaned back in the G-plan chair with its frayed right arm and shrunken antimacassar and took a long, deep swig instead.

It was nearly 6 p.m., after all, and he was finally off duty after an exhausting twenty-four hours, which had started with last night's phone call from the police to say that Lily had been found. Joe had never prayed in his life, since in his view the Bible simply didn't add up, but to his astonishment he found himself sending a note of thanks to whatever computer was up there, sorting out their numbers.

Then had come the phone calls, and not just from the tabloids. Reporters from responsible newspapers wanted comments from him on whether safety procedures had been followed, and why it was that despite new guidelines on school trips, a four-year-old could go missing.

When they put it like that, he himself found it hard to understand.

Then a pair of policemen had marched up to his room, much to Joyce's consternation until she recognised one of them as the son of a friend. So she'd insisted that they held their meeting in her kitchen, where there was more room. Joe could almost read the policemen's minds. What was a grown man in his thirties with a good job doing in a rented bedsit that was too small to hold three people?

'Can you explain exactly what happened that day?' asked one of the policemen. 'I know you've already given a statement, but there might be some details you've forgotten. And can you also shed any light on why no one realised that Lily was here under false pretences?'

So he did. But the more Joe tried to explain that he honestly hadn't known that Lily was a girl called Natasha, and that the necessary registration procedures had been followed as far as he knew, the more he felt that the police considered him partly responsible for the child's disappearance.

'So what's the score now, lad?' asked Brian, taking off his specs, which were held together with brown tape, polishing them on his new moss-green jumper and replacing them in the same slightly askew position.

Joe began to feel slightly dizzy from the whisky and lack of sleep. 'They're still making their inquiries.'

'But what about her so-called mother, Dilly Dalung?'

'The police are questioning her as well. It all seems extremely complicated.'

'And Gemma? Can she throw any light on the situation?'

Joe felt himself flushing, which was most unlike him. 'Actually, I bought her some get-well flowers but when I knocked on her door, there wasn't any answer. My landlady said she'd gone to stay with her friend Kitty up in London.'

'Humph.' Brian didn't sound impressed. 'And what about that fancy boy of hers, the son of your landlady?'

Joe moved to the window so Brian couldn't see his face. 'Joyce said that Barry was going up tomorrow to visit, so he could take the flowers and any messages if I wanted.'

'You've lost a good one there,' muttered Brian.

Lost a good one? Joe experienced a mixture of surprise and recognition of a feeling that he had been trying to quell for some weeks now, despite himself. 'What do you mean by that?'

'Think you know, lad. Now how about another?'

'No really, I can't, but thanks for the offer.' Joe yawned, knowing he didn't have to try and conceal it. 'I must get back for an early night although – blast – I've just remembered something. I have to stop off at Puddleducks to pick up some paperwork which Miriam has left for me.'

Brian looked concerned. 'Not going to take your bike, are you, lad? You've got to be over the limit with my servings!'

'No way.' Joe shook his head. That was one thing he was very careful about. One of the boys at his previous school had died thanks to a drunk driver, and it was something he'd never forget. 'Mind if I leave it outside your house until tomorrow morning?'

Brian beamed. 'Delighted. I'll try not to have a go. Don't look like that, lad! Can't you see I'm pulling your leg? I don't know. Just as I thought you'd lightened up a bit, you go all serious on me!'

It wasn't any wonder, thought Joe as he walked to Puddleducks. He felt very confused, and not just because of Lily. Still, the cold winter evening helped clear his head, allowing him to do some mental calculations.

It was the way he worked when things were worrying him. In his head he would draw a column on the left, headed Pros. On the right, he had a column headed Cons. He used it as a means of solving a problem, or sometimes as an end-of-week summary in order to reassure himself that his world was still stable. Ed used to sarcastically call it his 'mental ledger'. What was wrong with that?

So far in the Pros column, there was the following:

Danny's life possibly saved by transfusion.

Lily found safely.

Both were major reasons to feel pleased, Joe told himself, rounding the corner towards the playgroup with its brightly painted exterior that now seemed jolly rather than gaudy, as he'd first thought.

But then there was the Cons column.

Guilt over Lily's disappearance.

Possible retribution, which might affect his career, if his leadership skills during the farm trip were questioned.

Gemma and Barry.

Joe paused, surprised. How had that last one slipped in? It didn't belong there. It didn't belong anywhere. OK, he admired Gemma for stepping in and being a bone marrow donor, but wasn't that what any decent person with the right match would have done?

Not Ed. She had been disparaging at the disco when he had mentioned he'd gone to have his blood checked but hadn't been a match. What did you want to do that for? she had said. It's not as though it was your own child.

The irony of the last sentence didn't appear to have occurred to her. If it hadn't been for her actions, carried out without any reference to him, they might have had a child just like Danny. If that child had fallen ill, Joe would have been indebted for life to someone who helped him get better.

She didn't see it like that, Ed had said at the disco, and in a way, her words made him feel much better. They proved, beyond doubt, that he had done the right thing in leaving a woman whose values were so far removed from his own. Maybe that was one to add to the Pros column.

Joe got out his key to open the playgroup door and then realised it was already unlocked. There was a light on inside, too.

'Who's there?'

There was a banging noise as though someone was hitting something against a wall. Another crash and then, from the kitchen area at the back, a small woman appeared in a floral housecoat like one his mother used to wear.

'What you here for?' she demanded in a foreign accent.

'May I ask the same?' But even as Joe spoke, he realised. It was the Eastern European cleaner whom Gemma had mentioned briefly. The noisy one whose

English wasn't great, but whose skills in erasing felt-tip marks and mopping up vomit and unmentionables in the loo were legendary. Presumably she was doing her evening shift.

'I am Mr Balls.'

She was frowning at him and holding the mop handle towards him, like a defence weapon. 'The head of Reception at the big school,' he added quickly.

The woman's face cleared. Now she had stopped looking so ferocious, he could see that she was less bird-like in appearance than he'd thought. She was also older than he'd assumed; about Joyce's age, in fact.

'I need to talk to you.' She was stabbing her mop towards him again.

'I'm afraid this isn't the time to discuss pay rises.' He spoke slowly, in case she didn't understand him.

'You are insulting me! I no want more money!' The mop handle was getting agitated. 'I need to talk about Natasha.'

'Natasha?'

The woman sighed heavily and, to his relief, put down her mop.

'The girl who calls herself Lily. I not responsible, you understand. I do not talk much here. But I hear things. See?' As if to make her point, she tapped her ear. 'I hear Natasha when she plays. She talks to herself. Good in her head, she is. Makes up stories.' She grinned, showing gaps in her teeth. 'When I hear her language is the same as mine, I talk to her. Now I hear rumours about why she go missing. But I know. I know the truth. I tell you now. There is a reward. Yes? Because I do not want it.'

Chapter 49

The cleaner was named Anna. Her story was so remarkable that Joe could hardly believe it.

'I want no reward,' she kept saying. 'I just tell truth. Natasha tell me her story. Then I see her at my church and I ask the mother, "Is it true?" She swears me to secrecy.' She crossed herself. On her chest two small gold crosses already hung on chains. 'May God forgive me for telling you now.'

Speaking rapidly, the cleaner explained that Natasha/Lily came from the same Eastern European country as she, Anna, did. So too did her real mother, who was not Dilly Dalung, but a young girl who worked as an assistant cook for the singer. She happened to have a daughter who was not only the same age as the celebrity's child but also looked quite similar, with dark hair and very white skin.

Dee-lee, as the cleaner called her, was terrified of her daughter being kidnapped by her estranged and possibly violent husband and whisked off to the Middle Eastern country from which he came. So Ms Dalung hatched this elaborate plan whereby she enrolled her real daughter Lily in a nursery on the border of Bedfordshire under another name and paid her assistant cook a large sum of money to substitute her own child, Natasha, as a decoy.

'She even tell newspapers about this place,' Anna had said, stabbing her finger in the air. 'Dilly Dalung wanted the papers to think her daughter was here, at Puddleducks, so she gave them anonymous tip-off. She thought it would take attention away from her real daughter.'

Somehow Joe persuaded Anna to come with him to the police station. 'We need to tell them about this,' he urged.

The cleaner looked scared. 'I no want to get into trouble.'

'You won't, I promise you.'

Even so, he felt a wave of concern for her when they got to the police station and he explained to the tight-faced policeman on the desk that Anna had some information about Dilly Dalung's so-called daughter. 'We'll need to take a statement, madam,' said the officer. Anna was escorted into another room, looking back at Joe, who felt as though he had delivered her into the hands of the enemy. Naturally, he waited for her – her interview took over an hour – and then made sure she got home safely.

The following day a best-selling tabloid ran the whole story under the headline SCANDAL AT SUBURBAN PLAYGROUP.

Why, it demanded, hadn't anyone checked that the adult enrolling a child was indeed its legal carer? Joe had asked himself the same thing before finding out that a carer only had to produce a birth certificate on registration, and to obtain nursery vouchers. He/she wasn't required to show proof of parentage.

There was also a piece written by the women's page

editor, about peer loyalty and how touching it was that Lily had been trying to take her sick friend a present.

Then there was a scathing article in his own broadsheet, asking why and how Natasha's mother could have put her child at risk by allowing her to be a decoy. The journalist had gone into considerable detail, portraying the mother as a woman who had come from a difficult background and entered Britain with papers that possibly weren't legal.

Joe's stomach began to churn when he read that. What would happen to Lily now? Proceedings were bound to be set in motion.

There was something else, too. Something which he didn't want to allow himself to think about, but he had to accept. None of this was good publicity for Puddleducks in its bid to win the Top Ten Playgroup Award. As the implications began to sink in, his mobile went.

'Joe. Are you all right? I've just seen the papers.'

It was Gemma.

'What are you doing on the phone? You're meant to be resting.'

'I know, but like I said, I've just seen the headlines. Look, I know what you're thinking and I'd feel the same but you don't have to worry, Joe. You honestly don't.'

Despite the gravity of the situation, he couldn't help smiling. 'How do you know what I'm thinking?'

'Because any decent person would wonder if they had done everything they could to make sure that none of the kids went missing, and I just know, Joe, that you would have. Lily wasn't on your list of children; she was on Miriam's. You mustn't beat yourself up, Joe. You really mustn't.'

'Thanks.' Her words made him feel better. She was right. Of course he felt responsible, but only another teacher – a kind, caring one like Gemma – would have understood this. Why hadn't he realised at the beginning of term that she was such a genuinely nice person? Why had he been so determined to see the worst in her, and indeed in everyone else?

'There's one more thing. Don't start worrying about the Playgroup Award. I know this might affect it, but if we don't get it, we don't get it. The most important thing is that Lily is safe.'

He nodded, forgetting she couldn't see him. 'You're right.'

'Good.' The relief in her voice was audible. 'I thought you might try to argue me down like you used to do.'

'Argue you down?'

'Well, you know what I mean.' She sounded as though she wished she hadn't said that. 'Listen, I must go. Kitty's coming up the stairs with dinner – aren't I being spoiled? Now, keep your chin up, OK?'

After she rang off, Joe felt considerably better. Gemma was right in everything she'd said, including the fact that he used to argue her down, as she put it. She was honest, kind and generous. Ed would be having a right old moan if she'd been a donor. In fact, she wouldn't have volunteered in the first place. Meanwhile, there was one vital phone call he had to make which might just help, although he knew how painful it would be.

There was so much to do that week that Joe almost forgot that Mike and Lynette were coming up for the weekend with the boys. The fevered atmosphere both in the main school and at Puddleducks, where the Lily/Natasha saga was even surpassing the bulletins on Danny, had to be calmed down. There was also the nativity play to sort out. Miriam, who had stepped in to 'help' during Gemma's recuperation, had managed to give the part of Joseph to two different boys, and had increased the number of wise men to five in order to prevent tantrums.

'What's wrong with wise women?' Di had asked, in what was meant to be a jokey aside. Brilliant idea! Joe patted her on the back, which almost made her choke on her custard cream, and promptly enrolled three girls from his year. If they were going to do a nativity play, he might as well make it different.

Then there was the not-so-small matter of the deadline for the award. The mural could have been abandoned altogether, but Nancy's tutor, a man called Doug who seemed to have taken a bit of a shine to her from the admiring way in which he spoke, had organised a working party. They had all made gargantuan efforts, and the project was almost finished.

That was another thing he had to admit he'd been wrong about. The mural was most impressive, and completely recognisable. There was the canal wending its way through the north side of town. There was the high street with its row of shops, both pretty and practical. There was the park with the sports centre on the other side of the road. And there was Puddleducks, round the corner from Corrybank.

Annie had been doing a photography course and had taken pictures during the making of the mural. The plan was that when it was finished – hopefully by next Monday, said the workers – the final pictures would be taken and sent off to the award organisers.

Meanwhile, he and Brian had almost finished the *MY SKOOL!* book. Joe had been going to find an online publisher but, with everything else going on, hadn't had the time, so Brian had volunteered to check some out.

'It's not as though I'm rushed off my feet, lad,' he said with a twinge of regret in his voice. Then his eyes twinkled. 'Mind you, did I tell you I've started going to salsa class? Two ladies, not so distantly connected to Danny, insist on escorting me every Tuesday and Thursday afternoon. I always wanted to dance but my Mavis, bless her, wasn't that keen on account of her bunions.'

On the whole, Joe told himself as he mentally totted up his Pros and Cons columns, life wasn't going too badly. And then he received the letter.

Chapter 50

'I agree,' said Mike as they walked along the towpath after a very filling lunch at one of the warm, busy pubs on the high street, which was already adorned with Christmas decorations even though there were a good three weeks to go. 'It does seem a blow, especially when they had all but promised you the job.'

Joe felt a wrench just under his ribs. It still hurt as much as when he had opened the envelope on Friday morning. He wasn't used to rejection in his working life, and this had come as a surprise.

'Unfortunately, the position which we originally discussed is no longer available . . .'

There was no reason given, but Joe couldn't help wondering if it was because his name had been in many of the reports about Lily/Natasha vanishing from the farm trip.

'What are you going to do?' asked Lynette as she fell into line next to him. Joe's arm accidentally brushed against hers, and he stiffened in case she had thought it was intentional.

'Apply for something else, I suppose, although there's not much being advertised at the moment. I may have to wait until after Christmas and, if necessary, take a few months off until the autumn.'

'Sounds good.'

Was that a hint of envy in Lynette's voice? 'I can't remember the last time Mike and I had a holiday.'

You don't need one when you live by the sea, he was about to say, but then, as he looked ahead and saw the boys swooping and diving in some make-believe game near the canal edge, stopped himself. That visit to Danny's hospital had taught him quite a few things. One of them was that you needed to appreciate what you had. Another was that you couldn't really understand a parent's hopes and fears until you were one yourself. A proper one. Not a nearly one.

'Tell you what,' he began, but then there was a splash.

Lynette was there before either he or Mike moved, yanking out Fraser, who had tried to push his brother into the water and then fallen in himself.

'It was your fault!'

'No, it was yours!'

'It was both of yours.' Lynette's voice had a tone in it that he hadn't heard before. It was relief mixed with anger. How did parents do it? It was such a responsibility, making sure that a small person stayed alive all day.

'It's OK.' He put a reassuring hand on Lynette's shoulder before remembering, and taking it off quickly. 'No one is hurt. How about going back to my place and drying off in the bathroom?'

Joyce loved an emergency. It made her, as she told them all, feel useful, especially now she didn't have any small children at home to look after. If she wasn't mistaken, she had some spare clothes left over from when Barry had been that age.

Both boys emerged dry and slightly subdued in warm jerseys and jeans that had once been worn by the perfect Barry. Joe found himself feeling slightly irritable.

'Uncle Joe, Uncle Joe! You promised to take us to the ice-cream parlour on the high street. The one with the chocolate fountain.'

Mike cut in. 'I'm not sure you deserve that now.'

'Pleease, Dad. Pleease, Mum.'

Joe glanced at Lynette as though seeking approval. Ever since that misunderstanding on the beach he'd been feeling horribly awkward in front of her, and somehow he sensed she felt the same.

'If Uncle Joe wants to treat you, that's up to him.' She gave him a quick smile, and Joe hoped that meant he was forgiven.

'We could go on to the Puddleducks mural after the ice-cream parlour,' he suggested as they walked down Joyce's stairs, the boys leaping down two at a time. 'I'd like to show it to you. You know I wasn't very keen at first, but actually, it's turned out to be amazing.'

Mike sounded amused. 'Like the book you showed me, the one you and your predecessor have been writing? Boys, don't do that. You've got so many bruises that I'm amazed social services haven't been on to us.'

He turned back to his friend. 'You might say you want to leave this place, Joe, but to my mind, you seem to have settled in rather well. By the way, you were going to tell me something about Ed. You said she'd done something really surprising.'

Lynette's nose wrinkled in disgust. 'After what you told me about her complete lack of regret for . . . for what she did, I've lost any sympathy I might have had for her. Think I'll let you two walk ahead and have some boy time while I get the kids their ice creams.'

'No, please let me,' Joe insisted. 'It's my treat.' He gave an affectionate look at the boys, who were trying to arm-wrestle as they walked along the street. 'They may be the closest I ever get to having children of my own.'

After a good fifteen minutes at the ice-cream shop ('Yes, you can have a double scoop if that's all right with Mum and Dad'), Joe finally got a chance to walk side by side with Mike while Lynette hung behind with the boys. His heart began to thump as he tried to work out the best way to talk about what had been eating away at him ever since that day on the beach. It had been a mistake. A silly mistake. At first he had thought he could just brush it over but since then, every time he'd spoken to Mike, he had felt a horrible burning guilt that wouldn't go away.

He didn't know what he would do without his two closest friends. But at the same time, he knew they couldn't have the relationship they'd enjoyed before unless he came clean.

'There's something I need to tell you,' he began as they walked along the high street.

Mike raised his eyebrows. 'There is?'

'It's about . . .'

372

'Hi, Joe!'

He almost didn't recognise her. She was sporting a sweet white hat that clung to her head, looking rather like a twenties flapper. She also wore high black boots under a white coat and was hanging happily on Barry's arm.

'Gemma! Are you feeling better? Did you get my flowers? How is Danny?'

He felt his words spluttering out of him like an awkward, embarrassed adolescent.

'I'm much better, thanks. The flowers were lovely. Thank you.' Then her face darkened slightly. 'Nancy phoned me this morning to say that Danny has a bit of an infection, but that happens sometimes. I'm so relieved about Lily, though.'

Joe nodded as Barry made to move on, but Gemma stopped him as Lynette and the boys caught up. 'Are these your godsons?' she grinned, looking down at two faces smeared with chocolate and ice cream.

'Yes, we are!' announced Charlie proudly. 'Uncle Joe's the best. He got me a bigger ice cream than Fraser.'

'No he didn't.'

'Yes he did!'

Gemma laughed. Barry, Joe noticed, was squeezing her arm again as though to move her on, but she was holding out her hand to Lynette before he could properly introduce them. 'Hi. I'm Gemma. I work with Joe; he's my boss and also my next-door neighbour.'

'Really?' Lynette's voice had an interested lilt to it. 'So you're the Puddleducks playgroup leader! I'm a teacher – maths – and so is my husband, Mike.'

Barry was looking bored now. Couldn't Gemma see that this was the kind of man who needed the conversation to revolve around him? thought Joe.

'I've always admired pre-school teachers,' Lynette was saying.

'And I've always admired anyone who can teach maths!' laughed Gemma. She gave him a wicked look. 'It's not one of my strengths, is it, Joe?'

Barry was looking really impatient now.

'Got to get back to write the next newsletter – maybe see you back at Joyce's later,' Gemma called out over her shoulder as she allowed herself to be moved on.

The boys had already shot ahead in a running race with Lynette close behind them. 'Better catch them up or they'll get lost,' said Joe, glancing at Mike. 'What are you looking at me like that for?'

'If I wasn't mistaken, I'd say you secretly fancied that girl.'

'Rubbish! We have nothing in common apart from our jobs, and besides she is at least ten years younger than me.'

'I know the signs.' Mike's voice took on the 'I've got something to tell you' tone that Joe had learned to spot over the years. 'It's different from the way you look at Lynette.'

Joe's blood froze.

'That's what you wanted to talk to me about, isn't it? It's all right. Lynette told me. We don't have any secrets. She gave you a comfort hug on the beach the other month and when you went to kiss her cheek, you accidentally brushed her mouth. Is that the long and the short of it?'

'Yes,' Joe mumbled.

'It's OK. Honest. I know you're not after my wife. You're not that kind of guy.'

Joe didn't know what to say. Mike and Lynette had talked about the kiss? He wanted to curl up with embarrassment. And now Mike thought that he had the hots for Gemma? Ridiculous!

But, somehow, what really haunted him, as they made their way down the hill towards the playgroup and its mural, was that Mike and Lynette had a relationship where they could talk about things like that.

And that was just the kind of relationship he wanted with someone. Whoever she might be.

'Uncle Joe! Uncle Joe! Are we nearly at the mural?'

'Nearly. Just round the corner and . . .'

No. He couldn't believe it.

Aghast, the five of them stood there, staring at the wall. Yesterday it had been virtually completed, apart from one square where the team were still working on the cinema.

Now it was an awful indistinguishable mess, smeared with red paint and an obscenity which Joe could hardly bear to look at, sprayed in big sprawling letters.

It was ruined. Absolutely ruined.

THE PUDDLEDUCKS PLAYGROUP NEWSLETTER DECEMBER ISSUE

Isn't it amazing how time flies when we're having fun? It doesn't seem a minute, to us at Puddleducks, since term started in September. And now it's nearly Christmas!

As you know, we've got some exciting events planned in the lead-up to the festive season. However, we'd like to put out a gentle reminder that next Monday is the final dress rehearsal for the Nativity Play. So all you kind mums who have volunteered to do your own children's costumes need to bring in the clothes by Friday.

If you don't list costume-making amongst your many skills, please let us know as soon as possible so we can find an outfit for your little Puddleduck.

Meanwhile, Nancy Carter Wright has asked me to pass on her thanks for all the lovely cards and gifts you have sent to Danny. Thanks also to the mural team for all their splendid efforts. Fingers crossed that we win the award!

One last thing. I know you are all busy but if you have time, please could you help your children learn the following song.

THE PUDDLEDUCKS SHARING SONG

We're the little Puddleducks
We're trying to learn to share!
It's really hard to lend our toys
But we know it's only fair!

Chapter 51

Was that OK? Gemma, flushed from her short walk with Barry when they'd bumped into Joe and his friends, reread the draft for the December Puddleducks newsletter that she was about to finalise and email out. It was later than usual but then again, as Barry said, she had every excuse.

'I still think you should be resting instead of working,' he chided gently as she sat on the floor, laptop on her knee and her head leaning back against him. 'Sure you're doing the right thing in going back tomorrow?'

Absolutely! The doctor had said she could, providing she felt better. And she did. It was incredible, really. When she'd read about people donating bone marrow, she'd presumed they were hospitalised for weeks. But nowadays it was apparently a couple of days and then anything between two and four weeks off. She'd had more than a fortnight and that had been plenty. Now she was itching to get back to her small Puddleducks. Seeing Joe just now in the high street with his lovely godchildren made her even keener. It was obvious that they adored him – clearly poor Joe, who was still grieving for the baby he could have had, was a real hands-on godfather. She could just imagine him arriving at Christmas with his arms full of goodies from Hamleys.

Still, enough of that. She had to get on. 'I'm not sure whether I ought to refer to Lily in my newsletter,' she mused out loud.

'Lily?'

She felt slightly irritated.

'Lily,' she repeated. 'My little girl who went missing.'

'*Your* little girl?' Barry teased her. 'I knew you were married, but you didn't tell me you had kids.'

Her skin began to prickle the way it had once when she'd put on an angora cardigan of Kitty's. Your colour, her friend had said, but if it doesn't feel right you shouldn't wear it. The weird thing was that, usually, Barry did feel right. Really right. But every now and then he'd say something jarring, like just now. If there was one thing she couldn't joke about, it was having children. She'd have thought he'd have understood that.

'I see all the Puddleducks as my children,' said Gemma, hurt. 'Their parents put them in my care.'

Barry wrapped his arm around her and she couldn't help snuggling in to him; it felt so good to be loved. Besides, didn't everyone have tiffs?

'Someone clearly didn't care very well for Lily or Natasha or whatever her real name is.' He bent to kiss the top of her head. 'It would have been different if *you* had been there to supervise.'

Would it? Gemma had briefly wondered that. Joe wasn't used to dealing with under-fours and Miriam was still in a post-natal stupor, from all accounts. She felt concerned for Joe. She'd heard through Bella that he had felt obliged to shoulder the responsibility himself, even though Lily (as she still thought of her) had been in Miriam's group and not his.

As for the Dilly Dalung story, she could hardly believe it. Sometimes mothers did some really irresponsible things.

Gemma pressed Send and jumped up. 'Right. That's done. I went without mentioning Lily in the end. It occurred to me that as there are legal implications, it's safest not referring to her.'

'Good point. Now come here and allow Dr Barry to check if you really are on the mend.' He put his hand in his pocket. 'Actually, I've brought you a present.' I saw it in the antique shop on the high street and thought it was perfect for you. May I? Here, let me take off that old silver chain.'

But I've always worn it, she wanted to say, although at the same time she could almost hear her grandmother's voice in her head. *It doesn't belong to you any more, just as Sam can never belong to you. Not now he has a partner and child.*

'Thank you.' She stood in front of the mirror with Barry behind her, fastening the pretty pale-pink coral necklace round her neck. It felt different from the chain. Heavier.

'It suits you!' Barry's eyes met hers in the mirror. 'There's something I want to tell you.'

As he spoke, there was the sound of footsteps running up the stairs and children's voices. 'I'll knock first.'

'No. Me. *Me.*'

Barry's voice was firm as he opened Gemma's door. 'Wrong one, mate. Your godfather lives next door.'

The pair of freckled faces stared up at both of them. 'We know that. Uncle Joe is on his way up behind us. He needs to tell Gemma something.'

The other one nodded. "Shreally important.'

Joe was puffing slightly as he came up the stairs, something that Barry – who worked out twice a day in his mother's sitting room – clearly noticed too.

'Gemma.' His eyes flickered across to Barry and then back again. 'I'm sorry to bother you. But we've just been up to see the mural.'

His voice was wobbling. Joe never wobbled. 'I'm afraid it's been vandalised.'

'No!'

Gemma was aware of someone putting their arms around her. Not Barry. Not Joe. They belonged to a woman who sensed her distress and knew that she was trying hard, so hard, not to break down in front of the children, because an adult should never do that.

'Tell you what, Gemma,' the kind auburn-haired woman was saying. Gemma remembered her name was Lynette. 'Why don't we all walk up and you can see for yourself? Then maybe we can work out what to do.'

Barry wanted to drive her there, but she refused politely. It was only a ten-minute walk and she needed the time to come to terms with what she'd just been told. But nothing could have prepared her for the huge red slashes of paint on the mural that had been so close to completion.

'Vandals again,' she said in disgust. 'They smashed up the front window of the chemist last week. And a newsagent the week before.'

Mike looked shocked. 'I didn't think this sort of thing happened out here in Hazelwood.'

She smiled sadly. 'I'm afraid it does.' She looked at Joe. 'What are we going to do?'

He didn't sound optimistic. 'Mike's already rung a decorator friend from Dorset who's suggested a few things. He's going to come up tomorrow to have a look.'

Barry's deep voice cut in. 'Dorset? That's miles away! I'll see if I can find someone local. We must be able to salvage it somehow.'

'Doug the mosaics tutor might have some ideas too,' Gemma said, as they all stood looking sombrely at the mural. Whoever was responsible had been thorough. The red paint had been smeared on thickly, while the obscenity had probably come from an aerosol can and was unlikely to come off easily.

'Mum, what does that mean?' asked Charlie, pointing to it.

Lynette put her arm around both her sons' shoulders and drew them to her, an action which made Gemma's heart churn. 'It's a very rude way of saying go away.'

How calm she was. And honest, too. If she ever became a mother, thought Gemma, she'd like to be like that. 'The deadline for the award is in a week's time,' she said quietly. 'We'll never get another one done by then.'

The taller boy piped up brightly. 'Don't worry, Gemma. Uncle Joe will think of something! He always does!'

Chapter 52

It turned out that restoration would be almost impossible. Both the local tradesman whom Barry found and the decorator who came up from Dorset had shaken their heads and said that if a different kind of paint had been used, the mural might have been saved. This stuff, however, dried almost immediately.

Doug, a nice steady man who asked Gemma to pass his best on to Nancy, spent some time observing the damage and said he'd put his thinking cap on.

Meanwhile, Gemma and her team had to reassure the horrified parents and Puddleducks who were met by the red mess when they came in on Monday morning.

'Shocking, Miss Merryfield. Absolutely shocking.'

'Mrs Merryfield, can Father Christmas order another muriel?'

'Mrs Merryfield? Why are walls hard?' Good question, Sienna.

'Just as well I took some pictures of your mural, Gemma. We can always send them in instead,' said Annie.

Gemma and Joe, who had come down from Reception to help her with the inevitable questions, stared at each other. Of course!

'I took pictures right up until Friday morning,'

Annie announced proudly, handing over her memory stick. 'Feel free to use them as you like. Don't forget to credit me, though. It might help.' She smiled shyly. 'I've decided to set up as a part-time photographer. I've been looking for something to do and now I think I've found it.'

Good for her! Meanwhile, something else was troubling Gemma as she set about sorting out costumes for the rear half of a cow and front half of a sheep, not to mention finding a wise man's missing staff and a shepherd's robe.

Danny's temperature was still up. 'It might mean,' Nancy had said in a trembling voice during a message she'd left earlier on Gemma's answerphone, 'that he's rejecting the bone marrow.'

The local paper picked up the news of the vandalism first, and then the nationals. Gemma hadn't thought it was the kind of story that would attract such wide attention, but she was wrong. At this time of the year, Joe informed her, newspapers were keen to plug anything with a heart-tug factor.

It might seem calculated, he went on, but he had a friend on the *Sunday Telegraph* (for someone who was a Colin Firth with attitude crossed with Mr Grumpy, that man seemed to have influential friends) who had written a piece which had been picked up by other papers. The results were mixed.

THUGS DESTROY PRIZE-WINNING MURAL AT DILLY DALUNG SCANDAL PLAYGROUP!

OK, so it hadn't won a prize yet, but it caught the eye.

RED PAINT PUTS PAID TO PLAYGROUP'S BID FOR TOP AWARD

That was more like it.

PUDDLEDUCKS LAND IN HOT WATER WITH RED PAINT VANDALS

Another eye-catcher. It would be good publicity, Joe assured her, and, judging from the sympathy letters and cheques for new equipment, it seemed to be working.

Meanwhile, Joe had sent in his own entry for the Reception year, which apparently he'd been working on with Brian. Gemma hadn't known about that until Di at the big school had let it slip. 'Oh yes, the two of them get on like a house on fire,' she'd assured Gemma importantly. 'Joe visits him regularly, he does. In fact, he's a much nicer man than we gave him credit for. Such a shame he's leaving.'

Talk about hypocrisy! Di had always been one of Joe's biggest critics, constantly dissing him to Beryl.

Mind you, hadn't she, Gemma, thought he'd been difficult at times, until she'd found out about the tragedy in his past? Even so, that only went some way towards condoning the head of Reception's critical attitudes, which, it had to be said, weren't nearly so critical nowadays. It was so confusing!

Still, perhaps she should try to push her mixed feelings to the back of her mind. There was too much else to concentrate on. For a start, Lily had been taken into care. The staff at Puddleducks had been asked to write reports on whether, in their view, she had been properly looked after at home, which hadn't after all been the Dilly Dalung mansion, but a canal boat without hot water or heating.

Gemma and Bella had no hesitation in writing glowing reports. Lily had always come into play-group looking immaculate and had perfect manners, which said a lot for her upbringing. She was also extremely bright, and should be allowed to stay in an environment in which she'd clearly thrived and made friends.

There was another thing that Gemma mentioned in her report, and that was Lily's feverish excitement at being a twinkling star in the nativity play. And now it wasn't going to happen. Gemma's heart lurched at the thought of Lily being in a foster family some-where while her mother was still in custody.

Honey, who had been the front end of the third cow, was now going to replace Lily, while Edward the Second, as distinct from Edward the First (there were two Edwards in the playgroup), was going to replace Honey.

As Gemma checked her cast list while Bella sorted out the Pyjama Drama session that morning, she knew that despite everything, hers was the only job in the world that could ever make her happy. This time of the year in pre-school was manic, and yet she loved it.

The chaos also helped to take her mind off the legal documents that had arrived that week, which she had duly signed with a slight pang, it had to be said, and sent off to the lawyer. With any luck, Sam would have managed to sign his bit too without Nancy knowing.

'Rather ironic that you've finally found each other,' the lawyer had said crisply, after her talk with Sam, as though it was her fault. 'If you had done so earlier, you could have had a divorce in two years, instead of waiting five.'

But if they had, she thought, they might not have tied up the loose ends during the last extraordinary three months.

Yet had those loose ends really all been tied up? She wasn't sure.

Chapter 53

It wasn't long now until the play, and excitement amongst the Puddleducks was rising to fever pitch.

'Mrs Merryfield, Mrs Merryfield, are we doing the play today?'

The staff were on edge, too. Would Beth's mum get those alterations to the star done in time? Would Joseph wet his pants again? And, oh dear, Bella's broken a nail!

Johnnie, who kept getting his singulars and plurals muddled, thanks no doubt to his au pair who did the same, only had one line. But you never knew what it was going to be until it came out. Yesterday, during practice, he announced that he'd lost his 'sheeps', and then looked around with a delighted beam, as though knowing that might raise some laughs in the audience.

Clemmie was beside herself with excitement because she was playing Mary. 'My daddy's coming with his new girlfriend and their baby,' she said, tugging at Gemma's black Topshop trousers to make her point.

Poor Clemmie's mum. Did she know? Edward the Second had been word-perfect until he'd come down with a cold and lost his voice. Still, as Bella pointed out, even if he wasn't well enough for the big day, it shouldn't be too difficult to coach someone else to go 'Moo'.

Tatiana, who had dreams of going on *Britain's Best Talent* when she was old enough, was hyper hyper because Miss Merryfield's friend Kitty was coming down to play the part of the fairy queen. In order to take in other religious beliefs and accommodate non-believers, the nativity script which Gemma and Bella had written between them had become somewhat unorthodox.

'Was that the same Kitty Macdonald whom I saw on television the other night?' asked Tatiana's stepdad. 'She was singing like an angel and playing that recorder of hers like a flute.'

Yes, it was! Since the summer, when her first album had been released, Kitty's career had soared off the ground. She was everywhere! Gemma couldn't have been prouder of her friend. She deserved a break, she told her. 'So do you,' Kitty had replied sternly during their latest phone conversation. They both preferred phoning to texting or email, which were, they agreed, so impersonal. 'Now what's happened to that handsome paratrooper of yours?'

Gemma, who was sitting as usual with her back against the wall dividing her from Joe's room, hoped, for some reason she couldn't put her finger on, that he couldn't hear. 'We're having dinner tonight,' she said quietly.

'Speak up, Gemmie. I can't hear.'

'We're having dinner tonight,' she said, wondering why she felt slightly awkward.

'Anywhere posh?'

Gemma named a new restaurant in the town that had just opened.

'Wow! That's impressive. We've got one in Chelsea too. Have fun and don't forget to tell me all about it tomorrow morning, providing you're not snuggled up in bed together.'

Gemma tried to laugh this off, not entirely successfully. Since Sam, she hadn't allowed herself to have a 'proper' relationship with anyone, partly because, deep down, she couldn't help wondering if he might come back. But now, things had changed. Hadn't they?

Two hours later, Barry knocked on her door to see if she was ready. Every time she saw him, she was struck by his height and piercing blue eyes. When he looked at her, he made her feel special, something she hadn't experienced for a very long time.

'You look gorgeous,' he said, taking in the classic cut of her violet shift dress, which she'd found in the second-hand designer shop in town. The style suited her, the manageress had assured her, although it wasn't easy walking in the heels which the woman had suggested she wore with them. As they went into the restaurant, Gemma felt slightly embarrassed when one, no two, men smiled at her.

'It's because you look stunning,' whispered Barry, who'd noticed their reaction, quickly pulling out her chair before the waiter could get there first.

He looked very handsome in beige chinos and a brown checked shirt, which he wore open at the neck without a tie. A woman at a neighbouring table was sending him admiring glances. I'm a lucky girl, she told herself as the waiter whipped out a pink starched napkin, placing it in front of her.

After they ordered, they made small talk. At first, Gemma felt slightly nervous. This was a proper date, after all. She didn't want to say anything that would put him off or make her appear boring.

'How was your day?' he asked.

Gemma let out a mock groan. 'Let's see! The front half of the ox performed an impromptu puddle in her excitement, and then the second wise woman refused to leave the messy corner to practise.'

Barry did a double take. 'What's the messy corner?'

She was just about to explain when their food arrived. Barry had perfect manners, waiting for her to pick up her knife and fork before he did. But there was a reticence about him this evening that didn't seem quite right. Years of uncertainty about Sam had taught her that she needed to know the score in a relationship: she had to find out what was on his mind.

'Is something wrong?' she asked nervously. 'Am I boring you?'

He put down his cutlery and dabbed his mouth. Gemma's heart plummeted. He doesn't care for me any more, she thought. He's going to say we're not right for each other after all.

'The truth of it is, Gemma, that I've got to go back earlier than I had thought. I've got a posting in . . . well, I can't say where at the moment. But it's a long way away, I'm afraid.'

Really? She hadn't been expecting that. In one way, his announcement made her feel hugely relieved, because it meant he hadn't been about to dump her. Then the implications of what he'd just said sank in.

He was being sent abroad again. Where would that leave her?

'I've got to report back on Christmas Eve,' he added gently, reaching out for her hand.

She felt tears prick her eyes. It was so unfair! Just as she'd found a man who seemed to care for her and who made her tingle whenever she saw him, he was leaving. He wouldn't be here for Christmas Day when most couples were together. What was wrong with her? Why did she always attract men who didn't stay?

Barry squeezed her hand. 'I feel the same as you, Gemma. I can't bear the idea of being apart.'

She hadn't actually said those words, even though her face might have indicated as much. Yet it was proof that he knew what she was thinking. Did that mean they were soulmates? She felt confused, and only took in snatches of what Barry was now saying.

'Understand that it would be unfair to expect you to wait without any kind of commitment . . . The sort of girl I've always been looking for . . . My mother thinks you're wonderful . . . So would you do me the honour of being my wife?'

His wife! He was proposing to her? Stunned, Gemma looked at the man kneeling beside her, holding a ring in an open box. The woman at the next table was staring with undisguised envy. Barry is actually asking me to marry him, thought Gemma, thrilled and amazed. She'd found him at last! The perfect husband. Was this really happening?

But you're married, said a small voice inside her.

Rubbish, she told herself. It's only on paper and besides, I'm virtually divorced, aren't I?

Barry's right knee was still firmly on the ground as he held the ring up to her. He was beginning to look concerned. 'Gemma,' he said in a steady voice, 'I understand this might be a bit of a surprise and believe me, it's a revelation to me as well. But I love you and I want to share the rest of my life with you. Will you accept?'

She lowered her voice. 'Do you want to have children, one day?'

He gave a decisive nod. 'Of course.'

That was all right then! The handsome Barry who turned heads and made her tingle and who wanted to marry her also wanted her babies! How amazing was that?

'Yes,' she heard herself saying excitedly. 'Yes please. I do want to marry you!'

'She's said yes,' someone yelled, and then the whole restaurant was filled with the sound of clapping.

They had to tell Joyce first, of course, even though it was gone midnight when they got back. She whooped with excitement, hugging Gemma.

'I knew you'd be a perfect match,' she crowed. 'I just knew it from the minute I met you, sweetie!'

'Hey, Mum,' Barry had joked. 'Gemma will think you've set us up.'

Then Joyce made the kind of face that suggested she felt she might well have had a hand in it, and insisted they all toasted the engagement with a bottle of champagne that she'd been saving for her grandson's christening but which could always be replaced.

Later, when Barry walked Gemma upstairs to her

room, she stopped at the door. The light under Joe's door, she noticed, was out. He was probably asleep or maybe away for the night, as he had been the other evening.

'Would you like to come in?' she heard herself say quietly.

Barry looked surprised, and for a minute she wondered if she should have waited for him to take the initiative. If it hadn't been for the shock proposal and the champagne she wouldn't have been so forward, but they were engaged now, weren't they? Besides, she wanted him to hold her close and run his tongue down her neck as he had started to do the other evening. Since then, she'd spent several nights on her own, wondering what it would have been like if he had continued.

'I would love to come in,' said Barry firmly. Before she could say any more he picked her up in his arms, just like a romantic hero in a black and white film. 'Gemma Merryfield,' he said, looking down at her, 'I am going to make you the happiest girl in the world.'

Then, still holding her, he somehow opened the door and went inside, kicking it shut behind them.

Chapter 54

Gemma woke up early because of the sun streaming in through the thin curtains. Stretching out diagonally, she slowly opened her eyes. And then remembered!

Had she dreamed it? Or had Barry really scooped her up outside her door and carried her in? She glanced down at her left hand. Clearly she hadn't dreamed the bit about getting engaged. She adjusted the sapphire ring, which was slightly tight on her finger.

Gemma knew what Bella, who was an expert on engagement rings, would say about it. In Bella's view, diamonds – preferably large ones – were the only suitable kind of stone, since they 'went with everything'. But it was the man who was important, wasn't it? Not the ring.

Just at that moment the door opened and Barry walked in, fully dressed. 'You made me jump,' said Gemma, instinctively holding the sheet against her chest.

Barry came and sat on the edge of the bed. 'Sorry. I didn't think about knocking.' His hand caressed her shoulders. 'Not after last night.'

He kissed her lips lightly and Gemma tried to respond, but it simply didn't feel right. Just as it hadn't really felt right last night. It was all coming back to her now. Gemma had never been one for talking about sex to girlfriends, but both she and Kitty had always agreed that if you didn't feel fireworks the first time, it wasn't a good sign.

Gemma hadn't felt fireworks with Barry. She *should* have done. He ticked all the right boxes: attentive, steady, loyal, good son, hard worker, fantastic looking. And she'd definitely been attracted to him *before* last night. So why didn't she feel the same way now?

'Hope you didn't mind me leaving you in the middle of the night.' Barry was cradling her in his arms now, which made her feel slightly trapped. 'The bed's too small for the two of us, don't you think, and besides I always get up at 5 a.m. to do my exercises.'

He smiled in a slightly preening way, clearly expecting a compliment along the lines of 'how dedicated' or 'you don't need to work out'.

Indeed, it was on the tip of Gemma's tongue to say something polite, but just at that moment her mobile went.

Barry raised his eyebrows. 'A phone call? At 7 a.m.? Who's ringing my beautiful fiancée at this time?'

He said the words 'beautiful fiancée' loudly, as though he wanted everyone in the house to hear. That was a thought. Had Joe heard everything last night through the thin walls? She didn't like the idea of that.

'It's a missed call from an unknown caller.'

'Really?' Barry leaned over to look at the screen. Part of Gemma wanted to say that it wasn't any of his business, but maybe he was just being caring.

'There it goes again,' he said unnecessarily. 'Aren't you going to answer it?'

'Hello?'

'Is that Gemma?'

The caller was well spoken and sounded familiar. She also sounded distressed.

'Yes.' She was feeling worried now. Had something happened to Mum? 'Who is this?'

'It's Patricia, dear. Sam's mother. I do apologise for ringing so early. Nancy asked me to call before you left for school. She felt you should know, after everything you've done for us.'

Her voice was cracked and wobbly, as though it was walking on a tightrope and trying desperately not to fall. Yet her words were coming out quite clearly, without her usual mistakes. 'It's Danny. He's taken a turn for the worse and has been rushed into the operating theatre. Unfortunately he seems to have rejected your bone marrow, so they're trying another match.'

There was a silence, as though she was about to fall off the rope. 'If that doesn't work, there's not a great deal of hope.'

Gemma's eyes filled with tears.

'What's wrong?' Barry kept saying.

She waved her hand to shush him. 'I'm so sorry. Please tell Nancy and . . . and Sam that I'm thinking of them. Would you ring when he comes out of theatre? Thank you.'

She turned to Barry. 'Did I hear you mention Sam?' he asked coolly.

Gemma nodded, tears pouring down her face. 'Oh, Barry. Poor Danny's rejected my bone marrow. He's been rushed into theatre.' Weeping, she buried her head in his shoulder. 'I'm terrified he's going to die.'

'There, there.' Barry patted her gently on her back. 'You had me worried there. For a moment, I thought it was a relative or close friend.'

Gemma lifted her head. 'What do you mean? Danny's special. He's one of my children.'

'Sure he is, Gem.'

Gem? No one called her Gem! Gemmie, yes, but that was only close friends and family. Still, Barry now fell into that category, didn't he?

'But it's not like he's your real child, is it?' Barry stood up. 'And I must say that now we're engaged, I'd rather you distanced yourself from his parents.' He looked at her carefully. 'Sam *is* past history now, isn't he?'

'Of course he is.' Gemma felt hurt. 'He's got nothing to do with my feelings for Danny.'

Barry nodded as though satisfied. 'That's all right then. Now hadn't you better get ready for work? I'll leave you to get on.'

How could he not have understood? It wasn't as though they had just had a one-night stand. Barry knew how important her Puddleducks were to her. Yet he had brushed off her distress about Danny with a crass comment about past history. Was it because he was jealous of Sam? Maybe she should have tried to reassure him more about that. Meanwhile, poor Danny's life was hanging in the balance again. Poor, poor Nancy. It wasn't fair.

Still weeping, Gemma went out of her bedsit, locking it behind her. As she did so, she could hear movement inside Joe's room. So he hadn't left yet? Impulsively, she knocked on his door.

'Gemma! What's wrong?'

She could see his eyes taking in her tear-stained face. 'Come in.' He shut the door behind them, speaking urgently. 'Has someone hurt you?'

Shaking her head, she told him about Danny. As she spoke, Joe's arms closed around her. It felt so good. So safe. Joe was one of the few people who would understand. And right now, still bruised by Barry's reaction, she desperately needed someone who would understand.

'He might not live,' she ended, as they finally drew apart and she fumbled in her sleeve for a bit of loo roll. 'How would his poor parents cope if he died? I feel so helpless, don't you?'

He nodded, handing her a proper handkerchief from one of his drawers.

'Thank you.' She blew her nose, noticing in his mirror that she looked really piggy-eyed and puffy. 'I'm sorry but I knew you would understand.' She almost told him that she'd also told Barry, but then she squashed that idea. Perhaps she wasn't being fair to the man who was now her fiancé. It would take him time to understand her job and all that came with it, just as it would take her time to understand his.

'I'm sorry,' she repeated. 'I didn't mean to be silly.'

As he shook his head, she could see there were tears in his eyes too. 'You're not. And actually, there *is* something we can do.' Joe's voice sounded firm and reassuring. 'We can be strong together. If anything does happen to Danny, we need to help the other children through this. I had some experience of this at my old school when a boy died. It affects everyone.'

399

That was true. She liked his honesty. It was solid, like the rest of him.

He gave her a smile. 'My bike's got a puncture. That's why I'm still here. I had to dash back to get some more change for the bus. I don't suppose there's any chance of a lift into school?'

She sniffed and nodded. 'Of course.'

As they walked out of the house together, towards her car, she felt Joe glancing down at her left hand. 'I heard Joyce last night,' he said in a cooler voice than the one he had used when comforting her earlier.

Gemma's heart raced. What else had he heard? Those walls were so thin!

'I believe congratulations are in order,' he continued evenly.

She nodded. 'It's all a bit sudden.' She felt an overwhelming need for him to know that she wasn't the kind of woman who would jump into bed with a man whom she hardly knew. 'I haven't even had a chance to ring my parents yet.'

Joe made an understanding face. 'Sudden can be good,' he said. 'You never know when you're going to meet the right person, do you?' His eyes were fixed steadily ahead. 'If you're not brave enough to make a commitment, that person could just slip away.'

He was right. Maybe that was why Barry had been jealous about Sam. He just didn't want to lose her. So he wanted to make a commitment to make sure that she didn't slip away or go back to her old love. In some ways, that was rather flattering. Wasn't it? Or slightly controlling? The fact that she couldn't decide was unnerving.

They didn't say much during the short drive to school. Joe looked as though he had as much on his mind as she did, even without the added worry of Danny. Then, as she was about to ask his advice on the seating arrangements for the nativity play, his mobile rang.

Looking apologetic, he answered it. 'Ed!' he said in what was clearly a relieved tone. 'I'm so glad you rang. Listen, I can't really talk at the moment. May I call you back in exactly three minutes?'

Clearly he couldn't wait to leap out of the car as soon as she'd parked. 'Thanks for the lift,' he said, dialling a number on his phone. 'See you later on, I expect.'

Well, thought Gemma wryly as she made her way towards the Puddleducks building, it just went to show, didn't it? No wonder Joe had made that comment about the right person slipping away. From the sound of it, he might just be getting back together with his ex-wife.

Chapter 55

Nancy sat silently in the ward next to Danny's empty bed. In her hand she held a small rubber in the shape of a pink and blue striped cow. Joe had brought it in last week when they had still thought Danny might be getting better.

Lily, he explained, had bought the rubber from the farm gift shop just before she had disappeared. She'd been trying to get to London to visit Danny and give it to him as a present. Poor mite had had it clutched in her cold hand when they'd discovered her on the canal boat.

Nancy now swallowed back the sobs in her throat at the thought of Lily, who had been used as a pawn in some celebrity game. Even so, she had a sneaking sympathy for Dilly Dalung, who had evidently shared her own concerns about child security.

But at least Lily was still alive and healthy, while her son was, at this minute, undergoing another transfusion, this time receiving a complete stranger's bone marrow.

'Hello, dear.'

Nancy didn't even look up. No prizes for knowing it was Patricia, who took it in turns with her own mother to come in on a daily basis. They had organised a rota, they told her rather smugly. One would visit and the other would stay at home in Hazelwood to tidy up.

'Is Danny still having his confusion?'

Transfusion, you silly woman, she wanted to snap. Stop muddling your words up.

She nodded.

'And are you all right?'

How could any mother be all right, in the circumstances? The older woman was taking her hand and stroking it rhythmically, just like she had stroked Danny's before he'd gone into theatre. 'You know, dear, that we haven't always seen eye to eye, and I will confess that I didn't immediately think you were right for my son.'

You don't say.

'But I can see that I was wrong. I've watched you both over the last few weeks and seen how close you are now.'

There was the sound of the old woman blowing her nose. Nancy really didn't want to look up. She just wanted to concentrate on the rubber. It might be her last link to Danny.

'Do you see this?' Nancy stared at the cow, which was grinning at her. 'Danny refused to let go of it, right up to when he had his anaesthetic. His friend Lily bought it for him.'

Patricia blew her nose again. 'So sweet.'

'Danny has two good friends,' continued Nancy slowly. 'Lily and Billy. Both have their problems, but Danny's were different.'

Patricia's hand continued stroking hers. 'He has been rather too much of a mummy's boy, if you don't mind me saying.'

Nancy's first instinct was to deny it, but she knew deep down that Patricia had a point. 'That's because of Sam and me. We were the problem. Neither of us were good at coping with the responsibility of a child – or each other.'

Her fingers tightened over the rubber so her nails dug into it. 'I tell you this, Patricia. If my prayers work and Danny gets through this, I'm not going to be a fussy mother ever again. I'm going to let him have his own life without worrying so much, and I'm going to do something for myself so I'm a more interesting person.'

Patricia nodded in agreement. 'If you don't mind me saying so, I've always thought that was important in a marriage. An interesting wife will keep her husband interested too.'

Nancy jumped up off her chair. 'That's not the point. Don't you get it? If Danny survives, I'm going to make myself a more exciting person for *me*, in order to let him be his own man. I've realised now. It's not healthy to live my life around being a mother.'

She glanced towards the bed previously occupied by the daughter of the woman in pink slippers. The poor woman had quietly and tearfully gone home now, without her daughter. 'And if Danny doesn't survive, I'm still going to do the same thing. Just for me.'

That night, long after Patricia had gone, leaving a box of home-made chocolate-chip cookies that she couldn't eat, the doctor came.

Sam was there by then and they sat, holding hands, as he gave them the news.

* * *

404

A week later, Nancy and her mother were in Joe's flat, tidying everything up before Nancy and Sam returned home. As Christabel had said, it was a good deal cleaner than it had been. 'Not that your Mr Balls is a dirty man,' she added hastily. 'Indeed, those piles of music magazines by his bed have been filed carefully in chronological order. Did you notice that?' She nodded approvingly. 'Shows a very orderly mind, in my opinion.'

As a thank-you, they had filled Joe's fridge with all kinds of nutritious goodies. When they'd arrived it had been totally empty, apart from an eye-cooling pack in the freezer. 'Rather strange, don't you think?' Christabel had said. 'Not really the kind of thing you'd expect from a man. Maybe he's not that way inclined, if you know what I mean.' She threw the pack into the bin before Nancy could stop her.

Nancy had chosen to ignore the innuendo. Frankly, she didn't care if Joe was gay or not. All she knew was that it had been very kind of him to lend them his apartment. He must be looking forward to getting back to it now they no longer needed it.

'By the way,' said her mother as she put away the Hoover, 'I've found this amazing book in the hospital charity shop. It's called *The Joy of Living* and trust me, Nancy, it really helps to put life in perspective. I'll lend it to you if you like.'

Please, Nancy wanted to say. The last week had all been too much; she needed time to think now. Time alone.

Her American parenting magazine had, by some freak coincidence, run a piece on post-traumatic stress.

It had been accompanied by haunting interviews with a mother whose eight-year-old son had died of cancer, and a dad whose ten-year-old daughter had survived the disease. The man still got stressed because of the 'what might have beens'.

One of the signs of PTS, as it was called, was a reluctance to speak. So too was not being able to form words properly. Sam said his mother had started getting her words wrong after his father had walked out unexpectedly. Nancy resolved to be more accepting of the woman in future.

'Sorry, dear,' said Christabel, as though reading her mind. 'Am I talking too much again?'

Stepping towards her, she gave Nancy a big hug. Nancy felt as though she was being suffocated. She didn't want to sound ungrateful but she really wished her mother would go home now, to her real home in the States, and let her get on with her own life. Maybe, she thought with a jolt, that was how Danny had felt when she kept hanging behind at playgroup instead of leaving him to have fun with his friends.

'Hadn't you better get going now, dear?' Her mother spoke gently, as though she was a child, which made Nancy feel suffocated all over again.

'I'll go in my own time, thanks.'

Christabel looked hurt. 'Up to you, dear. I'll be getting off now myself, if it's all the same to you. Patricia and I have arranged to meet back in Hazelwood. See you later. And don't worry about dinner; we've got that under control!'

Nancy stood at the window of Joe's sitting room overlooking a narrow street with cars parked on either side, displaying permits. Three streets away, she could see the market where she'd bought some fresh oranges that morning, and a cake from the bakery over the road. If she stood here for ever, she could freeze her life so that nothing would ever go wrong again.

On the other hand, her life might never go right if she didn't allow it to move, taking her along for the ride. There was, after all, that ad for Birkbeck College that she'd seen on the Tube today. It was offering exactly the kinds of courses she could be interested in if she made herself move on.

The question was, *could* she?

Her pocket began to hum with the vibration of her mobile, but she ignored it. It stopped and then rang again. Sam's signal. She picked it up.

'Nance? We're almost ready. Are you coming over now?'

Chapter 56

It had been the nurses' idea. It was, after all, Danny's fourth birthday. Carefully holding the small bakery box in one hand containing the cake (chocolate had always been Danny's favourite), Nancy took the lift to the fourth floor where she'd spent so many weeks in the children's ward.

She'd got some small presents too for the nurses, who had been so selflessly devoted to Danny, and with whom she was on first-name terms.

'Nancy, that's so kind of you!'

No, she told Deirdre and Chris and all the others. It was they who had been kind.

Now up to the bed where Danny had been for so long. The curtains were round it. Gingerly, she opened them. Sam was sitting on the chair by the bed where she had left him in order to help her mother and get the cake.

And there, in the bed itself, was Danny! Not the pale Danny who had gone in for the operation. Or the over-rosy-cheeked Danny who had had a temperature. But the Danny she remembered before any of this had happened.

'Mum!' He reached out his arms and she nestled into his neck, breathing in his own smell, which, according to her American parenting magazine, was unique to each child. 'You were ages!'

'I had to get some surprises,' she teased and then looked at Sam, hardly daring to believe their son was there. When the doctor had come to them to say that the transfusion had been completed and now they could only wait and maybe pray if they felt able to, they had slept in each other's arms on the narrow hospital camp bed that someone had found for them, clinging together for comfort.

During the next few days, Danny was definitely looking better. He was brighter than he had been after the first transfusion, too. And now he was well enough to be eating his birthday cake. Just a small slice, said the nurses, and yes, they wouldn't mind a piece themselves. Thank you.

'Can I have my present now? asked Danny.

Nancy looked across to Sam. Usually it would be him telling Danny off for being impatient, but now she would do it. She needed to take a firmer line. That was another of her resolutions. 'Small boys shouldn't ask for their presents. They should wait until they are given them.'

Sam was already reaching into his pocket. 'But since you haven't been well, we'll make an exception, won't we, Mummy?'

He beamed up at her and Nancy felt that warm glow which had started to develop between them in Vietnam and had grown even stronger during Danny's illness. She'd heard the nurses say that when a child's life was threatened, parents either split up or got closer.

'If you say so!' She watched as Sam took the white envelope from his pocket and handed it to their son, who was now jumping up and down with excitement. Nancy felt her heart quicken as she watched Danny pull the photograph out of the envelope.

'We weren't allowed to bring him with us,' said Sam, 'but he'll be there waiting for you when you get back.'

Danny looked as though he had seen the five wise men, the three wise women, the star and Baby Jesus (plus his understudy) all in one. 'Pongo?' he said in a voice that was laced with magic. 'You've bought me Pongo? My dog with the funny tail?'

Not so much bought, Nancy almost said, as given him a good home. Toby's dad had originally sold the puppy along with the others in the litter, but Pongo had gone to a couple who had recently split up and could no longer have him. Toby's dad had then texted Nancy soon after Danny's successful transfusion to ask if she'd be interested. He didn't want to sell Pongo. Instead, he just wanted a commitment that the puppy would go to a good home and a loving family.

She'd talked it over with Sam, but they both knew the answer already.

'Pongo won't be coming to live with us until you're home and properly better.'

Danny's face fell a bit.

'And you'll have to help us look after him,' she warned. 'That means taking him for walks whatever the weather.'

Danny was still jumping up and down on the bed. 'I will. I will.'

410

Sam and Nancy shot each other a look that said we'll see about that. 'He seems better all the time,' whispered Sam as they watched Danny unwrap his other presents. There was a pair of pyjamas from Granny Christabel and a book called *Happy Children: How to bring up confident kids*, which was clearly designed for her rather than the birthday boy. A small toy train from Granny Patricia. A DVD from Billy which Brigid had dropped round. And a colouring book with crayons.

'That's from Gemma,' pointed out Nancy.

Sam's face seemed to change. 'You know, I'm actually quite glad that Danny has someone else's blood. It might have seemed odd if he'd had his playgroup teacher's blood inside him, mixing with ours.'

'Really?' Nancy didn't feel that way. Personally, she didn't care whose blood it was so long as it worked, and so far, according to the doctors, all the signs were good.

'Mum?'

'Yes darling,' they both said at once.

'Can you help me write a letter to Father Cwismas?'

Danny never used to lisp like that! The nurses said that was something that could happen after a serious illness. The recovering child learned that he or she had been in danger, and often began acting younger in order to continue getting attention. That was one she needed to watch.

'Of course I'll help. But it's Christmas, not Cwismas.'

Danny was already getting out the crayons that Gemma had given him. 'I want to write it now.'

Sam laughed. 'OK, son. What do you want to say?'

'I want to ask him for one present.'

'Another one?' joked one of the nurses.

Danny nodded solemnly, suddenly producing the pink and blue striped rubber which he must have had in his pyjama pocket. 'I want to ask Father Cwismas to bring Lily back.'

There was a short silence. 'You know, son, Father Christmas can't always do everything,' said Sam quietly.

'Yes he can, Dad! He's magic. He can do whatever he wants!'

Nancy went back to Hazelwood on the train. Now Danny was so much better, she and Sam had felt it was only fair to give Mr Balls back his flat. They no longer needed a London base. Instead, she and one or other grandmother would come up daily, and Sam, who had gone back to the London office, would visit at lunchtime when he could.

It would be so nice to be back in her own home, she thought as she walked up the hill from the station and put the key in the front door. Putting down her bags in the hall, she looked around disbelievingly. Where was the desk? Where was the stool which had stood in the space under the stairs?

Shocked, Nancy went into the kitchen and then into the back room which had acted as Sam's study until he had gone away, and then as her mosaic room. None of it was recognisable. At first she thought they'd been burgled, but then realised that everything was all there. It had just been changed around.

'We both thought it needed a bit of a sort-out,' said a voice from upstairs. 'Much better now, don't

412

you think? The sofa is less obtrusive where Christabel and I put it and as for your room at the back, it took us ages to sort out all those bits of glass and stone. You don't mind, do you? We followed Christabel's new feng shui book: amazing what a difference it makes!'

The old Nancy would have swallowed hard and said nothing. But Danny's illness had changed her. In fact, so had lots of things. 'You had no right,' she said as her mother came down the stairs looking slightly shamefaced, as though she knew she had gone too far. 'You had no right to move things about. It's my home. Sam's and mine. I wouldn't do this to your place!'

Her mother took her arm and led her into the sitting room, which didn't seem like her sitting room at all with that horrid maroon throw over a rocking chair that she'd never seen before. 'Talking of Sam, my dear, there's something I think you ought to know. Something that Patricia told me about his past.'

'Christabel!'

There was the sound of someone running down the stairs. Patricia appeared. 'I don't think that Nancy needs to be bothered with all that stuff now, do you?' To her surprise, Nancy saw Patricia look daggers at her mother. 'What's going on?'

'Nothing, dear,' said her mother hastily. 'It's just that we might have done something we shouldn't have done.'

'We found some old papers and photographs from when Sam was younger.' Patricia was looking really shifty now. 'And I'm afraid we threw them away.'

'By mistake,' said Christabel quickly.

They shouldn't have done that. But in the scheme of things, it wasn't really important. The only thing that Sam and she were concerned about was Danny getting better.

'I know you meant well,' she said, pulling the maroon throw off the chair, 'but please don't rearrange my home. I wouldn't do that to yours.'

'What are you doing, dear? Patricia and I spent ages choosing that.'

'I'm getting my own house back in order.' She turned round to face the two women. 'Don't get me wrong. Sam and I are really grateful for your help. But we think it's time you went back to your homes. Both of you.'

Chapter 57

Joe was in a grumpy mood. This was obvious to everyone both at the main school and at Puddleducks, where the impending nativity play and of course the good news about Danny had resulted in a permanent high.

The worst thing, Joe told himself grimly as he tried to instil some order into Reception by giving them a fun maths quiz before the final rehearsal, was that his grumpiness was obvious even to him. He could not discount the fact that his mood was not unrelated to Gemma Merryfield's recent engagement.

Ridiculous. He hadn't even found her attractive back in September. Then again, it hadn't been her face he'd been looking at when they'd first met. It had been his bike. The whole silly incident had got them both off to a bad start. It wasn't as though his Harley had even been damaged. But he'd spoken sharply, instead of thinking first.

Brian's help and advice had softened Joe. Over the months, he had inexplicably found himself drawn to this girl who somehow managed to combine a sense of fun at Puddleducks with good organisational skills.

Then, when she'd started seeing that oaf of a paratrooper with his baby face and lithe body that could bound up the staircase like an over-eager puppy, he began to see Gemma in a new light. Gone were the brown trousers and cardigans that she tended to wear during the day at Puddleducks. He watched her leaving her room at Joyce's in knee-length dresses and slinky tights with long black boots, and looking at Action Man as though she was star-struck.

Yes, of course it was admirable that the man was fighting for his country, as Joyce was always reminding everyone.

And yes of course he was a heel to loathe him. But, thought Joe, as he collected in the fun maths quiz answers from a highly energised Reception, he realised now that he had been a fool to dismiss Gemma so easily at the beginning. She had, he could see now, all the traits he admired in a woman. She was feisty, kind, honourable, fun to be with (mostly), and stubborn just like him. If they hadn't got off to the wrong start over his bike and if he hadn't still been licking his wounds over Ed, it might have been very different. Now she'd gone and got herself engaged and it was too late.

'Mr Balls, Mr Balls!' shouted Elsie, her face shining with excitement as she jolted him back into the present. 'They're coming.'

So they were. Joe looked out of the window along with thirty pairs of eyes and saw Gemma and Bella, her rather aloof assistant who wore heels that were too high for the classroom. She spotted him, waved and nearly dropped the box of costumes she was carrying.

Joe had never flushed in his life, but felt he was in danger of doing so now. Unless he had caught Joyce's menopausal symptoms, which she was all too ready to discuss, this was one more piece of evidence that he was no longer in control of his feelings.

Not good. Something had to be done about this.

'No one,' he said in that quiet 'I mean business' tone which had usually worked on even the most unruly kid in his inner-city school, 'I repeat no one is to move until they have tidied up their table. Only when I have inspected them will you be allowed to line up at the door to go down to the main hall where we will be having the rehearsal.'

Who's in a bad mood then? He could almost hear Ed's voice in his head. OK. She was right. And maybe she was right about that other thing which they'd been talking about almost every evening this week. Had Lynette been right, too, to say he should give his ex-wife one more chance to prove that she wasn't so bad after all? Only time would tell.

'So the thwee withe women followed the thtar until they found Baby Jeeeethus.'

Joe rolled his eyes as he sat awkwardly on the floor. Someone had moved the adult-sized chairs, and although it was all very well for Gemma with her small frame to sit on one of the kiddy chairs, he wasn't physically able to even if he had wanted to. The seat would only have taken one half of his rear end. Maybe it was time to join a gym: if Brian could do it, so could he.

'Then they that down under the thtar and had a west.'

Why choose a child with a lisp to be one of the narrators? Diversification was all very well, but not at the expense of clarity. Lisping seemed to be catching at the moment: a few of them were doing it, he'd noticed. Perhaps it was in the water.

Gemma was leaning forward with that encouraging smile of hers, which was almost as dazzling as that vulgar stone on her left hand. 'Very good, Darren.'

Very good? Who was she kidding? Joe prided himself on not belonging to the band of teachers who praised children for all and sundry. Brian had said he was with him on that one. There was a kid the other year who'd got a certificate for getting on and off the bus. Ridiculous.

Now a boy with purple glasses was piping up. 'The three wise women walked for miles and miles.'

'Excuse me.' Joe awkwardly got to his feet. 'Could we have a word?'

He gestured to Gemma that they should go to the back of the hall. Never criticise a member of staff in front of the children, Mike had advised when Joe had first started.

'Why did you pick the first narrator, with his lisp?' he demanded.

Gemma gave him a cool look. When he spoke like that, she seemed to say, it was as though the kind, understanding Joe, who'd been so comforting about Danny, hadn't existed. Immediately, he wanted to apologise.

'Darren didn't have one at the beginning of term,' she said softly, 'but his parents are in the middle of a divorce and he's started talking in a babylike way. It can happen when a child feels insecure.'

Ouch. 'Sorry. I can see that. But what about this

"miles and miles" stuff? We've been metric for years. It ought to be kilometres and kilometres.'

Gemma snorted with laughter. 'Are you joking? It's always been "miles" in traditional scripts.'

'Traditional? With three wise women?'

Gemma put her head on one side as though considering something. 'You might have a point. Can we talk about it later? I don't want to delay proceedings any more. Not when Billy is about to perform as the front half of the ox. You never know what's going to happen.'

Good point. Joe wasn't looking forward to that particular whirlwind joining his class next year.

'Oh no.' Gemma pointed to the white sheet that was waiting in the wings. Underneath it, two pairs of shoes were kicking each other impatiently. But that wasn't what she was looking at. Underneath the back legs was a brown circle of cow pat. Except it wasn't from a cow.

'Sorry, Mrs Merryfield,' came a small voice from the rear end. 'I couldn't wait.'

After that, it all went to pieces. A shepherd did a bunk in order to scale the wall bars at the other end of the hall. The Virgin Mary declared that her mother had just had her colours done and that this particular shade of blue didn't suit her because she was spring and not autumn. One of the stars went to pieces, literally, in a costume that had been tacked together by Toby's dad, who'd also managed to sew dog hairs into the tinsel. And Johnnie kept saying 'sin' instead of 'inn', probably due to the male au-pair influence.

'It will be all right on the night,' said Bella bouncily

as they tried to get the children to tidy up after it was all over. 'They're just excited because it's so near Christmas. I must say, I do think that this term seems much longer than it usually does.'

She was waving her hands around as she spoke, and Gemma caught a flash. 'Bella, is that a ring on your finger? I mean a different finger?'

Bella glowed, proffering her left hand. The diamond which had been on her used-to-be-engaged-but-not-any-longer finger was now back on the usual fourth finger. 'We made up,' she cooed happily. 'Just in time for Christmas.'

Joe made a noise at the back of his throat as a warning signal. 'Excuse me, ladies, but we do have ears here.'

It was an expression he'd picked up from Lynette, warning him and Mike not to say certain things in front of the children. Instantly, both women stopped and gave each other a look he couldn't read. Why did women have this secret language and more importantly, how could he download the phrase book?

'You're right,' said Bella with a glossy smile. 'If you don't mind me saying so, you're picking up the lingo rather nicely.'

Not long ago, Joe would have said something about picking up the lingo faster if everyone had been more welcoming at the beginning. Now, too late, he could see that things might have been different if he, too, had made more of an attempt to fit in.

'Thanks.' He nodded at Bella's ring. 'Congratulations.'

Then he nodded in the general direction of Gemma's left hand. 'Looks like you're all doing it!' It was meant to be a joke, but it seemed to come out more like sarcasm. 'Right, my class. Line up by the door please, ready for lunch.'

Behind him he could hear Bella giggle and say something about being in the army. Gemma was whispering something back. Something, if he wasn't wrong, about him having a firmer hand than Brian and that it wasn't a bad thing.

That made him feel more uncomfortable. In a way, he told himself as he marched the children along the corridor, he preferred it when there'd been cool hostility between them. It made it easier to shut out his feelings; feelings which he'd allowed to creep in, despite himself.

Maybe it was time to go back to the old Joe and stick to numbers instead. At least you couldn't get them wrong. Not where the heart was concerned, at any rate.

Chapter 58

It would be a relief, Joe told himself that evening, as he got on his bike in the school car park to make his way down the motorway to London, a real relief to get back to normality for two days. Now the Carter Wrights no longer needed his apartment – such good news about Danny, even though it had gone against all the statistical odds – he could go back to normal Saturdays. A browse round Portobello Road; an afternoon at the Science Museum maybe, and, as it was so near Christmas, an hour or two at Hamleys to get his godsons' presents.

Anything was better than staying in his lonely room at Joyce's and listening to music coming through the wall from Gemma's room, where she and Action Man were no doubt pawing on the bed. Anything rather than being cornered by Joyce on the stairs and being told that it was wonderful, really wonderful, that Gemma was going to be her daughter-in-law.

'Mr Balls! Mr Balls! How fast does that go?'

It was Juan, the only kid in his class who had any natural ability with numbers, as far as he could see.

'Very fast, Juan. Too fast for you.'

This wouldn't be the first time that one of the children had asked for a ride.

'I don't want to go on it.' The boy's eyes darkened. 'It belongs to you. I just want to see the numbers.'

He reached up on tiptoes and pointed to the speedometer. Joe was tempted. Lynette allowed him to pick up the boys and put them on his knee while he sat on the bike so they could see the dials, but they were his godchildren.

'Shouldn't you be in After-School club?'

'It's finished and I'm waiting for my dad. He came to pick me up but then told me to wait here while he went to get some cigarettes. Please, Mr Balls.'

Just quickly, then. He reached down and lifted the boy on to the seat, thinking to himself that this was what he might be doing now if he and Ed had had the baby. 'You see these numbers? They're in kilometres and miles as well. And this dial means . . .'

Later, as Joe tried to explain, he didn't know how it had happened. All he knew was that Juan simply slipped sideways from the seat and fell on the ground with a thud.

Thank heavens Gemma had been there, supervising the end of After-School club. If it hadn't been for the calm, reassuring way in which she'd taken charge of the situation, he didn't know what he would have done.

'Are you sure he wasn't unconscious, even for a second?' she had asked him while sitting Juan on her knee and mopping up his tears.

Joe nodded tightly. 'Absolutely certain. Well, 99 per cent sure. Maybe 98.'

'That's good then,' said Gemma as though she was

trying to be reassuring, but she said it in a way that made him realise he shouldn't have let Juan get on the bike in the first place. 'I know it's only a scrape on the side of his face, but I still think we need to get him to Casualty just to make sure he's all right. We'll need to ring his father too. I'll drive us. You sit in the back with Juan. Is that all right, poppet?'

For a minute, he had thought the last sentence was addressed to him. When they got to the hospital and he had to explain to the girl at A&E what had happened, he felt even more of an idiot, although Juan was, by now, happily sitting up on one of the chairs and chatting to Gemma over a comic. If she hadn't been there, he told himself again, he would have felt even worse than he did already.

'Juan,' called out a nurse, and Gemma, signalling to Joe that it was all right and that she'd take him in, went with her into another room down the corridor.

'The nurse will take him to the obs,' said the girl at reception, noticing his anxious face. 'You know. Observation room just to see if everything is all right.'

Minutes later, after Gemma had returned, a voice rang down the corridor. 'Where is my son? I demand to see him! What have those crazy idiots done to my son?'

A small wiry man reeking of cigarettes, in dirty jeans and a fluorescent labourer's jacket, appeared. Gemma and Joe watched him being taken down the corridor and into the observation room where Juan was.

So far, they'd been told, there was no sign of injury apart from the scrape, but a blow to the head was

424

always considered potentially serious, and Juan would need to be kept in for a few hours at least.

'Here he comes,' said Gemma under her breath.

The man was scurrying angrily towards them. 'Who is the idiot that put my son on his bike?'

Joe took a deep breath. Was that his imagination, or had Gemma touched him lightly on his side in support? 'I'm afraid that was me, sir.'

'You?'

The man's lip curled with disdain.

'You did a very foolish thing.'

'I know, sir. I am sorry.'

'You are lucky my son is not hurt badly.'

'I agree.'

The man's lip curled again. 'I could report you for this, you know.'

'I realise that.' The other patients in Casualty were looking at them curiously. 'The truth of the matter is, sir, that your son is very gifted with numbers. In fact he is very gifted all round. When he started asking me questions about the speedometer, he couldn't see properly so I made the mistake of lifting him up so he could.'

The man was looking at him as he spoke enthusiastically, and so was Gemma, as though she hadn't seen him in this light before. 'You must be very proud of your son, sir. You have done a good job.'

It was then that something incredible happened. The man began to cry. Tears trickled down his face which he didn't bother to wipe away. 'I have been looking after Juan since his mother died.'

His mother was dead? That wasn't on his record card.

'I have done my best but it is difficult.' The man reached out for Joe's hand. 'She was very clever at numbers, his mother. The boy takes after her. It is extremely fine that he has a teacher now who cares about him. We will say no more about the incident. Unless . . .'

He stopped.

Please, no, thought Joe. Don't change your mind.

'Unless one day, it might be possible for you to show me your bike too.' The man's eyes glinted. 'I have always wanted to ride a bike such as the one that Juan tells me about.'

Joe had phoned Beryl from the hospital to tell her what had happened and to report that Juan was being discharged. It had not been an easy call. For his part, Joe had not attempted to make excuses for himself. For hers, Beryl had listened without comment and then said that she would like to see him in her office within the hour. Gemma had sweetly offered to come with him, but he had explained that although he was very grateful, this was something he needed to take on his own shoulders.

Beryl was waiting for him at her desk when he arrived. She shook her head when she saw him, sighed and indicated that he should sit down. Once more he was faced with the photograph of a blond toddler grinning at him from inside a silver frame. He turned away.

Beryl clasped her hands in front of her and leaned towards him. 'You're both a very lucky man and an extremely stupid one.'

Beryl wasn't one to beat about the bush, thought

Joe. He admired her for that, just as he despised himself right now. 'I know.' He hesitated. What he really wanted was to tell the head that he had only let the boy get on the bike because if he'd had a son, Juan was the sort of kid he would have liked. They would have been bike-mad together. They would have explored the Science Museum together. They would have played maths quiz games. But somehow, it didn't seem right to mention this.

'What on earth was in your mind, letting a child get on to your bike?' demanded Beryl. There was a sharper sound to her voice now.

'I suppose,' said Joe awkwardly, scratching the back of his neck which he sometimes did when put on the spot, 'it was the bloke thing in me. Boys love bikes!' He looked across at Beryl and at the photograph. 'Yes, I know it was dangerous, but it didn't seem like that at the time. I was holding him and the engine wasn't switched on.'

Beryl snorted. 'Didn't stop him falling off though, did it? And in this day and age, a male teacher holding a kid round the waist can be misconstrued. Anyway, it looks as though you're off the hook. I've already rung Juan's father and he isn't going to take the matter further.'

Joe recalled the promise he had made to let Juan's father come round and take a closer look at the bike which had caused all the trouble, and decided that it might complicate the issue to mention this.

'Nevertheless, I will have to report the incident through the official channels,' continued Beryl. 'If it was up to me, I would let it pass but rules are rules, as you know.'

Joe's heart sank. That would really scupper his chances of getting another job. So far, his applications hadn't got anywhere. It seemed that there was a surplus of maths teachers at the moment, all with more experience than him.

'Still, if I were you, I would put it behind you.' Beryl's voice sounded less schoolmistressy now. 'You're a good teacher, and we've had some excellent feedback from parents. Your weekly maths tests have produced some extremely good grades.'

There was the sound of someone at the door. 'Hello!' Gemma put her head round. 'Sorry. I don't want to barge in on your meeting but I had to come into school to get something, and I thought you might like to know that Juan and his father are back home and really do seem all right.'

Gemma had stayed at the hospital with them until Juan had been sent home, which was far beyond the call of duty, thought Joe, considering the pupil was in his year and not in the playgroup. But Gemma wouldn't see it like that, he realised now. She didn't like to see any child upset – or adult.

'I couldn't help overhearing what you said just now about Joe's abilities as a teacher,' added Gemma, still standing at the doorway. 'Have you heard about his maths quizzes, Beryl? They're legendary. Fun and informative, or so I've heard.'

She flashed him a smile. 'In fact I wouldn't mind some myself. Words are my thing, not numbers.'

Beryl beamed. 'Then you're a good match, I'd say. That is,' she added quickly, 'in a professional context.'

Gemma was going pink. 'Got to dash now. I've got a date.'

Beryl beamed again. 'Thanks for coming in and supporting your colleague, Gemma. It was very good of you.'

She looked at Joe pointedly.

'Yes, thanks,' he added quickly. 'Look, both of you. I just want to say that I'm really sorry about all this. I know I'm leaving anyway, but believe me, I've learned so much here. I won't make the same mistake again.'

Beryl nodded. 'We're all human, Joe. By the way, you know we talked about my grandson?' She indicated the photograph of the blond boy. 'He broke his arm last weekend, climbing a tree. Guess who was meant to be looking after him? That's right. Silly old Granny who just happened to take her eye off him for one second. Maybe that might make you feel a bit better.'

Chapter 59

Ed was waiting in her car outside his flat when Joe arrived. 'I've been sitting there for ages,' she snapped, displaying, as she got out, those beautifully shaped legs which could have belonged to a model instead of a City high-flyer. 'Didn't you get my texts?'

Although in one way he was glad to see her, Joe couldn't help groaning inside. Ed was one of those people who didn't mind keeping others waiting, but didn't care for anyone else being late. If past history was anything to go by, she wouldn't let up until she'd extracted a full and unabridged apology.

'Look, I'm really sorry but a kid at school had an accident – it was my fault in a way – so I had to take him to hospital and . . .'

Ed waved a hand in the air before tucking it into his arm and walking with him towards his door. 'I don't want to know. It's been a long hard day and I am gasping, absolutely gasping for a drink. Please tell me you have some ice.'

She spoke as though this was a social visit, so, not wanting to offend her in case she walked out in a huff (something she was quite capable of doing), as soon as they got in he poured her a large vodka and lime with ice. He then poured himself a cold lager.

'Sit down,' she said, waving him to his own sofa,

'while I tell you what I found. I have to say that it's looking hopeful. More hopeful than I had thought.'

They spent nearly an hour talking it over, by which time she had got through two more vodkas. 'You won't be able to drive now,' he pointed out.

Ed stretched so that her taut brown stomach was on display between the top of her skirt and the bottom of the lacy camisole under her jacket. 'I could always stay the night,' she purred.

'Sorry.' Joe was already on the phone. 'I've got plans, I'm afraid. But I'll get you a taxi and you can pick up the car tomorrow.'

'Tomorrow?' Ed looked hopeful. 'Does that mean you'll be asking me over for dinner as a thank-you?'

Joe shook his head. 'Ed, we agreed that all this is strictly business, didn't we?'

She pouted. 'Spoilsport.' Then she staggered across to his fridge. 'By the way, I think I left one of my gel eye packs in here. Don't tell me one of your new girlfriends has pilfered it.' She waggled a finger. 'You owe me one.'

There was a loud beep outside. 'Your taxi's here,' he said with relief.

'I'm going, I'm going.' As she passed him, she caught hold of his jacket lapels, forcing him to look at her. 'And don't forget, Joe. Not a word about our so-called business arrangement to anyone. Not until I'm certain. We don't want anyone to be disappointed, do we?'

Then she departed, leaving Joe to breathe out a deep sigh of relief.

* * *

For the first time since he'd lived in London, Joe found himself at odds with everything that weekend. He did all the things he had promised himself. Portobello. Again. The Science Museum. A film in Leicester Square. But it all seemed to have lost its charm. He found himself yearning for the quiet evening walks along the Hazelwood canal which he regularly enjoyed. He missed the coffee shops where you could get a seat and where you were bound to bump into a parent or someone from school. And he missed Gemma, dammit, with her sparkly eyes and knock on the door saying she was terribly sorry but she'd run out of chocolate powder again.

All in all, he wasn't sorry to come back on Sunday night. As he went into his room he could hear raised voices through the wall between him and Gemma. It wasn't difficult to hear what they were saying.

'If you hadn't been late on Friday, we wouldn't have missed it. Frankly, I call it selfish.'

That was Action Man. Not the cool suave Action Man he had grown to dislike for no particular reason, but an angry cold Action Man who was being decidedly rude to a lady.

'I couldn't help it, Barry. It was an emergency. Beryl was glad of my support.'

That was definitely Gemma! An upset Gemma who made him want to march next door and tell this man/ boy to cool it.

'I'm sorry, Barry. But you know how important my work is.'

She was apologising? It ought to be stroppy Action Kid.

432

'I just feel that you put everyone first at that place, and that I come second every time. It's not right, Gemma. Don't you want to be part of a couple?'

There was the sound of someone crying, and Joe had to clench his fists to stop himself bursting in. How dare that oaf talk to her like that?

The voices softened then, and he could hear low murmurings. Joe didn't like the sound of that at all. They were making up. And from what he'd heard, Joyce's son didn't deserve that. Selfish, he had called Gemma. She was the least selfish person he knew, but he also knew that when someone was constantly criticised by their partner (as Ed had criticised him), their self-esteem plummeted and they believed what the other person said.

The next day, Joe took care to get to the bathroom even earlier than usual. The last thing he wanted was to bump into Gemma's fiancé. If he did, he couldn't trust himself not to give him a piece of his mind. He also wanted to get to his classroom early in order to sort out his number-project display, which was going on the wall for the parents to admire after the nativity play.

'Mr Balls! Mr Balls!'

When Joe first arrived at Corrybank he'd been irritated by everyone's habit of saying everything twice, whether they were children or adults. Now he was getting used to it.

'Yes, Di.' He did a double take at her bright red outfit. 'I must say, that's very fetching.'

She glowed at the compliment, which Joe hadn't intended but which had somehow come out, and was making him feel surprisingly good about himself. 'Thank you.' She was waving an envelope in front of him. 'It's come! It's come!'

'What's come?'

This was silly, thought Joe as he opened the envelope. They were beginning to sound like a bad panto-mime script, although, in his opinion, you couldn't get much worse than the one that was to be performed on Thursday night. Three wise women, indeed!

'Have we won? Have we won?' Di was jumping up and down now as though she was on the small mini trampoline in the hall.

Joe read the letter carefully, in case he had made a mistake.

'I think,' he said, handing it to her – it was headed TOP TEN PLAYGROUP/TOP TEN RECEPTION YEAR – 'you might want to read this one for yourself.' He smiled weakly. 'Just to make sure I haven't read it wrong.'

Chapter 60

Gemma thought about Joe as she put the finishing touches to a donkey's tail with the help of wire wool and a spot of Blu-tac. She wished now she hadn't complained to Beryl about him in the early days. She had butted in on the meeting after Juan's accident in order to back Joe up. Still, it looked as though it was all too late now. He was leaving, even though he didn't have another job. If only she'd known earlier that his rather brash, brusque exterior shielded the personal problems he had told her about in their illuminating coffee-shop chat a few weeks ago.

Perhaps, she told herself, Barry was more insecure than he seemed. Maybe she shouldn't have got so upset when he had called her selfish. It was just, as he'd explained when they'd kissed and made up, that he wanted her all for himself. She should really take that as a compliment.

Meanwhile, he had promised to understand that she might be preoccupied with the nativity play. Relations were at crisis point amongst the Puddleducks at the moment. The second angel had fallen out with the first angel because the third angel had become best friends with the first instead of the second, and not asked the latter to her birthday party. That in turn had led to a heated exchange amongst the mothers the other day at pick-up time.

So difficult! Gemma could remember not being asked to someone's birthday party at school once, and feeling awful.

'We'll have to stand them at different ends of the stage,' suggested Bella, who kept twirling her ring just in case anyone hadn't noticed its new position.

Then there was the tricky situation with one of the wise men, who kept sucking his costume. *Could* sequins go straight through?

The day before the big night, a real calamity occurred. 'I've lost Baby Jesus!' wailed the Virgin Mary. 'I can't sleep without him.'

Gemma had warned Clemmie's mother that it might not be a good idea for Clemmie to bring in her favourite doll, but both had insisted. The doll was bone china and had belonged to a famous designer whom Mummy had once worked for.

In the end, the doll was found in the messy corner, where the understudy for the Virgin Mary had been trying to wash its hair in the jelly bowl in retaliation for not clinching the role herself.

'Mrs Merryfield? Why is jelly green?'

'Good question, Sienna. It can be other colours too, depending on how it's made.'

Only twenty-four hours to go! 'Barry, I'm really sorry,' she said when she rang from school on her mobile. 'I just can't go out tonight. Bella and I have to stay late to finish the stage scenery.'

There was a tight silence at the other end. 'But you know I've only got a few days before my leave ends.'

His voice was clipped and even. Even worse, she could hear Joyce in the background. 'What's wrong, dear? Has she stood you up again?'

This was ridiculous, thought Gemma, feeling cross now. He was a grown man. Why didn't he tell his mother to mind her own business?

'Perhaps you could explain to Joyce that I have to work in order to pay my rent,' she snapped.

Bella raised her eyebrows at the conversation, and Gemma turned her back in order to get some privacy. 'Look, sorry. I didn't mean to be rude but I did warn you, Barry, that I've got to work late this week. Otherwise the play simply won't be ready.'

She could imagine him nodding that short, sharp nod at the other end of the phone. 'We can't have that, can we?' he replied cuttingly before hanging up. A nasty cold feeling crawled down Gemma's spine. She'd have some making-up to do when she got back that night – to both mother and son. Except that, she didn't feel this time that it was up to her to apologise. Barry should understand, just as she had to understand about *his* job. And Joyce should stay out of it.

Meanwhile, she couldn't spare any time to dwell on it. If she was ever going to get home tonight, she needed to push on with the scenery. Ah good, here was Joe. That would give them three sets of hands to get the job done.

'Isn't it fantastic about the award?' chirped Bella as she put the finishing touches to the large sheet of cardboard that was meant to be a tree.

Everything was fantastic in Bella's book now that

the ring was back in situ, but yes, it *was* amazing about the award.

'I can't believe they made a special category just for us,' she continued.

Gemma smiled at Joe. 'It is incredible. If you hadn't sent those pictures in and emailed all those news-papers, it might not have happened.'

Three months ago, she thought, he'd have said something about it being an obvious business strategy, but now he was looking almost shy, as though he was embarrassed at being praised.

'It's a shame that your book didn't get a prize,' sympathised Bella, who, at the moment, was feeling magnanimous towards the whole world.

'*Our* book,' he reminded her. 'It was Brian's idea in the first place, but as he says, prizes aren't everything.'

Bella made a cooing sound. 'Such a sweet old man. He reminds me of my grandfather.'

'He's not that old,' said Joe quickly, 'although I suppose that at your age anyone over thirty is ancient!'

'Course they are,' said Bella and somehow, Gemma had a feeling she wasn't joking.

'Have you thought about getting the book printed and selling it to the parents?' she suggested.

Joe nodded. 'Beryl has already given the go-ahead and it's with the printers now. Might even be ready for the spring bring-and-buy.'

'Pity you won't be there to see it.' Bella squinted at her representation of a tree to see if that made it look any better. It didn't. 'Do you think this tree looks lopsided?'

'Yes,' said Joe and Gemma together, and found themselves laughing helplessly, like children when they got a fit of the giggles.

'What's the joke?'

Gemma turned to find Barry at the door.

'The tree,' she said, starting to laugh all over again. 'We're admiring Bella's artistic skill.'

'Or lack of it,' added Joe. 'Want to join us? We could do with a hand.'

Barry took a step back. 'Decorating's not my thing. I was just wondering how long you were going to be, Gemma?'

'Ahhh,' cooed Bella. 'How sweet. He's missing you. You two go ahead. Honestly. Joe and I will finish off, won't we?'

Chapter 61

'You didn't say that Joe was going to be staying late too,' said Barry briskly. They were walking back down the hill to the restaurant where he had booked dinner. He'd announced this fact soon after collecting her from school, as though expecting praise, even though she had made it clear she couldn't go out that night.

'He did it as a favour so we could finish the scenery,' Gemma retorted in an equally short, brisk manner. 'Now the two of them are going to have to do it on their own.'

'When you do the kind of job I do,' he said carefully, reaching for her hand, 'you realise that each minute counts when you're with your loved ones. You never know how much time you have left.'

Kitty had warned her about that. Of course she was pleased for her, about her engagement. But after spending years waiting for her first love to turn up, did she really want now to wait months at a time for a man whom she didn't know very well and who might, with the uncertainties of war, not even return?

'Or,' Kitty had asked with her usual ability to strike a nerve, 'is that part of the attraction? You have the security of a relationship without it being on your doorstep.'

'Of course I don't want a long-distance engagement

or even marriage, but that's just the way it is,' Gemma had replied.

Kitty hadn't sounded convinced. Maybe it was because of her own army brother that Gemma understood more about the demands made by Barry's job than he did about hers. Besides, men like Barry, she told herself, were doing a brave thing, unlike most other professionals. Take that poor kid who had been blown up last week from friendly fire. He was only nineteen. Her heart had bled for his parents and his too-young pregnant fiancée, staring blankly out from the front page of her newspaper.

'I'm sorry,' she said now, reminding herself of this. 'I know we don't have much time left. It's just that I feel I'm being pulled in all kinds of directions at the moment.'

They'd reached the restaurant by now and Barry had, rather overzealously she thought, reached over and unfolded her napkin for her. 'By the way,' he said, with a smile which irritated her, for no apparent reason, 'your friend Kitty rang when you were at work. Apparently your mobile was playing up again so she left a message with me instead. She's really sorry but she can't make it after all, because she's got a last-minute booking that her agent says she's got to do.'

No! Kitty couldn't possibly let her down like that!

'She said there was no point ringing her,' added Barry, watching her fish for her mobile in her bag. 'She's filming tonight. But she did suggest that you might step in as the fairy queen instead.'

'Me? But I've got to supervise the children. And I've got nothing to wear.'

Barry passed her the menu. 'She said you'd say that. So she told me to tell you that you could always wear your dress from Las Vegas. Something about it being a test.' He frowned. 'Any idea what she was talking about?'

Clever, clever Kitty. The dress would be a test, in more ways than one. Three, in fact.

Kitty clearly thought it would be a test for her, Gemma, to see if wearing her wedding dress made her feel as she had about her silver chain. If so, it might mean she still had feelings for Sam.

Obviously she couldn't come between a man and his not-wife, especially as there was a child at stake. But if she did feel twinges about wearing the dress, she shouldn't marry Barry. After all, it would mean that she hadn't progressed emotionally since taking off the necklace.

The second test would be Sam's reaction. What would he say when he saw the dress? Would he recognise it? And if so, would he suggest that they reconsider their future?

And the third test would be Barry's. If she told him that her fairy-queen costume was her wedding dress, how would he react? If he accepted it, it meant he could accept her baggage. If not, then did she really want a man who was, she was beginning to feel, a bit of a control freak? It wasn't just that he checked her phone every time it rang. It was also that he questioned her whenever she mentioned Sam's name, despite also mentioning Nancy and Danny at the same time. And now he didn't like her working late.

It was all those things, plus several smaller niggles that couldn't be set aside easily. Not to mention the fact that she *still* wasn't experiencing any fireworks.

Maybe, she told herself shakily, her body was trying to tell her something that her mind refused to recognise: the uncomfortable truth that Barry wasn't the right man for her after all.

Chapter 62

'Hiiiiic. Hiiiic. Hiiiiiiiiiiiiiiic.'

Dick Whittington's cat had got hiccups.

Puss wouldn't have been there at all if it hadn't been for one of the parents who had written in to complain about the nativity play being 'biased towards one religion'. Why can't you include other fairy tales too? she had demanded. There was no pleasing everyone! Gemma herself always got a thrill from the Christmas story. It wouldn't have been the same without it.

'Try drinking from the other side of a mug, dear,' said Helpful Mum, as Miriam used to call her. 'We did that in my day. It's meant to help you stop. Whoops. Oh dear. Has anyone got a cloth?'

'Mrs Merryfield, Mrs Merryfield, my daddy's going to be here!'

'That's nice.'

'No it's not. Mum doesn't want him near us.'

'Miss Merryfield, I'm terribly sorry to bother you but is it possible for Sienna to stand a bit nearer the front than she did at the dress rehearsal? It will give us a clearer view for the camcorder.'

'Mrs Merryfield, Mrs Merryfield? Are you getting married?'

Gemma looked down to feel Clemmie stroking her

dress. 'It's beautiful.' The child's eyes were full of wonder. 'You look like a princess.'

One of the mums, who was hastily stitching up the ox's tail, nodded, her mouth full of pins. 'It's gorgeous. Billy, will you stand still?'

Thank you, Gemma wanted to say. It was my wedding dress. Not that she could ever tell anyone that, but it was a revelation that she could think those words without feeling so much as a tiny ripple of regret. She had passed Kitty's test! It didn't hurt to wear the dress again that she had once worn with so many hopes and dreams. It was proof that she had finally moved on.

At that moment, Joe walked by and she saw his eyes widen as they took in her appearance. She felt a slight flush of pleasure. If Joe approved, that meant she really did look all right. Still, she mustn't forget that this evening wasn't about her. It was about the children around her, and of course their parents.

'Mrs Merryfield, Mrs Merryfield, my mum's just sent me a picture text to say she can't come. But our au pair is coming instead.'

'Mrs Merryfield, Mrs Merryfield, I need a wee wee.' Too late.

'Anyone got a cloth? And a spare pair of pants?'

'Gemmie, darling?'

Gemma blinked. When she'd casually issued an invitation to her parents, she hadn't thought they'd come. What was it her father had said again? Something about a first-class degree being wasted on a nursery career, if her memory was right.

'Mum! You came!'

'Yes, dear. A nice man called Mr Balls showed us where to sit. He said he worked with you.'

It was then that she noticed her mother's eyes were damp with tears. Don't say something had happened to Tom! Gemma reached out for her arm. 'What's wrong, Mum?'

'Nothing, darling, nothing.' Her mother blew her nose. 'It's just that we didn't realise, your father and I, how much they all love you here.'

Thank heavens the tears weren't due to her brother. A huge tide of relief went through her as her mother babbled on. 'Every time we mention that you're our daughter, all the parents tell us how amazing you are Look at your father over there with your head-mistress!'

Dad was talking to Beryl, who was nodding animat-edly and glancing over in her direction with approving smiles.

'Actually Mum, I'd quite like you to meet someone.' Gemma looked around for Barry, who was also meant to be here. She should have told them about her engagement before but something had stopped her. Was it because, deep down, she'd always had doubts? Or was it, as she'd told herself, there was too much going on at school and she'd wanted to wait until she saw them? Well, now the time was finally here. 'Remember me telling you about the paratrooper I'd met?'

Her mother blew her nose. 'Goodness me, dear, you don't want to get distracted by some young man. Not when you've got a career like this. Now, what time does the curtain rise? I just can't wait!

By the way darling, you look lovely. Absolutely lovely.'

Gemma wove her way through the demands, pleas and compliments towards the children's loos. She remembered the time she had caught Joe in there. Poor man had been mortified! How cruel she had been to laugh about it afterwards. It was only a few months ago, but now, she told herself, standing in front of the mirror over the basins, it seemed like a lifetime.

Gemma had been wearing the dress for an hour now, and had merely felt a very small twinge when she had slipped into it. It was slightly tight round the waist, but the only other difference was in her state of mind. When she'd worn it for her wedding, she had felt sick with excitement and a sense of daring.

'Let's get married,' Sam had said five long years ago, and because she hadn't expected this and because everything seemed so new and full of possibilities now exams were over and they were able to go off back-packing, she had found herself saying yes and then buying the dress from a shop whose windows were dominated by glittery Elvis Presley outfits.

Now, as she looked in the mirror, she felt sorry for the dress and its previous owner, a different Gemma who had literally leaped before she had looked.

'We've grown up, you and I,' she told the dress. 'We've learned a lot, don't you think?'

There was a knock on the door. 'Gemma,' called Bella. 'Are you there? You're first on, remember?'

Smoothing down the cream silk, she swished her

way out – bang into Sam. 'What are you doing here?' she gasped.

He took a step backwards. 'I'm so sorry but I needed to find you. To tell you something.'

He glanced behind him to check no one was listening. Bella had gone. 'The doctors said Danny could come and watch the play. That's why we're here. He got so upset at missing it that they said it might do him more harm than good not to come. He's got to go back tomorrow, just for a day or so, and then they reckon he can be discharged.'

Gemma almost wanted to hug him. 'That's amazing.'

Sam was looking nervous. 'There's something else too. Nancy. She mustn't know. About us. I hope that's not being cowardly but somehow, after Danny, we've managed to sort ourselves out and . . .'

Another wave of relief. 'I absolutely agree.' The last thing she wanted was to break up a family. 'It wouldn't be right.'

Sam was still shifting from foot to foot. 'But I also wanted you to know how grateful I am. We are. For what you did.'

Gemma bit her lip. 'It didn't work though, did it?'

'But you tried.'

'Maybe I should have tried to make us work too,' she said, glancing around to make sure no one was there. 'I was just so upset when you said you didn't want children. Now I can see that we should have talked about it first.'

'Gemma.'

He was taking her hands now. It didn't feel right. 'Gemma, we were so young then. Mere babies. We

448

shouldn't have got married on the spur of the moment like that. It was crazy!'

He was hugging her now.

'But it all worked out,' he added, finally stepping back. 'I have my family and, from what I hear, you've got engaged, so it won't be long before you have yours. I just want you to know that Nancy and I will never forget what you've done for us.'

And with that he had gone, wending his way back through the curtain to the audience. What about the dress? Gemma could almost hear Kitty hissing. No problem. Sam hadn't even noticed it.

'Gemma!' Not another interruption. She was on the stage now, behind the closed curtains which were about to go back any minute. Besides, weren't you meant to give flowers *after* the performance and not before?

'I wanted you to have them now.' Barry stood before her with a bunch of stargazer lilies. He knew they were her favourite but not now, not right now. 'Thought you might like to carry one along with that wand of yours.' His eyes swept over her dress. 'You look lovely.'

Go on, urged Kitty in her head. Tell him. See what he says.

'It's my wedding dress.' Gemma tried to speak casually.

Barry went quiet for a moment, and then threw back his head and laughed. 'You've bought it already?'

'No.' Gemma tried to keep her voice steady over the rise of excited backstage chatter. 'No, it's the dress I got married in. The first time round.'

Barry's face tightened. 'You kept it?'

Gemma nodded.

'Then it must mean something to you.'

She paused. 'I thought it did but actually, now I find it doesn't.'

Barry's eyes narrowed. 'I'm not sure I believe you.'

Was this the same man who'd just given her flowers? Not only did his voice sound completely different, but his angry face looked like that of a stranger.

'In fact,' he continued, 'I'm not really sure I believe your story about not finding your husband after your marriage split. It sounds suspiciously to me like you still feel something for him, and that's why you didn't look hard enough in case he rejected you. This way, you still had some hope.'

A few weeks ago, he might have been correct. Yet now, as he blustered on, and some of the mums helping backstage looked at them with undisguised curiosity, she felt different. 'There's nothing between us now.'

'Then take it off.' Barry's eyes were flashing. 'If it doesn't mean anything to you, take it off and wear something else.'

A voice called out from the wings. 'Two minutes until curtain up, Gemma.'

'I can't,' she whispered. 'There isn't time.'

'Can't or won't?'

'Both.' As she spoke, Gemma felt her chest lighten as though someone had just burst a huge balloon inside it, allowing her to breathe again. 'I've got to be honest, Barry. I don't like being told what to do, and you don't like it when other people don't do as you think they should.' Gently, she eased his ring off her finger. 'I think you'd better have this back. I'm sorry, but you'll thank me in the long run.'

'Gemma! Thirty seconds.'

Feeling amazingly calm, she stepped out towards the curtain just as it was drawn back. In front of her was a sea of faces, and there in the middle of the second row were Sam, Nancy and Danny, staring at her as if they had seen magic, pure magic.

'Welcome to the Puddleducks nativity play,' she said. And as she spoke, she could see a tall, lean man with a short army haircut make his way up the side of the hall and out through the back door of her life.

Chapter 63

Welcome to our nativity play!
We hope that later you will stay
For a cup of tea and a biscuit or two
Although there may be a bit of a queue!
But now please sit back and enjoy tonight.
We've been practising with all our might!
There's plenty to entertain you all
No matter whether you're big or small!

Nancy watched Gemma standing on the stage as she recited the 'welcome' rhymes in that beautiful dress that made her, as Danny had whispered, look like a fairy princess. One of the other mothers had said that Gemma had written the script herself. Nancy wished that she could have been like Gemma, so sure of what she was doing and so nice with it.

Who else would have donated her bone marrow so willingly after being tested, without being asked? Sam was grateful to Gemma, too. When Nancy had gone backstage just before the curtain went back because Brigid urgently needed a safety pin for Billy's outfit, she'd seen Sam give Gemma a thank-you hug. If there was one good thing that had come out of Danny's illness, it was Sam being able to show his emotions.

Her heart melted to see him now, with Danny on

his knee sitting up bright-eyed and excited. Sam had his arms around his son's waist to make sure he didn't slip. Yes. There was no doubt about it. The two had definitely become closer during Danny's illness.

Her mother leaned towards her, talking in what the English called a stage whisper. 'Nancy! I'm still not happy about Danny being here. It's very cold outside. Supposing he catches consumption?'

Her mother had been adopting what she saw as English mannerisms and vocabulary ever since she arrived. The trouble was that the vocabulary belonged to English books published in the 1950s or even earlier. No one used the word 'consumption' nowadays, as far as she knew. Besides, they'd been through all this before.

'The doctor said it was all right,' whispered Nancy, nodding towards the platform where the Puddleducks were doing a dance. Couldn't her mother see that they ought not to be talking? Clearly not. Just as she hadn't taken Nancy's point the other day that it was time for both her and Patricia to go back to their respective homes.

'We do love Hazelwood,' they had chorused when she'd raised the subject. The shops are so pretty, Christabel had said wistfully, while Patricia had made noises about not wanting to go back to an empty house when she could be with her grandson.

'Shhh,' said a father in the row in front, turning round to glare at their murmured conversation.

'Sorry,' mouthed back Nancy.

Just then a telephone rang, with that shrill tone of a mobile pretending to be a landline. 'Whoops!' said a pretty woman in a smart black suit with glossy heels. Getting up from the seat next to the father in front, she noisily made her way past jutting-out knees towards the back. 'It's my call from head office in Toronto,' she exclaimed happily. 'I do apologise!'

That was Honey's mother, who'd gone back to work and was now taking conference calls in the middle of her daughter's nativity play.

'Sshh.'

That man in front again! Just as it looked as though he was going to say something, a ripple went through the audience as a small, slightly bowed figure bounced on to the stage, wearing a red costume with what looked like maroon jumper sleeves underneath.

'It's Bri . . .' began Patricia excitedly.

'Mum!' This time it was Sam shooting his mother a look.

Danny was sitting so far forward that he was in danger of falling over. 'Father Christmas,' he said in a hushed, reverent voice.

He leaned across his two grandmothers and grabbed Nancy's arm. 'Do you think he's got my letter?'

Nancy didn't need to worry about the disturbance this time. Santa's appearance on stage had got everyone excited. The children in the audience, who didn't seem to recognise Brian, were leaping up and down in their seats, while the children on stage seemed equally mesmerised.

Brian's surprise appearance was also causing ripples amongst some of the adults who had spotted the former teacher, and were giving him a warm 'welcome back' clap. His popularity couldn't have been easy for Joe, his successor, to live up to. Joe was, so she'd heard, leaving after only one term. She'd never be able to thank him enough for giving up his apartment to them.

'Cuts a very fine figure, I must say,' murmured Christabel, patting back an imaginary stray hair.

'If you don't mind me saying so, there's nothing like an Englishman,' retorted Patricia, getting out her powder compact and bright red lipstick. She smiled at her rival, completely unaware that she had left a trace of Elizabeth Arden on her front teeth. 'We know how to make them in this country, and they, in turn, know the value of a good Englishwoman.'

Brian had left the stage now and it was time for the three wise women to take over.

'They're girls!' hissed Patricia in horror.

'Shhhhhh,' said the man in front, turning round and glowering again.

'Three wise women?' repeated Christabel. 'I can see you feel as I do, Patricia. It simply isn't on. Frankly, I'm thinking of becoming a Buddhist.' She reached into her terracotta-coloured tapestry knitting bag. 'I've got this wonderful new book about it. You can borrow it if you like.'

Sam sent Nancy a look that said we'd better let them get on with it, and she sent one back to say she agreed. One look at her son's face proved that none of this mattered if he was happy and, touch wood, on the mend.

Meanwhile, Toby and Giles, dressed as shepherd boys, were walking together across the stage, and there was a collective 'ahhh' from the audience. 'We're looking for . . .' began Giles. He stopped.

'Baby Jesus,' whispered Jean loudly from the wings.

But Giles was moving away from Toby, giving him a disdainful look. 'Ugh! He's farted,' he announced loudly and the audience cracked up with laughter.

Thankfully there was the interval after that, which might, Nancy hoped, give the two grannies time to compose themselves after the excitement of seeing Brian. Ever since the charity disco, she'd been hearing nothing but that man's name from both of them. Brian seemed a nice enough man, but a maroon jumper? Bet he had patchy hair under that hat. Yes, she was right! He was coming towards them now without his Father Christmas costume, wearing brown cords, that jumper and a shirt with a collar that had seen better days.

'Christabel,' he was saying. He was actually kissing her mother's hand. 'And Patricia!' Now it was Sam's mother's turn.

'May I buy both of you lovely ladies a nice polystyrene cup of coffee?'

Open-mouthed, Sam and Nancy watched him leading the two women towards the back of the hall, where refreshments were being served by adult-sized angels. One of them waved gaily to Nancy and, abandoning her duties, skipped over to them.

'So lovely to see you!' Annie bent down next to Danny. 'And how's the brave soldier doing?'

Danny eyed her wings distrustfully. 'I'm not a soldier.' He pointed to the stage. 'I was going to be a shepherd.'

Annie clasped her hands together. 'And you will be, I'm sure. Maybe next year.'

Nancy looked up at Sam, who seemed to know what she was thinking. Since Vietnam and the hospital, they had begun to read each other's thoughts.

'Think I'll take Danny off to get some juice,' Sam said. 'Leave you two girls to have a natter.'

Nancy waited until their son was out of earshot. 'The thing is, Annie, that we're going.'

'Going? Where?'

Nancy felt as thrilled as she had when Sam had come back the other evening and told her about his promotion. 'Sam's being moved to Boston. It's a great package and we'd be crazy to turn it down. Of course, we won't go until Danny is completely better, but we're due to make the move by February at the latest. We've found a great school for Danny right next to the university, where I'm going to be doing an art course. I've never done anything that's not purely academic before, and I'm really excited about it.'

Annie's eyes filled with tears. 'I'll miss you.' She moved towards Nancy and gave her a hug. 'I take it Danny doesn't know yet?'

Nancy shook her head. 'I'm worried it's going to upset him. He won't want to leave his friends. And then of course there's the puppy.'

'What puppy?'

'Didn't I tell you?'

Just as she was about to explain, someone tapped her on her back. It was Tracy's mum, who some time ago she'd mistakenly thought was pregnant. Tracy's mum had lost a lot of weight, and wore a tight smile on her face to say she knew it.

'I'm so glad your boy is better.'

'Thank you.'

The smile faded. 'However, I think there's something you ought to know. Something I overheard at Parents' Evening actually, between Miss Merryfield and your mother-in-law.'

Nancy felt a strange prickle down her spine, just as Patricia herself loomed up behind Tracy's mum with a grim expression on her face.

'Excuse me, young woman, but I couldn't help hearing what you said. Contrary to what some people think, my ears are as sharp as they used to be. And my eyes, too. So if you don't mind, I'd like a word with you.'

Amazed, Nancy watched as Patricia virtually escorted Tracy's mum out of the door.

'What was that all about?' she asked her own mother, who'd come up with a cup of tea for her.

Christabel put an arm around her. 'I wouldn't worry about it, dear. Probably something to do with Early Years Goals. Dear Brian has been telling me all about the British learning system. I must say, it's rather bizarre, isn't it?'

A bell rang, and everyone started going back to their seats.

'No thank you,' her mother was saying to a large cherub helper. 'I won't have another drink. I've had an elegant sufficiency.'

Nancy snorted with laughter at her mother's feeble grasp of English idiom, but somehow managed to turn it into a cough.

Annie was nudging her in the ribs. 'I've got a new venture,' she was hissing excitedly. 'You know, a

458

project. Something to do now the kids are at school. So has Brigid. I'll have to tell you later. If I don't get back to the washing up, I'll get the sack. Fallen angel and all that. Byeeee.'

Then Patricia came back, sliding into her seat next to Christabel, and Tracy's mother took her place in front, looking extremely subdued, and it was time for the second half to begin.

Chapter 64

Part Two of the nativity play reminded Nancy of that strange art exhibition she had gone to in London last week, while the grandmothers had been on Danny duty at the hospital. A real mixture to please everyone, with a meteorite as well as the stars, a rainbow, Dick Whittington, and seven dwarfs looking for Snow White.

'In my day,' sniffed Patricia, 'we stuck to the facts.'

Christabel clucked her tongue. 'Are you saying that everything in the Bible is a fact?'

'Sshhh,' said the man in front. He turned round and glared just as the singing started.

'Away in a manger,
No crib for a bed . . .'

There wasn't a dry eye in the house as the audience focused their attention on the group of children singing as though their lives depended on every word.

Then it was the turn of the wise men, which didn't seem very chronological, after Snow White and the dwarfs. Oh well. Who was this kid with ginger hair and freckles, carrying a box covered in painted newspaper? Nancy leaned forward. It looked like the son of Hippy Mum as the others called her, and he was speaking very slowly with long pauses between each word.

'We got you a present. It's . . .'

He stopped and looked around the audience, as though about to burst into tears.

'Frankincense and myrrh,' impatiently hissed the prompt behind the curtain, who sounded very like Bella.

'Franky sense and mermaids,' announced the boy. There was a ripple of laughter and a burst of clapping, which made him beam around the hall. Buoyed up by even more clapping from someone at the back, he carried on enthusiastically. 'Then the wise woman gave birth to Jesus.'

Chronology had definitely gone out of the window! Another round of clapping until an arm came out from the curtain and gently pulled him back out of sight. Clearly the fourth wise man was too much of a liability.

Then there was a burst of music which Nancy immediately recognised. It was the tune for the various versions of the Puddleducks song. But although she knew the music, she didn't know these words as well as the rest of the audience, who were rocking from side to side and clapping in time with Di's piano-playing.

We are the little Puddleducks
Happy Christmas to you all.
We hope you have enjoyed our show
We've certainly had a ball!
But we've something else to tell you
Before you all depart.
And that's to say we love you
With one big Puddleduck heart!

461

Nancy's heart filled with emotion. To think how frightened she'd been about Danny coming here in September. Now it was as though he was part of one big happy family – and she felt the same. It was going to be so hard to leave it all. Still, if there was one thing that Puddleducks had taught her, it was that you could always make new beginnings.

Sam leaned towards her. 'Danny's getting tired,' he whispered. 'We need to get him home.'

She agreed but then an oversized elf bounced on to the stage. Standing in front of the assembled cast, he said he had some announcements to make.

'That's Mr Balls,' giggled Danny. 'Doesn't he look funny?'

Everyone else clearly thought the same, as it took a while for the giggles to subside. Actually, thought Nancy, it wasn't every man who could carry off a pair of green tights so well.

The elf cleared his throat. 'As you know, back in September, all the parents were asked to come up with an idea for the Top Ten Playgroup Award. One of our mothers had a bit of a brainwave. I wonder if Mrs Carter Wright would mind standing up.'

Nancy felt her legs wobble and her face burn as she awkwardly got to her feet. Everyone began clapping enthusiastically. Mr Balls continued. 'Mrs Carter Wright, who also happens to be Danny's mum, had the idea of building a mural at Puddleducks which would depict the whole town. Unfortunately, as you will know, it was vandalised. Nevertheless, the award administrators saw fit to make a special category for the mural, which has resulted in a very

462

generous cheque and lots of good publicity for the school.'

Another round of applause. Sam was beaming at her. 'Well done,' he mouthed.

'Meanwhile, you might recall that you were asked to send in one-line statements about what our schools, past and present, mean to us, for inclusion in a book we called *MY SKOOL!* Mr Hughes and I had the task of editing it – we didn't win a prize but one of our parents, who wishes to remain anonymous, has kindly offered to print it so we can sell copies in aid of both Corrybank and the school. The book was Mr Hughes' idea so I think he deserves a clap, don't you? He's helped me see that prizes aren't everything. Where are you, sir?'

Brian appeared beside Joe, and everyone cheered.

'Finally, just before we start the second half, I'd like to say on behalf of everyone that we are thrilled to have Danny Carter Wright with us this evening,' smiled Joe.

Another round of applause. Three months ago Danny would have hated being thrust into the limelight, but now, as he got down from his father's knee and waved at his friends on stage, he seemed to be lapping up the attention.

'Of course, I was always in the high-school production,' murmured Christabel. 'He takes after me.'

Patricia snorted. 'Acting was always considered rather low in my family. Did I tell you I've offered to pay for Danny to have pee-yarno lessons?'

Sighing at their endless bickering, Nancy tried to ignore them. To her amazement, Danny walked up to the stage. Gemma, who was standing next to Joe in her lovely dress, grabbed the microphone. 'Is that all right, Danny's parents, if he comes up?'

They both nodded as they watched Danny run up the steps at the side of the stage and link hands with Billy, who had been remarkably quiet during the performance.

'Blimey, I forgot to tell you,' whispered Brigid, who'd now abandoned her washing-up duties and was sitting next to Nancy in the aisle, her coat-hanger wings lying by her side. 'When we went to see you at the hospital last time, one of the doctors asked if we were interested in enrolling Billy in a trial for what he called challenging children. He doesn't have to take pills. It's a sort of behavioural therapy combined with something called brain gym. Gemma says she's going to incorporate it into the musical movement activity.'

'Shhhhh,' said the man in front angrily.

One of the mother helpers had just come on to the stage and was whispering something to Mr Balls. He looked surprised, and then conferred quietly with Gemma. An apprehensive ripple ran through the hall, and finally Gemma took the microphone. 'We've just received some news that we thought you might like to share,' she began.

It was then that Danny grabbed Billy's arm and began pointing excitedly to the back. Nancy tried to turn round, but her view was blocked.

'He did it!' Danny was shouting. 'Father Christmas got my letter. He did it!'

A small, delicate-featured dark-haired girl, clutching

the hand of a thin pale woman in a blue anorak, slid into the empty seat next to Nancy. 'Hi,' she said shyly.

It was Lily! Or rather Natasha.

'I hope we not miss too much,' said her mother in an Eastern European accent. 'My daughter wants to come. It is OK. Yes?'

Chapter 65

Ed had pulled it off! One of the mothers had picked up Joe's mobile, which kept ringing persistently backstage, and taken the message. It was, the caller had insisted, urgent, and yes, Mr Balls had to know, whether he was on stage or not.

Somehow, his ex-wife, whose considerable ability in the field of human rights was enhancing her reputation in the legal profession, had persuaded the court that Natasha's mother had acted in the best interests for her child, in circumstances that were to remain undisclosed. You can only guess at them, Ed had said darkly. So Natasha had been returned from her foster family to her mother, and an application had been made for the two to stay in England permanently. Of course there were no guarantees, but if anyone could swing it, it would be Ed.

As for Dilly Dalung, she was still in trouble but she could afford the best legal brains available. Joe was proud of Ed for acting for Natasha's mother without payment, even if she had done it with an eye to impressing him.

'Fantastic news,' said Mike and Lynette, as they celebrated with non-alcoholic Christmas punch at the back of the hall after the show was over. Joe, feeling slightly out of it when all the other staff were bringing family, had invited them, along with his godsons.

Mike slapped Joe on the back. 'Nice tights. Great performance too – real Oscar stuff. No, really, I mean it! Had tears running down our faces, didn't we, Lynette?'

Lynette nodded. Moving away from her husband, she took Joe to one side. Despite having cleared the air with both of them about the beach incident, it still made him feel a bit awkward to be talking to Lynette in a low voice in the corner of the room.

'I do hope,' she said, her long auburn hair falling over her face like a Pre-Raphaelite model, 'that this breakthrough with Lily doesn't mean you're thinking of giving Ed another chance.'

The thought had only occurred to Joe for a split second. People did get back together. Take Clemmie's mum, who was there holding hands with her ex. Don't even ask, he had heard someone mutter, before adding darkly that nativity plays did some very strange things to people.

Joe saw Juan and his father waving at him. 'I couldn't go back to someone who had got rid of our baby,' he said quietly, waving back.

Lynette nodded her approval. 'I liked Gemma, by the way.'

Joe gave her a warm grin. 'That's not very subtle.'

'It's not meant to be subtle.'

He moved closer so he could whisper. Ears were everywhere, big and small. 'She's taken. Engaged to Action Man, who happens to be my landlady's son.'

Lynette gave him one of the quizzical looks that

she usually reserved for one of his godsons when they'd promised her, hand on heart, that they'd already cleaned their teeth. 'Are you sure? Because I heard them having quite an argument backstage, after Fraser had insisted that we tried to find you before the show started.'

She winked. 'Not that I was listening, of course. Although I did happen to hear something which sounded as if she was giving him back his ring.'

'Really?'

'Really!'

If he hadn't known better, he'd have said that Lynette was flirting with him, when in fact she was giving him a 'what are you waiting for' twinkle.

'Ah, there you are, you two!'

Joe gave an awkward smile as Mike strode up, looking slightly on edge. The last thing he wanted his best friend to think was that he was making a play for his wife.

'Has Lynette told you about this plan of hers?' Mike said.

'Sorry.' Joe dug his hands into his pockets the way he sometimes did when feeling cornered. Inviting Gemma to dinner was a crazy idea. 'I just don't think I have the nerve.'

Mike looked taken aback. 'Really? But you've offered to do it before? It's only for four days just after Christmas.' He draped his arm around his wife. 'We haven't had any time to ourselves since the boys were born, and neither of us would trust them with anyone else.' He gave a small sigh, and Joe noticed that he looked rather more tired round the eyes than usual.

'To be honest, both of us could do with a bit of a break.'

Lynette was laughing now. 'Joe and I were talking about Gemma! I hadn't got round to asking him about the boys yet.' She gently touched Joe's arm. 'I found this great deal in the paper; it's a four-day trip to Venice, and we wondered if you could possibly . . .'

'Have the boys?' Joe understood at last. 'I can think of nothing that I'd like to do better. Well, only one thing, and to be honest, I'm pretty sure that's out of the question.'

'Uncle Joe, Uncle Joe! Are you going to look after us in your cool London flat for two days squared?'

He'd taught them well!

'Uncle Joe, Uncle Joe, can we go to Madame Two Swords?'

'May', corrected Lynette. 'May, not can.'

'Uncle Joe, Uncle Joe, can we go to bed really, really late?'

What had he got himself into? Four glorious days with his wonderful godsons. He couldn't wait.

Chapter 66

It was nearly nine o'clock when they'd finally finished clearing up. Both Joe and Gemma, who was rather quiet, had insisted that Bella left early as she was having yet another engagement drinks do with her friends. 'It's much better the second time round,' her assistant assured them both with all the confidence of a twenty-three-year-old. 'We've matured. Honest.'

Natasha's mother had come up to them to say that if it was all right with them, she would like her daughter to continue at Puddleducks next term.

'I've got a new book,' said Natasha, whom he still couldn't stop thinking of as Lily. Solemnly, she handed them a well-thumbed book with cardboard pages and brightly coloured illustrations, the text in a foreign language.

'It was Mama's when she was small.' Natasha/Lily gripped her mother's hand. 'I am teaching her some English words too.'

That child's English was better than that spoken by many of the kids around here who came from wealthy backgrounds. Feeling moved and needing to root himself in reality, Joe helped gather up all the left-behind shoes and sandwich boxes and mobile phones for the Lost Property box, and then Gemma said a subdued goodnight, leaving him to lock up.

Had Lynette been right about the argument she'd overheard, or was Gemma just tired?

'Very well done,' said Beryl, as she left with him. 'Actually Joe, I wonder if I could have a word. I was going to leave it until tomorrow, but as you're here, I thought I'd ask. Have you got another job yet?'

If this had been yesterday, he'd have said no. But even as she spoke, he felt in his pocket for the envelope that was tangible proof. His old school, after rejecting him, had gone for someone else, which had hurt. But a similar school, in Brixton, had made him an offer.

'I have, actually.'

Beryl's face fell. 'That's a shame. Oh well. Just thought I'd ask. Goodnight. And well done.'

You silly oaf, Joe thought as he went out into the car park in the cold dark night air. You could at least have asked her the reason for her enquiry. It would have been nice to have heard her say that she wanted him to stay on.

Swinging his right leg over the saddle, he turned the key in the engine. He might still have said no; in fact, he would definitely have said no, but on the other hand . . .

What was that? Joe felt the vibration pass right through him as the bike reversed. No. Please no. He'd hit something. Even worse, there was the sound of someone weeping.

Chapter 67

'You idiot! Didn't you see me?' Gemma could hardly believe what had just happened. Joe had shot straight into her as though she hadn't been there!

'Are you all right?' His voice rang through the night, sounding panicky, not like cool, self-possessed Joe at all.

'Luckily I am,' she said tearfully, bending and running her hands over her poor car's dented bonnet. 'But Gran's lights are smashed and there's a horrible bump in the front.'

'Your grandmother?' repeated the voice, coming nearer. 'What's she doing here?'

'She's not, you twit. She's dead. That's the whole point. This was my gran's car and she's ancient. I mean the lights are ancient.' Gemma sniffed, wiping her nose on the sleeve of her lovely wedding dress in the absence of a tissue. 'Morris is one of the few things I've got left of her – even if I can replace the lights, they'll cost a fortune.'

It was no good. On top of everything that had happened this evening with Barry, this was too much. Sinking to the ground, Gemma put her head on her knees to shut out the rest of the world and sobbed. She cried for her grandmother. She cried for Sam, whom she'd waited for, in vain, for so long. She cried for Danny and Lily out of relief. And she cried for Barry, who, although he ticked all the right boxes, had turned out to be another false hope.

'I'm sorry.' Joe sounded as though he really meant it. 'I know what it's like to lose something precious.'

Then suddenly she felt something warm around her. Gemma stiffened. It was Joe's arm. He was actually sitting down on the ground next to her, with his arm around her, stroking her shoulder and gently pulling her towards him so that she was leaning into his body.

'What on earth do you think you're doing?' she began to say, but the rhythmic stroking motions were doing something to her; something which she could hardly put into words. Was she imagining all this? Was it possible that Joe Balls, head of Reception, who could still at times annoy her with his 'I know best' attitude, was giving her a cuddle? And if so, why wasn't she pushing him off and telling him that he was the last person in the world she thought of in that way and that he honestly wasn't her type?

'Thank heavens you weren't hurt,' he was saying now in a voice that was gentle and yet firm at the same time. 'I couldn't have forgiven myself if I had done that. And don't worry about your car. I'll pay whatever it takes to put it to rights, I promise you.'

The stroking stopped, and Gemma felt surprisingly regretful. In the light that was just about reaching them from the school building, she could see Joe getting up and holding out his hand. Hesitating slightly, she took it and found herself being pulled to her feet. He was looking down at her now and – there was no doubt about it this time! – Gemma felt a delicious shiver pass through her.

'Could I ask you something?' he said, his eyes fixed on hers but not in a stern way.

She tried to find her voice. 'That depends.'

'Will you come with me to the friendship circle?'

Gemma gave him a quizzical look. 'The one that, if I am correct, you said was unnecessary at the beginning of term?'

'I was wrong. Sorry.' He scratched the back of his neck in embarrassment. It was a gesture she'd started to notice only recently. Quite endearing, really. 'It's a good idea, but I didn't know it then.' He grinned uncertainly. 'To be fair, I was still getting to know you all in those days.'

The cheek of the man! 'And now you think you do? Personally, I'm still getting to know myself.'

He laughed. A nice warm friendly laugh, not like the short sarcastic ones which had seemed his trademark when she first knew him.

She nodded at his monster of a bike. 'Aren't you going to check it first to see if you've hurt it? I seem to recall that when I reversed into you, back in September, your bike was more important to you than any limb, let alone a friendship circle.'

'No, I'm not.' His voice was firm, although he gave the bike a quick glance as if he would indeed like to check out any damage. 'No, this is more important.'

He was actually slipping his arm around her waist as they walked up towards the circle of stones. She had thought that him sitting on the ground with her and stroking her shoulder was merely how a comforting friend would behave, but putting an arm round her waist? And why was this tingle spreading through her bones? Surely she wasn't falling for Joe?

'Do you want to jump inside or shall I?' he asked, grinning at her.

'Jump?' she repeated. 'You mean you can jump as well as do a reverse turn in personality? What happened to the tough Joe Balls we used to fear?'

He looked hurt, and instantly she wished she could take the words back. 'I'm sorry,' she said, moving towards him and, without meaning to, taking his hands in hers. 'It's just that I'm confused. You seem different now.'

He nodded. 'That's because I *am* different, and part of that, Gemma Merryfield, is thanks to you.'

If his face hadn't looked so serious, she would have laughed. None of this made sense. None of this was logical. None of this added up. None of this explained why she was still holding his hands and he, hers.

'Please.' He indicated the circle of stones which she and the children had so painstakingly laid at the beginning of term. 'I want us both to stand in it. Unless, of course, there is something stopping you.'

As he spoke, he let go of her left hand and looked at it carefully, as though searching for something.

'I broke it off,' she said quietly. 'I gave Barry his ring back.'

'Wise move!'

That was definitely a smile passing across his lips. 'How do you know?'

Joe gave a shrug. 'Just didn't feel right, either to me or Bella.'

'You talked about it to *her*?'

'Didn't have to. That girl's face says it all, although I did hear her make some comment to someone about engagement rings. Afraid she didn't seem to think much of yours.'

'It's the person who matters, not the ring,' replied Gemma.

His hand tightened on hers. 'Exactly.' Then he moved closer again, closer than before so she could smell him: a sort of lemony woody mixture which made her want to breathe him in.

'Is this all right?' he murmured, and she nodded. 'Just so long as you don't think I make a habit of moving from one man to another,' she told him.

'Surely not?' He glanced at his watch. 'It's been at least, let's see, at least two hours twenty minutes.'

'What about you?' she retorted. 'Do you make a habit of bringing your ex-wife along to social occasions?'

'Nope.' He shook his head in an exaggerated, playful fashion. 'I promise that if you agree to go out with me, I will keep my ex-wife firmly locked up.'

Go out with him? That was insane. So why was her heart thumping like that? 'That's all right then,' she said, smiling.

His face was coming nearer. And now his lips were pressing hers. She felt her mouth melting into his as though it recognised his touch; as though they had done this before. Don't stop, she urged him silently, with an urgency and heat that matched his. Don't ever stop. These, finally, were the fireworks which Kitty had spoken of with such authority. And maybe, said a sudden small voice inside her head, this was why she hadn't been able to commit herself to Barry. Perhaps, deep down, she had been secretly harbouring a passion for Joe.

'Mummeeee,' piped up a shrill voice. 'Look! Mrs Merryfield is kissing Mr Balls. And she's married!'

Instantly they stopped, whipping round to see who had caught them out.

'Sorreee!' called out a well-modulated, embarrassed voice. 'Honey left her tiara behind so we've come back to find it.'

Joe's voice sounded hoarse, as though he'd been smoking. 'There's one in the Lost Property box. Can it wait until tomorrow?'

'Of course!' Honey's mother trilled. 'Have a nice evening, both of you.'

The moment had gone, thought Gemma in despair. Little Honey had unwittingly blown it for both of them. Now Joe would act all embarrassed and apologise and say he hadn't meant it. He was certainly looking awkward enough, shifting from foot to foot like that.

'Never try to act with children or animals,' he said, clearly trying to introduce a note of levity. 'By the way, I've been meaning to say. It's very sweet the way the kids call you Mrs instead of Miss.'

Gemma felt a stab of uncertainty. 'Actually,' she began, but he was going on talking, sounding a little flustered.

'Now,' he predicted, 'it's going to be all over school that I've been caught kissing a married woman.'

OK. It was time to come clean. 'Joe, there's something I've got to tell you,' she said. 'But not here. Do you mind if we go back to your room? I'd rather tell you there.'

His finger was tracing the outline of her lips now, so she could barely get the last words out. 'Whatever it is,' he murmured, 'it can wait, don't you think?'

As his mouth closed over hers, sending hot urgent waves pounding through her body, another small voice inside Gemma's head told her that he was right. Her confession could wait. Sam was her past now, and so was Barry. If she was lucky, Joe might just be her future. And that, after all, was what mattered.

PUDDLEDUCKS END-OF-TERM SONG

Now our term is finally over
But do not shed a tear.
We Puddleducks will soon return
For the start of a new year!

Chapter 68

Shortly after Christmas

'Sure you don't mind?'

Gemma, who had been lying with her head in Joe's lap, looked up at him sleepily. 'Course not. I'm looking forward to it.'

Joe gave her one more kiss. 'Lynette and Mike need a break. Actually, it sounds like they're here!'

Two pairs of hands were already hammering on Joe's door. They opened it to two boys who, Gemma could swear, had grown since the nativity play. They rushed in past her, hurling themselves at Joe.

'Uncle Joe, can we go now, right now to Madame Two Swords?'

'It's Too So, silly.'

''Snot.'

Lynette gave Gemma a 'do you know what you're letting yourself in for' look.

'And can we have loads of ice cream and stay up really late to hear Big Ben strike midnight?'

Mike chipped in. 'Listen folks, please don't think we're rude but we're going to miss our plane if we don't go. I know we're late, but . . .'

Gemma interrupted him. 'It's fine. Don't worry.

They'll be safe with us. I cut my teeth on my brother; well, not literally, but you know what I mean.'

Lynette looked slightly startled. 'I think so. Bye then. Ring if there are any problems.'

'Uncle Joe, Uncle Joe. What's this?'

Charlie, ignoring his parents' departure, was pointing at the red and white cage on the side table.

'That's the Puddleducks hamster,' said Gemma proudly. 'He's called Hammie. One of the children was going to take him home for the holidays, but her mummy is having a baby so I've got him instead.'

The boys were poking their fingers in through the bars. 'We've got hamsters,' said Fraser. 'Our neighbour's looking after ours. We know lots about hamsters cos we get them every two years. That's when they die, you know.'

Gemma raised her eyebrows at Joe, who shrugged.

'Ours is a she hamster cos she leaves specks of blood on the sawdust sometimes,' butted in Charlie. 'Mum says that means she can reprojuice, like this one.'

'I don't think so,' said Gemma, feeling for Joe's hand and marvelling that the tingly touch of his skin now felt the most natural thing in the world. This would have been as likely as a blue moon three months ago. 'Hammie is a he, not a she.'

'No way!' Charlie was jumping up and down so the cage was rattling. 'Look. Hammie's got babies!'

Gemma and Joe stared at the three, no four, tiny pink noses now emerging from the sawdust, the nostrils twitching madly. Too late, Gemma remembered that three-year-old Molly, who had had Hammie for the weekend recently, had, so she told Gemma, put him in the cage with her own hamster so they could 'play'.

'A hamster's gestation period is between sixteen and twenty-three days,' announced Fraser importantly. 'Gestation is the time between boiling the egg and giving birth.'

'Swot,' said Charlie, elbowing him. 'You only know cos we've just had a sex project at school and you Googled it. Anyway, it's not boiling the egg. It's infertilising it.'

'Fertilising, silly.'

Gemma didn't know whether to laugh or cry. 'How come we didn't notice?' she said quietly, leaning back into the man standing behind her.

Joe ruffled her hair. 'Because we've been doing other things for the past twenty-four hours,' he whispered back.

Gemma flushed. Kitty reckoned she'd always secretly fancied Joe, and that he'd always secretly fancied her. It was why, she said, they had each been so anti the other at the beginning. Couples who were fiercely mutually attracted often started off by loathing each other.

'Is it fireworks?' Kitty had pried when Gemma had rung to tell her all about it.

'Absolutely,' Gemma had replied, feeling both embarrassed and also remarkably lucky at the same time. Joe had been so understanding when she had told him about her complicated history with Sam. He'd nodded at the parts which Barry had previously frowned about, and gave her comforting squeezes when she'd got to the bit about discovering Sam was Danny's father.

'You must think badly of me,' she had said with a slight tremor in her voice, 'starting a full relationship with Barry so soon after meeting him.' She'd looked away shyly. 'It might sound like a cliché, but I'm really not that sort of girl.'

'I know you're not.' Joe had taken her into his arms. 'That's one of the reasons why I love you. But we can all make mistakes, and it's better to realise that before it's too late.' He began to give her small butterfly kisses all over her face. 'Just think how awful it would have been if you'd married Action Man, as I'm afraid I call him. Then you'd have had to wait for *another* divorce!'

He was right. What a narrow escape! Joe then admitted that he'd always been attracted to her sparkly eyes and wit. She confessed that she couldn't resist a smouldering northern Colin Firth, mixed with Mr Grumpy.

Could that really only have been a few days ago? It felt as though they'd been together for ever. Joe put his arm around Gemma as the boys continued to examine the hamster cage and its contents. They'd agreed that when his godchildren came to stay she would go back home every night. It wouldn't have been right for her to sleep over too. But it didn't mean they couldn't show affection to each other. It was one of the many things they had discussed, along with Gemma's decree absolute, which would make her free in three weeks, and Joe's decision to turn down the new job offer and return to Corrybank, as Beryl had suggested.

'You've got babies! You've got babies!' chanted Fraser, jumping up and down.

'No they haven't, silly. Uncle Joe and Gemmie are humanoids like us. Not hamsters.'

'Babies,' Joe repeated. His eyes searched hers, and she felt her insides melt like the chocolate ice cream, which – she now remembered – she'd taken out of the freezer and forgotten about. 'I rather like the sound of that. Don't you?'

PUDDLEDUCKS PLAYGROUP
NEWSLETTER
JANUARY ISSUE

Welcome back everyone to the start of a new session! A special welcome to all new parents who might be feeling nervous!

We've got all kinds of activities organised for young and old. Please keep the following dates free in your diary:

February 14: Parents' Social.

March 17: Kite Flying Competition. A former parent has provided us with a kite for each Puddleduck and his/her parent. We will be meeting at the park at 4 p.m., weather permitting. This will be a joint activity with the Reception class, led by Mr Balls, the year head.

We've also got some changes to announce! Miss Gemma Merryfield will be taking over permanently as Puddleducks leader, now Miriam Thomas has decided to stay at home and be a full-time mum.

Sadly, Miss Bella Hick-Huckman is leaving us to join a public relations firm in London. We trust that the negotiating skills she learned at Puddleducks will be put to good use in the business world! She will be replaced by Maggie, otherwise known as Alex's mum, who has recently completed her degree in Early Years Management.

Finally, some of you may have read about brain gym in newspapers and magazines. This is a series of exercises that can help with behaviour skills. If you would like to know more, please see Miss Merryfield.

PS. If you wish to contribute to the collection for Brian Hughes, please see Di in the main school office. Brian has made an amazing recovery following his illness and is now planning a round-the-world trip during his retirement, starting with a stopover in Westport, Connecticut, where he will be visiting Danny's American granny, along with Danny's British granny!

PUDDLEDUCKS PLAYGROUP
NEWSLETTER
APRIL ISSUE

Welcome back to the summer session! A special welcome to all new parents who might be feeling nervous!

We've got all kinds of activities organised for young and old. Please keep the following dates free in your diary:

April 23: The grand opening of the Puddleducks mural. As some of you will know, the original was spoilt by vandals but it has now, thanks to our terrific mural team, been rebuilt.

May 19: Parents' Social. We will be selling copies of the award-winning book MY SKOOL!, which was edited by Mr Balls, Reception year head, and his predecessor Brian Hughes. We will also be holding an auction. So far, donations include twenty boxes of sweets, a mobile phone, and a vintage wedding dress from Las Vegas. Proceeds from the book sales and the auction to go to the Aplastic Anaemia Foundation.

June 5: International Day. Parents of different nationalities will be coming in to tell us about traditions in their countries. Our guest list includes Johnnie's au pair Lars on Sweden, and Mikey's grandmother on Australia.

We don't usually allow adverts in the newsletter,

but two of our mothers have asked if we could make an exception. Annie Worth has set up her own photography business and is available for family portraits. Brigid Harris has started an employment agency called Part-Time Parents for parents who can only work limited hours.

We also thought that former friends of Danny Carter Wright and his mother Nancy might like to know that they have settled well in Boston and that Danny is expecting a baby brother. They thank everyone for their good-luck cards and emails and hope that you will visit one day. Pongo has adapted well to life in the USA and even has an American pet passport!

Danny's grandparents have self-published a book! It's called Grannies: How to Work Together. If you'd like to order a copy, please see Jean.

Meanwhile, we are looking for entries for the Top Ten Playgroup Award for this year. So if anyone has any bright ideas, please see Maggie. So far, suggestions include a maths quiz championship for parents and children.

Finally, some wonderful news! We'd like to announce the engagement of Miss Gemma Merryfield to Mr Joe Balls! This is the very first Puddleducks/Corrybank wedding!

To celebrate, the happy couple would like to invite all the little Puddleducks and those in Reception to their reception, which will take place at . . . Yes, you've guessed it! Puddleducks Playgroup on August 5.